TIME MAGAZINE 100 BEST FANTASY BO

NPR FAVORITE SF&F BOOKS OF THE

WORLD FANTASY AWARD WINNER · BI

AWARD WINNER · CRAWFORD AWARD WINNER

LOCUS AWARD FINALIST · NEBULA AWARD FINALIST

LOCUS RECOMMENDED READING

★ "Samatar's sensual descriptions create a rich, strange landscape, allowing a lavish adventure to unfold that is haunting and unforgettable."—*Library Journal* (starred review)

"Sofia Samatar's debut fantasy *A Stranger in Olondria* is gloriously vivid and rich."—Adam Roberts, *The Guardian*, Best Science Fiction

"It's the rare first novel with no unnecessary parts—and, in terms of its elegant language, its sharp insights into believable characters, and its almost revelatory focus on the value and meaning of language and story, it's the most impressive and intelligent first novel I expect to see this year, or perhaps for a while longer."
—*Locus*

"The excerpt from Sofia Samatar's compelling novel *A Stranger in Olondria* should be enough to make you run out and buy the book."—K. Tempest Bradford, NPR

"With characteristic wit, poise, and eloquence, Samatar delivers a story about our vulnerability to language and literature, and the simultaneous experience of power and surrender inherent in the acts of writing and reading."—Amal El-Mohtar, Tor.com

"Books can limit our experiences and reinforce the structures of empire. They can also transport us outside existing structures. The same book may do both in different ways or for different people. Samatar has written a novel that captures the ecstasy and pain of encountering the world through books, showing us bits and pieces of our contemporary world while also transporting us into a new one."—*Bookslut*

"A richly rewarding experience for those who love prose poetry and non-traditional narratives. Sofia Samatar's debut novel is a fine exemplar of bibliomancy."
—Craig Laurence Gidney (*Sea Swallow Me*)

"Vivid, gripping, and shot through with a love of books."
—Graham Sleight, *Locus*

"If you want to lose yourself in the language of a book, this is the one you should read first. Samatar's prose is evocative and immediate, sweeping you into the complex plot and the world of Jevick, a pepper merchant's son."—xojane

"A journey that is as familiar and foreign as a land in a dream. It's a study of two traditions, written and oral, and how they intersect. Samatar uses exquisite language and precise details to craft a believable world filled with sight, sound and scent."
—*Fantasy Literature*

"A book about the love of books. Her sentences are intoxicating and one can easily be lost in their intricacy. . . . Samatar's beautifully written book is one that will be treasured by book lovers everywhere."—Raul M. Chapa, BookPeople, Austin, TX

"The novel is full of subtle ideas and questions that never quite get answered . . . such as what is superstition and what is magic? How much do class and other prejudices affect how we view someone's religion? . . . Samatar gives us no easy answers and there are no villains in the book—simply ordinary people doing what they believe is right."— io9.com

"As you might expect (or hope) from a novel that is in part about the painting of worlds with words, the prose in *Stranger* is glorious. Whether through imaginative individual word choices—my favourite here being the merchants rendered "delirious" by their own spices . . . Samatar is adept at evoking place, mood, and the impact of what is seen on the one describing it for us."
—*Strange Horizons*

A STRANGER IN OLONDRIA

A STRANGER IN OLONDRIA

Being the Complete Memoirs of the Mystic, Jevick of Tyom

by

SOFIA SAMATAR

Small Beer Press
Easthampton, MA

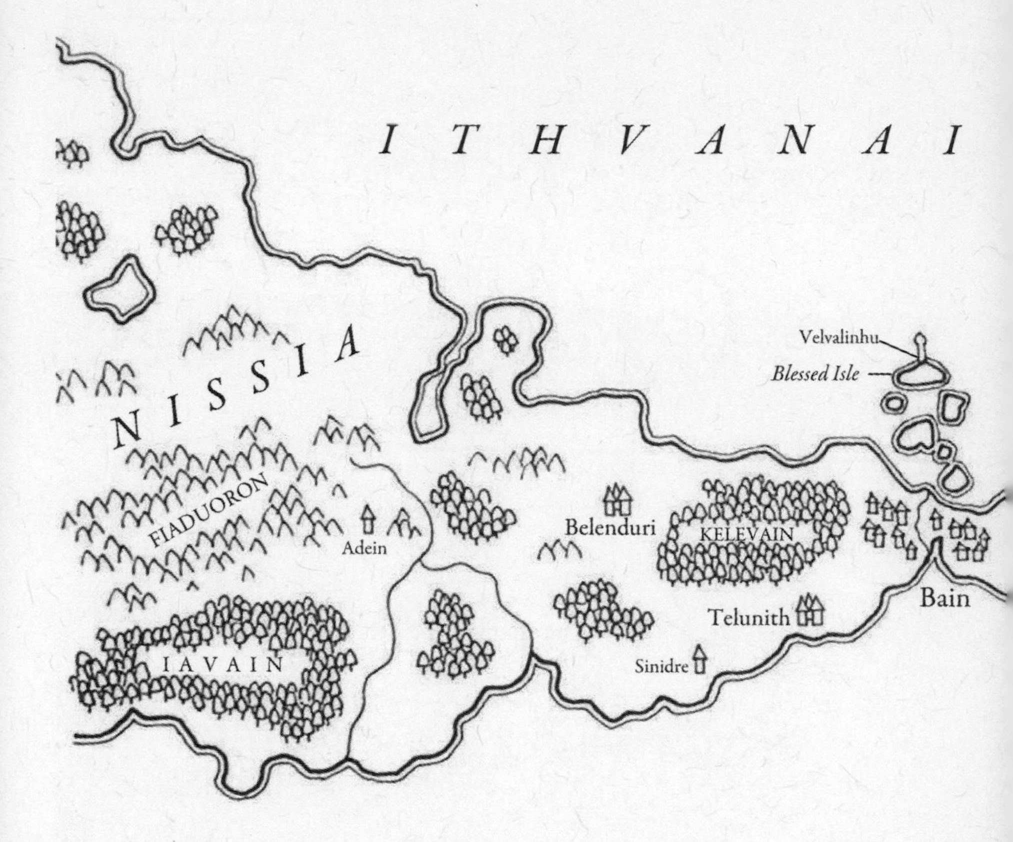
ITHVANAI
NISSIA
FIADUORON
Adein
IAVAIN
Belenduri
KELEVAIN
Telunith
Sinidre
Bain
Velvalinhu
Blessed Isle

ITHNESSE

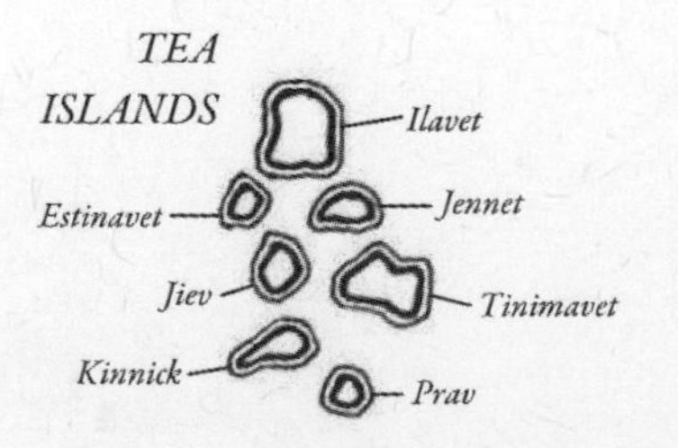
TEA ISLANDS
Ilavet
Estinavet
Jennet
Jiev
Tinimavet
Kinnick
Prav

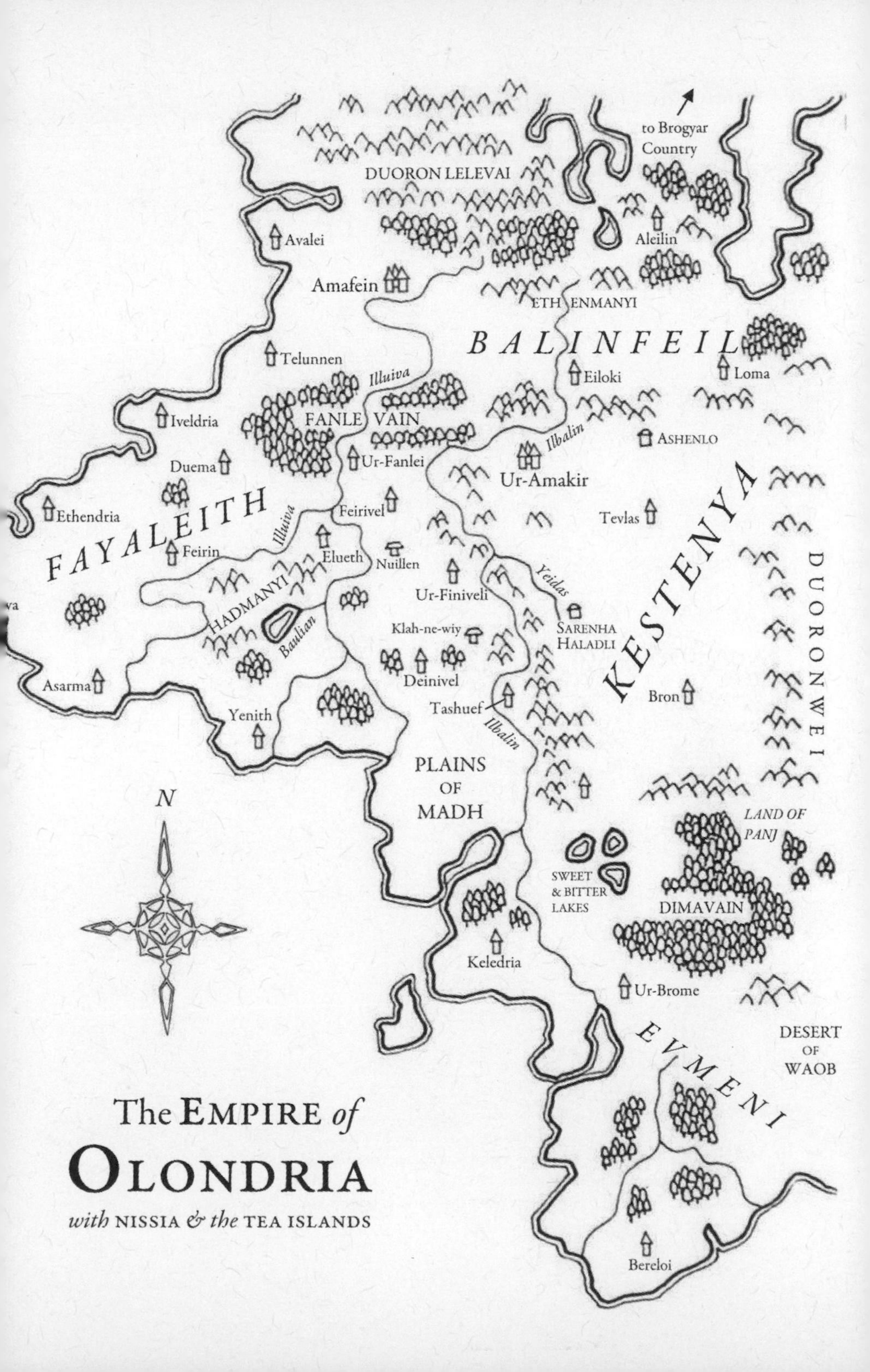

The EMPIRE *of* OLONDRIA

with NISSIA *&* *the* TEA ISLANDS

This is a work of fiction. All characters and events portrayed in this book are either fictitious or used fictitiously.

sofiasamatar.com

Small Beer Press
150 Pleasant Street, #306
Easthampton, MA 01027
bookmoonbooks.com
weightlessbooks.com
smallbeerpress.com
info@smallbeerpress.com

Distributed to the trade by Consortium.

Library of Congress Cataloging-in-Publication Data

Samatar, Sofia.
A stranger in Olondria : a novel / Sofia Samatar. -- 1st ed.
p. cm.
ISBN 978-1-931520-76-8 (alk. paper) -- ISBN 978-1-931520-77-5 (ebook)
1. Books and reading--Fiction. I. Title.
PS3619.A4496S77 2012
813'.6--DC23

2012020482

First edition 4 5 6 7 8 9

Text set in Centaur 11.5 pt.

ISBN: 9781618730626 (hardcover); 9781931520768 (trade paper); 9781931520775 (ebook)

Printed on 55# 30% PCR recycled Natures Natural paper by the Versa Press in East Peoria, IL.

For Keith

BOOK ONE

The Wind of Miracles

Chapter One

Childhood in Tyom

As I was a stranger in Olondria, I knew nothing of the splendor of its coasts, nor of Bain, the Harbor City, whose lights and colors spill into the ocean like a cataract of roses. I did not know the vastness of the spice markets of Bain, where the merchants are delirious with scents, I had never seen the morning mists adrift above the surface of the green Illoun, of which the poets sing; I had never seen a woman with gems in her hair, nor observed the copper glinting of the domes, nor stood upon the melancholy beaches of the south while the wind brought in the sadness from the sea. Deep within the Fayaleith, the Country of the Wines, the clarity of light can stop the heart: it is the light the local people call "the breath of angels" and is said to cure heartsickness and bad lungs. Beyond this is the Balinfeil, where, in the winter months, the people wear caps of white squirrel fur, and in the summer months the goddess Love is said to walk and the earth is carpeted with almond blossom. But of all this I knew nothing. I knew only of the island where my mother oiled her hair in the glow of a rush candle, and terrified me with stories of the Ghost with No Liver, whose sandals slap when he walks because he has his feet on backwards.

My name is Jevick. I come from the blue and hazy village of Tyom, on the western side of Tinimavet in the Tea Islands. From Tyom, high on the cliffs, one can sometimes see the green coast of Jiev, if the sky is very clear; but when it rains, and all the light is drowned in heavy clouds, it is the loneliest village in the world. It is a three-day journey to Pitot, the nearest village, riding on one of the donkeys of the islands, and to travel to the port of Dinivolim in the north requires at least a fortnight in the draining heat. In Tyom, in an open court, stands my father's house, a lofty building made of yellow stone, with a great arched entryway adorned with hanging plants, a flat roof, and nine shuttered rooms. And nearby, outside the village, in a valley drenched with rain, where the brown donkeys weep with exhaustion, where the flowers melt away and are lost in the heat, my father had his spacious pepper farm.

This farm was the source of my father's wealth and enabled him to keep the stately house, to maintain his position on the village council, and carry a staff decorated with red dye. The pepper bushes, voluptuous and green under the haze, spoke of riches with their moist and pungent breath; my father used to rub the dried corns between his fingers to give his fingertips the smell of gold. But if he was wealthy in some respects, he was poor in others: there were only two children in our house, and the years after my birth passed without hope of another, a misfortune generally blamed on the god of elephants. My mother said the elephant god was jealous and resented our father's splendid house and fertile lands; but I knew that it was whispered in the village that my father had sold his unborn children to the god. I had seen people passing the house nudge one another and say, "He paid seven babies for that palace"; and sometimes our laborers sang a vicious work song: "*Here the earth is full of little bones.*" Whatever the reason, my father's first wife had never conceived at all, while the second wife, my mother, bore only two children: my elder brother Jom, and myself. Because the first wife had no child, it was she whom we always addressed as Mother, or else with the term of respect, *eti-donvati*, "My Father's Wife"; it was she who accompanied us to festivals, prim and disdainful, her hair in two black coils above her ears. Our real mother lived in our room with us, and my father and his wife called her "Nursemaid," and we children called her simply by the name she had borne from girlhood: Kiavet, which means Needle. She was round-faced and lovely, and wore no shoes. Her hair hung loose down her back. At night she told us stories while she oiled her hair and tickled us with a gull's feather.

Our father's wife reserved for herself the duty of inspecting us before we were sent to our father each morning. She had merciless fingers and pried into our ears and mouths in her search for imperfections; she pulled the drawstrings of our trousers cruelly tight and slicked our hair down with her saliva. Her long face wore an expression of controlled rage, her body had an air of defeat, she was bitter out of habit, and her spittle in our hair smelled sour, like the bottom of the cistern. I only saw her look happy once: when it became clear that

Jom, my meek, smiling elder brother, would never be a man, but would spend his life among the orange trees, imitating the finches.

My earliest memories of the meetings with my father come from the troubled time of this discovery. Released from the proddings of the rancorous first wife, Jom and I would walk into the fragrant courtyard, hand in hand and wearing our identical light trousers, our identical short vests with blue embroidery. The courtyard was cool, crowded with plants in clay pots and shaded by trees. Water stood in a trough by the wall to draw the songbirds. My father sat in a cane chair with his legs stretched out before him, his bare heels turned up like a pair of moons.

We knelt. "Good morning father whom we love with all our hearts, your devoted children greet you," I mumbled.

"And all our hearts, and all our hearts, and all our hearts," said Jom, fumbling with the drawstring on his trousers.

My father was silent. We heard the swift flutter of a bird alighting somewhere in the shade trees. Then he said in his bland, heavy voice: "Elder son, your greeting is not correct."

"And we love him," Jom said uncertainly. He had knotted one end of the drawstring about his finger. There rose from him, as always, an odor of sleep, greasy hair, and ancient urine.

My father sighed. His chair groaned under him as he leaned forward. He blessed us by touching the tops of our heads, which meant that we could stand and look at him. "Younger son," he said quietly, "what day is today? And which prayers will be repeated after sundown?"

"It is Tavit, and the prayers are the prayers of maize-meal, passion fruit, and the new moon."

My father admonished me not to speak so quickly, or people would think I was dishonest; but I saw that he was pleased and felt a swelling of relief in my heart, for my brother and myself. He went on to question me on a variety of subjects: the winds, the attributes of the gods, simple arithmetic, the peoples of the islands, and the delicate art of pepper-growing. I stood tall, threw my shoulders back, and strove to answer promptly, tempering my nervous desire to blurt my words, imitating the slow enunciation of my father, his stern air of a great landowner. He did not ask my brother any questions. Jom stood unnoticed, scuffing his sandals on the flagstones—only sometimes, if there happened to be doves in the courtyard, he would say very softly: "Oo-ooh." At length my father blessed us again, and we escaped, hand in hand, into the back rooms of the house; and I carried in my mind the image of my father's narrow eyes: shrewd, cynical, and filled with sadness.

At first, when he saw that Jom could not answer his questions and could not even greet him properly, my father responded with the studied and ponderous rage of a bull elephant. He threatened my brother, and, when threats failed to cure his stubborn incompetence, had him flogged behind the house on a patch of sandy ground by two dull-eyed workers from the pepper fields. During the flogging I stayed in our darkened bedroom, sitting on my mother's lap while she pressed her hands over my ears to shut out my brother's loud, uncomprehending screams. I pictured him rolling on the ground, throwing up his arms to protect his dusty head while the blows of the stout sticks descended on him and my father watched blankly from his chair. . . . Afterward Jom was given back to us, bruised and bloodied, with wide staring eyes, and my mother went to and fro with poultices for him, tears running freely down her cheeks. "It is a mistake," she sobbed. "It is clear that he is a child of the wild pig." Her face in the candlelight was warped and gleaming with tears, her movements distracted. That night she did not tell me stories but sat on the edge of my bed and gripped my shoulder, explaining in hushed and passionate tones that the wild pig god was Jom's father; that the souls of the children of that god were more beautiful, more tender, than ordinary souls, and that our duty on earth was to care for them with the humility we showed the sacred beasts. "But your father will kill him," she said, looking into the darkness with desolate eyes. "There is flint in his bowels. He has no religion. He is a Tyomish barbarian."

My mother was from Pitot, where the women wore anklets of shell and plucked their eyebrows, and her strong religious views were seen in Tyom as ignorant Pitoti superstition. My father's wife laughed at her because she burned dried fenugreek in little clay bowls, a thing which, my father's wife said with contempt, we had not done in Tyom for a hundred years. And she laughed at me, too, when I told her one morning at breakfast, in a fit of temper, that Jom was the son of the wild pig god and possessed an untarnished soul: "He may have the soul of a pig," she said, "but that doesn't mean he's not an idiot." This piece of blasphemy, and the lines around her mouth, proved that she was in a good humor. She remained in this mood, her movements energetic and her nostrils clenched slightly with mirth, as long as my father sought for a means to cure Jom of his extraordinary soul. When the doctors came up from the south, with their terrible eyes and long hats of monkey skin, she served them hot date juice in bright glazed cups herself, smiling down at the ground. But the dreadful ministrations of the doctors, which left my brother blistered, drugged, and weeping in his sleep, did not affect his luminescent soul and only put a shade of terror in his gentle pig's eyes. A medicinal stench filled the house, and my bed was moved out into another room; from dusk until dawn I could hear the low moaning of my brother, punctuated with shrieks. In the evenings my mother knelt praying in the little room where the family *janut,* in whose power only she truly believed, stood in a row on an old-fashioned altar.

The *jut* is an external soul. I had never liked the look of mine: it had a vast forehead, claw feet, and a twist of dried hemp around its neck. The other *janut* were similar. Jom's, I recall, wore a little coat of red leather. The room where they lived, little more than a closet, smelled of burnt herbs and mold. Like most children I had at one period been frightened of the *janut,* for it was said that if your *jut* spoke to you your death was not far off, but the casual attitudes of Tyom had seeped into me and diluted my fear, and I no longer ran past the altar room with held breath and pounding heart. Still, a strange chill came over me when I glanced in and saw my mother's bare feet in the gloom, her body in shadow, kneeling, praying. I knew that she prayed for Jom and perhaps stroked the little figure in the red jacket, soothing her son from the outside.

At last those unhappy days ended in victory for my brother's soul. The doctors went away and took their ghastly odor with them; my father's wife reverted to her usual bitterness, and my bed was moved back into my room. The only difference now was that Jom no longer sat in the schoolroom and listened to our tutor, but wandered in the courtyard underneath the orange trees, exchanging pleasantries with the birds.

After this my father took a profound and anxious interest in me, his only son in this world; for there was no longer any doubt that I would be his sole heir and continue his trade with Olondria.

Once a year, when the pepper harvest was gathered and dried and stored in great, coarse sacks, my father, with his steward, Sten, and a company of servants, made a journey to Olondria and the spice markets of Bain. On the night before they left we would gather in the courtyard to pray for the success of their venture and to ask my father's god, the black-and-white monkey, to protect them in that far and foreign land. My mother was very much affected by these prayers, for she called Olondria the Ghost Country and only restrained herself from weeping out of fear that her tears would cause the ship to go down. Early the next day, after breakfasting as usual on a chicken baked with honey and fruit, my father would bless us and walk slowly, leaning on his staff, into the blue mists of the dawn. The family and house servants followed him outside to see him off from the gateway of the house, where he mounted his fat mule with its saddle of white leather, aided by the dark and silent Sten. My father, with Sten on foot leading the mule, formed the head of an impressive caravan: a team of servants followed him, bearing wooden litters piled high with sacks of pepper on their shoulders, and behind them marched a company of stout field hands armed with short knives, bows, and poisoned arrows. Behind these a young boy led a pair of donkeys laden with provisions and my father's tent, and last of all a third donkey bore a sack of wooden blocks on which my father would record his transactions. My father's bright clothes, wide-brimmed hat, and straw umbrella remained visible for a long time, as the caravan made its way between the houses shaded by mango trees and descended solemnly into the valley. My father never turned to look back at us, never moved, only swayed very gently on the mule. He glided through the morning with the grace of a whale: impassive, imponderable.

When he returned we would strew the courtyard with the island's most festive flowers, the *tediet* blossoms which crackle underfoot like sparks, giving off a tart odor of limes. The house was filled with visitors, and the old men sat in the courtyard at night, wrapped in thin blankets against the damp air and drinking coconut liquor. My father's first wife wept in the kitchen, overseeing the servants, my mother wore her hair twisted up on top of her head and fastened with pins, and my father, proud and formidably rich after four months in a strange land, drank with such greed that the servants had to carry him into his bedroom. At these times his mood was expansive. He pulled my ears and called me "brown monkey." He sat up all night by the brazier regaling the old men with tales of the north; he laughed with abandon, throwing his head back, the tears squeezing from his eyes, and one evening I saw him kiss the back of my mother's neck in the courtyard. And, of course, he was laden with gifts: saddles and leather boots for the old men, silks and perfumes for his wives, and marvelous toys for Jom and me. There were musical boxes and painted wooden birds that could hop on the ground and were worked by turning a bit of brass which protruded from under their wings; there were beautiful toy animals and toy ships astonishing in their detail, equipped with lifelike rigging and oars and cunning miniature sailors. He even brought us a finely painted set of *omi*, or "Hands," the complex and ancient card game of the Olondrian aristocracy, which neither he nor we had any notion of how to play, though we loved the painted cards: the Gaunt Horse, the Tower of Brass. In the evenings I crept to sit behind a certain potted orchid in the hall which led from the east wing of the house into the courtyard, listening to my father's tales, more wonderful than gifts, of terraced gardens, opium, and the barefoot girls of the pleasure houses.

One night he found me there. He walked past me, shuffling heavily, and the moonlight from the garden allowed him to spot my hiding place. He grunted, paused, and reached down to pull me upright. "Ah—Father—" I gasped, wincing.

"What are you doing there?" he demanded. "What? Speak!"

"I was—I thought—"

"Yes, the gods hate me. They've given me two backward sons." The slap he dealt me was soft; it was terror that made me flinch.

"I was only listening. I wanted to hear you. To hear about Olondria. I'll go to bed now. I'm sorry. I wanted to hear what you were saying."

"To hear what I was saying."

"Yes."

He nodded slowly, his hands on his hips, the dome of his head shifting against the moonlight in the yard. His face was in darkness, his breathing forced and deliberate, as if he were fighting. Each exhalation, fiery with liquor, made my eyes water.

"I'll go to bed," I whispered.

"No. No. You wanted to hear. Very good. The farm is your birthright. You must hear of Olondria. You must learn."

Relief shot through me; my knees trembled.

"Yes," he went on, musing. "You must hear. But first, younger son, you must taste."

My muscles, newly relaxed, tensed again with alarm. "Taste?"

"Taste." He gripped my shirt at the shoulder and thrust me before him through the hall. "Taste the truth," he muttered, stumbling. "Taste it. No, outside. Into the garden. That way. Yes. Here you will learn."

The garden was bright. Moonlight bounced from every leaf. There was no light in the kitchen: all the servants had gone to bed. Only Sten would be awake, and he would be on the other side of the house, seated discreetly in an alcove off the courtyard. There he could see when the old men wanted something, but he could not hear me cry, and if he did he would let me be when he saw I was with my father. A shove in my back sent me sprawling among the tomato plants. My father bent over me, enveloping me in his shadow. "Who are you?"

"Jevick of Tyom."

A burst of cackling rose to the sky from the other side of the house: one of the old men had made a joke.

"Good," said my father. He crouched low, swaying so that I feared he would fall on me. Then he brought his hand to my lips. "Taste. Eat."

Something was smeared on my mouth. A flavor of bitterness, suffocation. It was earth. I jerked back, shaking my head, and he grasped the back of my neck. His fingers tough and insistent between my teeth. "Oh, no. You will eat. This is your life. This earth. This country. Tyom."

I struggled but at last swallowed, weeping and gagging. All the time he went on speaking in a low growl. "You hide, you crawl, to hear of Olondria. A country of ghosts and devils. For this you spy on your father, your blood. Now you will taste your own land, know it. Who are you?"

"Jevick of Tyom."

"Don't spit. Who are you?"

"Jevick of Tyom!"

A light shone out behind him; someone called to him from the house. He stood, and I shielded my eyes from the light with my hand. One of the old men stood in the doorway holding a lantern on a chain.

"What's the matter?" he called out in a cracked and drunken voice.

"Nothing. The boy couldn't sleep," my father answered, hauling me up by the elbow.

"Nightmares."

"Yes. He's all right now."

He patted my shoulder, tousled my hair. Shadows moved over us, clouds across the moon.

Chapter Two

Master Lunre

My father's actions were largely incomprehensible to me, guided by his own secret and labyrinthine calculations. He dwelt in another world, a world of intrigue, bargains, contracts, and clandestine purchases of land all over the island. He was in many ways a world in himself, whole as a sphere. No doubt his decisions were perfectly logical in his own eyes—even the one that prompted him, a patriotic islander, to bring me a tutor from Bain: Master Lunre, an Olondrian.

The day began as it usually did when my father was expected home from his travels: the house festooned with flowers and stocked with coconut liquor. We stood by the gate, washed and perfumed and arrayed in our brightest clothes, my mother twisting her hands in her skirt, my father's wife with red eyes. Jom, grown taller and broad in the shoulders, moaned gently to himself, while I stood nervously rubbing the heel of one sandal on the flagstones. We scanned the deep blue valley for the first sign of the company, but before we saw them we heard the children shouting: "A yellow man!"

A yellow man! We glanced at one another in confusion. My mother bit her lower lip; Jom gave a groan of alarm. At first I thought the children meant my father, whose golden skin, the color of the night-monkey's pelt, was a rarity in the islands; but certainly the children of Tyom were familiar with my father and would never have greeted a council member with such ill-mannered yells. Then I remembered the only "yellow man" I had ever seen, an Olondrian wizard and doctor who had visited Tyom in my childhood, who wore two pieces of glass on his eyes, attached to his ears with wires, and roamed the hills of Tinimavet, cutting bits off the trees. I have since learned that that doctor wrote a well-received treatise, *On the Medicinal Properties of the Juice of the Young Coconut,* and died a respected man in his native city of Deinivel; but at the time I felt certain he had returned with his sack of tree-cuttings.

"There they are," said Pavit, the head house servant, in a strained voice. And there they were: a chain of riders weaving among the trees. My father's plaited umbrella appeared, his still, imposing figure, and beside him another man, tall and lean, astride an island mule. The hectic screams of the children preceded the company into the village, so that they advanced like a festival, drawing people out of their houses. As they approached I saw that my father's face was shining with pride, and his bearing had in it a new hauteur, like that of the old island kings. The man who rode beside him, looking uncomfortable with his long legs, kept his gaze lowered and fixed between the ears of his plodding mule. He was not yellow but very pale brown, the color of raw cashews; he had silver hair, worn cropped close to the skull so that it resembled a cap. He was not the leaf-collecting doctor but an altogether strange man, with silver eyebrows in his smooth face and long, fine-knuckled hands. As he dismounted in front of the house I heard my mother whispering: "Protect us, God with the Black-and-White Tail, from that which is not of this earth."

My father dismounted from his mule and strutted toward us, grinning. I thought I caught an odor off him, of fish, seasickness, and sweat. We knelt and stared down at the bald ground, murmuring ritual greetings, until he touched the tops of our heads with the palm of his fleshy hand. Then we stood, unable to keep from staring at the stranger, who faced us awkwardly, half smiling, taller than any man there.

"Look at the yellow man!" the children cried. "He is like a frilled lizard!" And indeed, with his narrow trousers and high ruffled collar, he resembled that creature. My father turned to him and, with an exaggerated nonchalance, spoke a few foreign words which seemed to slip back and forth in his mouth, which I later learned were a gross distortion of the northern tongue, but which, at the time, filled me with awe and the stirrings of filial pride. The stranger answered him with a slight bow and a stream of mellifluous speech, provoking my mother to kiss the tips of her fingers to turn aside evil. Then my father pointed at me with a gesture of obvious pride, and the stranger turned his piercing, curious, kindly gaze on me. His eyes were a mineral green, the color of seas where shipwrecks occur, the color of unripe melons, the color of lichen, the color of glass.

"*Av maro,*" said my father, pointing to me and then to himself.

The Olondrian put one hand on his heart and made me a deep bow.

"Bow to him," said my father. I copied the stranger ungracefully, provoking hilarious shrieks from the children who stood around us in the street. My father nodded, satisfied, and spoke to the stranger again, gesturing for him to enter the cool of the house. We followed them into the courtyard, where the stranger sat in a cane chair, his long legs stretched out in front of him, his expression genial and bemused.

He brought new air to our house: he brought the Tetchi, the Wind of Miracles. At night the brazier lit up his face as he sat in the humid courtyard. He sat with the old men, speaking to them in his tongue like a thousand fountains, casting fantastic shadows with his long and liquid hands. My father translated the old men's questions: Was the stranger a wizard? Would he be gathering bark and leaves? Could he summon his *jut*? There were shouts of laughter, the old men grinning and showing the stumps of their teeth, pressing the stranger to drink our potent homemade liquor and smoke our tobacco. He obliged them as well as he could, though the coconut liquor made him grimace and the harsh tobacco, rolled in a leaf, sent him into a fit of coughing. This pleased the old men enormously, but my father came to his rescue, explaining that allowances must be made for the northerner's narrow ribcage. In those days we did not know if our guest were not a sort of invalid: he vastly preferred our hot date juice to the liquor the old men loved; he ate only fruit for breakfast and turned very pale at the sight of pig stomach; he rose from his afternoon sleep with a haggard look and drank far too much water. Yet his presence brought an air of excitement that filled the house like light, an air that smelled of festivals, perfume and *tediet* blossoms, and drew in an endless stream of curious, eager visitors, offering gifts to the stranger: yams baked in sugar, mussels in oil.

My father swelled like a gourd: he was bursting with self-importance, the only one who was able to understand the illustrious stranger. "Our guest is tired," he would announce in a grave, dramatic tone, causing his family and visitors to retreat humbly from the courtyard. His lips wore a constant, jovial smirk. He spoke loudly in the street. He was moved to the highest circle of council and carried a staff with hawk feathers. Most wonderful of all, he seemed to have lost the capacity for anger and ignored annoyances which formerly would have caused him to stamp like a buffalo. The servants caught his mood: they made jokes and grinned at their tasks, and allowed Jom to pilfer peanuts and honeycombs from the back of the kitchen. Even my father's wife was charmed by the northerner's gift of raisins: she waited on him with her smile drawn tight, an Olondrian scarf in her hair.

My mother was most resistant to the festival air in the house. On the night of the stranger's arrival she burned a bowl of dried herbs in her room: I recognized, by their acrid smoke, the leaves that ward off leopard ghosts. They were followed by pungent fumes against bats, leprosy, and falling sickness, as well as those which are said to rid human dwellings of long-toed spirits. Her face as she moved about the house was exhausted and filled with suffering, and her body was listless because of her nightly vigils by the clay bowls. My father's wife, strutting anxiously about in her Bainish pearl earrings, lamented that my mother would shame us all with her superstition, but I think she secretly feared that the stranger was in fact some sort of ghost and that my mother would drive him away, and with him our family's new status. "Talk to your nursemaid," she begged me. "She is making a fool of your father. Look at her! She has a ten-o'-clock face, like somebody at a funeral." I did try to speak to her, but she only looked at me mournfully and asked me if I was wearing a strip of charmed leather under my vest. I tried to defend the stranger as nothing more than a man, though a foreigner, but she fixed me with such a dark, steady look that my words died out in the air.

The Olondrian tried, in his clumsy way, to set my mother at ease, knowing that she was the wife of his host—but his efforts invariably failed. She avoided his shadow, kissed her fingers whenever she heard him speak, and refused his raisins, saying in horror: "They look like monkey turds!" Once, in the courtyard, I saw him approach her, at which she hurriedly knelt, as we all did in the first days, being unfamiliar with his customs. I had already seen that the northerner was disturbed by this island tradition, so I hid myself in the doorway to see how he would address my mother. He had learned to touch the servants on their heads to make them rise but seemed reluctant to do the same with my patiently kneeling mother; and indeed, as I now know, to his perplexed Olondrian mind, my mother was in an exalted position as a lady of the house. A sad comedy ensued: the northerner bowed with his hand on his heart, but my mother did not see him, as she was staring down at the ground. Evidently he wished to ask for something, but knowing nothing of our language, he had no means of making himself understood but through gestures and facial expressions. He cleared his throat and mimed the action of drinking with his long hands, but my mother, still looking down at the ground, did not see, and remained motionless. At this the Olondrian bent his long body double and mimed again, trying to catch her eye, which was fixed studiously on the flagstones. Seeing my mother's acute distress, I emerged at this point from the doorway. My mother made her escape, and I brought our guest a clay beaker of water.

It was proof of the stranger's tenacious spirit that, through his friendship with Jom, he convinced my mother that he was, if not of this earth, at least benevolent. In those early days it was Jom, with his plaintive voice of a twilight bird, with his small eyes of a young beast, who was at home in the stranger's company. Jom was my mother's child: he wore strips of leather under his clothes, iron charms on his wrists, and a small bag of sesame seeds at his waist, and she had so filled his clothes and hair with the odor of burning herbs that we thought our guest would be blown back into the sea if he went near my brother. Yet Jom was excited by the stranger and sought every chance to speak to him—of all of us, only he did not know that our guest could not understand. And the stranger always met him with a smile of genuine pleasure, clasping his hand as Olondrians do with their equals and intimates. In the green bower of the shade trees with their near-transparent blue flowers, the two spoke a language of grunt and gesture and the eloquent arching of eyebrows. Jom taught the northerner his first words in the Kideti tongue, which were "tree," "orange," "macaw," "finch," and "starling." My brother was fascinated by the stranger's long, graceful hands, his gold and silver rings, his earrings set with veined blue stones, and also, as we all were, by the melodies of his speech and his crocodile eyes: another of Lunre's early words was "green." One afternoon Lunre brought a wooden whistle from his room, brightly painted, with three small pipes like the flutes of western Estinavet. On these he could play the calling notes of the songbirds of the north: music which speaks of vineyards, olive trees, and sacred rivers. At the strange music my brother wept and asked, "Where are the birds?" The stranger did not answer him but seemed to understand: his smooth brown face was sorrowful, and he put the whistle away, brushing the leaves with his fingertips in a gesture of despair.

I do not know when my mother first joined them under the flowering trees. She must have begun by watching to see that no harm came to her son; sometimes I saw her pause, a tall pitcher balanced on her hip, staring into the trees with alarm in her lovely eyes of a black deer. Bird sounds came from the shadows, the Olondrian's low chuckle, the sound of my brother's voice saying patiently: "No, that one is blue." Somehow my mother entered the trees, perhaps to protect her son—and somehow the Olondrian's humble expression and sad eyes softened her heart. In those days she began to say: "May good luck find that unfortunate ghost! He sweats too much, and those trousers of his must keep his blood from flowing." She no longer knelt when she met him, but smiled and nodded at his low bow, and one morning pointed firmly to her chest and said: "Kiavet."

"Lunre," the stranger said eagerly, tapping his own narrow chest.

"Lun-le," my mother repeated. Her sweet smile flickered, a feather on the wind. Soon after this she presented him, shyly, yet with a secret pride, with a vest and a pair of trousers she had sewn for his lanky body. They were very fine, the trousers flowing and patterned with rose and gold, the vest embroidered in blue with the bold designs of both Tyom and Pitot. The stranger was deeply moved and stood for some time with his hand on his heart, his silver head bowed, thanking her earnestly in the language of raindrops. My father's wife did not fail to sneer at my mother's kindness to her "ghost," but my mother only smiled and said serenely: "The Tetchi is blowing."

When the miracle wind had blown for a month, my father dismissed my old tutor, a dotard with hairy ears who had taught me mathematics, religion, and history. The Olondrian, he explained to me as I sat before him one morning, was to take the old man's place, tutoring me in the northern tongue. His eyes contracted with pleasure as he spoke, and he waved the stump of his narrow cigar and patted his ample stomach. "My son," he said, "what good fortune is yours! Someday, when you own the farm, you will feel at ease in Bain and will never be cheated in the spice markets! Yes, I want you to have a Bainish gentleman's education—the tall one will teach you to speak Olondrian, and to read in books."

The word for "book" in all the known languages of the earth is *vallon,* "chamber of words," the Olondrian name for that tool of enchantment and art. I had no idea of its meaning but thanked my father in a low voice as he smoked his cigar with a flourish and grunted to show that he had heard me. I was both excited and frightened to think of studying with the stranger, for I was shy around him and found his green gaze disconcerting. I could not see how he would teach me, since we shared no common language—but I joined him dutifully in the schoolroom that opened onto the back garden.

He began by taking me by the wrist and leading me around the room, pointing to things and naming them, signing that I should repeat. When I had learned the names of all the objects in the schoolroom, he took me into the kitchen garden and named the vegetables. If there were plants he did not know, he pointed and raised his gull-gray eyebrows, which meant that he wished to learn the Kideti word. He carried with him always a leather satchel of very fine make, in which he kept another leather object, dyed peacock-blue; when he opened it, sheets of rich cotton paper spread out like a fan, some of them marked with minute patterns which he had made himself. The satchel had a narrow pocket sewn to an outside edge, fastened shut with a metal clasp and set with bits of turquoise, and in this my new master kept two or three miraculous ink pens, filled only once a day, with which he made marks in his *vallon.* Whenever I told him a word in our language, he took out his blue leather book, wrote something in it rapidly, and thanked me with a bow. I was puzzled, for though I admired the book as more cunning than our wooden blocks, I could not understand why he wished to keep track of the number of words he had learned.

At last one morning he brought a wooden box with him into the schoolroom, a splendid receptacle covered with patterns in gilt, paint, and mother-of-pearl. Orange flowers danced on its dark blue lid, and in a cloud of golden stars a pair of ivory hands floated: the hands of spirits. I knew that the box had come from my master's heavy, ornate sea chest, with which my father's servants had toiled through the damp forests of the island, in which he was said to keep the awful trappings of a magician, as well as the bones of his wife, her skull as flawless as a bride's. He set the box on the round, flat stone that served us as a table. I knelt on my mat with my elbows on the stone, cupping my chin in my hands. My master preferred to sit on a stool, hunkering over the table, his legs splayed out, his crooked knees rising above the level of the stone. He did so now, then removed his satchel and set it on the table, and drew from it a slim book bound in red leather.

"For you," he said in Olondrian, sliding the little book toward me.

I felt a rush of excitement and a tightness in my throat. I took up the book and tried to put my gratitude into my eyes, while my master grinned and cracked his spider's knuckles, a habit he had when pleased.

The schoolroom was already warm. The long light came in through the garden archway, and the voices of the servants reached us from the kitchen next door. I turned the little book tenderly in my hands, fingering the spine, and at last, with a sharp intake of breath, I opened it. It was empty.

I touched the blank paper and looked at my master reproachfully. He chuckled and squeezed his knuckles, apparently charmed by my disappointment. I knew enough of his speech to ask at last: "What is it, Tchavi?"—addressing him, as I always did, with the Kideti word for "Master."

He held up a finger, signaling for me to wait and pay attention. He opened the book before me at the first page and smoothed the paper. Then he unlatched the ornate box, revealing a neat shelf suspended inside the lid, flecked with diamonds of yellow paint. Humming cheerfully to himself, he removed several small clay jars, each with a tiny cork in it, and a little red cut-glass bottle. His fingers hovered over the shelf for a moment before selecting an engraved silver pen from an ivory case. Swiftly, with fluid, dexterous movements, he unstoppered one of the jars, releasing the dark odor of rust and aloes. He added a few drops from the glass bottle, which made the room smell of pollen, and stirred the resultant brew with a slender reed. The reed came out very black, and he rested it in a shallow dish. Then he filled the pen from the jar by turning its tip. He wiped its nib on a silken cloth much stained by streaks of ink; then he leaned toward me, bent over my book, and wrote five intricate signs.

I understood now that my master meant to teach me the Olondrian numbers, and how to record accounts, as he did, in neat, small rows in a book. I leaned forward eagerly, imagining how it would please my father when he saw his son writing numbers on paper just like a Bainish gentleman. I had my own secret misgivings, for though the book was easy to carry, much more so than the blocks on which we wrote with a piece of hot iron, it seemed to me that the pages could be easily ruined by seawater, that the ink could smear, and that this was a flimsy way of keeping records. Nevertheless the strange signs, fluted like seashells, captivated me so that my master laughed with pleasure and patted my shoulder. I moved my finger slowly under the row of graceful figures, memorizing the foreign shapes of the numbers one through five.

"Shevick," my master said.

I glanced at him expectantly at the sound of his familiar mispronunciation of my name.

"Shevick," he said again, pointing down at the signs on the page.

I said to him proudly, in his own tongue: "One, two, three, four, five."

He shook his head. "Shevick, Shevick," he said, tapping the paper. I frowned and shrugged, saying, "Forgive me, Tchavi. I don't understand."

My master put up his hands, palms outward, and pushed gently at the air, showing that he was not angry. Then he bent forward patiently. "*Sh*," he said, pointing with his pen at the first sign on the page; then he moved the pen to the second sign and said distinctly: "*Eh*." But only when he had described all the signs several times, repeating my name, did I understand with a shock that I was in the presence of sorcery: that the signs were not numbers at all, but could speak, like the single-stringed Tyomish harp, which can mimic the human voice and is called "the sister of the wind."

My back and shoulders were cold, though a hot, heavy air came in from the garden. I stared at my master, who looked back at me with his wise and crystalline eyes. "Do not be afraid," he said. He smiled, but his face looked thin and sad. In the garden I heard the sound of the Tetchi disrobing herself in the leaves.

Chapter Three

Doorways

"A book," says Vandos of Ur-Amakir, "is a fortress, a place of weeping, the key to a desert, a river that has no bridge, a garden of spears." Fanlewas the Wise, the great theologian of Avalei, writes that Kuidva, the God of Words, is "a taskmaster with a lead whip." Tala of Yenith is said to have kept her books in an iron chest that could not be opened in her presence, else she would lie on the floor, shrieking. She wrote: "Within the pages there are fires, which can rise up, singe the hair, and make the eyelids sting." Ravhathos called the life of the poet "the fair and fatal road, of which even the dust and stones are dear to my heart," and cautioned that those who spend long hours engaged in reading or writing should not be spoken to for seven hours afterward. "For they have gone into the Pit, into which they descend on Slopes of Fire, but when they rise they climb on a Ladder of Stone." Hothra of Ur-Brome said that his books were "dearer than father or mother," a sentiment echoed by thousands of other Olondrians through the ages, such as Elathuid the Voyager, who explored the Nissian coast and wrote: "I sat down in the wilderness with my books, and wept for joy." And the mystic Leiya Tevorova, that brave and unfathomable soul, years before she met her tragic death by water, wrote: "When they put me into the Cold, above the white Lake, in the Loathsome Tower, and when Winter came with its cruel, hard, fierce, dark, sharp and horrible Spirit, my only solace was in my Books, wherein I walked like a Child, or shone in the Dark like a Moth which has its back to a sparkling Fire."

In my room, in my village, I shone like a moth with its back to a sparkling fire. Master Lunre had taught me his sorcery: I embraced it and swooned in its arms. The drudgery of the schoolroom, the endless copying of letters, the conjugation of verbs—"*ayein, kayein, bayeinan, bayeinun*"—all of this led me at last through a curtain of flame into a world which was a new way of speaking and thinking, a new way of moving, a means of escape. Master Lunre's massive sea chest did not hold the bones of a murdered wife, but a series of living lovers with whom he lay down voluptuously, caressing the hair of each one in turn: his books, some written by hand and some from the printing press, that unearthly invention of the wizards of Asarma. I soon understood why, when I went in to call him for the evening meal, my master could always be found stretched out on his pallet in the same position: his head on his hand, his bare chest gleaming, a thin sheet over his hips, his earrings glinting, his spirit absorbed in the mists of an open book. I, too, soon after I read my first book, Nardien's *Tales for the Tender,* succumbed to the magical voices that called to me from their houses of vellum. It was a great wonder to me to come so close to these foreign spirits, to see with the eyes and hear with the ears of those I had never known, to communicate with the dead, to feel that I knew them intimately, and that they knew me more completely than any person I knew in the flesh. I confess that I fell quite hopelessly in love with Tala of Yenith, who was already an old woman when the printing press was invented. When she heard of it, she is said to have danced in ecstasy, crying out, "They have created it! They have created it!" until she fell down in a dead faint. Her biographer writes: "When she rose she began her rapturous dance again, shouting 'They have created it!' until her strength was wholly exhausted. She continued like this, beyond the control of the people of her House, who feared to subdue her with force, for seven days, whereupon she died. . . ."

The books of my master's sea chest were histories, lyrics, and romances, as well as a few religious texts and minor philosophical works. In their pages I entered, for the first time, the tree-lined streets of Bain, and walked in the Garden of Plums beside the city's green canal. I fought with the rebel Keliadhu against Thul the Heretic, and watched the sky fill with dragons, unfurling fires like cloth of gold. I hunted mushrooms in the Fanlevain and fleet wild deer on the plains, and sailed down the swift Ilbalin through the most radiant orchards on earth; I stood in a court in Velvalinhu, the dwelling place of the kings, and watched a new Telkan kneel to receive the high crown of black and white silk. My dreams were filled with battles, haunted woods, and heroic voyages, and the Drevedi, the Olondrian vampires whose wings are like indigo. Each evening I lay on my pallet, reading by the light of an oil lamp, a tear-shaped bowl made of rust-colored clay—a gift from Master Lunre.

My master's gifts to me were those whose value cannot be reckoned. The education he gave me was erratic, shaped by his own great loves; it was not the traditional education of wealthy Olondrians, which consists of the Three Noble Arts of riding, music, and calligraphy. It was more like the education of novices dedicated to Kuidva, yet still it deviated, rejecting some classics for more obscure texts: I knew almost nothing of Telidar's seminal *Lectures on Poetry* but had read many times a small volume entitled *On the Nine Textures of Light*. Thus, while my father imagined that I was becoming a Bainish gentleman, I was in fact ignorant of almost all that such gentlemen know. I had only seen horses in pictures, I could not play the flute or guitar, my handwriting was neat but uninspired, and I knew only five classic writers. What I knew, what I learned, was the map of a heart, of the longings of Lunre of Bain: I walked in the forests of his desire and bathed in the sea of his dreams. For years I walked up and down the vales of his heart, of his self-imposed exile, familiar with all he loved, looking out of his eyes, those windows of agate.

He was as reticent as a crab. Or he was reserved about certain subjects: there were things of which, in the course of nine years, I could never persuade him to speak. One of these was his former trade, the one he had followed in Bain: he would never say what he had been—a tutor, a printer, a merchant, a thief? My boy's mind dreamed up fierce romances for him, but he would not be baited and only laughed when I said he had been a sorcerer or a pirate. When I asked him why he had left, he quoted Leiya Tevorova: "I was spoken to by a god, and I found myself unworthy of Him."

His face, neither old nor young, grew dark as an islander's with the sun, and his brows and close-cropped hair were bleached like sand. With his gangly limbs, in his island clothes, he resembled a festival clown, but he had too sad an air to be truly comical. He grew to love our valleys and forests and spent many hours outdoors, roaming the slopes with a staff of teak wood or exploring the cliffs by the sea. He would come home with completely ordinary flowers or shells and force me to look at them while he praised their inimitable loveliness. "Look at that!" he would say, elated. "Is it not finer than art? Is it not like a woman's ear? Its curves are like notes of music. . . ." On subjects such as the beauties of nature, books, and the colors of light, he spoke with an unrestrained passion which often drove me to groan with exhaustion. He spoke to my mother as well: he studied our language doggedly, until he could praise the trees and the play of light and shade in the courtyard. When my mother explained how the shadows echoed the pelt of my father's god, he rubbed his hands with delight and jotted some notes in his private book. "Let me tell you," he said to me once, resting a hand on my shoulder after drinking a glass of our liquor, to which his tastes had become accustomed: "Let me tell you about old men. Our appetites grow like vines—like the hectic plants of the desert, which bear only flowers and have no leaves. You have never seen a desert. Have you not read Firdred of Bain? 'The earth has a thousand thirsty tongues.' That is what old age is like."

He never seemed old to me, though he certainly had a great appetite—for sights, for the sounds of birds, for the smell of the sea, for the words of our language. And sometimes, too, he would take to his bed, his body wracked with fevers, with the stricken expression of one who has not long to live and whose life is unfinished. I nursed him through his fevers, reading aloud from the *Vanathul* because he believed words had the power to cure all ills. I loved him as if we were partners in exile, for only with him could I speak of books, enjoying that conversation which Vandos calls "the food of the gods." And yet there was something unyielding in him, something unconquerable, an unknown center which he guarded with care, which was never revealed to me, so that, while I knew him best, he seemed to hold me at a distance. Even in his delirium he let fall no shining thread.

In the islands the old word *tchavi,* by which I always called my master, originally referred to a teacher of ancient and cryptic lore. The *tchanavi* were few, and their houses were built on mountains so that those who sought them could only reach them after prolonged struggle. They were strange, solitary, at home in forests, speakers of double-voiced words, men without *jut,* for they cast their *janut* to the sea, a symbolic death. Their disciples passed down laments in the form of sighing island chants, bemoaning the dark impenetrability of the *tchanavi*'s wisdom: a Kideti proverb says, "Ask a *tchavi* to fill your basket, and he will take it away." They were difficult spirits, and made men weep. Yet the greater part of their pupils' laments do not mourn the enigma of wisdom but rather the failure of the disciples to find their masters at all: for the *tchanavi* were known to melt away into the forests, into the mists, so that those who had made hard journeys discovered only the mountain and silence. These songs, the "Chants of Abandonment," are sung at festivals and express the desperate love and grief of the followers of the *tchanavi*. "*Blood of my heart, on the mountain there is no peace in the calling of doves / My master has pressed a blossom into the mud with the sole of his foot.*"

My people called Lunre "the yellow man" or "the stranger." Their stares in the village hurt me, the old men's grins, the shouts of the children who followed us through the streets. Sometimes they even called him *hotun*—a soulless man, an outcast, a man without *jut*. I coaxed him away from them, away from the broad clean roads. He knew it, regarding me amused and compliant as I led him through knotted patches of jungle and onto the dangerous cliffs, through heavy forests where cold air rose from the earth, where I breathed raggedly, striking dead vines away from us with a stick. Leaves split under my weapon, spraying milk. When we broke through at last and emerged on the cliffs, my vest was so wet the sea wind chilled me. About us the crags lay tumbled and white with guano, and beyond them a sea the color of spittle moved in regular heaves.

"How do you bear it?" I muttered.

Lunre stood calm in the midday glare, chewing a shred of ginger root. "I am not sure what you mean."

"You know what I mean. This place."

"Ah. This place."

"You've been to Bain, to the great library. You're Olondrian. You've been everywhere."

"Everywhere! Indeed not."

"Other places."

"Yes." He shrugged, looking out to sea. The breeze was growing cooler, and fat clouds blocked the sky. In places the sun shone through them, silver, making them glow like the bellies of dead fish. Every day, I thought, every afternoon, this rain.

Lunre slapped my back, chuckling. "Don't be so gloomy. Look!" He darted back to the edge of the forest and plucked a bell fruit from the undergrowth. "Look around you!" he went on, returning to wave it under my nose, dispersing a sickening odor of hair oil and liquor.

I batted his hand away. He laughed as if it were a game but at once regained his usual pensive look, his hair standing up in the wind. The sky turned the color of dust while in my mind there were porcelain tiles, medallions embossed with the seals of Olondrian clans, monuments of white chalk. I longed for wide streets loud with the rumble of carriage wheels, for crowded markets, bridges, libraries, gardens, pleasure houses, for all that I had read of but never seen, for the land of books, for Lunre's country, for somewhere else, somewhere beyond. Thunder broke in the distance, and the afternoon darkened around us. Lunre spat out his scrap of ginger root, and it whirled on the wind. We hurried home beneath the shrieks of agitated birds, arriving as the storm fell like an avalanche of mud.

At home the archways were full of sound. In the hall I looked at Lunre, barely able to see him in the rain-dark air. He lifted one pale hand and spoke.

"What?"

"I'm going to read," he repeated, louder.

"Me, too," I lied and watched him melt away in the south wing.

When he had disappeared, I went to the stone archway that gave on the courtyard. A low gleam pierced the storm from a window on the opposite side: my father was in the room where he kept his accounts. I dashed across the courtyard, soaked in seconds, and pounded on the locked door.

A click, then a juddering sound as the bolt slid back. Sten, my father's steward and shadow, opened the door and stepped aside to let me in. I rubbed my hand over my face, throwing off water, and blinked in the dull radiance of the little brazier at my father's feet.

He was not alone. Two elderly men from the village sat with him beside the brazier, men of high rank with bright cloaks on their shoulders. Their beaky faces turned to me in surprise. My father sat arrested, an iron rod in his hand, its tip aglow. A servant knelt before him holding a sturdy block of teak wood; similar blocks were stacked beside him, ready for use. Behind the little group, silent and ghostly, arranged in rows as high as the ceiling, were other blocks, my father's records.

I threw myself on my knees on the sandy floor. "Forgive me, Father!"

There was a pause, and then his expressionless voice: "Younger son."

I raised my eyes. He had not touched my head, but he was too far to reach me, the brazier and the kneeling servant between us. I scanned his face for anything I could recognize: anger, acceptance, disappointment. His eyes were slivers of black silk in the fat of his cheeks.

I waited. He lowered his iron rod to the brazier, turning it in the coals. "This is my son Jevick," he explained to the old men. "You'll have forgotten him. He doesn't compete in games. I brought him a foreign tutor, and now they spend all their time gossiping like a pair of old women."

One of the men laughed briefly, a rasp of phlegm.

"Father," I said, my arms taut at my sides, my fists clenched: "Take me with you when you go to Olondria."

He met my eyes. My heart raced in my throat. "Take me with you," I said with an effort. "I'll learn the business. . . . It will be an education. . . ."

"Education!" he smiled, looking down again at the rod he was heating. "Education, younger son, is your whole trouble. That Olondrian has educated you to burst in on your father in his private room and interrupt his business."

"I had to speak to you. I can't—" I stopped, unable to find the words. Rain roared down the roof, pounding the air into the ground.

"Can't what?" He lifted the rod, the tip a ruby of deep light, and squinted at it. "Can't speak to your age mates? Can't find a peasant girl to play with? Can't run? Can't dance? Can't swim? Can't leave your room? What?" He turned, drawing the burning iron briskly across the block his servant held. Once, I remembered, he had slipped, searing the man's arm, leaving a brand for which he had paid with a pair of hens.

"I can't stay here."

"Can't stay here!" His harsh, flat laugh rang out, and the old men echoed him, for he had too much power ever to laugh alone. "Come now! Surely you hope and expect that your father will live for a few more years."

"May my father's life be as long as the shore that encircles the Isle of Abundance."

"Ah. You hear how he rushes his words," he remarked to his companions. "It has ever been his great failing, this impatience." He looked at me, allowing me to glimpse for the first time the depths of coldness in the twin pits of his eyes.

"You will stay," he said softly. "You will be grateful for what you are given. You will thank me."

"Thank you, Father," I whispered, desolate.

He tossed the hot iron aside, and it fell with a thud. He leaned back, searching under his belt for a cigar, not looking at me. "Get out," he said.

I do not know if he was cruel. I know that he was powerful; I know that he loved power and could not endure defiance. I do not know why he brought me a tutor out of a foreign country only to sneer at me, at my tutor, and at my loves. I do not know what it was that slept inside his cunning mind, that seldom woke to give his eyes, for a moment, a shade of sorrow; I do not know what it was that sprang at last at his heart and killed him, that struck him down in the paradise of the fields, in the wealth of pepper.

The morning was cool and bright. It was near the end of the rains, and the wind called Kyon rode over us on his invisible serpent. The clustered leaves of the orange trees were heavy and glistened with moisture, and Jom stood under them, shaking the branches, his hair dusted with raindrops. His was the voice we heard, that voice, thick with excess saliva, calling out clumsily: "There is a donkey in the courtyard!" His was the voice that brought us running, already knowing the truth, that hoofed animals were not brought into houses except in cases of death. I arrived in the doorway to see my mother already collapsing, supported by servants, shrieking and struggling in their arms, whipping her head from side to side, her hair knotting over her face, filling the air with the animal cries which would not cease for seven days. In the center of the courtyard, under the pattern of light and shade, stood a donkey, held with ropes by two of my father's dusty field-workers. The donkey's back was heaped with something: a tent, a great sack of yams, the carcass of an elephant calf—the body of my father.

The body was lashed with ropes and lolled, dressed in its yellow trousers, the leather sandals on its feet decorated with small red beads; but the ceremonial staff, with its arrogant cockscomb of hawk feathers, had been left behind in the fields, as none of the field-workers could touch it. I brought that scepter home, resting its smooth length on my shoulder, climbing the hill toward Tyom as the wind came up with its breath of rain, followed by the fat white mule who had been my father's pride, whom the field-workers had abandoned because a death had occurred on its back. When I reached the house, I stepped through an archway into the ruins of the courtyard, where every shade tree had been cut down and every pot smashed on the stones. I stood for a moment holding the staff in my arms, in a haze of heat. From the back rooms of the house came the sound of rhythmic screaming.

That screaming filled my ears for seven days and seven nights, until it became a drone, like the lunatic shrilling of cicadas. The servants had gone to the village to fetch eleven professional mourners, ragged, loose-haired women who keened, whipping their heads back and forth. Their arrival relieved my mother, who was hoarse and exhausted with mourning, having screamed unceasingly ever since she had seen my father's body. The mourners sat in the ravaged courtyard, five or six at a time, kneeling among the broken pots, the dirt, the remains of flowers, grieving wildly while, in our rooms, we dressed in our finest clothes, scented our hair, and decorated our faces with blue chalk.

Moments before we left for the funeral I passed my mother's room, and there was a *tchavi* there, an old man, sparse-haired, in a skin cloak flayed by storms. He was crouching by my mother where she lay face-down on her pallet, and his thin brown hand was resting on her hair. I paused, startled, and heard him say: "There now, daughter. There, it's gone out now. Easy and cold, like a little snake." I hurried back down the passage, guilty and frightened as if by a sign. My mother appeared soon afterward, unrecognizable under the chalk. I could not tell if her grief was eased by his visit, for she was like a shape etched in stone. As for the *tchavi,* he left the house in secret, and I did not see him again.

The women keened, their voices mixed with the raucous notes of horns, as we walked through the village slowly, slowly, under the gathering clouds, we, my father's family, blue-stained, stiff as effigies, with our blank, expressionless faces and our vests encrusted with beads. We walked in the dusty streets, in the cacophony of mourning, followed by the servants bearing the huge corpse on a litter. Master Lunre was with us, in his Olondrian costume, that which had caused the village children to call him a "frilled lizard." His face, unpainted, wore a pensive expression; he had not mourned, but only clasped my hand and said: "Now you have become mortal. . . ."

He sat with us for the seven days in the valley, beside the ruined city, the city of Jajetanet, crumbling, cloaked in mists, where we set my father's body upon one of the ancient stones and watched his flesh sag as it was pelted by the rain. "*Where shall I go to find the dawn?*" the hired singers chanted. "*He has not pricked his foot on a thorn, he leaves no trail of blood.*" My father's *jut* was beside him, potbellied like him, kept bright through years of my mother's devoted polishing, its feathers drooping.

Because of my father's high position, the mourning was well-attended: most of the people of Tyom were there, and some had come from Pitot. The green and gentle slope that led down into the ruined city was covered with people sitting cross-legged on mats under broad umbrellas. Harried servants walked among them bearing platters of food, begging them not to refuse nourishment in the ritual phrases of mourning. The people turned their heads away, insisting, with varying degrees of vehemence, that they could not eat; but at last they all accepted. "May it pass from me," we said, swallowing coconut liquor, sucking the mussels from their shells, the oil dribbling down our chins.

Before us rose the ancient ruins of Jajetanet the Desired, that city so old that none could remember who it was that had desired it, that city of ghosts inhabited by the ashes of the dead, where damp mists crept along the walls and a brooding presence lingered. At night when the fires were lit and the mourning rose to a frenzied pitch, the women with their knotted hair imitating the throes of death, Jajetanet rose above us, massive, blocking out the stars, She, the soul of loss, who knew what it was to be forgotten. The mourners shrieked. My father's body lay on a block of stone, surrounded by lighted torches, in his gold trousers and beaded sandals. Did his hands still smell of pepper? I thought of him, inspecting the farm, while within his ribs his death was already waiting, coiled to spring.

All at once, through the shadows of drink, I realized that I had not wept, and recognized the strain in my heart as the secret elation of freedom. I saw, looking into the blur of fires in the night, how it would be, how I would descend like a starling into the country of guitars. I trembled with excitement as, on the block of crumbling stone, my father's *jut* was consumed by a burst of flame; I felt within me the moment when I would bid my mother good-bye and canter down into the drowning valley, riding toward the north. I had that moment within me, and many other moments as well: the moment of touching my father's wife on the top of her head as she knelt, weeping and imploring me not to cast her out of the house; the solemn moment of taking snuff with the old men of the village; the moment when I would pack my satchel, moths about my lamp. My journey was already there, like a word waiting to be written. I saw the still, drenched forest and the port of Dinivolim. The ship, too, that would bear me away, arresting as a city, and beyond it, like light rising up from the sea, the transparent coast of the north.

The one thing I had not foreseen was that Lunre, my foreign master, would refuse the chance to return with me to the country of his birth. He shocked me when, with a small, hard smile, he shook his head and said: "Ah, Shev, that way is barred. 'I have cast my helmet into the sea.'"

"Ravhathos the Poet," I murmured numbly. "Retiring from the wars . . . secluding himself in a cottage made of mud, in the Kelevain. . . ."

"You have been a fine student," Lunre said. I glanced up at him. He was shadowed, leaning, framed in the archway, the bright kitchen garden behind him. A touch of light caught one earring with its blue stone, a silver eyebrow, the steady green of an eye, a shade of expression: resigned, resolute.

"I am still your student," I said.

He laughed and made a light, uncertain gesture, opening one pallid palm in the glow that came in from the garden. "Perhaps," he said. "I have been a student of Vandos all my life, and I believe your *tchanavi* tended not to release their disciples."

His teeth flashed in a smile; but seeing my still, crestfallen look he added gently: "I will be here when you return."

I nodded, recognizing the secret iron at my master's core, the adamantine vein that never yielded to my touch. I narrowed my eyes, looking into the sun, my lip between my teeth. Then I asked: "Well—what can I bring you from Bain?"

"Ah!" He drew in a sharp breath. "Ah! For me? Don't bring me anything. . . ."

"What?" I cried. "Nothing? No books? There were so many things you wanted!"

He smiled again, with difficulty: "There were so many things I *spoke* of—"

"Tchavi," I said. "You cannot refuse a gift, something from your homeland."

He looked away, but not before I saw his stricken expression, the anguish in his eyes, the look he wore in the grip of fever. "Nothing," he muttered at last. "Nothing, there's nothing I can think of—"

"It can't be, Tchavi, there must be something. Please, what can I bring you?"

He looked at me. He wore again his grim, despairing smile, and I saw in his eyes the sadness of this island of mist and flowers. And I thought I saw, as well, a tall man walking along a windy quay and spitting the stone of an olive into the sea.

"The autumn," he said.

Book Two

The City of Bain

Chapter Four

At Sea

The ship *Ardonyi*—in Olondrian, "the one who comes out of the mists"—bore me northward along the coast of Jennet, the still hours punctuated by the sound of the captain's gong announcing meals of odorous fish stew clotted with bones. I stood at the front of the line with the other paying passengers while my steward, Sten, and our laborers waited behind, shifting their feet and snacking on the crescent-shaped rolls the sailors called "prisoners' ears," which were abandoned, rather than served, in a row of sacks. A great heat came from the galley next door, a rough voice singing, the clanging of metal, a creeping odor of rot and a reddish glow, while outside, on the smooth sea, which was both dark and pale in the moonlight, the Isle of Jennet floated by with its peaks of volcanic stone. We took no passengers from that tortured island of chasms and ash, where double-tongued salamanders breed among flowers shaped like pitchers, and where, according to island lore, there dwells Ineti-Kyan, the Devourer of Mouths, who runs up and down the black hills with his hair in the wind.

I had almost fought my way through the stew by the time Sten joined me with his own bowl. He set it down with the tips of his fingers, his nose creased in distaste. About us the walls vibrated with the movement of the ship, the old wood gleaming in the light of whale-oil lamps.

I nodded in greeting and spat a collection of bones into my hand. "Come," I laughed, "it's better than what we had at the inn."

"At the inn there was breadfruit," Sten replied, looking gloomily into his bowl.

"Breadfruit dulls the brain. Try this—there's eel today."

"Yes, Ekawi," he said. The title, uttered in a quiet, resigned, and effortless tone, made me start: it was the way he had addressed my father. That title now was mine, along with the house, the forests, the pepper bushes, the whole monotonous landscape of my childhood.

And it means nothing to me, I thought, crunchy spiny morsels of fish, my momentary unease absorbed in a rush of exultation. The sacks of pepper we've stuffed in the hold, the money we'll make, the farm—to me all this weighs less than the letter *fi* pronounced in the sailors' dialect. . . .

They pronounced it *thi*; they whistled their words; they sang. They hunched over other tables, tall rough men, their ruffled white shirts stained dark with sweat and tar. Some wore their hair cut short in the Bainish fashion, but others left it to fly out over their ears or knot itself down their backs. They raised their bowls to their bearded lips and threw them down again empty, and when they turned their heads their earrings flashed in the light. They were nothing like my master: they told coarse stories and wiped their mouths on their sleeves, and laughed when one of their fellows struggled against a bone in his throat. "The Quarter," I heard them say. "You drink with the bears. Gap-toothed Iloni, the smell in her house." In their speech ran the reed sounds of Evmeni and the salty oaths of the Kalka; they used the Kideti words for certain fruits and coastal winds, and their slang throbbed with the sibilant hum of the tongue of the Kestenyi highlands. At last they rose, one after the other, spitting shells on the floor. As they passed our table I lowered my head to my dish, my heart racing, afraid they might notice me and yet longing to be one of them, even one of the galley slaves who wore their crimes tattooed underneath their eyes.

When I looked up, Sten was watching me.

"What?"

He sighed. "It is nothing. Only—perhaps you would ask the cook if there is fennel."

"Fennel! What for?"

"Prayer," he replied, raising his spoon to his lips.

"Prayer."

"The old Ekawi was accustomed to pray while at sea."

"My father prayed." I laughed, flicking my bowl away with a finger, and Sten's narrow shoulders rose and fell in a barely perceptible shrug. The light of the lamp shone on the implacable parting in his hair and the small white scar that interrupted one eyebrow.

I rested my elbows on the table, smiling to put him at ease. "And where will our prayers go?"

"Back to the islands. To the nostrils of the gods."

"My poor Sten. Do you really believe that a pinch of dried fennel burned in my cabin will keep the gods from crushing this ship if they choose?"

Again his shoulders moved slightly. He drew a slender bone from his mouth.

"Look," I argued. "The Kavim is blowing. It blows to the north, without turning! How can the smoke move backward?"

"The wind will change."

"But when? By that time our prayers will have disappeared, inhaled by the clouds and raining over Olondria!"

His eyes shifted nervously. He was not *hotun*, after all, not one of that unfortunate class who live without *jut*: he had *jut* at home, no doubt in one of the back rooms of his strong mud house, a humble figure of wood or clay, yet potent as my own. Naturally it would not do to bring *jut* northward to Olondria: to lose one's *jut* in the sea would be the greatest of calamities. Burnt fennel was said to make the gods favorable to keeping one's *jut* from harm; but it shocked me to think that my father had held any faith in such superstition. Sten, too: his iron features were softened by dejection. He looked so forlorn that I laughed in spite of myself.

"All right. I'll ask for fennel. But I won't say what I'm going to do with it. They'll think they've picked up a cargo of lunatics!"

I stood, took my satchel from the back of my chair, and left him, swinging myself up the steep stairs to the deck. The wind tossed my hair as I emerged into the sunlight where the great masts stood like a forest of naked trees. I walked to the edge of the gleaming deck and leaned against the railing. As the wind was fair, the rowers were all on deck, slaves and free men together, the slaves' tattoos glowing like blue ornaments against their flesh, their hands sporting rings of carefully worked tin. They crouched in the sails' shadow playing their interminable game of *londo,* a complex and addictive exercise of chance. The planks beneath them were chalked with signs where they cast small pieces of ivory, first touching them to their heads to honor Kuidva the God of Oracles. Some went further: they prayed to Ithnesse the Sea or to Mirhavli the Angel, protectress of ships, whose gold-flecked statue stood dreaming in the prow. The Angel was sad and severe, with real human hair and a wooden trough at her feet; as a prayer, the sailors spat into the trough, calling it "the fresh-water offering." When a man ran off to perform this ritual, the soles of his bare feet flashing chalk-white, the others laughed and called merry insults after him.

I drew a book from my satchel and read: "*Now come, you armies of glass. Come from the bosom of salt, unleash your cries in the conch of the wind.*" All through that journey I read sea poetry from the battered and precious copy of *Olondrian Lyrics* my master had sent with me. "*Come with your horses of night, with your white sea-leopards, your temple of waves / now scatter upon the breast of the shore your banners of green fire.*" I read constantly, by sunlight that dazzled my eyes, by moonlight that strained them, growing drunk on the music of northern words and the sea's eternal distance, lonely and happy, longing for someone to whom I might divulge the thoughts of my heart, hoping to witness the pale-eyed sea folk driving their sheep. "For there is a world beneath the sea," writes Elathuid the Voyager, "peopled and filled with animals and birds like the one above. In it there are beautiful maidens who have long, transparent fins, and who drive their white sheep endlessly from one end of the sea to the other. . . ." Firdred of Bain himself, that most strictly factual of authors, writes that in the Sea of Sound his ship was pursued by another; this ship was under the sea, gliding upon its other surface, so that Firdred saw only its dark underside: "Its sails were outside of this world." In Tinimavet there are countless tales of sea-ghouls, the ghosts of the drowned, and of magical fish and princesses from the kingdoms under the sea. I wondered if I would see any of them here, where the sea was wildest—if at night, suddenly, I would catch in the depths the glow of a ghostly torch. But I saw no such vision, except in my dreams, when, thrilled and exhausted with poetry, I stood on deck and watched the glow worm dances of the ghouls, or caught, afar off, the rising of a dreaded mountain: the great whale which the sailors call "the thigh of the white giant."

Above me, on the upper deck, the island merchants sat: men of my own rank, though there were none as young as I. There they yawned through the salt afternoons under flapping leather awnings, drank liquor from teacups, predicted the winds, and had their hair oiled by their servants. The Ilavetis, slowly sipping the thin rice wine of their country, also had their fingers and toes dyed a deep reddish-brown; the smoky scent of the henna drifted away with the fog from their Bainish cigars, while one of them claimed that the odor of henna could make him weep with nostalgia. I despised them for this posturing, this sighing after their forests and national dishes mingled with boasts of their knowledge of the northern capital. None of them knew as much as I; none of them spoke Olondrian; their bovine heads were empty of an appreciation of the north. The Olondrian boy who knelt on a pillow each evening to sing for their pleasure might as well have sung to the sails or the empty night: the merchants would have been better pleased, I thought, with a dancing girl from southern Tinimavet, plastered with ochre and wearing mussel-shells in her hair.

The boy sang of women and gardens, the Brogyar wars, the hills of Tavroun. He knew cattle-songs from Kestenya and the rough fishing songs of the Kalka. The silver bells strung about his guitar rang gently as he played, and the music reached me where I sat beneath the curve of the upper deck. I sat alone and hidden, my arms clasped about my knees, under the slapping and rippling of the sails, in the wind and the dark. Snatches of murmuring voices came to me from the deck above, where the merchants sat under lamps, their fingers curled around their cups. The light of the lamps shone dimly on the masts and rigging above; the lantern in the prow was a faint, far beacon in the darkness; all was strange, creaking and moving, filled with the ceaseless wind and the distant cries of the sailors paying their *londo* forfeits in the prow. The boy broke into his favorite air, his sweet voice piercing the night, singing a popular song whose refrain was: "*Bain, city of my heart.*" I sat enchanted, far from my gods, adrift in the boat of spices, in the sigh of the South, in the net of the wheeling stars, in the country of dolphins.

Halfway through the voyage a calm descended. The galley slaves rowed, chanting hoarsely, under a sky the color of turmeric. The *Ardonyi* unrolled herself like a sleepy dragon over the burnished sea, and sweat crept down my neck as I stood in my usual place on deck. The pages of my book were limp with heat, the letters danced before my eyes, and I read each line over and over, too dull to make sense of the words. I raised my head and yawned. At that moment a movement caught my eye, an object beetle-black and gleaming in the sun.

It was a woman's braided hair. She was climbing up from below-decks. I closed my book, startled by the strangeness of the image: a woman, an island woman with her hair plaited into neat rows on the crown of her head, aboard an Olondrian vessel bound for the city of Bain! She struggled, for she grasped a cotton pallet under her arm which made it difficult for her to climb the ladder. Before I could offer to help, she shoved the pallet onto the deck and climbed out after it, squinting in the light.

At once she knelt on the deck, peering anxiously into the hole. "Jissi," she said. "You hold him. Jissi, hold him." I detected the accent of southern Tinimavet in her speech, blurred consonants, the intonation of the poor.

Slowly, jerkily, an elderly man emerged from below, carrying a young girl on his back. The girl's head lolled; her dry hair hung down in two red streams; her bare feet dangled, silent bells. She clung to the old man's neck with a dogged weariness as he staggered across the boards of the deck toward the shadow of an awning.

Several sailors had paused in their duties to stare at the strange trio. One of them whistled. "*Brei!*" he said. *Red.*

I turned my back slightly and opened my *Lyrics* again, pretending to read while the woman dragged the pallet into the shade and unrolled it. The girl, so slight, yet straining the arms of the others like a great fish, was set down on it, the end of the pallet folded to prop up her head. Her thin voice reached me over the deck: "There's wind. But there aren't any birds."

"We're too far from the land for birds, my love," the older woman said.

"I know that," said the girl in a scornful tone. Her companion was silent; the old man, servant or decrepit uncle, shuffled off toward the ladder.

Ignorant of my destiny and theirs, I felt only pity for them, mingled with fascination—for the girl was afflicted with *kyitna*. The unnatural color of her hair, lurid against her dark skin, made me sure of her malady, though I had never observed its advanced stages. She was *kyitna*: she had that slow, cruel, incurable wasting disease, that inherited taint which is said to affect the families of poisoners, which is spoken of with dread in the islands as "that which ruins the hair," or, because of the bizarre color it gives, as "the pelt of the orangutan." Not long ago—in my grandfather's time—the families of victims of *kyitna*, together with all of their livestock and land, were consumed by ritual fires, and even now one could find, in the mountains and wild places of the islands, whole families living in exile and destitution, guarding their sick. Once, when I was a child, a strange man came to the gate of the house, at midday when the servants were sleeping, and beat at the gate with a stick; he was grimy and ragged and stank of fear, and when I went out to him he rasped through his unkempt beard: "Bring me water and I'll pray for you." I ran back inside and, too terrified to return to him by myself, woke my mother and told her that someone was outside asking for water. "Who is it?" she asked sleepily. "What's the matter with you?" I was young and, unable to name my fear, said: "It is a baboon-man." My mother laughed, rose, rumpled my hair and called me a dormouse, and went to the cistern to fill a clay pitcher with water for the strange man. I kept close to her skirts, comforted by her smell of dark rooms and sleep, her hair pressed into her cheek by the pillow, her gentle voice as she teased me. I felt braver with her until, just outside the courtyard, she started and gasped, kissing her fingertips swiftly, almost upsetting the pitcher of water. The man clung to the gatepost, looking at us with a desperate boldness. His smile was a grimace and had in it a kind of horrible irony. "Good day to you, sister!" he said. "That water will earn you the prayers of the dying." My mother gripped the clay pitcher and hissed at me: "Stay there! Don't move!" Then she took a deep breath, strode toward the man, handed him the pitcher, turned on her heel without speaking, walked back to the house, and pulled me inside. "You see!" I cried, excited to see my fear confirmed in hers: "I told you it was a baboon-man! He stank, and his teeth were too big." But my mother said sadly, gazing out through the stone archway: "No, he was not . . . He was one of the *kyitna* people who are living on Snail Mountain."

The thought of any kind of people living on Snail Mountain, where the earth breathed sulfurous exhalations and even the dew was poisonous, shocked and terrified me. How did they live? What did they eat? What water did they drink? But my mother said it was bad luck to think of it. Later the empty pitcher was found standing beside the gate, and my mother had the servants break it in pieces and bury it in the back garden. And some days after that we heard that a party of men from Tyom, armed with torches and spears, had driven the *kyitna* people away: "They had a small child with them," whispered the women in the fruit market: "Its hair was red, they could see it in the torchlight—as red as this palm nut!" I wished, at the time, that I had been able to see the *kyitna* child. Now I studied the girl who lay motionless in the shade of the awning, who took up so little space, who seemed without substance, a trick of the light, who flickered under the flapping shade like the shadow cast by a fire.

She was not as young as I had thought her at first. She was not a child, though from a distance she appeared to be so—she was small even for an islander. But her waist, showing between her short vest and the top of her drawstring trousers, was gently curved, and the look in her face was too remote for that of a child. She seemed to be wandering, open-eyed; her skin was dark, rich as silt; the crook of her elbow, dusky in the shade, was a dream of rivers. She wore a bracelet of jade beads which showed she belonged to the far south, to the rice-growers and eel-fishers, the people of the lagoons.

I think she had spoken to me twice before I realized it. She struggled to raise her voice, calling: "Brother! You'll get sun-sick." Then I met her gaze, her tired, faintly mocking smile, and smiled back at her. The older woman, no doubt her mother, hushed her in a whisper.

"It's all right," said the girl. "Look at him! He wouldn't harm anyone. And he isn't superstitious. He has the long face of a fish."

I strolled toward them and greeted the mother, whose eyes darted from my gaze. She had the flat, long-suffering face of a field-laborer and a scar on her forehead. The young girl looked at me from inside the fiery cloud of her hair, her lips still crooked in a smile. "Sit down, brother," she said.

I thanked her and sat in the chair beside her pallet, across from her mother, who still knelt stroking the girl's long hair and would not meet my eye. "The fish," said the young girl, speaking carefully, her breathing shallow, "is for wisdom. Isn't that right? The fish is the wisest of the creatures. Now, most of our merchants here are shaped just like the domestic duck—except for the fat Ilaveti—the worst of all, he looks like a raven. . . ." She paused, closing her eyes for a moment, then opened them again and fixed me with a look of such clarity that I was startled. "Ducks are foolish," she said, "and ravens are clever, but have bad hearts. That is why we came up here now, at noon, when they're asleep."

I smiled. "You seem to have had ample time to study all of us. And yet this is the first time that I have seen you come out of your cabin."

"Tipyav," she answered, "my mother's servant, tells me everything. I trust him absolutely. He has slow thoughts, but a very keen eye. My father—but I am talking too much— you will think me poorly behaved—"

"No," I said. But she lay very still and silent, struggling for breath.

"Sir," said her mother in a low voice, looking at me at last, so that I saw, surprised, that she had the deep eyes of a beautiful woman: "My daughter is gravely ill. She is—she has not been well for some time. She has come here for air, and for rest, and this talking taxes her so—"

"Stop," the young girl whispered. She looked at me with a trembling smile. "You will forgive us. We are not accustomed to much company."

"It is I who should ask forgiveness," I said. "I am intruding on you—on your rest."

"Not at all," said the girl, in a manner peculiarly grave and formal. "Not at all. You are a very rare thing: a wise man from the islands. Tell me—have you been to this northern ghost-country before?"

I shook my head. "This is my first visit. But I do speak the language."

"You speak their language? Olondrian?"

"I had an Olondrian tutor."

I was gratified by the older woman's look of awe; the girl regarded me silently with an expression I could not read.

"We have heard that one can hire interpreters," her mother said.

"I am sure one can," I answered, though I was not sure of it at all. The woman looked relieved and smoothed her dark dress over her knees, moving her hand down to scratch discreetly at her ankle. Poor creatures, I thought, wondering how they would fare in the northern capital. The woman, I noticed, was missing the two smallest fingers of her right hand.

The girl spoke up abruptly. "As for us," she said in a strange, harsh tone, "we are traveling to a place of healing, as you might have guessed. It is called A-lei-lin, and lies in the mountains. But really . . ." She paused, twisting the cloth of her pallet. "Really . . . It's foolish of us. . . ."

"No, not foolish," her mother interrupted. "We believe that we will find healing there. It is a holy place. The temple of a foreign goddess. And perhaps the gods of the north—in the north there are many wonders, son, many miracles. You will have heard of them yourself. . . ."

"It is certainly said to be, and I believe it is, a place of magic, full of great wizards," I said. "These wizards, for example, have devised a map of the stars, cast in brass, with which they can measure the distance of stars from the earth. They write not only in numbers, but words, so that they may converse across time and space, and one of their devices can make innumerable replicas of books—such as this one."

I held out the slim *Olondrian Lyrics* bound in dark green leather. The women looked at it but seemed loath to touch it.

"Is that—a *vallon*?" the girl asked, stumbling slightly over the word.

"It is. In it there are written many poems in the northern tongue."

The girl's mother gazed at me, and I guessed that the worn look in her face came not from hard labor but from an unrelenting sorrow. "Are you a wizard, my son?"

I laughed. "No, no! I am only a student of northern letters. There's no wizardry in reading."

"Of course not!" snapped the girl, startling me with her vehemence. Her small face blazed, a lamp newly opened. "Why must you?" she hissed at her mother. "Why? Why? Could you not be silent? Can you never be silent even for the space of an hour?"

The woman blinked rapidly and looked away.

"Perhaps—" I said, half rising from my chair.

"Oh, no. Don't *you* go," said the girl, a wild note in her voice. "I've offended you. Forgive me! My mother and I—we are too much alone. Tell me," she went on without a pause, "how do you find the open sea? Does it not feel like freedom?"

"Yes, I suppose—"

"Beautiful and fearsome at the same time. My father, before he stopped talking, said that the open sea was like fever. He called it 'the fever of health'—does that not seem to you very apt? The fever of health. He said that he always felt twice as alive at sea."

"Was your father a merchant?"

"Why do you say that—was? He isn't dead."

"I am sorry," I said.

"He is not dead. He is only very quiet."

I glanced at her mother, who kept her head lowered.

"Why are you smiling?" asked the girl.

My conciliatory half-smile evaporated. "I'm not smiling."

"Good."

Such aggression in a motionless body, a nearly expressionless face. Her small chin jutted; her eyes bored into mine. She had no peasant timidity, no deference. I cast about for something to say, uneasy as if I had stepped on some animal in the dark.

"You spoke as if he were dead," I said at last.

"You should have asked."

"I was led astray by your choice of words," I retorted, beginning to feel exasperated.

"Words are breath."

"No," I said, leaning forward, the back of my shirt plastered to my skin with sweat. "No. You're wrong. Words are everything. They can be everything."

"Is that Olondrian philosophy?"

Her sneer, her audacity, took my breath away. It was as if she had sat up and struck me in the face. For an instant my father's image flared in my memory like a beacon: an iron rod in his hand, its tip a bead of fire.

"Perhaps. Perhaps it is," I managed at last. "Our philosophies differ. In Olondria words are more than breath. They live forever, *here*."

I held out the book, gripping its spine. "*Here* they live. Olondrian words. In this book there are poems by people who lived a thousand years ago! Memory can't do that—it can save a few poems for a few generations, but not forever. Not like this."

"Then read me one," she said.

"What?"

"Jissi," her mother murmured.

"Read me one," the girl insisted, maintaining her black and warlike stare. "Read me what you carry in the *vallon*."

"You won't understand it."

"I don't want to understand it," she said. "Why should I?"

The book fell open at the *Night Lyric* of Karanis of Loi. The sun had moved so that my knees were no longer in shadow, the page a sheet of blistering light where black specks strayed like ash. My irritation faded as I read the melancholy lines.

Alas, tonight the tide has gone out too far.
It goes too far,

it stretches away, it lingers,
now it has slipped beyond the horizon.

Alas, the wind goes carrying
summer tempests of mountain lilies.
It spills them, and only the stars remain:
the Bee, the Hammer, the Harp.

"Thank you," said the girl.

She closed her eyes.

Her mother took her hand and chafed it. "Jissi? I'm going to call Tipyav."

The girl said nothing. The woman gave me a fearful, embarrassed glance, then stumped across the deck and called down the ladder.

"Brother." The young girl's eyes were open.

"Yes," I answered, my anger cooled by pity. She is going to die, I thought.

A puff of air forced itself from her lungs, a laugh. "Well—never mind," she murmured, closing her eyes again. "It doesn't matter."

Her mother returned with the servant. I stood aside as the old man knelt and the woman helped the girl to cling to his curved back. The old man rose with a groan and staggered forward, his burden swaying, and the woman rolled up the pallet, avoiding my eye. . . . I pulled my chair farther into the shade of the awning and opened my book, but when they reached the ladder the girl called back to me: "Brother!"

I stood. Her hair was vibrant in the sun.

"Your name."

"Jevick of Tyom."

"Jissavet," said the dying girl, "of Kiem."

In my twenty-ninth year, having lost my heart to the sea, I resolved to travel, and to come, if I might, into some of the little-known corners of the World. It was with such purpose in mind that I addressed myself to the captain of the Ondis*, as she lay in the harbor of Bain; and the captain—a man distinguished, in the true Bainish style, by an elegant pipe and exquisitely fashioned boots—declared himself very able to use the extra pair of hands on board his ship, which was to go down the Fertile Coast.*

We would stop at Asarma, that capital of the old cartographers, and go on to fragrant, orange-laden Yenith by the sea, and finally travel up the Ilbalin, skirting the Kestenyi highlands, into the Balinfeil to collect our cargo of white almonds. The arrangement suited me perfectly: I planned to cross into the mountains and enter the formidable country of the Brogyars. I little knew that my wanderings would last for forty years, and bring me into such places as would cause many a man to shudder.

I will not, O benevolent reader, spend time in describing Bain itself, that city which is known to lie in the exact center of the world—for who, indeed, who reads this book will be unfamiliar with her, incontestably the greatest city on earth? Who does not know of the "gilded house," the "queen of the bazaars," where, as the saying goes, one can purchase even human flesh? No, I begin these modest writings farther south and east, at the gates of Asarma, which, seen from the sea, resemble a lady's hand mirror. . . .

I lay on my pallet, surrounded by the rocking of the sea, reading Firdred of Bain in a yellow smear of candlelight. But I could not keep my mind on the words: the letters seemed to shift, rearranging themselves into words which did not exist in Olondrian. *Kyitna.* And then, like a ruined city: *Jissavet of Kiem.* I laid the book aside and gave myself up to dreams of her. I remembered the clarity of her eyes, which were like the eyes of Kyomi, the first woman in the world, who had been blessed with the sight of the gods. I thought of the city whose name she had said so carefully, A-lei-lin, Aleilin, Leiya Tevorova's city, the city of violent seasons. What I knew of that city was Leiya's story of how she was declared mad and shut up there for the winter in a great tower of black bricks. I looked at the city on Firdred's map, which, like all Olondrian maps, showed painted cities of exaggerated size. Aleilin: a city like the others. The Place of the Goddess of Clay. And near it the moon-colored oval of the Fethlian, the lake where Leiya had drowned, where a nurse, as I knew from the preface to her autobiography, had found her with her shoe caught in the weeds. There, after long torments, the girl from Kiem would die—for was it not futile to struggle with *kyitna,* the just punishment of the gods? "And perhaps, the gods of the north—" the mother had said, hesitant, desperate; but what had the gods of the north to do with us? They were tales, pretty names. I turned on my side, restless, thinking of the strange girl with sadness. The bones of her face as she lay beneath the awning like a jade queen. She came from the south, from the land of doctors, wizards, and superstition, from the place which we in Tyom called "the Edge of Night."

At length I blew out the candle and slept, but did not dream of the girl, as I had hoped I would; she had fled with the tiny light of the candle. I dreamed instead of the sea, raging, crushing our fragile boat, drowning the spices, splintering planks and bones with its roaring hands. . . . And then of the monkey, leaping from tree to tree, weighing down the branches. The way it looked over its shoulder, the way its tail hung, teeming with lice. And last of all the courtyard, patches of sunlight, the sound of hurried footsteps, closer now, the sound of breath. *Jevick.* My mother's voice.

Chapter Five

City of My Heart

On the bridge of Aloun I gave up the great sea
Bain, city of my heart
That I might never weep for the memory of thee
Bain, city of my heart.

Let me gather the light that I saw in the square
Bain, city of my heart
And the jewel-haired maidens who walked with me there
Bain, city of my heart.

Oh the arches, the lemons, the cinnamon flowers!
Bain, city of my heart
What we abandon must cease to be ours,
Bain, city of my heart.

Bain, the Gilded House, the Incomparable City, splits the southern beaches with the glinting of her domes. On either side the sands stretch out, pale, immaculate, marked with graceful palms whose slender figures give no shade. Those sands, lashed by rain in the winter, sun-glazed in the summer, give the coast the look of a girl in white, the Olondrian color of mourning. Yet as one approaches the harbor this illusion is stripped away: the city asserts itself, Bain the exuberant, the exultant. And the vastness of the harbor mouth with its ancient walls of stone, with its seemingly endless array of ships, blocks out the southern sands.

From this raucous, magnificent port the Olondrian fleet once set out, adorned with scarlet flags, to conquer the land of Evmeni; from this port, ever since the most ancient times, "before the Beginning of Time," long merchant ships have embarked for the rivers, for apples, for purple, for gold. Still they come, laden with copper and porphyry from Kestenya, with linen and cork from Evmeni, with the fruits of the Balinfeil, ships that have sailed north as far as the herring markets of the Brogyar country and south as far as the jewels of the sea, as far as Tinimavet. Here they gather, so many that the sea itself is a city, with rope bridges thrown between ships so that sailors can visit one another, with the constant blasts of the brass horns worn in the belts of the harbor officials, the *sinsavli* weaving among the ships in their low yolk-colored boats. "Forward!" they cry. "Back! You, to the left, a curse on your eyes!" And before them, around them, rises that other city: a glittering mosaic of wind towers, terraces, flights of white-washed steps, cramped balconies and shadows hinting at gardens of oleander.

Bain is, of course, the name of the Olondrian god of wine, whose eyes are "painted like sunflowers," who plays the sacred bone flute. "Come before him with honey," exhorts the *Book of Mysteries,* "with fruits of the vine both white and red, with dates, with succulent figs." Perhaps it was the presence of this strange god with the ruddy cheeks, who bewilders men with his holy fog, that dazzled my eyes and brain—for though I thrust myself against the rails and gulped the air, though I looked wildly about me, staring as if to devour the harbor, my first few hours in Bain—and indeed, the whole of that first day—I dwelt in a cloud pierced now and then by images like sunbeams. There was the great neighborhood of ships, most of them almond-shaped, blue and white, the Olondrian river boats with their cargoes of melons; there were the shouts, the clankings, the joyous, frenzied activity as we made our way to the bustling quay and the gangplank rattled down; there was the heat, the brilliance of the light, the high white buildings, the shaking of my legs as I stood at last on the quay, on land, the way the stone seemed to roll beneath my feet, the shifting trees, and the sudden, magical presence of what seemed more than a hundred horses. Olondrians love these noble beasts and harness them to carriages, and the city of Bain is full of them—their lively, quivering noses, the ammoniac smell of their hides, their braided manes, their glittering trappings, the clop of their hooves, and the piles of their dung steaming on the cobblestones. My fellow Kideti merchants and I disembarked under jostling umbrellas with our clusters of servants and porters, eyeing the carriages anxiously, and at once a number of slit-eyed, disheveled youths with leather knapsacks descended on us, crying out "*Apkanat*," the Kideti word for "interpreter." One of them clutched my arm: "*Apkanat!*" he said eagerly, pointing to himself and breathing garlic into my face. When I shook my head and told him in Olondrian, "There is no need," he raised his eyebrows and grinned, showing a set of narrow teeth. For a moment there was the vivid sight of his black, greasy curls, his head against the blinding white of the sunlit wall behind him—then he was gone, bounding toward the others of his mercenary trade who crowded around the gangplank, shouting.

The success of our journey lay entirely in the hands of Sten, who seemed immune to the charms of that exotic capital. While I stood gazing stupefied at the towers, the glazed windows, he arranged for one of the large open wagons to carry us and our merchandise. When he plucked at my sleeve I followed him numbly and climbed the wooden steps into the wagon where my fourteen servants crouched among sacks of pepper. The wagon driver leaped into his seat and snapped the reins on the backs of his horses. "Ha!" he cried, and the tall vehicle lurched into life. I came sharply out of my daze for a moment, long enough to gasp, long enough to think, now it is true, we are leaving the harbor, long enough to turn and look back at the elegant *Ardonyi*, floating against the quay, her gangplank thronged with interpreters. Another ship was unloading fruit; the air reeked of oranges. In the crowd I made out the Tinimaveti woman: she was arguing with the interpreters. And there, being borne away on a sort of litter, the sick girl with the coppery hair. . . .

The wagon turned a corner and the ship disappeared from view. The harbor receded after it, shrinking between the walls of the buildings. Sten, sitting at my side, neat, drab, and unruffled as ever, touched my knee. "Ekawi, you will soon be able to rest. Your father always frequented a particular hotel, not far from the harbor and also conveniently near the spice markets. I hope that it will suit you as well. The price is not overly high, and nearby there are smaller inns, very cheap and, I think, ideal for the men. . . ."

I stared at him and muttered: "Of course, of course." His face was the same, dark, triangular, with the pale scar over one eye; yet it was framed by the passing white walls, the walls of the city of Bain with their wrought-iron gates, their carved doors crowned with amaranths. We rattled under narrow stone bridges connecting these high, solemn buildings, raised walkways with curved parapets above the echoing street, we passed under balconies trailing languid white and indigo flowers, through sunlight and abrupt shadows cast in that stone-paved passageway. With a shock that came over me as a physical chill, making me feel faint, I recognized the moment in which the imagined becomes visible. For these were the streets, despite their carefully cultivated blossoms, of which Fodra had written: "There it is autumn, and always deserted." The old iron gates were eaten by rust, the walls streaked with green moisture, the buildings encircled by empty alleys too narrow for carriages; these were the streets which that doomed, exalted, asthmatic youth from the Salt Coast, whose poetry seduced a nation, called "the unbearable quarters." "*O streets of my city,*" I whispered, "*with your walls like faded tapestries.*" Sten glanced at me swiftly with a trace of alarm in his eyes. I clutched the rough material of the sacks on either side of me and breathed the hot, dry, scented air of the passageway. Eternal city of Bain! We turned a corner, the street went on, we burst into a secluded square with walls of rose-colored stone; a flock of swallows, disturbed by the wagon, lifted into the air; and the statue of a young girl watched us go by, her arms stretched out.

The Hotel Urloma, the "Arch of the Dawn," stands in the Street of Copper, in the lively mercantile district to the north of the Great Harbor. Here the walls of the buildings are thin, so that one can hear voices and thuds from inside, feet clattering up and down the stairs, flute-playing, the cries of cats. The hotel is a tall old building of wood and stone with a roof of coppery slate, one of those roofs, turned greenish now, which gave the street its name. As we drew up before its wide, pillared porch flanked by a pair of cypresses, a fresh burst of sweat bloomed over my skin like a cool dew, and I shivered.

"The hotel," said Sten, looking at me with veiled eyes, gauging my approval. I nodded and tried to smile, my dry lips cracking. Then the door flew open and a tall, portly Bainishman emerged and hurried down the steps, clumsy in loose leather slippers.

"Welcome, welcome!" he cried out in abominable Kideti, waving his arms in their billowing white shirtsleeves. He hastened toward the wagon as the driver took down the wooden steps and placed them at the side for our descent. "Welcome," shouted the gentleman. His mild, gold-colored eyes flickered nervously across my servants' faces. "*Apkanat?*" he asked, again mangling the word in Kideti. "No *apkanat*? You have no *apkanat*?" Meanwhile the driver, ignoring the gentleman's impatient cries, looked up at me with black and steady eyes, reached out his hand, and stamped one boot on his steps with an almost scornful confidence, as if declaring that I might trust them absolutely. I gripped his hand and rose, swaying, surrounded by worried murmurs, the sound of the servants and Sten, who placed his hand on the small of my back; the strange hotel and the dark, bristling spears of the cypress trees seemed to leap and swing in the sunlight as I clambered down from the wagon. When I reached the ground and the driver released me, I stumbled. The portly gentleman supported me with a large hand on my shoulder. "Welcome," he said; and then, in Olondrian, shaking his head as he spoke to himself: "Poor soul! Nothing but a boy! And he calls himself an interpreter!"

I felt that I should correct him but could not find the words in his language. I looked up into his ruddy face and compassionate topaz eyes; his gray hair, sculpted so that a curl lay precisely on either temple, exuded a powerful odor of heliotrope. I felt that sensation of smallness which our people must feel in the north: my head barely reached the scented gentleman's shoulder. I was fascinated by his great hands, so moist, with their moon-white nails, on which he wore several rings set with aquamarines.

"*Apkanat*," he said slowly, peering down into my face. I cleared my throat and opened and closed my mouth. He sighed, turned, then rolled his eyes in despair at the sight of Sten and the wagon driver, who were communicating with energetic gestures. This method, however, seemed to succeed, for Sten hurried toward me and said: "Ekawi, I will escort the servants to their own inn. After some days you may wish to see their accommodations yourself—but for now I suggest you rest and await me here. . . ." He looked at me uncertainly, then glanced at the Bainish gentleman, who was looking at us both with intense interest. I felt, like a heavy blow, the shame of being unable to speak—of proving, at the great moment, such a poor student.

I summoned my courage and nodded. "Of course! I shall see to our rooms." Sten looked relieved and hurried back into the wagon, but I saw him kiss the tips of his slender fingers as he went, and his lips moved rapidly as if in prayer.

The reins struck the backs of the horses. I turned to the Bainishman beside me, squared my shoulders, and said: "Good afternoon."

His gold eyes widened. "Good afternoon! What!" He reached out his hand, smiling, and enveloped mine inside it. "Good afternoon to you, *telmaro*!" He leaned in closer, searching my face for any sign of comprehension. "Do you speak Olondrian? Are you the *apkanat*?"

I laughed and answered him clumsily enough, but with delight: "I am a merchant from the Tea Islands. My father—he used—he was coming—"

"Yes, yes!" said the gentleman. "But come in out of the sun." He ushered me toward the hotel along a pathway of pink slate. "So you are the son of the bald gentleman! Yes, I expect him every year! I hope no misfortune . . ." He trailed off as we went up the stairs to the porch.

"He is dead," I said.

"Ah!" The gentleman's brow was creased with such a look of pain that I was sorry I had not spoken with more delicacy. "That is dreadful, dreadful! And he no older than myself! But forgive me—I am called Yedov of Bain." He put his hand on his heart and bowed, showing me the round patch of pink skin at the top of his skull; when he had risen I bowed also, saying: "Jevick of Tyom." At this he gave a rich, merry laugh. "Marvelous! Such an education! Ah, but your father was shrewd! Come, step inside."

He clasped the brass ring on the door and pushed it open, leading me into a vast, cool room, empty but for a vase of white roses on a table. His leather slippers smacked on the tiles, and the tails of his light-green morning coat fluttered as he passed through this hall and into the gloomy corridor beyond. The entire hotel possessed, like its owner, an odor of cedar, old carpets, and heliotrope. Somnolent parlors yawned on either side of the passage, each with a high, marmoreal fireplace gleaming in the shadows and shapeless pieces of furniture pushed against the walls. At length we came through a set of peaked double doors onto a veranda flooded with sun, and I stood blinking in the robust sea light of Bain. "I'm here," I murmured in the tongue of the north, gripping the ornate curves of the balustrade. The iron was cold on my palms, unyielding, foreign, delightful.

My host offered me a chair—a long, low object covered with a green silk shawl—and hurried off to fetch me "a drop of the country." I reclined on the chair, breathing in the scent of the garden, the perfume of exhausted pansies mingled with the odors of dust and ancient plaster. The sky was deep blue, the balconies like necklaces. I lowered my gaze: the arm of my chair with its cover of pear-green cloth seemed to pulse in the tireless light. There was my hand, narrow, dark, languid. In Olondria. When my host returned with the wine, I had drifted into a blissful sleep.

I awoke rumpled and sweaty and sat up, evening light on my face, thinking of books. It was the *kebma* hour, named for the bread that is eaten at dusk: across the garden I could see lights in the windows, and in one overgrown yard a woman's voice called insistently: "Valeth, come in." I started up, turned, and went into the hotel, knocking against furniture in the gloom until a light in the corridor led me to my host. He sat at a table laden with food, his face and oiled hair shining in the rays of a splendid table lamp in a netting of pink crystal.

"Come in, come in," he cried, beaming and standing up so swiftly he bumped the table, provoking a gentle clatter of glass. "I didn't like to wake you, but I'm glad you've arrived at last. I don't mind telling you that our conversation has been strained!"

With a wave of his hand he indicated his sole dinner companion: my steward, Sten. Colorless, doleful, looking shrunken beside the tall Bainishman, Sten sat before a plate heaped with an array of foreign delicacies, rose-colored claws and forbidding blobs of aspic.

"Sten," I said, trying not to laugh.

"Ekawi," he returned in a mournful tone. "The gentleman insisted I sit. I felt I could not refuse."

"No, no, you did right. Listen, Sten, I need money, Olondrian money. Just give me half of what you've got in the purse."

The Bainishman, still standing, resting both hands on the table, glanced from me to Sten and back again with a look of indulgent good humor, but when he saw Sten pull out the purse and count a number of bright triangular coins into my hand, his brows contracted in dismay.

"What! What's this? What do you want with money? You don't need money in my house," he exclaimed, either forgetting that his house was a hotel, or overcome with native hospitality to the extent that he intended not to charge me for the meal.

"I'm sorry. I can't stay."

"But where are you going? I have *sefdalima,* real *sefdalima* from the country, either with or without anchovies! Come, *telmaro,* I beg you, you haven't eaten!" And at last, in despair, as I opened a door: "Not that way! The other door, if you want the street. . . ."

"Thank you," I called out over my shoulder, hurrying down the passage, my pockets jingling. I soon came out into the antechamber with the white roses. Then all I had to do was open the door, and there it was: sea air, long cypress shadows, the racket of carriage wheels, Bain.

I ran down the front steps of the hotel and into the light of the evening, dazed as a moth released from a dark bedroom. Strangers jostled me, merchants in short cloaks with well-fed, shaven cheeks, students in colorful jackets and the tasseled shirts of scribes. The glad spirit of the *kebma* hour was awakening under the trees: the cafés were crowded with diners laughing through clouds of cigar smoke, tearing the flat, oily loaves of *kebma,* rinsing their fingers in brass bowls, clapping their hands to call the waiters. I darted across the street, dancing to keep away from the carriages, and pressed my face to a window where books lay blanketed in dust. There they were, just as I had imagined, open, within easy reach. I pushed the door, setting off a soft bell, and entered the shop.

Then it was like those tales in which there are sudden transformations: "He found himself in a field, and felt that it was a very vast country." It was like the story in which Efaldar awakes in the City of Zim: "There were walls of amethyst round him, and his couch was upon a dais." In the shop there was a dim, ruddy light and little space to move, for the shelves rose everywhere, filled with books with their names written on the spines: *The Merchant of Veim. Lyrics Written While Traveling on the Canals. The Secrets of Mandrake Root and the Benefits Derived Therefrom.* I ran my fingers over the books, slid them from the shelves, opened them, turned the pages, breathing in line after line of mysterious words, steeped in voluptuous freedom like Isvalha among the nymphs of the well, a knot in my throat with the taste of unswallowed tears. There were so many books. There were more than my master had carried in his sea chest. The shop seemed impossible, otherworldly, a cave of wonders; yet it was not even a true bookshop like the ones I would discover later, lining both sides of the Street of Poplars. It was one of those little shops, tucked into various corners of Bain, which sell portraits of popular writers and tobacco as well as books, whose main profits come from the newspapers, whose volumes are poorly bound, and which always seem to be failing, yet are as perennial as the flowers. It is unlikely that anyone before or since has experienced, in that humble establishment, a storm of emotion as powerful as mine. I collected stack after stack of books, seizing, rejecting, replacing, giddy with that sweet exhalation: the breath of parchments.

At last I found a leather-bound copy of the *Romance of the Valley* with which, once they had touched it, my hands refused to part. It was a "two-color copy": the chapter titles were ornamented with elaborate flowers in blue and crimson ink. The cover was also embossed with a pattern of blooms; the paper, though not of the best quality, was of pressed cotton beautifully textured; and through the pages danced the mysterious tale, the enchanted hawks and the sorrowful maiden transformed into a little ewe-lamb. Clutching this prize I approached the bookseller's desk, that hallowed region central to every bookshop, however lowly, in Olondria. This one, like many others, was piled with books and scattered papers, and behind it, in the glow of a lamp, sulked a young girl of great beauty. She had the amber skin of the Laths, the people of Olondria's wine country, and masses of coarse brown hair that snaked among the towers of books. Her hands, grimy and capable with broken fingernails, wrapped up my purchase and clenched my fifteen *droi* with frank eagerness. I thanked her, but she did not look up. Instead she yanked a curl of hair impatiently from among her charm necklaces. I walked out into the last light of the evening. Bells tolled in the Temple of Kuidva, and over its dome the first stars were coming out.

If you love Bain as I have loved it, then you will know its spell, a heady mixture of arrogance and vitality, which has in it a great sigh, as of an ocean that has been crossed, the sigh of its terrible age from the depths of its stones. You will know the arcades underneath the Golden Wall where the old men sit, playing at *londo* and sipping their glasses of *teiva,* that colorless, purifying fig alcohol which has no scent, but whose aftertaste is "as chewed honeysuckle." You will know the wood-sellers, the midnight trot of the horse of the nightsoil wagon.

You will know also the great glow of the Royal Theater, huge as a castle and lit for its gala events like a temple on fire, with its wide tiered terraces going down to the canal. And you will know the white walls, the smell of sumac, the smell of dust, of coffee roasting, of eggplant fried in batter, the "unbearable quarters" where there is the feeling that someone has been interred, that people cannot live among such ancient towers. All of this I discovered in Fanlei, the "Month of Apples," one of Olondria's happiest and most careless months. There may still be a few in Bain who remember me as I was then: an aristocratic young foreigner in a gray silk suit.

My days began with a carriage ride through the humid morning streets to the great spice markets. Housed on the site of ancient horse and cattle auctions, the vast covered markets, with their arched leather roofs made to keep out the rain, form a jumbled labyrinth that stretches almost to the harbor. Here in the shadows the lavish, open sacks display their contents: the dark cumin redolent of mountains, the dried, crushed red pepper colored richly as iron ore, and turmeric, "the element of weddings." One wanders among the cramped, odorous, warren-like enclosures, among elderly men and women, fresh from the country, who sip glasses of tea as they sit beside their wares, their hands smelling perpetually of cinnamon. There are younger merchants, too: slow-voiced men, gentlemen farmers, who dab at their eyes with muslin handkerchiefs; and in one corner a Kalak woman, one of Bain's old fishing people, sells the wind out of a great brass bell. There are herbs, fresh and dried—mint, marjoram, and basil; there are dark cones and mud-like blocks of incense; there are odors in the air that seem to speak to one another, as though the market were filled with violent ghosts. Wandering vendors offer tea and odorless "water of life," which revives those who succumb to the spice madness: for here there are treacherous substances, ingredients for love-philters, and spices used in war and assassination. I have seen them selling the powder called *saravai*, the "hundred fires," with which prisoners are executed for treason; and there is also the nameless spice which, carried on the wind, infects one's enemies with the falling sickness. There is crushed ostrich eggshell, the "beckoner of women." It seems as if the odors cloud the air—as if, in the half light, the breath of spices rises up like smoke and wreathes the faces of the merchants.

Here I sat with Sten, bargaining, arguing, and laughing, pouring pepper into sacks for my customers, awaiting with growing impatience the hour of noon, the end of the market day, when I would walk out alone into the city. When that moment came, and my servants tied up the sacks and rolled down the door of the stall, I stood and brushed the pepper from my clothes, and with hardly a word I left them, walking out with the last of the Bainish citizens, mingling with them, no longer a foreign merchant.

It was the season of sudden rains. The wild summer storms came out of the west, pouring on the slate roofs and the white wind towers, swaying and bowing down the poplar trees in the Street of Booksellers and rolling in sheets from the awnings of the cafés. These were the rains that drove people close to the walls, under the balconies, or sent them dashing madly through the squares, and drenched the fluttering ribbons and bright trappings of the horses so that their flanks were streaked with delicate watercolors. The storms washed the streets so that little streams of brown water went roaring along the gutters toward the sea, and thundered on the roofs of the cafés where people were crowded together laughing in the steam and half darkness. I loved those rains; they were of the sort that is welcomed by everyone, preceded by hot, oppressive hours of stillness; they came the way storms come in the islands but did not last as long, and often the sun came out when they had passed. I was happy whenever the rain caught me walking about in the streets, for then I would rush into the nearest café, along with all the others who were escaping from the weather, all of us crushing laughing through the doors. The rain allowed me to go anywhere, to form quick, casual friendships, forced to share one of the overcrowded tables, among the beaming waiters who pushed good-naturedly through the throngs carrying cups of steaming apple cider. In this way I was thrown together with students or dockworkers or tradesmen, or the *huvyalhi*, the peasants in their old robes, with their belts of rope and tin earrings and tough shoes caked with dung, and the pipes they smoked carefully in their cracked misshapen hands. As the rain poured down outside, we leaned together over our drinks, and there was always the weather to talk about for a beginning, and everyone was glad for the sudden excuse to have a drink and for the wild release from the stillness of the air. The cafés smelled of cider, wet clothes, steaming hair, and tobacco. The lamps burned valiantly in the storm's darkness; often there was someone playing the northern violin, which is held upright between naked feet and moans like the wind in the towers.

After the rains the city was tranquil and glittering, freshly washed, the high roofs shining, the trees iridescent with moisture, and all seemed calm and quiet because of the passing of the storm. The clear air sparkled with the cold light of diamonds. The winds coming off the sea were cool, and there was no dust in the city; it had all been washed away with the heat and discomfort, and the sky had been washed as well and rose in pale, diaphanous layers of ether, streaked with gauzy clouds in blue and gold. Slowly the cafés emptied and the waiters sat down to play *londo*. Children came out to race painted boats in the gutters; they laughed and shouted down the wet streets in the opalescent air, while above them white-shawled grandmothers dragged chairs out onto the balconies. In these transparent hours I would set off again on my walk, down the Street of Booksellers or toward the intricate trees of the Garden of Plums, often with a girl on my arm, perhaps a student drawn to my strangeness or one of the city's cheerful lovers for hire.

There was never an end to Bain. I never felt as though I had touched it, though I loved the book markets under the swinging trees, the vast array of books on tables, in boxes, stacked on the ground, and the grand old villas converted into bookshops. I loved the Old City also, which is called the "Quarter of Sighs," with its barred windows and brooding fortified towers, and I loved to watch the canal winding below the streets and bridges and the stealthy boats among the shadows of trees. Laughing, replete, I raised a glass of *teiva* in a café, surrounded by a bold crowd of temporary companions, a girl at my side, some Ailith or Kerlith whose name I no longer recall, for she was erased like the others by the one who followed.

"Perhaps I'll stay," I shouted over the singing from the next table. "Perhaps I won't go home. I'd like to know every corner of Bain."

The girl beside me giggled and tossed her hair, her earrings jangling. "Bain!" she said. "You won't know Bain until you've been to the Feast of Birds."

Chapter Six

The Feast of Birds

I think I still do not know Bain. The Feast of Birds taught me of no city on earth, but of another, deeper territory.

It began as all holidays begin, though stamped with the special gaiety of Olondria: the city prepared for the celebration for two days. Revelers spilled from the overcrowded cafés and thronged the streets; when the outdoor tables were filled they sat on the curbs, uncorking bottles of *teiva*. From the balcony of my hotel room I looked down on garden parties, women in brilliant clothing laying tables among the oleanders, stout grandfathers bellowing for more wine, and children everywhere shrieking, trampling the marigolds, chasing one another. All the children held flexible wooden wands with tissue-paper birds attached to the ends, their gauzy feathers strengthened with copper wire; when the children played, these magical creatures trembled as if about to take flight for the trees, and at night they lay discarded on the lamplit grass. Many houses, I noticed, were dark, without a sign of joy; I once saw a child who was watching the streets pulled in from a balcony and scolded. But the streets were alive, flamboyant, crowded with vendors, vintners, and flower girls who had burst all at once from the markets to conquer the world.

On the day of the procession I put on a clean shirt with a pearl button at the throat and went downstairs, curious to observe the famous holiday. Yedov was in the antechamber, peering out a window, and he turned toward me with a grave look as I entered.

"Where are you going, *telmaro*?"

"Out to see the procession," I answered cheerfully.

He frowned. I observed that he was not dressed to go out himself: he wore a plain white morning coat, a modest jasper in one ear, and what we in Tyom would have called a ten-o'-clock face.

"Oh, you don't want to go out today," he said.

"Why not?"

"It's the Feast of Birds, *telmaro*. The streets will be full of nasty people, thieves! Your father always took my advice and stayed indoors on the Feast."

I needed no more encouragement. "Good-bye!" I laughed, flinging the door wide.

The Feast of Birds is dedicated to Avalei, the Goddess of Love and Death, of whom my master had said: "Not all that is ancient is worthy of praise." In my readings, Avalei's shadow had passed most often at moments of crisis; I thought she must be like the vegetable gods of the islands, mute and beyond appeal. Yet her great feast day appeared to involve no sacrifice or grief. The cafés were crowded with groups of students pounding the tables and singing, and a boisterous crowd of country people possessed the Garden of Plums, dressed in shades of blue and smelling of charcoal fires.

When the procession began, the musicians scrambled down from their makeshift stages and the crowd pressed eagerly toward the Grand Promenade, and I went with them, forcing myself among the straining spectators opposite the gray façade of the Autumn Palace. Drums boomed, deep and solemn. In the gardens of the palace, where in the last century a famous general had hanged himself for love, people climbed up the bars of the wrought-iron fence for a better view, waving banners above an aviary of tissue-paper macaws. "Can you see it?" someone shouted near me, almost into my ear. "No!" I replied. There was the dark march of the drums. Both sides of the street were thronged with people watching from under the trees, and stiff-legged soldiers patrolled the edges of the crowds.

The procession came down the street, heralded by a trembling sigh, a sigh released all at once by the waiting crowd, and then by bursts of music which erupted along the street like waterspouts, and by loud cries and the waving of scarves. The women were waving their scarves in the air, slow flags of colored silk, waving them with their bare arms, even from the balconies, and singing strange, exhilarating songs that rose and throbbed in the heated air like melodies from the depths of the earth. The drums came into sight, huge, decorated with bells, made from the skins of sacred bulls raised in the temples, creatures fed on wheat and basil and turned to face the west before they were slaughtered, their massive horns preserved in bronze. The drummers wore masks of painted wood and nodded their heads as they struck. Behind them walked young eunuchs with silver censers, their mellow, eerie voices entwined in ethereal cadences, mingling with the dark fumes that billowed around them. . . . The air was filled, all at once, with a strong smell I could not place, an elemental odor like frankincense and charred bone, and under the influence of this scent, more powerful than that of the spice markets, I saw the priests strutting in their skin skirts. They were naked to the waist, and their chests were shaved and painted with ochre; they were crowned with the bronzed horns of the slaughtered bulls, and behind them came the priestesses in cloaks of lion skin, bearing lilies and decked with garlands of cornflowers.

In the winter I go to the Land of the Dead,
I belong to Telduri my brother;
In the spring I belong to Tol,
The God of Smoke and Madness;
In summer only shall I be yours,
O youth with the reddened cheeks,
O player of flutes,
O star who sleeps beneath a tree on the hill.

So sang the priestesses, and with them the women among the crowd. And the goddess came into view, she or her image, hewn from a great stone and borne by twenty men on a litter, a vast figure spangled with old gilt.

Where is the hunting knife
with which I slew the milk-white deer?
For I see it not: neither beside my arm, nor under it.

This was the song of the priests, which the men around me sang with them, the notes lifting into an impassioned thunder, pleading and terrible and underscored by the bells and drums. The air was erased by the odor of incense and flowers. The goddess passed slowly, a thing of such unbearable weight, of such gravity, that I could scarcely look at her and could not read the expression in her face of indifferent stone. She was a moon: there was nothing animal about her. Her litter was heaped with lilies, jonquils, anemones, and narcissi amid flames which were barely discernable in the sunlight; they were the flames of scented candles, and there were urns about her, and carpets, and the men who bore her sweated a scarlet ooze through dyed faces. Behind her came another, smaller litter borne by hooded priests, in which, underneath seven layers of sumptuous brocades, the *Book of Mysteries* slept in its silver casket as if under the sea, in its dim and fragrant grotto studded with pearls.

All at once the women sang: "*The hunting knife is within my heart, the hunting knife is the ornament of my heart.*" And the music swelled, the voices of men and women together now, the men asking *Where is the hunting knife,* and the women answering them in ardent notes like shot arrows: *The hunting knife is the ornament of my heart.* Faces twisted with ecstasy. A woman near me looked toward the trees, arching her back, her bright face wet with tears; and other women opened their mouths and flung hard, trilling melodies at the procession, songs that jarred with the sacred music. Elsewhere there were cries, sobs, the chattering shrieks of someone who was speaking in a language without words; and as the goddess passed away, a great convulsion of weeping wracked the crowd, pierced with inarticulate cries.

My own cheeks were wet. I was still gazing at the disappearing goddess, Avalei of the Ripened Grain, when a second tremor went through the crowd—not as profound as the first, but signifying some change, some new excitement. "The Wings!" someone cried. At once the shout was taken up; people were running, but not closer to the procession. They were running back into the square, into the garden, into the alleys, pressed together and laughing, glancing behind them. Children were snatched up quickly and borne away, women picked up their skirts, and a few men climbed the trees of the Promenade, while the balconies above the street grew crowded with curious figures looking eagerly downward, half laughing and half afraid.

"The Wings!"

I stood looking at the street. My face was strangely warm, as if I had drunk a pitcher of new wine. The crowd had grown thin; there were only a few of us who watched, transfixed as if by the track of an errant comet. And we saw them come: young men, running, roaring, linked together, their arms interlocked so that they moved like a wave, like a thick tumultuous flood or else like a dragon, some single beast of a hundred parts, deranged, obliterating the pavements. They moved as if they were running downhill at the mercy of gravity, as if they could crash through forests, armies, stone, and as they came they shouted and some were singing and others wore grimaces of pain, or else of an alien ecstasy. The street performers began to scatter belatedly toward the alleys, but the youths came into their midst with the force of a deluge, and those whom they could touch they seized and drowned in their living river, compelling them to run or be crushed underfoot. I watched them, shivering, feeling something like terror, or perhaps longing, seeing their sweat-dampened hair as they came closer, and seeing also that some of them had blood smeared on their foreheads and others were soaked as if they had come through a sheet of rain. Near me a man, his face radiant with tears, released a fearsome cry and plunged like a diver into the moving mass. I saw myself for a moment, a small figure under the trees; and then they cracked over me, and I was with them.

They were students, poets, and lovers of the goddess Avalei, and they were mad with the love that drove them through the streets. Love made them bound up and down among the walls in a rhythmic dance, clinging to one another, chanting hoarsely: "Riches and glory I do not desire, nor do I wish to be king; I ask nothing more than to be your lover and slave, to remain with you; only stay with me in the hills and you shall fulfill all my desire. . . ." Their dance was like those which are danced on the eve of battle. They tore through the streets with the savagery of an inferno until their passion exhausted itself like a sheaf of lightning among the alleys, and they stumbled, still clutching one another's arms like frightened children, into the shelter of an ill-lighted café. Then I saw for the first time the faces of those who had been my companions in terror, and they were thin and drawn, their expressions stunned, and their bodies wore the shabby clothes of those who drink under the bridges, and their gestures were vague, and they held one another's hands. They were true devotees of the goddess and had spent the day in the temple drinking heady liquors made from fermented flowers, and some of them had made love to the temple harlots behind the screens and wore the lost and shimmering look of new-slain warriors. The café where we found ourselves, fatigued and sore, our lungs aching, was a great stone room with a domed and blackened ceiling, with smoky lamps along the walls which made me realize that the sun had set and only the blue dusk came through the doorway. Evidently the "Wings" were known there, for a fire was quickly kindled and sleepy girls materialized from the darkness, one with a large pewter basin from which she splashed the face of a boy who had fainted. We looked at each other in the firelight.

"Where are we?" I asked the slight, grimy youth who was holding my hand.

He shrugged. "Somewhere in the Quarter."

"Are you hurt?"

"No," he said, looking at me as if I had asked an odd question, though there was blood mixed with the dirt on his brow and hair. We sat at a table with some of the others on wooden chairs strengthened with twine, and the girls, moving as silently as witches, brought us wine and *teiva* and held out their hands which we pressed with coins, and then melted away, yawning, into the gloom. "I need a drink," said the boy who sat opposite me in a trembling voice. Tears welled up in his eyes, though he was smiling. . . . The others patted his back, and one of them said, "Yes, by the gods, I've a dragon's thirst!" and there was a light pattering of laughter. Outside, in the streets, beat the music of fifes and drums, the continuing festival, which we had stepped out of, if only for a moment; and I found myself wishing fervently, with desperation and sadness, that these strange youths would let me remain among them.

We were young and had been through a fire, and so we were shy. We did not exchange names, but after a time we began to behave like young men, and our talk grew louder in that dim room where pork and rabbits crackled above the hearth and the drowsy girls went dragging their feet. Our eyes shone; a boy took a violin from against the wall, removed his boots, and began to play, cradling the instrument; when the meat was done we ate it ravenously, grease on our lips, and the strength it gave us was potent like that of the wine. I found myself in an earnest conversation with two of the youths, explaining things to them I had not known myself, connections between the poets I had never seen before, a clear architecture rising out of excitement and *teiva*. The youths who listened were students at the School of Philosophy, and they argued eagerly, with fiery humor. They rolled cigarettes for me and we bent close together, smoking, their eyes alive and sparkling in the dimness. I had answers to all of their contradictions; they looked at me admiringly, they laughed, they began to call me the Foreign Professor. And I felt myself at the height of human bliss as I protested, "No, not foreign. I've been raised on the northern poets. . . ."

The night brought music. A band from the festival invaded the café, armed with raucous pipes, guitars, and swollen drums, filling the room with a reek of sweat, demanding money and wine, releasing a deafening, jaunty cacophony of sound. The whole room glittered with girls, perhaps the same ones who had served us earlier, but now they wore long earrings and shrieked with laughter, and the young men caught them and whirled them about the floor in popular dances, their shadows huge in the redness of the firelight. The music called in a troupe of Kestenyi dancers from the street, who were greeted with ragged cheers from the drunken students—they were lithe young men with rouged cheeks and hats that were round at the brim and square on top, made of the piebald skins of goats. They wore long purple tunics that reached to their boot-tops and were slit at the sides to show their voluminous embroidered trousers, and they skipped wildly on their heels and toes, their bodies motionless from the waist up, their faces fixed in sublime hauteur. I watched everything through the deep, resplendent mists that surrounded me, watched the rise of an arm, the toss of a head, watched even the shoulder of the girl who had come to sit on my lap through a starry haze—it was cool to the touch, as if made of enamel. She turned her head to look at me. I was happy and exhausted, feeling as I had felt on the open sea: as if the world had drowned and something new had taken its place, a ringing brilliance, fathomless and transparent.

The cool girl moved her lips, saying something I could not hear. I told her that no, she was not heavy at all. My desire for her had no beginning; I felt it had always been there, blind and torrential like my desire for the city. She took my arm and led me into the rooms, the elusive corridors, the hanging stairs, the ineluctable darkness, into a room with walls as thin as if they were made of cardboard, where a single candle winked crazily in the gloom. There was music from downstairs. I believe the girl was talking to me, but I could not understand anything she said, not until she drew close to me and I heard her voice distinctly as she whispered: "Cousin, this is what the gods eat."

I awoke to glare and silence. And then, beyond the silence, sound—the sounds from the street which I realized had awakened me, sounds of talk and footsteps, a burst of laughter, the whine of a door, the scrape of a wooden table across the pavement. My mouth was dry, but I felt no pain until I tried to move, and then I began to ache in every limb, the agony concentrated in my skull, which throbbed rhythmically as if in time to the ringing of my ears. With the pain came the realization that I was in a strange room, and that the silence of the room was the first thing I had heard, a blankness that made me uneasy because it was not like other silences: it was the dead sound of abandonment and squalor. I opened my eyes. I lay on a narrow pallet that smelled of ammonia and mice, wearing only my shirt, on a floor of wooden slats that had long ago been green, in a very small room dazzlingly lit by the sun. There was no sign of the girl, and no sign that the room belonged to anyone. I sat up, groping weakly for the trousers lying over my feet. I saw my boots against the wall, but my waistcoat had disappeared, and I soon realized that my purse was gone as well. The single pearl button that had once closed the throat of my shirt had been removed, plucked away with a surgeon's skill.

Trembling, my body clammy with a poisonous film of sweat, I opened the door and limped into the hall, a twilit region down which there echoed a shriek of coarse laughter. A door opened to my right, and a girl stumbled out. She slipped and fell, naked but for a green shawl clutched about her, turning her back to the wall, screaming with laughter, facing the open door at which she yelled: "Don't you do it!"—and a pair of slippers was flung at her from inside. I stood, swaying, sick with rage, wondering if it was she, and about to demand the return of my belongings, when she looked up at me and shouted in a flatly insulting tone: "*Vai!* If it's not the camel of Emun Deis." Her own witticism sent her into transports of braying laughter. I turned away, walking unsteadily down the hall, refusing to believe that this could be my companion of the previous night, and lacking the strength for a fight.

As I turned a corner I nearly walked into one of the Kestenyi dancers, who stood urinating calmly against the wall. He wore the long split skirt but was missing the trousers underneath, and the front of his skirt was looped up over his arm. He was very tall, and he turned to stare at me with his hot black eyes, a stare of vivid and terrible attentiveness which made me stop short, looking back at him, my heart racing. He looked like one whose thoughts are not those of others. There was something in his eyes, a look both vacant and profound, which made me certain he was no mere lunatic; his gaze of inspired singleness of purpose, combined with his handsome, bestial face, gave him a look of precise evil. I opened my mouth but could not find anything to say to his stare. At last he shook himself and released his skirt, which swirled below his knees, a voluptuous and dusky purple, and turned away, swaggering down the hall.

"Horrible!" I whispered, unable to help myself. I was now shivering violently with fever, and the ringing in my ears had grown into a persistent whine. I moved on down the empty passage. This hall seemed narrower, more constricted than the others, and it was quiet, as though at the center of the building. I was shaken by my encounter with the dancer and glanced back often, making sure that I was not being followed. Soon you will be outside, I told myself, but I did not believe it, no longer believed anything that I told myself, no longer believed that there had been sunlight, festivals, screens of poplars beside a canal. The air was dancing before my eyes. A stairway opened in front of me, and I shuffled down, trying to cling to the wall, which was smooth and cold and offered me no support; and at last, overcome by exhaustion, I sank to my knees and leaned back against the stairs, my mind reeling in the stillness.

And then, suddenly, she was there. She did not appear, as a person would, but at once the world became aware of her presence. With a violence, a blinding rupture, she was there at the foot of the stairs, and the air opened, trembling, to receive her. The city wept. I cried out from the intense pain in my head, throwing up my arms to protect my face. . . . But she was there, I could still see her, just as she had been on the ship, with her childlike shape, her long red hair, and her face, unclear in the brilliance. The air shuddered, flashing with the strain of having to hold her, humming like sheets of steel, like sheets of lightning. There was the chaos in the hall of a disturbed geography, of a world constrained to rearrange itself.

She raised her small hand. There was the shock of opening vistas, of landscapes over which I hurtled, helpless; and she said, in a voice as intimate as if she were pressing her fingers on my brain: "Rise! Rise, Jevick of Tyom!"

Chapter Seven

From a Somnambulist's Notebook

Our islands are full of ghosts.

I wrote those words. I scribbled them down after I had found my way back to the Hotel Urloma, after waking on the steps of a brothel in the city of Bain, a haunted man. Three words in Olondrian. In Kideti, they are five.

I wrote in a paperbound record book, a book I have with me still. Soft leather covers, a string to wrap around the whole and keep it shut. I had purchased the book to keep track of my transactions in the market, and I used it for this purpose for several weeks. So there are pages with lines of Kideti numbers, bold compartments, rows of accounts. And then on the last few sheets this eruption, this disorder. Newspaper clippings stuffed inside, hurried copies from the books in Yedov's library. A true mirror of my life in Bain.

Our islands are full of ghosts. They come from the flowers and from the water. They are those who are always waiting, outside on the paths. There are the Sea Dead and the Rotted Dead whose bodies have never been burned, the Poisoned Dead, and the Animal Dead—the ghosts of the sacred beasts. They are the reason we walk under trees, avoid the shapes made by the moonlight, never toss seeds carelessly over our shoulders in the darkness. They haunt the hills and crossroads and are implacable on the beaches where the Sea Dead hold their ragged, ungraceful dances at festival time. If you see one you must kiss your fingers and pray, you must back away slowly, and above all you must never ask its name. Your house must be purified with smoke, and you must have smoke in your hair, wear strips of charmed leather about your ribs, underneath your clothes, rub your chest and neck with peppermint oil, avoid the ocean, keep fires burning close to you, and chew dried pumpkin-flower. If you are pursued, then you must consult the doctors, who will treat you with hot needles, purges, the constant rattling of gourds.

I have heard them chanting from a nearby house: "Take back your beads, Ghost, take back your fan, take back your sandals."

I have seen her three times—perhaps four.

First, on the steps. Then in the warren of streets where I wandered, asking strangers the way to the canal. She bloomed into life in a nearby wall, like a cancer of the stone. I threw myself backward, screaming, and collapsed in a gutter.

I must have lost consciousness for a time. The stealthy hands of a beggar woke me. He abandoned my pockets when I sat up, and showed me his broken teeth. His eyes were crushed dried figs. "Tobacco," he hissed, tugging the hem of my shirt. "Tobacco for the beloved of the gods."

In the Street of Owls I saw her again: the ghost of the Kiemish girl. She looked at me with the eyes of one born into the country of herons. With a lift of her hand she dispelled my reason; I gibbered into the sunlight; I ran, shrieked, struck my head against walls, seeking the merciful dark. My terror was stronger than shame. When I awoke again, a couple were passing me, and the woman twitched her skirt away from my prone body. Her dress was pale pink, her hair secured with pins. "Shocking," she said, and her companion replied: "It is to be expected, after the Feast."

Is there some connection between the Feast of Birds and this apparition? I wish I could find one of my companions from that night—one of the Wings. Are they all haunted like me? I cannot believe it. There were so many of them. Even here in the hotel I would hear their screams.

I said I had seen her "perhaps four times." Now I must call them five.

I was not sure, at first; I thought it was only a nightmare caused by the horrible events of the Feast. Now I know she pursues me when I sleep.

I have seen her again. There is no escape. I pace the room, boil coffee, drink glass after scalding glass. I speak to myself in the mirror. I say: "Wake up. Open your eyes. Look at me. My curse on you if you bow your head."

Sten has told Yedov that I am suffering from a fever.

Sten knows all. I told him at once. I said: "It is a jeptow*."*

He kissed his fingertips at the word. Jeptow*—a wild spirit, a ghost, a citizen of the ghost country,* jepnatow-het*. But he is not superstitious. He keeps to the quiet and ordered religion of his forefathers who have served my family since the War of the*

Crows. As I write he is tending a fire in a clay bowl, burning fenugreek against ghosts, and rosemary, "the salt herb," a prayer to the winds.

What is she?

She arrives in chimes. The air tolls and bellows. Now I understand that light has a sound. She is an absolute stranger to me: she is stranger than the effulgent sea, more alien than the pale coast, the foreign city. In vain I sob: "Ghost, begone, your hair is under the mountain"—the chant of frightened children under far trees.

"Help," I scream. To no one.

And the ghost answers: "No. You help me."

Her voice metallic, a harp of light.

"You help me." What does she want?

I have asked her. I cried: "How? Tell me how." But I cannot bear her voice and presence for very long. Her small mouth opens and closes, a cave of light. And night falls down around me like a temple of broken glass.

What does she want? I think—

I write left-handed. The right is bandaged: last night I put it through the window. I woke to find Sten bending over me, winding strips of a torn sheet around my hand, two tears on the burnt leather of his cheek. He told me he had tried to turn me before I reached the window, but I moved suddenly and he was too late. I told him not to blame himself. He has guarded me well on my dream walks, kept me from falling into the brazier or the fire.

He says we are going home today.

He is too weary to smile fully, his face a mask. Poor Sten—

I have not opened this book for three days. I have not had the strength. But I must think. I must act, or perish. I am alone. Sten and the others have gone back to the islands without me.

Some buried part of me suspected the truth. A hidden intuition whispered: "She will not let you get away." I ignored it. I concentrated on the coming voyage, on our plans for keeping my ailment secret until we arrived in Tyom. I was to board the ship wrapped in a cloak—for I know that my face reflects my suffering, and I appear to have aged ten years in as many days. Sten would take me quickly into the hold. We did not reveal my condition to the other servants, for fear that the tale of my haunting would reach the captain.

It was when Sten asked me what Olondrians think of ghosts, and how they manage in such cases, that I realized I did not know. Indeed, to my knowledge there is no word in Olondrian for "ghost." There is only the word nea, *which means "angel."*

And so we resolved to take no chances. There are few Kideti captains who would willingly allow a ghost on board, and I assumed an Olondrian captain would feel the same.

I am not sure of this, now. But in the end I was not permitted to see for myself.

It began in the Street of the Clocks. First, a tightness in my forehead. Then nausea, against which I clenched my teeth and prayed. Then headache, then loss of reason. Before we reached the harbor and the ship, pain cracked my mind like a pair of silver tongs.

"No," she said. A single word, a stab of pure and agonizing light.

The time that followed is vague in my mind, flickering like a storm. I know that I fought to get out of the carriage. I fought Sten, my good Sten. I said: "Let me out. She'll kill me." These words I remember well.

When I had come out of the carriage, she faded, and I could see again. A crowded street, curious dockworkers gathered around the scene. The horses stamped and rolled their eyes. Sten took me by the shoulders.

Even now I cannot believe that he is gone.

I must believe it. He is gone, and it was I, his Ekawi, who sent him away. I know that I did right. It is only a matter of weeks before the winds change and Olondrian ships stop sailing for the south. What would happen to the farm, to my mother and Jom, without Sten? He would have missed two full growing seasons had he stayed too long. He knew it, but still he tried to stay. He said: "We'll book a new passage next week." I told him it was no use. I said: "The ghost will not let me go."

The ghost will not let me go. I came back to the Hotel Urloma alone. I walked through the room of white roses and down the hall. Yedov looked up from his newspaper when I entered the dining room. A cigarette before him, a glass of tea.

I told him I was too ill to travel. He brought me here, to this room on the roof of the hotel.

He said he had already rented my former room. He did not look at me when he spoke. He unlocked the door to a cramped stairway and led me up to this chamber, the "student's quarters." It stands alone on the roof. He has not used it for some time. "Students, you know," he said, "furniture broken, strange women at all hours." I told him yes, I saw, I understood. I was suddenly anxious for him to leave. Unsure of how much he knew. Afraid.

"You help me."

I remember coming back through my beloved Bain. Passing the Street of the Saints, the Street of the Baths, where the air is perfumed with myrrh. The Street of Acacias, the Street of Red Eaves. The Street of Prince Kelva's Mistress. The Street of Harps, populated with echoes.

"Oh streets of my city," *writes Fodra,* "how you depart when I enter you."

I passed the Street of the Dead, the Cemetery of Bain. Its whitewashed ramparts glitter like spun sugar. There stand the miniature homes of the dead, tiled fantasies, like houses for children.

Beneath them Olondrian bones are falling to dust.

Somewhere, she is like that too. She must have died here, in Olondria, in the north. She was buried, then, not burned as is our custom in the islands. She is one of the Rotted Dead.

She must desire what all such dead desire: to be consumed. To be released.

"You help me."

"Do you want me to find your body?" I screamed.

My own voice frightened me: too harsh, too much. As I slipped into darkness, I heard swift feet downstairs. Dogs barked from a neighboring yard.

From The Starling, *a Bainish newspaper, just after the Feast of Birds:*

> The Feast of Birds is over, to the relief of all upright citizens. Small fortunes were lost, glass broken, reputations irreparably soiled—but this

will hardly come as news to longtime residents of the capital. What is more alarming is that, contrary to popular belief, the so-called Feast is no mere invasion, attended solely by outsiders. This writer observed, from a convenient window, a person very like Lady Olami of Bain wailing before the effigy of the Goddess.

Such displays are proof that despite the best intentions of the Telkan, whose wisdom in the matter is undeniable, the cult of Avalei persists in its more unworthy forms, and can be expected to do so for some time. Those who thought that the Telkan's decision to prevent the High Priestess of Avalei from attending the Feast would crush it, must admit themselves in the wrong. It seems that as long as Avalei's priests, bulls, eunuchs, and peasant hangers-on exist, chaos will clog our streets every Month of Apples.

But is there no solution, nothing to be done? Is our only response to be a sigh, and the sweeping of broken glass and refuse from our doorsteps? No! For it has been reported that letters are flooding the Blessed Isle, complaining of damages and requesting more guards. Respectable Bainish hearts must not lose hope! We must add our voices to the Telkan's, until the Red and White Councils answer our demands! Citizens, make your wishes known: no more harlots' festivals in Bain, no thieves' holidays, no Feast of Birds!

Letters respond in the next several issues. Agreement, approval, reports of crimes committed during the Feast. No challenge. No defense.

The windows in the student's quarters are all covered with boards. They must have been broken long ago. Prepared for me.

A door leads onto the roof, where herbs and vegetables grow in pots. Sometimes I step out for air. I lock the door at night.

A table. A candlestick so dented it looks as if it was used in a brawl. A fireplace wreathed in grinning figures, some missing a nose or a horn.

My satchel, my books. Olondrian Lyrics, *the binding stained with seawater. the* Romance of the Valley, *beginning to curl with use. Newspapers, pens. I have no talents, but unless my master failed, I am a decent scholar. That scholarship must serve me as sword, and shield, and friend.*

From The Lamplighter's Companion, *the Olondrian almanac and general encyclopedia, the entry on angels:*

> **Angels.** Hallucinations.
> Once believed to be the spirits of the dead, and to possess knowledge of the Land Beyond, the angels are now understood to be merely products of human minds which have become unbalanced through illness, shock, or intrinsic abnormalities. In the days of widespread ignorance and the reign of the cult of Avalei, diseased individuals were adored as saints rather than treated and returned to health. Suffering and folly ensued. The worship of angels, like geomancy and reading the taubel, was outlawed and registered as a crime in 939.

939. Three years after my master left Olondria.

A fruitless trip to the Library of Bain.

There are no books about angels. I countered my weakness with coffee and seared beef at a café and took a carriage to the great pillared edifice. How often I walked its halls in happier days! Now I clung to the banister as I climbed the stairs to the seventh floor. Here, in the Collection of the Rare and Unseen, I paged through discourses on magic and theological textbooks. Sometimes I found a word, a line, that seemed to promise discovery. "Breim may have been led to his profession by his mother, who was visited by an angel for six years." "According to the Angel of Berodresse, as reported by his mouthpiece Gerna, there will never be a machine capable of flight." But I found no treatises, no arguments, no explanations. Only a little white volume, Jewels from a

Stone, for the Edification and Uplifting of Eager Hearts, *which repeated what I had read in the* Companion*—there are no angels, only sick minds—and appended several prayers to restore order to the spirit.*

Even Leiya Tevorova's autobiography was absent.

I asked for it at the scribe's desk on the first floor. The scribe on duty, a dark, angry-looking girl with deep red cheeks, stared at me so coldly her lashes seemed to bristle.

What did I want with such a book?

I told her I had heard it praised as one of the greatest prose works in the language.

"Oh?" she said, her pen raised. "And who said so?"

"I don't know his name," I said. "I met him in the spice markets." And I turned around and left her.

I wish my master were here.

I wish Sten were here.

I don't want to be alone.

A pile of old cotton lies before me on the table. Yedov let me have the hangings on the skeletal bed in the student's quarters, which had fallen into rags. Each night I read till I feel the chime, the quiver in the air, that signals the ghost. Then I close my book and blow the candle out. I lock the door, force a wad of cotton into my mouth, and bind it in place with another strip to muffle my cries.

I ask myself: How long? How long can I bear it?

It is not only the light. The light brings pain, but the pain is not everlasting. When the force of it grows too strong, I drop into darkness. No, the pain is not the worst thing. The worst thing is the sense of wrong, *like the uncovering of a crime.*

Our two worlds scrape together like the two halves of a broken bone.

My world has changed forever, tainted by that touch. Jissavet, my countrywoman, is dead. She is now as vast as a cavern, as small as a bead on a woman's scarf, indifferent like a landscape. She has died in the city and in the gardens and in the unnameable forests, and in all the great plains and seas of the earth her death lies like a corruption.

She brings me images from her past, like a diabolical dowry. A window. A street.

I writhe against them. They are not mine.

From The Lamplighter's Companion:

Jewels from a Stone, for the Edification and Uplifting of Eager Hearts. A book of wisdom collected by Ivrom, Second Priest of the Stone, and published by the Imperial Press in 931. The book has been reprinted six times to date. Of particular interest are the chapters on the evils of luxury, idleness, and wine. The chapter on reading includes the verse "And I am helpless before thee like a child," which is said to have made the Telkan weep.

Ivrom, Priest of the Stone. The second to hold this holy office. Ivrom was born in Bain in 883. On the death of his predecessor, the First Priest of the Stone, in 928, he accepted the leadership of the cult at the Telkan's request. He has published over fifty books and pamphlets explaining the wisdom of the Stone his predecessor found in the desert of Ludyanith, including the popular and influential **Jewels from a Stone**. A widower with one daughter, he resides with the Telkan on the Blessed Isle.

Locked gates. Empty roads.

Leiya Tevorova. A deranged woman and moderately gifted writer. Her preposterous autobiography, used in schools for a century after her death, was denounced by the Priest of the Stone and banned in 934.

When I am too ill to go downstairs, Yedov brings me a bowl of soup on a tray. He never forgets me. I am grateful for this, and wary. At the sound of his foot on the stair I peel myself from the floor, clamber onto the bed, touch my head to find any bruises I must explain.

He enters, stiffening slightly at the smell of the chamber pot. He will send the scullery boy to take it down.

Thank you. Thank you for the kindness. Thank you for the soup.

Do not expose me. Do not send me away.

"Human minds . . . unbalanced through illness, shock, or intrinsic abnormalities."

A lie. She is no illusion.

Avalei. The Goddess of Love and Death, one of the Gods of Time. According to her legend she is the daughter of Leilin, the Goddess of Healing, and Heth Kuidva, the Oracle God. Her brother Eliya compared her in beauty to the goddess Roun, for which both he and his sister were banished to the Land of the Dead. Avalei is said to return every spring. She is called the Ripened Grain, and rules the summer according to the understanding of simple minds. Fanlewas the Wise, in his book **The Serpent and the Rose**, describes her in the following terms:

"The Goddess Avalei is a most mysterious figure, perhaps even more enigmatical than the Moon. She is the presence of grain, of the cultivation of the earth. She was there when first we put our hands into the soil. She is all laughter and love, she is the agreement of the wild things, the acquiescence of earth in our endeavors. . . . And like her mother, Leilin the Mother of us all, she has the strangeness of having been human clay before she was made divine. And yet—O wondrous mystery!—she is also the Queen of the Dead, who possesses, instead of hands, the paws of a lion. It is she who sits on that dark throne. Yet she also walks in the orchards. She is the mother of both kings and vampires. . . ."

> The cult of Avalei flourished during the reign of the House of Hiluen, until the ascendancy of the current Telkan. The goddess was worshipped in many forms, called Velkosri, the "Plague-Lily," in the north, and in the far south Temheli, the "Queen of Flutes." The crimes of this cult, their fleecing of the peasants, their lust for political power, and the gross wealth of their temples, are notorious. In recent years their influence has happily lessened, particularly since the outlawing of one of their most offensive practices, the courtship and worship of angels.

I have been to the Horse Market.

In the Street of Tanners a stinking breeze made me retch, and I drank the trickle from the mouth of a carved bat near the Architects' Prison. In the Market the painted beasts, half-tamed, driven out of the west, reared and snorted in the dread smell of skin become leather.

Merchants argued with dust-streaked horsemen. Horses and cattle jostled together, gazelles, wild ostriches, and the camel, that descendant of the dragon. At the Carriage House I reserved a seat in a coach bound for Ethendria. The first step on a journey toward the body.

I remember the name of the place she was traveling to: Aleilin. Named for the Goddess Leilin, patroness of healers.

Yedov: "Will you not have a doctor, telmaro? *I know a most gifted and discreet lady. It appears to me that your illness is a stubborn one."*

No. No doctors.

"Come, telmaro. *Try to be reasonable. Put yourself in my hands. Your suffering makes me suffer."*

He pulled a rickety chair to the table, set his bulk down carefully. His eyes like melted caramel in the candlelight.

"Trust me."
A curl on each shining cheek. An odor of heliotrope.
Tears filled my eyes. The desire to confide in him made me tremble.
"What is your trouble?" he whispered.
"A dead thing. Something dead."
He leaned close, urgent. "An angel?"
Yes. Yes, I said. An angel.

I hope I have not done wrong. I fear

The last words in the book.

They came for me the following afternoon. Yedov walked in first, twisting his hands in the strings of his morning coat. "I'm sorry," he blurted, stepping aside to make way for the soldiers.

There were two of them, one silver-haired, one young. Both wore the dark-blue coats and embroidered sashes of the Imperial Guard.

The silver-haired man moved toward me. His eyes, behind his enormous hooked nose, were not unkind. He cleared his throat, and the beads clacked on his plaited beard.

"What is your name?"

"Jevick of Tyom."

"Your trade?"

"I am a pepper merchant."

"Your business here?"

"The same that brings all manner of merchants to Bain."

He smiled, his eyes growing colder, green lakes in a glacial wind. "We have been told of a disturbance. Noise. Screaming. Can you explain?"

The younger soldier was writing in a book. He raised his head, expectant.

My mouth was dry. "I," I said, glancing at Yedov. He was busy examining the frame of the ancient canopy bed, running his finger along the wood as if checking for dust.

"You told me to trust you," I said.

"Pay attention, please," said the silver-haired soldier. "You are under suspicion of illegal acts. Be so good as to collect your things.

You are to come with us to Velvalinhu on the Blessed Isle, to be examined by the Priest of the Stone."

"What sort of examination?"

"Come," said the soldier. "Our time is short."

Then, as I did not move, he added: "Nothing's been proven yet, you know. The priest may dismiss your case altogether. But if you force us to take you in chains, it will make an unfortunate impression."

The younger soldier was trying to unclasp a length of chain from his belt.

"What are you doing?" snapped his superior. "That won't be necessary."

"I thought," the young man said, blushing.

"Nonsense," the older soldier snorted as I gathered my belongings. "You can see he's perfectly docile."

I stuffed my books and clothes into my satchel, adding Yedov's *Lamplighter's Companion* without a qualm.

"And what about me?" asked Yedov.

"You!" said the soldier. "You'll hear from the Isle."

"But I acted in good faith! I informed you the moment I suspected—"

"You can appeal if you don't like it," the soldier said.

I stood up and put my satchel over my shoulder. Outside the day was growing darker, light rain falling among the towers of the city. When the gray-haired soldier saw me looking at him, he flashed his teeth. "That's right!" he said. "We shall go together, as the lid said to the pot!"

Then, as if my expression touched him, he added: "Come, have courage. On the Isle we have two blessings. One is music. The other is clarity."

Clarity. "We have the sea, the forests, the hills," he said. "It is holy country. And ours is the Holy City."

BOOK THREE

The Holy City

Chapter Eight

The Tower of Myrrh

The Holy City: a city of pomegranates, of sounding bells. An incandescent city, a city of plumage. By day its lofty balconies are haunted by tame songbirds, and at night by cavorting bats and furred owls. It is peopled with silent figures painted on the walls and ceilings, or hunting elusive game through tapestries, or standing at the end of a passage: blind, with stone curls, but dressed in sumptuous robes with a coating of dust. Solitary, a young gazelle comes skittering down a hall, its dark eyes wide, wearing a ruby collar. It noses its way behind a curtain to eat its meal of mashed barley served in a dish of rare blue porcelain.

When Firdred of Bain was named to be cartographer to the Telkan, he wrote: "And so, in the way of the ancient sages, I retired at last from my weary life to a house perfumed with incense, in the land to the north of which all journeys end." This reflects the Olondrian belief that the dead dwell in the north, that the dead land is "the country north of the gods," and thus that the Blessed Isle is the gate between two holy empires, between Olondria and the place which "is not earth, and is not void." At certain times of the year the king and queen go to the northernmost tip of the Isle, there to make sacrifices of an unknown nature, on an altar within a hill so sacred that birds do not land on it. At such times it is customary to say: "They are meeting with the Grave King."

Perhaps it is the nearness of death, or the northern obsession with it, which gives the place its peculiar, drowning languor. The rich halls seem embalmed, and the air is saturated with scent. The beds are enclosed in boxes, like carven tombs. . . . And the extravagance, the gorging voluptuousness of court life, the nobles dreaming in baths of attar of roses, the dishes of quails' brains or of certain glands of polar bears, suggest a greed for life at the gateway of death. There are rooms of painted concubines sleeping in wanton poses. Behind the gardens the *iloki*, the saddlebirds, squat: those massive fowls the Telkans ride to war, riddled with parasites and stinking of death, whose wild cries ripen the fruit.

And is it death that gives the festive nights their vibrancy? Is it death that makes the ballrooms echo with laughter, adding a touch of fascination, as a piquant sauce of his enemies' eyeballs spiced the meat of Thul, the nineteenth Telkan? For sometimes the rooms explode with color, as if in a storm of tulips, and laughing faces are passed among the mirrors; the fountains in the square run gold with fermented peach nectar, and pleasure boats illuminate the lake. Courtiers smoke in the stairwells, their faces ruddy with wine and feasting, and princesses throw lighted tapers from the balconies. Everywhere there are handsome figures, drenched in scent and lavishly costumed—only the loveliest, only the brightest stars, gain this society.

And perhaps it is this, and not the nearness of death, which exhausts the atmosphere. Perhaps it is simply the grandeur, the over-refinement, the febrile nature produced by centuries of mingling a few exalted bloodlines, the oppressive stamp of the divine. Cries of rage echo down halls where antique paintings glitter. A marmoset is found strangled in an arbor. Two hundred years ago an anonymous court poet prayed: "Defend us from the persecution of our superiors."

And they, the superiors, the nobility—they are drunk with freedom, indulging their various tastes without restraint, riding out to hunt before dawn, whipping their favorite servants, or feverishly copying manuscripts in the library. The passions of the aristocrats are famous: there was Kialis, the princess whose experiments poisoned more than a thousand birds; there was Drom, who insisted on lancing his peasants' boils himself, and Rava whose craving for opals beggared the provinces. There have been Telkans who relished army life and filled the banqueting halls with soldiers who picked their teeth at the bone-strewn tables; there have been patrons of dramatists and musicians, patrons of guilds. And innumerable princes infatuated with roses.

The light slides down the corridors of that "City of Five Towers." In the east it strikes the Tower of Pomegranates, with its copper spires and gardens of flamboyant scarlet peonies, where the Teldaire dwells with her children and attendants. It passes on to the Tower of Myrrh, which houses shrines and temples, and gilds it with a pale marmoreal splendor; then it plays over the central Tower of Mirrors, turning the battlements dusky pink and flashing brilliantly through the galleries. In the west it drowns itself in the heavy jade of the Tower of Aloes, where the scribes sit at their desks in the Royal Library; lastly it warms the blue of the Tower of Lapis Lazuli, and the fragrant, shuttered chambers of the Telkan.

In a moment the sun has dropped behind the hills, like a lamp extinguished. In this city they say "the darkness falls like a blow." The gazelle looks up, then trots away down an avenue of brocades, leaving a trail of pellets like dark seeds.

They took me to that city, to Velvalinhu. We traveled on one of the barges of the king, a funereal-looking vessel lined with cushions. A black leather awning provided some protection from the rain, though the soldiers suggested I store my satchel in the hold. I sat with them on damp cushions while the bargemen, wearing dark hats trimmed with silver bells, poled their way down the canal. At the sea they exchanged their poles for oars. They sang: "*Long have I carried the king's treasures. But the corals of Weile are not so red as your mouth.*"

Bain drew away from me, vague in the mists. Then the rain stopped, the sky lightened, and the bright sea spread around me on every side. As Ravhathos writes in his *Song of Exile,* "I turned my face to the north"—and like his, my heart was "shivering like a stringed instrument."

Islands dotted the sea. The imperial barge slid past them in silence: the white, uninhabited knob called the Isle of Chalk, the lovelier islands with mountains and streams, where palaces stood in groves of cypress, the Isle of the Birds, the Isle of the Poet's Daughters. "Fair are the isles of Ithvanai," writes Imrodias the Historian, "but fairest of all is the Blessed Isle itself, the fallen star which all the waters of Ocean could not extinguish, the fragrant island, the asphodel of the sea." It glimmered, at first an indistinct shadow, a gathering of mists, then more solid, its pier a pale ray on the sea and its mountains cloaked in olive trees. We left the other islands behind, and it stood in serene majesty, like a white horn or an amethyst crown, like a city of alabaster.

A carriage met us at the pier, and we rumbled down the smooth Eagle's Road, the soldiers smoking, the windows obscured by an anise-flavored fog. I slid open the pane beside me for air. A clement countryside rolled past, its vineyards bedecked with grapes like beads of glass. The thought of the coming "examination" distracted me from those tidy fields, but I gasped when I saw Velvalinhu at last, forgetting everything for a shining instant in the iridescent glow of its pillars of Ethendrian marble.

In the islands we do not pierce the clouds, for fear of the goddess of rain. But the northerners are prey to no such dread. The pinnacles of Velvalinhu rose to heights I had never seen in the capital, and never imagined even in nightmare. They were varied, no two alike, formed by the separate wills of kings: smooth walls rose beside walls puckered with carvings, marble figures leaned from the balustrades and adorned the towers where spires of obsidian sprang up, somber, drinking the light. Mirrors flashed from conical roofs, jade dogs snarled on the battlements, flights of steps hung shimmering in midair, and ornamental trees grew in the gardens, impossibly high, that peeked from between the richly tiled walls. We crossed the magnificent square in front of the palace, as vast as a desert, and rumbled down a slope into a subterranean carriage house. I thought of the words of Tamundein's ode: "*O lamp of the empire, forest of marble, caravan of the winds, Velvalinhu!*"

In the carriage house our coachman opened the door, holding up a lamp. "What news?" he asked.

"All bad," the old soldier answered cheerfully as he stepped out. "Low pay, high taxes, and no prospect of war outside Brogyar country."

"I'd like to go to the Brogyar country," the younger soldier said.

"You!" his companion exclaimed with a laugh. "They'd pickle you like a herring."

The coachman chuckled appreciatively and tilted his head toward me. "What's this one for?"

"The Tower of Myrrh."

The coachman stepped away from me, and the soldier bade him good-day with a grim smile.

I followed him down a torchlit tunnel, the young soldier walking a pace or two behind me. We entered a hall with the dimensions of a temple. Three, perhaps four houses like my own in the islands might have been stacked inside it. Light filtered through its high windows, ladders of floating chalk. Such space, such silence. On one wall hung the triumphant painting of Elueth's wedding, one of the last masterpieces of Fairos the Divine, its gold paint mellowed by centuries of smoke. I knew the picture: I had seen it reproduced in my master's copy of *The Book of Time.* The human girl knelt in the foreground, wearing a smile of celestial happiness. Each fold in her dress was large enough to contain me. Her hair was "smooth as a shadow," and she held one palm turned outward, showing where she had been burned by the skin of the god.

A second hall. A third. The soldiers' boots clicked in the stillness. Each window let in, like a secret, a halo of misty light. We climbed a marble staircase, then another. No one accosted us, no one passed. It was as if the great palace were utterly deserted. Only when the halls narrowed and began to fill with an acrid smoke did we see a few figures, preoccupied men and women in long robes. They flitted past us without a word, like moths. At last, in an ill-lit room where urns smoked in the corners, the old soldier stopped with a cough.

"Well," he said, "we will leave you."

I nodded, my fingers tight on the strap of my satchel.

"Don't look so frightened," he advised me. "It never helps."

He turned to his young subordinate and jerked his head toward the door. "Come on. They'll give us bread and tea in the printer's shop."

They went out, the young soldier's chain clanking softly at his belt, and left me alone in the eerie and stifling darkness. I heard a rustle and turned. A tall, slim figure was moving toward me across the carpet, carrying something white in both hands.

I do not know what I expected: perhaps a priest in a belted robe or a green-cloaked scholar with the smug air of Olondrian medical men. Certainly not this tall woman in a dark dress, her delicate features lit from below by a lamp in a globe of frosted glass.

"Are you the petitioner?" she asked.

"*Teldarin,*" I answered, "I am a stranger."

She gazed at me closely. "But you have come to see my father."

"Is he the Priest of the Stone?"

"Yes."

"Then I am—I think—he is to examine me." I paused, unable to trust my voice.

"Welcome," she said. She balanced the light on one hand and held out the other; I clasped her fingers warmed by the lamp like heated wax. "My name is Tialon," she said. "My father is the Priest of the Stone. He's waiting for you; we received the letter yesterday."

"The letter."

"Yes. From someone called Yedov. You were staying with him, I think."

"Ah."

"Don't worry," she said, compassion softening her gaze.

I laughed: a short, hard sound.

"Your name?"

"Jevick of Tyom."

"Jevick. Come with me. He's waiting for you in his study."

I followed her. She was taller than I, and her curls were cropped short, as if she had been ill. There was nothing elegant in her cloth slippers, her plain wool dress; had she not introduced herself as the daughter of a priest, I would have taken her for some sort of superior servant. Yet she had a certain distinction, an air not of loneliness but of self-sufficiency. In the next room, where gray light filled the windows that dripped with returning rain, I saw that she was older than I had thought, perhaps thirty years old. Her left temple was tattooed with the third letter, against insomnia.

"Father," she said.

I did not see him at first; the room was crowded with desks, each covered by a landslide of books and papers. I only noticed him when he cleared his throat: a bent old man in a black robe, seated by the fire on a high-backed chair.

The knob of his head gleamed in the grainy light as he gazed at me. At the sight of his carven features my heart gave a throb of hope: he had the same arrogant, solitary look as the doctors of my own country, men who cured illnesses of the spirit, men who banished ghosts. Ivrom, Second Priest of the Stone—a holy man. "Greetings, *veimaro*," I said. "My name—"

I stopped, taken aback, as he moved toward me. He did not rise: the chair itself was moving. As it drew closer, I noticed the delicate wheels at its sides, spider-webbed with spokes.

The old man advanced with a slight ticking sound. When he reached me, his gaunt hand, resting on the arm of the chair, gave a barely perceptible twitch, and the vehicle stopped. He tilted his head back to read my face. His eyes were startling, large and light, rich signal lamps still burning in a shipwreck.

"So," he said. A single word, yet my heart sank at the sound. His voice was thick with phlegm, disdainful, the voice of a tyrant.

"Jevick, please sit down," his daughter murmured, pushing a stool toward me. I glanced at her and she nodded, her eyes giving back the light from the windows. Something in her gaze, so steady and frank, encouraged me, and I sat down.

"So," said the priest again. "You claim to have seen an angel."

"I claim nothing. It is the truth."

"So you say." He cocked his head as if observing a process of nature. "But it's original," he said. "A *ludyaval*."

Ludyaval—an "unlettered one." Illiterate: a savage.

"I can read and write," I said, stung, "and speak Olondrian fluently."

"Ah! And you are proud of yourself, no doubt." He shook his head, smiling so that his lips whitened, drawn against his teeth. "Well, well. Come, there is no need for this. The matter is a simple one. Tell me who has sent you, and you may go."

"No one sent me. I was brought here by soldiers."

"Do not toy with me," he said more softly. "Give me your master's name."

I swallowed. Rain rapped sharply against the windows, the fire stirred in its bed. The old priest watched me, clutching the arms of his enchanted chair. "I," I said. My blood sang in my ears; a strange sea, white and full of stars, seemed to be rising about me, filling up the room.

"A name!" barked the priest.

I blinked fiercely to clear my vision. His arm in its black sleeve flashed through the mists around me like a wing. Parchment crackled. He spread a map on his knees and jabbed it with a yellow fingernail. "Where did you go in Bain? Where were you corrupted?"

"Corrupted—"

"Yes! Was it Avalei's priests? I doubt it; they are too cunning for that these days. Was it a merchant? Was it the proprietor of your hotel? What was his name?"

"Yedov," I whispered.

"Was it he?"

"No—that is—I don't know what you're asking me. I don't know what you mean."

The priest turned to his daughter, who had drawn up a stool and sat near us, her chin in her hand, her expression thoughtful and tinged with pity.

"You see?" he said. "That's why they chose this *ludyaval.* He can claim he doesn't know anything, and we cannot prove he does."

"But perhaps he's telling the truth," she said.

"I am," I interrupted, seizing on this spark of hope. "*Veidarin*—"

"I am not a priestess."

"*Teldarin*—"

Again she shook her head, frowning. "No. Call me by name."

"Tialon, then—by the gods you pray to, help me!"

My cry hung in the air. The priest's daughter seemed moved by it: her cheeks grew pale, and she sat up straighter, setting her hands on her knees. "I will," she said. Her father groaned, wrinkling his map in a gesture of impatience. "I will," she repeated firmly, "but you must help me too."

"Anything. Anything you ask." I rubbed my eyes with a trembling hand. The mist of my faintness had receded, the room growing clear again. Beneath the windows, blue in the rain, Tialon leaned forward, her hands clasped, a streak of firelight on her cheek.

"Jevick," she said in a slow, earnest voice, "this is a serious matter. You have been brought here under suspicion of a crime. Do you know what it is?"

"No."

"Pretense of sainthood," she said and paused to watch me.

"Sainthood."

"Yes. The crime of claiming contact with the spirits of the dead."

"But I claim nothing," I said. "I have claimed nothing. I told no one but the keeper of the hotel, and he sent me to you." I turned from her clear green eyes to the glittering orbs in her father's face. "I am no saint. I would not call anyone with my affliction saintly."

"You see, Father," Tialon said.

"I see nothing," he snapped. "Nothing but a new ruse of the pig-worshippers of Avalei."

Tialon sighed and turned to me. "Tell us about your island. Tell us—"

"Tell us," the priest broke in with a sneer, "do your people worship angels?"

"No," I said. "That is—we have good spirits which we call angels. But they are not dead. They are not the same as the dead—that is something different. . . ."

My voice sounded very small in the room, but the priest leaned forward, intent, transfixing me with his pitiless gaze. "Not the same?"

In my mind there were vast forests, my mother's hands, smelling of flour. There were bowls of burning rosemary and *janut* on their dark altar. The wind sighing in the jackfruit trees, the sound of the doctors chanting, the sound of my elder brother being beaten behind the house. I struggled to put these images into words, looking at Tialon rather than the priest, strengthened by the candor of her gaze. The room grew slowly darker as I spoke. The rain had ceased, but there was a sound of distant thunder over the sea.

"In the oldest time," I said, "there was only the sea. There were no islands. At this time, the gods were there, but under the sea. And with them were their servants, the lower spirits, who are the angels, who are like the gods, always the same, neither increasing nor decreasing. . . . After the world was divided, they went to live on the Isle of Abundance, which is where we go after death—those of us who die well. Those of us who do not die well—belong to another place."

"Another place? Which place?" the priest demanded.

"*Jepnatow-het*," I said softly. "The angel—no, the dead country. Of those who are dead, yet alive. The one place that cannot be reached by sea."

"And what does it mean—to die badly?" Tialon asked.

"To die unburnt. To die at sea, or to rot, or to die in the midst of an evil passion. This angel, the one who haunts me, died in Aleilin in the north. Her body was never burned, and so she cannot rest."

Tialon nodded. "I have read, in the books of one of our scholars, a man called Firdred of Bain, about the island people burning their dead—"

"Yes!" said the priest testily. "My daughter adores the geographers. But let me ask you, *ludyaval*—do you communicate with the dead?"

"No."

"He shudders!" the priest exclaimed, sitting back and raising his eyebrows. "Well, that is something! That is out of the ordinary, at least! So your people do not seek to reach the dead; they are not grave-lovers. A splendid, a sensible people, you *ludyavan*! But our own people, as you may know, have a terrible passion for angels. At one time, one could scarcely dream of one's dead grandfather without being dragged to the temple. Those who claimed they could speak with the dead were revered, and people came to them with all sorts of questions, as if they were oracles. How will the maize crop be, where is the necklace my mother gave me, whom will I marry, who stole my brown horse—all nonsense, chicanery, a farce! Yes, the love of angels was once a canker of this country, and I am the physician who removed it."

We had arrived at a moment I must not lose. "If you are a physician," I said, "then cure me. Help me to find my countrywoman's body. I need to go to Aleilin, or to have the body exhumed and sent to me here. And I must burn it on a pyre."

The old man stared at me. For a moment a look of surprise and respect flitted across his face of a bleached old cormorant battered by the snows. Then he looked at Tialon, returned his gaze to me, threw back his head, exposing a skinny throat, and laughed.

"Marvelous!" he crowed. There was no true mirth in his laugh; it was a cruel sound, like the sharpening of a beak against a stone. "He asks me to send people traipsing across the country, to dig up graves, to make summer bonfires as our peasants do when the haymaking is over. What a festival it would be! And you, I suppose," he went on, bringing his head level to fix me with his predatory glare, "you, no doubt, would lead the procession, loved and revered by all, and we would not hear the end of it for a hundred years. No, *ludyaval*, it shall not be. I will not have my people duped. I will have them clean, and honest, and able to read the *Vanathul*. Words are sublime, and in books we may commune with the dead. Beyond this there is nothing true, no voices we can hear."

He turned to his daughter. "The Gray Houses, I think."

"Yes, Father," she murmured. She crossed the room and struck a gong, sending out a clang like a spray of ice. She remained in the shadows, her face like a wafer of stone, the firelight touching only her ankle and the black nap of one of her slippers.

Her father folded his map on his knees, pressing down each crease.

"*Veimaro,*" I said, but he did not look up.

A moment later we heard the tramp of feet, and I stood so abruptly my stool toppled over as the guard arrived to take me to the Houses.

Chapter Nine

The Gray Houses

> **The Gray Houses.** A hospital for the mentally afflicted, located at Velvalinhu, on the southern side of the Tower of Myrrh. Built in 732, it was reserved for members of the Imperial House until 845, when, having stood empty for some time, it was opened to other noble families. At present any person, noble or common, admitted by a priest or priestess not of the cult of Avalei may receive treatment there. The Houses are run according to the philosophy of Muirn of Feirivel, who emphasized light, air, and silence in the management and cure of lunatics.

I closed the book and looked up.

White walls, a white floor, a ceiling painted like the sky.

I remembered hearing the words before: *The Gray Houses.* A crowded café in Bain, scattered talk of an artist everyone knew. "Shut himself in the kitchen," they said. "Almost bled to death."

The young woman drinking with me waggled her head. "Poor boy! He's for the Houses."

"The what?" I said.

"The Gray Houses," she replied. Again that curious sideways waggle of the head, the roll of the eyes, the laugh. At the back of her dazzling smile, a single blue tooth.

I returned the book to my satchel—*The Lamplighter's Companion,* stolen from Yedov's library at the Hotel Urloma. The nurse who had brought me in had told me to use the shelves if I liked, but I would not. I would not make a home for myself in that white room. My books stayed where they were. The nurses had taken away my clothes: I wore the pale robe and sash of the Gray Houses. They had taken my purse, "for safekeeping," my pens and ink. But writing was encouraged. They gave me a soft pencil with a rounded tip.

There were other books on the shelf. I crossed the room in four steps and bent sideways to read the titles. *Kankelde, the Soldier's Discipline. The Evmeni Campaign. A Concise History of the War of the Tongues.* Fat tomes in brown calfskin, no doubt donated by some aging former soldier.

I looked up. I scratched at the wall with a fingertip, and some whitewash came off. I walked around the room for exercise, and to forget I was a prisoner. I could have gone out to the common room, where stained white couches lined the walls, but I recoiled from the society of the other patients. At *kebma* two of them had looked at me and whispered and giggled together: a man with a scarred head and a woman who wore a neat bandage on each fingertip. The woman had bright green paint on her eyelids, a smear of red on her mouth. When she caught my eye she waved those mysterious cotton-tipped fingers. . . .

No, I would not go there. I walked around and around, hopelessly, in an effort to tire myself before night arrived. A lamp burned above me on the lofty ceiling, too far to reach, enclosed in an iron cage so that no one could break the glass.

The door was locked, but the angel still came in.

I burst from sleep with a cry.

She was there, a rust-colored glow, her garment on her like a liquid.

I arched my back and writhed on my cot, the whole room suddenly a grave, my heart a mad instrument beating too hard to be borne. My fear was still an animal fear, immediate and unconquerable like the scream of a donkey that catches the smell of blood.

She said many things before I could hear her over the pounding of my heart. I think that she was speaking to me of the cold. But I only saw her moving hands, her head tilted to one side, the light from her picking out the lines of the volumes on the shelf. I watched her lips as they opened and closed, unreal, a trick of her light. I imagined her hollow inside, or filled with ashes or perfume. She had an earnest look, though her eyes were still inhuman, unreadable. She moved the way I imagined eels would, under water.

Her thoughts, her images, invaded me: I was as open as a field. I saw her mother's face, then a street corner somewhere in Bain. I knew it was Bain by the shape of the lamps. A lopsided carriage passed me in blue light. Rooftops, a midnight sky so cold the stars rang with it.

I rolled on the floor, threw myself into the walls, to escape that vision. The room went silver and tossed me to and fro like a boat. I fainted, and woke lying on the floor. A light moved above me: the mundane, greasy light of an oil lamp, so steady and natural it brought the tears to my eyes.

"There, he's coming back."

One of the nurses, the servants of Leilin, put his arm around my shoulders and helped me sit up. Another nurse held the lamp. The one beside me dabbed my temples with a cold handkerchief, filling the air with the odor of bruised ivy.

"There," he said. He helped me into bed. His companion watched us, her worried face lit from below, her mustache a thumbprint.

"Can we bring you anything?" she asked.

"You can bring me a dead girl's body."

"What's that?" said the other nurse, bending down.

"Nothing," I said.

"O benevolent reader," wrote Firdred of Bain from the road above Hadellon in the northern mountains: "Do not think that a man has ever finished his creation. A soul may always be forged in a new shape; and the fiery hand of Iva now took hold of me in earnest—nay, he even set upon me with his hammer. . . . Ah! you ladies of Bain, lovelier than mimosa flowers, what will you think if I tell you that I bent down, and crawled on my belly into the wretched hovel of a mountainside magician, who wore a cap made out of sheep's bladders? Only desperation caused me to submit to him, for the wound in my thigh now gave off an evil odor. I looked into his eyes smeared round with fat and told myself: A day has dawned that never was foretold. . . ."

I, too, was set upon with a hammer; and in the clash of it I was ready, like Firdred, to seize any hope of healing. And so when the priest's daughter, Tialon, came to my room and told me she thought she could ease my pain, I sat up on my cot and said: "Do it."

She paused. "You are very persuadable. Don't you want to hear my proposal?"

"I don't need to," I mumbled. My lip was swollen, cut by a fall in the night.

She pulled over a *bredis,* a scribe's stool covered with leather, from the wall, and sat, one slippered foot crossed on the other.

I lay down again. Her face was just above the level of mine, and I gazed at the whorl of her ear and the blue tattoo on her temple. She had brought a battered writing box with her, and now she opened it on her knees and took out a small book bound in white.

She cleared her throat. Her hands were very brown on the little book. Bars of shadow from the cage of the lamp passed over her when she moved. "It's really too early for this," she said, glancing at me, "but I thought it would help you understand the treatment I have in mind."

She opened the book and read: "*For you are following a thread. For you are cloaked in dawn. For in a field you have found a hidden treasure. Kneel, traveler, and take it. It is a word. Now stand, take up your staff, and travel on until you find another.*"

She closed the book, smoothed the cover.

"That's your father's book," I said. "*Jewels from a Stone.*"

She looked at me and smiled. "You know it."

"I saw it in Bain."

"Did you read it?"

"Only a line or two. I read what it says about angels."

A faint color warmed her cheeks. "Well. I've just read to you from the chapter on reading."

Reading, she said: this was her proposal. The passage she had read to me had dropped from the mouths of gods. The words were etched in the Stone her father's late master had found in the desert, where he had traveled at the bidding of a dream. To read the Stone, to take down the words, was her father's life's work, and her own work was to assist him. The chapter on reading was one of the first they had written down. She told me her father had groaned when he understood it, curled on the floor, as if in labor with the beauty of the blessing.

She said she would read to me.

"A fine idea," I said. "What is it supposed to do?"

She frowned, not offended but examining the question. Her face wore an inward look, as if she were listening. "I think," she said at last, "that what troubles you is an imbalance, a lack of order. And written words possess order, much more so than the words we speak. I believe you should read without stopping, read everything you can. And when you are tired, I will read to you. The method has had some success. I've tried it with others. One of them has now returned to her family."

"I haven't known many who read more than I," I told her. But I lay on my back, and she stood up and bent over me with a gilded pen.

"I beg your pardon," she said. She made two dots above my brows and measured the space between them with a piece of tape. Her lips pressed together in concentration. The touch of her hands was firm, though she was so thin. Her clothes had a dry smell, like earth heated by the sun. When she had finished, she jotted a few lines in a notebook from her box. "Ura's Conclusion," she explained. "On the effect of thought on the blood. It's never been proved."

She went to the bookshelf and crouched to read the titles. "Have you read any of these?"

"You're not going to read prayers? To guide me in the ways of the Stone?"

She smiled at me over her shoulder. "It doesn't matter what we read, but I'd rather not bore you." She looked at the titles again. "Let's try this. *A Soldier's Memoir.*"

She brought the thick volume with her to the *bredis*. The print was too small for her to read comfortably, so she took a pair of spectacles out of her box. They dangled from a chain she wore like a necklace. She pressed them onto her nose, opened the book at random, and began.

> *Of course it was an honor to fight under her, for which I thank Him Whose Face Is Hidden. I remember the midnight watch and how we would see that the lamp was still burning in her tent, or in the tent of one of her concubines. She took all forty-seven of them with her wherever she went, and they did not complain, although some of them were just boys, and their skin was chapped like ours was in the winter and if there was no wood to heat water they went without bathing just like we did. . . . But Ferelanyi was never the same after Drunwe died that spring, although she still had forty-six concubines to*

> *console her, which is why we soldiers say, if something in life has lost its savor, "it is just like the forty-six concubines of the general"*. . .

Naturally, the treatment was a failure.

Still Tialon's voice filled up the hours, and I waited for her with more impatience every day. I never heard her coming. She always knocked, then peered around the door, smiling and hesitant, carrying her box.

Clarity, I thought. Clarity and music. Her voice was low, expressive, not bell-like but vibrant like the *limike,* the Olondrian dulcimer. She read me the lyrics of Damios Beshaid and the letters of Skendho the Literate, the Brogyar chieftain who had asked to be buried under the Telkan's library. She read me the plays of Neavandis the Poet with great animation, altering her voice and features to suit the characters. She was disappointed to see no change in me. After a week I no longer needed to shake my head. She could read my face.

"Don't give up," I whispered.

She smiled. Her hand strayed toward my pillow, toyed with a wayward string. Propriety or shyness prevented her from touching my hair. Instead she tugged at the string until it broke. She brushed it against her skirt, where it clung, a strand of white against the black.

"Tell me something," I said, afraid she would go—afraid she would slip away to the place where she lived the rest of her life, a happy and structured region built of bookshelves, enlivened by colored ink, far from the drab misery of the Houses.

"All right," she said.

She spoke of Neavandis, the great poet-queen. "One of her legs was shorter than the other. Only slightly, but still, she never walked. Her servants carried her in a special chair—it's in the treasure vaults here. It's called the Chrysoprase Seat. The Old Teldaire used to bring it out on the date of Neavandis's death; I saw it several times as a little girl. It's covered with bright green gems, the color of sour apples. It's very lovely." She paused, pulled the *bredis* away from the cot, and faced me.

"They say she had a lover," she went on, thoughtful, her arms about her knees. "A groom from the Fayaleith. He was hanged for laming one of the king's war-horses. Now, of course, everyone says he was hanged out of jealousy—the king was Athrin the Pallid, famed for his cruelty. But they also say that Neavandis poisoned one of the king's dancing girls, the one called 'Feet like the Palm-Leaves.' So who can say? 'For there are more things under the Telkan's cloak,' as my nurse used to put it, 'than one could name from now to Tanbrivaud Night.'"

She pushed a tawny curl behind her ear and smoothed it down. Strips of shadow hung about her face. "It was on Tanbrivaud Night," she said, "that they hanged Neavandis's lover. He had been granted a last request, according to custom. He asked that he might be executed on Tanbrivaud Night. It was a severe blow to the king, who was superstitious—for those who die on Tanbrivaud Night, they say, can easily pass from the Land of the Dead to this one, and many of them become Angels of Persecution."

"And did he persecute the king?" My voice was very soft.

"It is not known. It is more likely that he persecuted the queen. For though she wrote several more plays, including *The Young Girl with Flowers,* and a ninth volume of poems after his death, she began to chew *milim* leaves—a hereditary vice—and died at the age of fifty, as you know."

"You don't believe in what you've just said—Angels of Persecution."

Her eyes held mine, steady and clear. "No, Jevick."

"Then how can you explain it? And don't say madness. *Don't.*"

A tiny sigh escaped her, slight as a memory of breathing.

I shifted away from her, facing upward toward my plaster sky. But she sat so still, for so long, that at last I turned back again. She was gazing at the foot of my cot, intent. "It would be too easy," she murmured. "Angels. For the gods do not speak as we speak."

And how did the gods speak?

In patterns; in writing.

But sometimes it seemed she could not hear them. Her manner was sharp and nervous; she banged the door behind her. She pressed her pen hard above my eye, scowling into my skin, locked in a fruitless effort to prove Ura's Conclusion. She thought there should have been some change, an increased heat in my bloodstream, an expansion of the brow, however slight.

"Do you *listen* when I read? Do you, Jevick?"

Once a tear dropped from her eye and landed on one of my cuts. It stung.

The Gray Houses are not cruel. They are kind. Each day begins with an outing for those not too distraught to stand and walk. Down the wide hall, where the lamps are always lit, each in its netting of wire, then out the big double doors into the garden. The garden is rough, a mere slope of grass surrounded by a wall. The sea is invisible but seems to be reflected in the sky. The air lively with iodine, strong. Once, at the bottom of the slope, the woman with bandaged hands found a gull with a broken wing.

Tialon came to see me there one morning. I sat against the wall with a book, and her long shadow darkened the page.

"Jevick," she said. "How are you?"

I squinted up at her. "As you see."

She sat beside me and laid her box in the sparkling grass.

"You're early," I said.

"It was so lovely outside, I couldn't stay in." She was in a blithe, expansive mood, leaning back to look up at the sky. "Everything is starting to smell of autumn, though it's still warm. It smells like stone, like in the old song. Do you know it?

Autumn comes with a whisper, smelling of stone.
I grow sad.
The days are coming when we will make a tea
of boiled roots.
Losha, Losha!
What have you done with the flower
that was my heart . . ."

She gasped with laughter: "At this point the song grows mawkish, really terrible! I only like the first lines, autumn, whispering, smelling of stone. . . . What are you reading?"

I held up my copy of *Olondrian Lyrics.*

She gazed at it for a moment without speaking. Then she advised me in a taut voice: "That's a rare copy. Old. You must take good care of it."

She sat with her back to the wall, suddenly subdued. I was not used to seeing her in such brilliant light. Her eternal dark wool appeared dusted with radiant powder; the chain of her spectacles dazzled me. I could not tell whether her lips were trembling or whether it was a trick of the sun.

All at once she said: "Tell me about your island."

"My island." The question was so unexpected, I stammered.

"Yes. What do you eat. What are your houses like." She counted on her fingers, not looking at me. "Who are your lords. What are the names of your seasons. How do you dance. Anything. Tell me anything."

"My island is called Tinimavet."

"Go on."

"We are farmers and fishermen, for the most part. Some of us grow tea. To be a tea-picker, you must first prove that your hands are as tender as flowers. For this reason it is usually work for young girls. . . ."

I faltered into silence. She had put her face in her hands; her shoulders were shaking.

After a moment she bent to her writing box. She took out a handkerchief, wiped her eyes, then crumpled the handkerchief back among her books and papers.

Still she did not look at me. Her profile looked peeled and wet. "I'm sorry," she said.

"No—It is—"

She held up a hand, cutting off my words. "Inexcusable," she said. "It is inexcusable, and I have no excuse. Let me ask—how old are you?"

"Twenty-two."

"Twenty-two." She looked at me, her eyes wet and green as celadon. "You are very young. I think that you have not built anything yet?"

I thought of my life: lessons, a journey, an angel. I shook my head.

"No," she murmured. "I thought not. It is dangerous to build. Once you have built something—something that takes all your passion and will—it becomes more precious to you than your own happiness. You don't realize that, while you are building it. That you are creating a martyrdom—something which, later, will make you suffer."

She shifted position on the grass, yanking her skirt into place. "Some would say it was built for me," she muttered. "And it is true, or partially true. I have never had a silk dress. Since I was eleven I've made all my clothes myself. Not even my nurse was allowed to help me. You should have seen some of my clothes—the skirts crooked, the armpits sagging or too tight. . . . And no one laughed. They did not laugh, because they were afraid. Afraid of my father and the Telkan. That made it worse for me. I was more alone. . . ."

She twisted a finger in the chain at her neck. "I don't know anything about it," she whispered. "All that I reject. Those things forbidden by the Stone. Fine clothes, dances, wine, the season of bonfires. I've never been to a ball. I've never been anywhere but the Library of Bain. Or yes—I went to the Valley once. Once! To the city of Elueth, where my grandfather had died. I was thirteen years old, and so frightened! So frightened I hardly remember the ride in the wagon, the look of the country. We had to relieve ourselves in the grass—it terrified me! And since then, never. I have no jewels but a necklace my mother left me. And I have never worn it, Jevick—not ever. Now you will ask: what does it mean? What have I built? If I've never decided—if I've only agreed with what was decided for me—"

I shook my head, but she seized my wrist and squeezed it fiercely, twice. "*Don't pretend.*"

Then she released me. The blood flowed into my wrist; it throbbed.

"Ura's Conclusion!" she said with a harsh laugh. Tears filled her eyes again. "My father was right. It's nonsense. I only thought if I had something of my own . . . I've never been to sea. I've never been to a foreign country. I've only read about it. I'll never go now. Do you hear me? I'll never go. But I have built something. You—you—"

She pointed at me, trembling. Her anger shocked me. "Where did you learn Olondrian?" she snapped.

"Olondrian? At home. I had a tutor."

It was as if I had dashed her with water. For a moment she froze; then she seized her writing box and got up.

"Tialon!"

She walked away swiftly over the dewy grass. She did not come to see me the next day, or the next.

Time unrolled in the Houses, monotonous as a skein of wool. I was known as the Islander and was almost a model patient. I ate my food. I took the required walks. The nurses liked me, and so did the patients: once the man with the scarred head gave me an autumn crocus.

So much for the days—but the nights, the nights. Sleep, we are often told, is the sister of death; for my ghost, it was more like a doorway hung with a silken curtain. She twitched the veil aside with her finger; I jerked like a fish on the line. Then lightning, screams, the swift feet of nurses in the hall.

I fell out of bed so often they pulled the mattress onto the floor and I slept there as if on one of the pallets of the islands. A nurse sat on a chair outside my door, the same reddish, blunt-nosed man who had come to my aid on my first night in the Houses. When I asked his name, he said I might call him Ordu, which means "Acorn." Once, when I lay exhausted, watching him clean my vomit from the floor, I asked if he believed in angels. He dropped his rag in his bucket, not looking at me. "I'll bring you some ginger tea," he said.

I wrote letter after letter to the Priest of the Stone, explaining my case and begging for mercy. I wrote to Tialon, asking her to come back. Ordu saw that my notes were delivered; he was an honest man; he told me frankly that no letter of mine would ever reach the mainland. Neither the priest nor his daughter answered my letters, but I went on writing them, for the act kept my mind from veering toward wild thoughts: a pencil pushed into a wrist. I paced in my chamber, barefoot and straggle-haired in my borrowed clothes, constructing logic, arguing with my own thin shadow.

Some nights the angel did not come, and I slept until Ordu opened the door and called me. After a time, only those mornings could make me weep. Having steeled myself to suffer, I had no defense against the simple light of day. I covered my face with my hands and sobbed.

All that could calm me then was my two-color copy of the *Romance of the Valley*. The flaking gilt on the spine, the woodblock illustrations. *Felhami Fleeing the Fortress of Beal. The King Encounters a Lion.* The creature's mane deep rose and symmetrical as a wheel. I crawled down into the story, immersed myself in the looping and formal plot, the wintry battles and magical transformations, the witch Brodlian like a slug in the forest surrounded by her four white swine, and Felhami, slain, stretched out on a bed of rue. "*Long he rode, and darkness fell, and the moon was his companion.*" The lines unchanged for eight hundred years, arrayed in their princely clarity.

Then one day a card fell out of the book, marked with a line in a hand I did not know. It said: "*Watch for us at midnight.*"

Chapter Ten

Midnight in the Glass Forest

A hiss woke me.

I sat up, hands clawed, every muscle taut, preparing to do battle with the ghost. But she was not there. Instead a shuttered lantern hung before me, emitting a single copper-colored ray.

I could just make out the fingers that held the light, and beyond them a shadow in a cloak.

The figure tossed something onto my mattress. "Put these on," it whispered.

I felt what had fallen beside me: trousers, a tunic, a pair of woven slippers.

"Who are you?"

My visitor raised the light to show me his face. His eyes were shadowed, but his smile was pleasant enough. "A friend," he said, his voice a breath. "A friend to you, and to the Goddess Avalei."

I asked no more questions, but dressed in the dark as quickly as I could.

When I was ready I stood, and the stranger leaned close to my ear, bending slightly because, like most Olondrians, he was taller than I. "Follow me, and don't talk until I tell you."

"Should I bring my things?"

He gripped my shoulder briefly. "Not tonight."

I followed him out. In the passage, tiny night lamps lined the wall, pale as fireflies. Ordu sat awake in his straight-backed chair. I stopped, but my companion took my arm and drew me onward, saying under his breath: "It's all right."

The nurse averted his eyes. It struck me that he had not answered when I asked him about angels, and I realized that he might have put the card with the strange handwriting into my book. The thought startled me, like a window opening in a dark house.

My companion led me through the common room, the dim beam of his lantern passing over the low ranks of deserted couches. We went down a corridor to the door, not the one that led to the garden but the other, the gateway to the Holy City. It was unlocked. We passed through like a wayward draft. My guide pulled the door behind us just so far that it appeared shut, but did not allow it to latch. Then we mounted a flight of lightless stairs and emerged onto a walkway where the night air met us, redolent with jasmine.

My companion threw back his hood. "Ah!"

He turned to me and grinned, opening his lantern so that the light swelled up between us. Then he held out his hand.

"Miros of Sinidre," he said. "Disgraced nobleman, temporary valet, and general layabout."

I took his hand. "Jevick of Tyom."

"You're a foreigner, aren't you?" he said, lifting the lantern and peering at my face. "And a battered-looking one, too. What have they been doing to you in the Houses? You look hag-ridden."

I glanced behind me. "I've been locked up. Shouldn't we be moving?"

Miros shouted with laughter. "*Vai!*" he swore. "Thank you for reminding me of my duty. It's easy to forget such things on a night like this. Right. Here's the official message: Mailar, High Priestess of Avalei, greets you and requests your presence at her salon."

I hardly knew what to make of him: his grin, his unkempt curls, the mixture of wariness and mischief in his manner. But his cheerfulness was as welcome to me as the breeze on that open walkway, and the Priestess of Avalei, I knew, was an enemy of the Priest of the Stone.

"I shall be pleased to attend," I said.

He clapped me on the shoulder. "Well done. The formalities are over. This way—and don't go to close to the edge. The railing, I warn you, was probably made in the days of worshiping milk, and it's a nasty drop into the garden."

We moved through the night palace. We walked across bridges, through halls where the painted statues looked startled in Miros's light, as if surprised in acts of darkness. Sometimes we found sentries drowsing in stairwells, leaning on their spears, or pacing the battlements with a weary stride. None of them stopped us to ask about our business. With some of them Miros exchanged envelopes or tobacco, and once a small bottle of *teiva*; but he seemed to receive as many gifts as he gave, so that the ritual looked less like bribery than like an arcane form of politeness. The night was cool and fresh, and on the terraces the wind came, lifting my hair, spreading the scent of nocturnal flowers. Between the towers where windows were lighted or lamps shone in the elevated gardens, bats veered fleet and precise in the light. We passed walls of whispering ivy, entered the peaked arch of a doorway. In the halls beyond, my sense of direction failed me. I knew only that we walked through one vast silence after another while the lamplight slid over frescoes and gilded floors.

At length we reached an indoor garden, its branches awash in moonlight. The only sound was the dripping of hidden water, and the ruddy glow of the lantern seemed indelicate, almost enough to wake the whorled flowers from their sleep. The waxy leaves of rhododendrons touched my hair in the scented gloom as we made our way down the tiles of the little path. At the end of this artificial jungle stood a door of dark wood flanked by tulip-shaped lamps, and Miros opened it for me with a bow.

"Here we are at last."

I stepped past him into an antechamber. A lamp burned on a table just inside, guarded by a retainer in the last stages of senility whose thin, silvery hair hung over his shoulders. He looked at me doubtfully and then immediately lost interest and stood plucking at the loose rosettes on his jacket. Miros greeted him, clearly without expecting a response, left his lantern on the table, and hung up his cloak.

In the next room, night had been dispelled. The globes of the lamps diffused a light that artfully mimicked the beaming of the sun; they shone, glazed and bulbous, from the sweetly scented tangle of flowering vines coaxed to grow across the ceiling. This canopy of dark green life melted into the verdure that covered the walls, winding among the branches of trees growing in pots, trees that glittered with a subtle life which I soon realized was not life at all: we were entering a forest of colored glass. A bird's wing flickered; the flowers around it tinkled. We crossed a bridge over a miniature canal that gleamed with carp. In the parlor beyond it a circle of figures sat or reclined on couches, enveloped in laughter, smoke, and the notes of a lute.

We approached them, and they grew quiet and looked at me. Their faces were proud, impassive, some of them beautifully painted. I knelt before them. Then a voice said: "Rise, dear boy!"—and I knew before I raised my head that it was the voice of the woman on the pink couch. Splendid, stupefying, she had already dazzled me with her breasts, almost completely uncovered, framed in a window of black silk. She was perhaps forty years old, her full throat powdered, encircled with diamonds and jet. Narrow eyes slumbered in her marmoreal face.

I rose, and she held out her arm. I stepped forward and took her perfumed hand. The curls of her armored coiffure shone like lacquer.

"Welcome, precious boy," she said in her deep voice, without smiling. "I am the High Priestess. You may kiss my shawl."

The High Priestess of Avalei was a prisoner on the Blessed Isle. She had not been to the mainland for over a decade. Yet she maintained a dignified, even a sumptuous, salon, entertaining guests from the noble families who still supported her failing cult. She made sacrifices to the goddess in one of the hillsides of the Isle; she was permitted the use of a ballroom in the Tower of Mirrors on feast days. Her shawl was of a silk so rare it felt heavy, like a live thing. When I pressed it to my lips, it left a flavor of mulberries.

"Sit down," she said.

I sank in the yellow upholstery of the chair she indicated. I found it difficult to meet her intelligent, faintly lascivious gaze. She said in a slow and liquid voice, each word a stone dropped into a pool: "You are safe here, my child. Don't be frightened. Someone bring him a drink."

A sullen girl stepped out of the decorative forest and lowered an object made of glass and silver filigree into my hands.

"Thank you," I said, holding it gingerly. It looked something like a lamp, having a round belly and four silver feet. Several others like it stood on the low table inside the circle; from each rose a curving pipe of glass.

"Have you drunk *los* before?" asked the High Priestess.

I shook my head.

"How fortunate you are to be trying it for the first time! Such is the priviledge of youth!"

A wire-thin, avid young lady opposite me, her skirts adorned with a fortune in peacock feathers, took one of the round vessels from the table, put her lips to the pipe, and sucked, winking a painted eye. A line of golden liquid filled the tube. I followed her example and took a cautious sip from my own vessel, drowning my tongue with the thick, sweet, and potent peach liquor which is the refreshment of the

Olondrian aristocracy. Its flavor and fiery texture were overpowering: I felt as if I had drunk undiluted perfume. However, after a brief wave of sickness, energy charged my veins. I thanked the High Priestess a second time, and she gave a low gurgle of laughter, barely parting her lips, which still did not smile.

The room dissolved in *los.* The lute player took up his instrument again and the unctuous air filled with its sorrowful notes, while the guests fell into conversation, laughed and sipped their drinks, too polite or too scornful to notice my existence. The lady who had come to my aid with the drink beat her hand against her flat chest so that her gold bracelets jingled, emitting a series of helpless shrieks, while beside her an odd-looking man, young but with spiky, dead-white hair, punctuated his story with disdainful shrugs. One youth was trying to set his boot on fire; another, flushed and handsome, lounged on the floor with his head pillowed on a hound. A furtive monkey curled up in the lap of a gilded beauty, and she scratched its ears with her whitened fingernails. There was a slender courtier in peach-colored silk, a middle-aged lady with bunches of violets above her ears whose cheeks collapsed with every swallow of *los,* and among the servants on the floor a Nissian slave of searing beauty, her cheek against the arm of an empty chair.

It was a pause in the room's noises, rather than any specific signal, which revealed the mystery of the tenantless chair. The gathered company took a breath and the player's lute fell silent, though only for a moment, a gap between notes. When the moment had passed, the music and laughter resumed, but by then I had seen him, the silent figure standing outside the circle, his back to us, one hand held behind him, covered up to the knuckles in the foamy lace that poured from his dark sleeve. He was bending forward to feed a monkey perched among the leaves of a potted tulip tree encumbered with glass fuchsias. He seemed as though he might have been there always, in the uncertain territory of the ornamental glade.

Then he turned, and an ugly chance, combined with the fumes of *los,* made me believe I recognized him. In the way he turned toward me, his feral mouth, his preoccupied gaze, I thought I saw the Kestenyi dancer of Bain. The ghastly shock made me choke; my skin was awash in sweat; I thought I saw him as he had been in the brothel, with his cruel handsomeness and lunatic air, somehow transported to this dainty chamber full of aristocrats. In another moment the dreadful resemblance dissolved, and I breathed again, as the dark-clad figure advanced and joined the circle, retaining no likeness to the dancer except for a certain purity of feature and striking grace and height.

He flung himself into the velvet chair and lit a cigarette. He was instantly the focus of darted glances and covert whisperings: conversation faltered, and an almost imperceptible depression entered the room, spoiling its atmosphere of an enchanted treasure chest. The young man who had caused the disturbance leaned back in his chair. He looked less and less like the dancer who had so unnerved me: his hair, though long, was tied in a knot on his neck; he wore a black skullcap, and the circle of glass in his right eye gave him the look of a jeweler or a young scribe. He seemed an arrogant, studious, slightly corrupt young man, well-born and long accustomed to being obeyed. Yet he shared with the Kestenyi dancer an electricity: the combination of beauty and the suggestion of menace.

"Refreshments!" the High Priestess intoned in her dark and somnolent voice. Four servant girls rose and melted into the forest. The priestess had drawn herself up, the light gleaming on the swelling expanse of her breasts, and was looking at the strange youth in the black skullcap. The servant girls returned with a cart, and cries of appreciation greeted the towers of candied passion fruit it carried, the pears poached in wine, the segments of preserved ginger impaled on peppermint swords, and the little swans carved from white chocolate. This fare dispersed the gloom which had arrived with the weary stranger. It was served with a different wine, sweet and red, poured in tiny golden cups and strewn with jasmine petals, and followed by a hot drink made from cocoa beans. Under the influence of these confections the guests grew even merrier than before, rose from their chairs, and changed places, balancing their glass plates on their knees and waving their little forks, to which there clung pale flecks of whipped cream. They spoke to me at last, and complimented me on my Olondrian. I learned the word for the *los*-vessel: *alosya*. The white-haired youth came to sit on the arm of my chair, and I told him about the island of Jennet, the world's greatest producer of chocolate.

When we were drinking our chocolate, the priestess announced abruptly: "Enough!"—and, still laughing and talking, the guests rose to their feet, carrying their steaming cups, and went out through the forest, the ladies shrieking when their hair caught in the glass buds. The servants followed them. The lute player straightened his supple legs, picked up his cushion, and departed with the confidence of one who makes his living by skill. Soon there were only five of us: the High Priestess, Miros, the courtier in peach-colored silk, the dark stranger with the lace cuffs, and myself.

The priestess arranged her skirts on the couch. An invisible monkey chittered.

"Well," said the courtier in a peevish, strangely querulous voice: "If we're going to hold a secret council, must we do it in such glaring light? My head has been throbbing for the past hour."

At a sign from the priestess, Miros brought out a fantastically ornate lamp, encrusted with claws and tendrils of old brass, and set it on the table. He climbed on a stool to extinguish the ceiling lamps, jumped down, and retired among the jingling leaves. In the newly mysterious room, the company looked theatrical, hollow-eyed. Faint laughter reached us from beyond the trees.

The courtier shook himself; the dimness seemed to restore his energy. He gave me his small pale hand and said: "Auram, High Priest of Avalei."

"Jevick of Tyom."

He laughed. His hair was so dry and black it reflected no light at all, his lips stark red in his powdered face. "I know who you are. We all know who you are. We expended some effort to see you in person, however. Delighted to meet you at last."

"Delighted," the priestess echoed. I looked at her. In the gloom she had grown, her breasts and throat monumental above her black dress. Her hair was like the ramparts of a city. "I have heard," she said, "that you have spoken with an angel."

Her features wavered in the light cast upward from the lamp. I wished fervently that I had not drunk so much. I wanted to ask the name of the strange youth in the dark suit but decided to concentrate on saving myself. "It is true," I said.

"Tell us," said the priestess. And I leaned forward and blurted out the tale of my haunting, my captivity, and the ways of the Rotted Dead.

When I had finished, the priest turned to the others and clutched the arms of his chair. "If it is true, we may hold a Night Market again!"

"Yes," said the priestess. "Still, it is too early to speak of that now. We must examine him thoroughly first. We must be sure."

"Of course," said Auram.

"What is a Night Market?" I asked.

The priestess turned to me, fingering the jet beads at her throat. In the sculptured mask of her face only her eyes, long and black, the lids painted with two streaks of apple-green, lived and brooded. "The Night Market, my child, is one of Avalei's multitude of blessings. It is held in the provinces, in the countryside. People come from far away to buy and sell, to eat and drink, to be merry together if only for a night. And always at the center of it there is the *avneanyi,* to answer their questions and comfort them in their distress."

Avneanyi—a mystic, a saint. "One ridden by angels."

My blood slowed. "What sort of questions do they ask?"

"All sorts of questions, my child. The angels know all."

"But I can't speak to her. I don't want to speak to her. I only want to be rid of her and go."

"Yes," she said. "Naturally you would like to return to your homeland. As we say, the fire of home is brighter than any other fire. And we also say, the cold of home is colder than any other. But an angel must be honored before it departs."

"Yes," the priest put in, in his soothing, quavering voice. "Like the Snow Child, whom we summon to cure fevers. It never departs without an offering. When the patient is cured we give it basil leaves and grain, and then it melts. . . ."

Sweat gathered on my brow. "I can't talk to her."

"Not yet," said Auram. "That is natural enough. You have not tried. Our lady will aid you in your first attempt. After that, slowly, it will become easier."

"No," I said.

The priest and priestess glanced at one another. As for the young man with the glass in his eye, he chuckled, lit another cigarette, and, with an ugly movement of his throat, blew smoke rings toward the glittering trees.

"But I think you will," the priest said then, smiling, his teeth perfect as a bar of silver. The black thatch of his hair whispered as he turned his head. He gazed at the priestess, repeating: "I think you will. For my lady is powerful. She has the power to do what you wish.

Did you not say that your countrywoman died in the mountains? How will you retrieve her body unless we help you? But with our assistance everything becomes simple, as in a play. Our enemies are strong, but our lady is stronger."

The priestess drew herself up. A gleam passed through the murky depths of her eyes. "It is true," she said. "I am a woman of no meager power. I have been since childhood a favorite of the goddess. I say this not, as another would, to frighten you, but to persuade you to accept my offer of help. You are far from home, and the attentions of an angel are at first difficult. You require guidance, guidance that Avalei can provide. You are unlikely, in these evil times, to escape the notice of those who shut you up in the Gray Houses, those whose blasphemous cult is becoming—"

I followed her gaze, for she was no longer looking at me, and saw the youth in the skullcap make a slight gesture. It was almost nothing: his hand, which had been relaxed on the arm of his chair, lifted an inch, the fingers spread out in warning. At once the priestess fell silent, and I wondered at the power of this stranger, who was only half her age. "But you know all that," she said. "You have already met them. It is I who can help you, I who can bring you the body of the angel."

Expectancy charged the air. They were waiting for me to speak.

"How will you do it?" I asked.

The priestess gave her low, heavy laugh. "If what you say is true, then while you hold the Night Market I will send my servants northward to Aleilin. They will obtain what you seek. They will come down into Kestenya, into the highlands, where it is easy to hide from the soldiers of the king. You will meet them there, in the village of Klahne-Wiy. Our Prince," she said with a soft, caressing glance at the silent youth, "has a house nearby."

The prince. His gaze met mine. One of his beautiful eyes was larger than the other, slightly magnified by the glass. His expression was at once disdainful and sad: yes, filled with regret. Seed pearls nestled in the lace at his throat.

I turned to the priestess. "If I do this for you—if I hold your Night Market—you'll give me the body."

"Yes," she said.

"How can I be sure?"

"You cannot be sure," she answered. "Nor can you be sure that in the end you will want the body destroyed."

I laughed. "I will burn it, I promise you."

"In the *Book of Avalei,*" the priestess said, "it is written: '*Like a wind upon the valley, like a dragon, like a sea of ambergris, and like the striking of a hammer: so is every spirit among the dead.*'"

Among the dead.

They took me through the trees, the way the others had gone, and we entered a pillared veranda filled with night. Steps led down to a terrace under the stars, where four lamps burned on brass posts, diffusing a freshening scent of resin. The terrace overlooked a small lake among the towers, a captive pool where lamplight and starlight played. There were other terraces bordering it, and balconies above it, but the others were all deserted, the lamps dark.

There was a shout from the water. I saw pallid bodies swimming there, the hard young bodies of Miros and the other gentlemen. Their clothes were strewn on the terrace along with the gowns of some of the servant girls, who were shrieking and splashing each other in the shallows. There was no furniture on the terrace but a table, and so the company sat above it, on the steps leading from the veranda, but they often rose to go to the table, where there was a bowl of sparkling liquid which they poured into their mouths with a ladle. The notes of the lute quivered. My heart, soaked in *los,* expanded at the sight of the two young ladies dancing on the terrace, their faces flushed in the lamplight, their beautiful gowns awry, their hair disheveled, hanging about their ears. They were singing a popular song of the type called *vanadel* whose refrain was: "*Gallop, my little black mare.*" The white-haired nobleman, luminous in the dark, had stepped into the trees beside the terrace and was gathering berries to pelt them as they whirled. He wore no shirt.

I entered that delirium. Later I would remember images but lose their chronology in the delusional air: someone shouts, another laughs, a wind disorders the quince trees—but I cannot place the events in their proper sequence. I see again the sharp, witty, mocking face of the lady in peacock feathers as she holds me by the collar, forcing my head back to empty the ladle into my mouth, the cold, tingling liquid soaking my clothes. She wears a bracelet of natural pearls which breaks during this struggle, the precious pellets scattering on the tiles. A rose-colored slipper drifts away on the water and slowly sinks. A servant girl is weeping among the pillars.

I see the High Priestess with her extravagant body raising her arms to release her hair, which springs outward in inky tendrils. The mask of her face is lifted. She bares her teeth, shrieks, runs, and plunges herself, still clothed, in the black water. Her arms rise, flinging drops. The company call her by her title, but also by the name Taimorya, which is the Queen of the Witches. The white-haired youth breaks the lake's surface, his hair a matted gray, and his arms encircle her astral shoulders. A naked servant girl slips in a puddle on the tiles; she falls to her knee with a cry, her dull flesh jiggling. And the prince is holding the Nissian slave by the wrists in the shadow of the veranda. They do not speak.

The last image, and the most powerful, concerns this enigmatic youth. It must be the end of the night, for the air is gray. He announces that he is leaving us. Slowly the revelers gather on the terrace, sopping, staggering, some of them naked. The youth has lost his curious single eyeglass and his skullcap. His face is sad; his hair falls on his shoulders. The assembled guests begin to bow. One by one they approach him, kneel, and touch their foreheads to the tiles. With each prostration the young man's face twitches, as if he is wincing, and an insufferable pride touches his plummy lips. The High Priestess kneels in a single arc, her wet gown clinging to the vastness of her hips. She cries out: "Father!"

I kneel too, close to his gleaming boots, almost swooning with my brow on the aching coldness of the tiles.

I do not remember returning to the Gray Houses. I woke with bile in my throat and a scrap of paper knotted in my hair.

Chapter Eleven

The Girdle of Avalei

We return on Tolie before the sun rises. Bury this note in the garden.

The angel did not come to me for two nights. Two whole nights, slow and splendid, undisturbed by the sound of light. The first was painful; on the second hope grew in me like a branch of thorns. *She knows,* I thought. I felt that some of my hope belonged to the ghost, that she was watching, that she knew I had set our destiny in motion, that she understood how I intended to save her. And those two nights, after so much suffering, filled me with a strength that came close to elation. I buried the little note I had pulled from my hair by the garden wall. Afterward I walked, spoke with a patient, tried to learn the words of a *vanadel.* I touched the cracks in the wall. I touched the trees. A crow took flight with the sound of a handkerchief in the wind. I could hear the world.

Three hours before dawn. The glade of the goddess, called the Girdle of Avalei, deep within the hills of the Blessed Isle. In the austerity of the Olondrian night, the olive trees painted black, we descend on thick uneven turf to the entrance of the shrine.

The hill is humped against the stars, covered with grass and small weather-beaten flowers that catch the lantern light. Facing us is the door, a jagged crack in the chalky stone, in that crumbling sand-colored rock with its channels of dust, its piled offerings. Leeks, a bird's nest, bundles of sweet hay tied up with ribbons. A flask of olive oil, a small white harp. We walk past the seashells of supplication, the mulberries of remorse, and enter the long slit in the wall of the hill.

One must turn sideways to enter. We wear the dust of the hill on our clothes. We: the Priestess of Avalei in her jeweled lionskin cloak, her lissome attendants with dilated eyes, carrying wreaths of bells, the nine silent priests in their masks of shrunken hide, their ivory beaks. And I. Clad in a white silk robe with turmeric on my cheeks, I scrape through the stone and am eaten up by the hillside. At the last I feel a tearing anguish, the agony of departure. Never have I been so far from home.

Darkness. The darkness of the old gods, gods who though foreign are like my own: gods of discord, pathos, and revelation. The tunneling entrance curves before it opens into this space and there is absolute, waiting, coiled, and sentient blackness. A blackness where something lives. I breathe in precious, pampered air, antique dust, the starveling ghosts of incense. Motionless, I feel the empty space around me tingle. There is a rustle, the loud rasp of a match. Then the darkness blooms: a dazzling light that makes me cover my eyes, and when I can open them a fire, a garden: a beauty that makes me cry out because it is lavish and unexpected, a bower of midnight roses, a cascade of gems. The cave is small and the walls are rough: its beauty is that of color. One by one the great pine torches are lit. They stand in iron brackets, lighting the orange of poppy fields and the scarlet of festive displays of lights and the gold on the walls. Under this glory the priests and the painted girls sit in a circle on the stone floor, crossing their legs in sublime silence. The high priestess stands before the crude altar hewn out of the wall with its flagrant, red-brown splashes, its smell of hot salt.

Our shadows are huge, unnatural; they seem to move more quickly than we. The priestess bids me kneel in the center of the circle. She takes the stone pitcher from the altar and pours something into a bowl: it is oily and oyster-colored, and tastes very sweet. After two swallows I gag. They wait in silence for me to finish. I hand the rough stone bowl back to the priestess. She dips her hands in another bowl on the altar and smears something rancid-smelling over my face and neck: clarified butter.

"*Anavyalhi,*" she says. "*I waited for thee in the snows of the mountain and thou didst not come, O dove with the crimson feet.*" Her voice is low, caressing and sad, as if she means the words, though she is only reciting from the book of her mind.

"*Anavyalhi, my love with red feet, aloe tree, cloud of saffron. Lost voice over the water, oh lost voice of my love! Will I never again hear the strings of thy throat,*

O moon-guitar? Nay, say the waters; for she has departed forever into the dark country. . . ."

The priestess steps back from me, her palms gleaming thickly with butter. Chrysolites wink among the coarse hairs of her robe. Above it her face is blank, heavy, watchful, the eyes like soot. Her gaze never wavers from me as she reaches a hand toward one of the girls.

A bird, a large dove violently beating its wings, is suddenly with us, drawn from the velvet bag in the girl's lap. It is a white fire in the hands of the priestess as she holds it toward the roof of the cave and thunders something in an unknown, dreadful language. Then she holds it over the shallow depression in the altar and removes a small stone knife from her plaited hair. The bird struggles; some of its feathers are stuck together with butter. She slits its throat with a smooth, voluptuous movement.

At that instant the cave is filled with sound: the girls are singing, chanting, beating their wreaths of bells on their bent knees, and the priests, their voices muffled by the stiff hide of their masks, are droning too and shaking beaded rattles. Some of them have small ceremonial mortars and pestles of stone, which they wear at their belts, and now beat rhythmically. I am too fascinated to understand what they are singing. The sound is that of furious bees, cicadas, rattling chains. The priests inspire horror in me with their yellowed beaks, their invisible eyes, the brittle antlers or ragged hares' ears sewn to the sides of their masks. They are like our doctors; they mean me ill. I look back toward the priestess and see blood running down a channel into a trench around the altar.

"*And wilt thou never return?*" she says, entreating me with her eyes, stretching out her hands, which shine darkly in the torchlight. "*Nay, say the snows; for the earth which spills the delights of her lap for thee is but a shade unto thy love, and the shadow of a closed door. Could my love not keep thee, Anavyalhi, body of water . . . the way of the sword, or the path of the deadly unguents. . . .*"

In a moment of pure lucidity I know that the liquid I have drunk is affecting my mind. Everything is clear in that moment. My vision is sharpened: I see the small hairs in the rigid mask of a priest, imagine how the hide would feel, hard and buckled, dried fruit. I see the bodies under the dark red dresses of the girls, secretive bodies, the ribs shuddering as they jangle their bells. I see more than it is given to the human eye to see, the sweat on their stomachs, their fear of the dark cistern, their fear of the dark. I see them washing their faces, becoming childish, pink, defenseless, crawling into their beds and speaking in code by touching fingers, passing gossip down the long row of beds, these girls called Feilar, Kialin, Kerelis, these young girls far from home. I can count the glimmering beryls scattered across the robe of the priestess, like copses in a field of tawny wheat. I think I can even catch the scent of them: they smell of mint. But the chalcedony smells like the bark of trees. I see her, Taimorya, the Queen of the Witches. I know that every night she eats a plate of snails, for eloquence. I see her sitting up by the lamp, painting a china apple. The prince is asleep in the shadow of her bed.

Then, as suddenly as it arrived, this clarity vanishes. My mouth goes slack; it is hard to keep my eyes from fluttering closed. The monotonous music, which never flags, which is now like a great company on horseback jingling and pounding through a gap between mountains, confuses me like a mist. It is the dust raised by the hooves. And far away, the echo of falling stones. I see the high priestess: only her face, beautiful, heartless, exalted. Her long black eyes reflecting the sparks of the torches. "My love," she says. Her voice is deep inside my ear, so deep that I do not know if it is she who has spoken or I.

"Where are you?"

Now I am sure that I am the one who has spoken. But it is also she; I feel her speaking through me. I struggle weakly against her, suddenly terrified, trying to rise, lifting my heavy eyelids to see the dove's body on the altar. I fight against the darkness but only think to myself, stupidly: They have put something on the torches. The smoke is strange. . . . Then it becomes too easy to sink, to abandon myself to oblivion. The slide to the bottom is effortless, enchanting. There, at the bottom, I see unimagined valleys of white fish. There are deserts too, dotted with blackened rose trees.

"Where are you?" I ask, or the priestess asks with my voice. "Why don't you come to me? Can't you hear me? I've been looking for you for so long. I'm lost. . . ."

Silence. A ripple of water which might be, far away, the bells of the girls in the cave.

Then I see her. And for the first time and the last, I know that I am seeing her when she is alone, before she knows I am there. She walks uncertainly, sometimes pausing as though she has dropped something.

She is far away, and her progress is very slow. She wears the same short, colorless shift, and her hair lies on her thin shoulders. She turns her head, bewildered, filling me with the desire to weep.

"I'm here," I say.

She looks up sharply and sees me. Her gaze burns. In the air, the insistent ringing, like flashes of light. "Jevick," she says.

"Yes."

She comes close to me, almost blinding me with her ocean of light, making me cry out, my eyes on fire; then she grows dim and looks at me anxiously and hungrily through the whirling cloud. "Jevick, you're here. You've come to find me. . . ."

"Yes," I whisper.

She frowns. "But you're strange. There are two of you."

"Yes. I have asked the aid of a northern priestess. Together we have come to find what it is that you desire. We have—I have done this for love of you—"

A blaze of scorn makes me scream again. My eyes are bleeding. "You do not love me," the angel says.

"Forgive me. It was the love which all of the living must have, for those who come from beyond the narrow grave, of which I spoke."

"Beyond the grave," the angel says. "That is northern talk."

"Yes," I whisper. I feel the words echo inside me. I am listening, and speaking, in two languages at once, translating. The mouth and ears of the Priestess of Avalei.

"Very well," says the angel. She looks at me in bitter disdain, and I grovel, writhing before the flame of her face. "This boy is weak," she says contemptuously. "He will not last long. You have asked what I desire, and I will tell you." She pauses, her indrawn breath a conflagration. Then she says: "Write me a *vallon.* Put my voice inside it. Let me live."

She draws close to me. "Write me a *vallon,* Jevick. Like what you read to me on the ship that day. You said they last forever."

Her voice is suddenly fragmented, broken with tears. She weeps like one who is dying of grief, and yet she cannot die; she weeps like one who has lost her dearest possession, her only love. "Jevick, my mother left me alone. Do you hear me? They buried me there, in the north. She was weak. She let them put me into the earth. In the graveyard—faugh!—in the huge graveyard on the hill. She let them put me there, to have my bones sink into the earth, and—oh, Jevick! I am one of the Rotted Dead."

Her face is transformed by the horror she feels—the horror that grips us both. In its clutches and for one moment she looks devastatingly human. Her face is close to mine, the eyes wide, the mouth aghast. I think I can see the pores in her skin, the beads of sweat, the terror . . . But of course it is an illusion, a wraith: her body is underground, sinking and putrefying, her youth and beauty mere bubbles of gas. As if she has read my thought, she shrieks, begins to wail, whipping her red hair to and fro, in mourning for herself.

"Jissavet," she cries. "Jissavet."

The priestess plucks the translation from my mind. Island of the White Flowers.

But I am falling now. I cannot speak for her, to answer the foolish question: "Yes, angel? What do you mean?" I know what she means, I think to myself, and the priestess does not hear me because I am already too far away, my body shivering, slick with sweat, riding the river of pain which bears me away to a new depth where I will not hear the grief-maddened shrieking of the angel. It is as if she moves away from me, weeping over the valleys. "Jissavet, Jissavet." Then silence. Then I know nothing, until I wake again in the holy cave and see the face of Auram bending over me.

"Don't sit up," he said. I looked up at him, at the thick locks of his hair in disarray against the craggy ceiling. His face was shadowed, but I could see that it did not have its usual chalky pallor: the skin was mottled, tense, excited. There was a sour odor: I guessed it came from his short leather skirt. An odor of ancient cabinets, ancient sweat. His mask was slung around his neck, and it looked at me too, leering downward, its hide in the torchlight criss-crossed with fine wrinkles.

"Brave one!" he said ecstatically. He caressed my hair; his palm was damp and heavily scented with musk. I lay motionless on the bare floor of the cave, close to his crossed legs, his plucked-looking, almost hairless shins, the brief flap of his skirt. Voices resounded in the air, the murmuring of the girls, and huge shadows moved to and fro on the walls. "*Avneanyi*," Auram whispered. His fingernail snagged my skin as he traced a circle on my brow with his index finger.

The shadows leapt and shrank to nothing, staggering drunkenly over the walls, those visions of glorious color. I lay still, my throat aching. The cavern throbbed, a forest fire, the lanterns of a carnival, a blossoming sky emblazoned with rare tulips.

At last Auram and another priest helped me sit up. My face felt stiff; the clarified butter had hardened. I looked about me dully. The girls, their beaded anklets rattling, were clustered around the high priestess, who lolled unconscious before the stone altar.

"Don't worry," Auram said. "With her it is always like this. You have had a splendid success, splendid! Ready! Up we go!" He chuckled, overflowing with high spirits. The girls were rubbing scented oil into the white temples of the priestess. One of them chafed her feet, her slender hands dwarfed by those great slabs of flesh. Another sponged the blood from her hands.

The priests wheeled me around and dragged me through the crack in the hillside, and we stumbled out into the cold, fragrant night. The moon was full and the shadows of trees lay black on the ghostly sward. Beyond them, a meadow furrowed like a pale sea. Auram crowed. He and the other priest told jokes, supporting me as they strode through the long grass toward the lights of the palace. The other priest was called Ildo; he told me about his niece who was a baker in the kitchens of the Telkan. Her brown-flour breasts. The two priests roared over their bawdy stories, like men returning from a hunting party. The masks bounced on the ropes around their necks. In the palace gardens among the yew trees we saw deer feeding on the grass.

Inside again, in the parlor, Auram served me a cup of chocolate without sugar. He wore a robe now, a lustrous garment of orange silk. "*Avneanyi,*" he whispered.

"Don't call me that."

"Drink," he soothed me. "All will be well."

He watched me drink, perched on the corner of his chair.

Write me a vallon, I thought. And I laughed, my muscles slow and sore. The priest had washed the clarified butter from my face with a rag, but I still felt as if I wore a mask. I laughed with stiff, uncooperative lips, with a raw ache in my throat, at the monstrousness of it, the sublime absurdity. Write *her* a book, set *her* words down in Olondrian characters! This ghost, this interloper, speaking only Kideti!

"No," I said aloud, gritting my teeth. I would not do it. I would not mingle the horror of death with what I most loved.

The chocolate was bitter as iron, the parlor gray in the dawn, the beaded lamps burnt out. "Drink," said the priest. "You need it after your supplication. But how brave you were! How fine! You have the makings of a priest of Avalei!"

"You will forgive me if I am not comforted."

He smiled. His flat, peculiar, blurred-looking features were lanced by the glittering points of his eyes. "I will tell you a story," he said. "Yes, before we return you to the Houses. Just a homely little story. Something to help you sleep.

"I was in Asarma at the time of the cholera. Not many years ago—a few years—a terrible time for us. I was only a child then. I was studying astronomy, and while I was at school they were throwing the bodies into the sea. . . . And the carts, the dead-carts were everywhere. You could see them from the windows. There was no place that did not have the smell of death. When we went out at night to read the stars, we choked on the smell of the city, and behind the sea wall the corpses floated and gave off their phosphorescence. . . . Well. There was a colleague of mine, a boy from the Fanlevain, a clockmaker's son, very clever and somewhat—lonely. That is, he kept to himself. We shared a room in the dormitory, and I used to hear him talking in his sleep. . . . Ah! Later I cursed myself for not having listened to him, for burying my head under the pillow! For you see, this boy—this boy was a saint. But it was not known until later. Who knows what we might have learned from him, had his power been known?"

The priest paused and turned up the palm of one hand despairingly. "Who knows? You see, *telmaro,* I was too slow. Only after strange things had happened—after he fell into trances at school, after I found a sheaf of poems he had written—only then did I mention what I had seen to one of our masters, and only then was the youth taken into the temple. But by that time the sign of the plague was on him. When he said good-bye to us he was already weak; as he went down the stairs he was clutching his stomach. And within the week he was dead. He had taken his wisdom into the grave. He had taken the angel's blessing away with him."

Auram leaned forward. The dawn in the window glowed on his shaven cheek. He gave me a long, deep glance, as of recognition. "I remember one night," he whispered, holding my gaze. "This young boy, *telmaro*, this boy conversed with a statue, alone in the dark."

My cup was empty; I passed it to him in silence. Then I said slowly: "Your story means nothing to me. Nothing. Do you hear?"

My voice gathered strength as he dropped his eyes and toyed with the enameled clasps on his robe. "*Nothing*. Your angels, your drugs, your filth, your Avalei! I want only to be rid of the spirit and go."

"But we can help," he said, raising his eyes. "We can give you the angel's body."

"In exchange for your Night Market. Where I'll be arrested again, no doubt, and dragged back to the Houses for impersonating a saint."

He laughed merrily. "Do you think my lady powerless? Oh, no. She has many friends still. Many friends. Day is breaking, and no one has reported your disappearance from the Gray Houses. And when you go back, it will be as if you had never left."

He slid forward, his eyes still bright with mirth, held my shoulder and rasped into my ear. "You will leave the Isle in a week or less." His smile had a childlike sweetness, and it struck me that he was, to some degree, mad—as our island doctors are mad, with the potency of transcendence. As the Priest of the Stone was mad: as I was mad. Such spiritual power was always capricious, not to be trusted, likely to scar. But latched to the power of this priest, clinging to Avalei's mantle, I might claw my way out of the Houses and to freedom.

I was grateful that he said nothing of the angel's ringing words: *Write me a* vallon. Perhaps he had not heard. Or perhaps what mattered to him was not what she said, but that I could communicate with her, that I was a true *avneanyi*. He took my arm and led me to the door, a dim heat in his fingers, a dark note in his breathing like a hidden sob. Long after I had returned to the Gray Houses, his stinging odor clung about me like the ghost of a struck match.

Chapter Twelve

Tialon's Story

I was cold the next day—so cold my teeth knocked together. Ordu touched my brow and removed the iron chamberpot after I vomited thin gray liquid. I did not join the others for the daily walk in the garden, but curled up and hid my face, wrapped tight in the sheets. When I slept I dreamt of the islands, my brother whistling, the shadows of birds, and when I woke I counted the minutes as if it could make my chills subside. Cries came from behind the wall: the groans of the mad, inarticulate and frayed at the edges, like prayers.

There Tialon came to see me. It was her first visit in several weeks. She carried her writing box and an umbrella beaded with moisture, for it was raining over Velvalinhu. Her hair was tightly curled and powdered with drops where the wind had blown rain under her umbrella. She placed her things against the wall and came unasked to sit on the edge of my mattress, bringing cold air that had gotten caught in the folds of her clothes, and smiled at me—a fragile smile, for her face was drawn and sickly and great shadows marred the skin under her eyes.

"Jevick," she said.

"Tialon."

"Are you unwell?" she asked softly.

"Are you?" I returned.

At that her smile grew warmer and tears came into her eyes. She patted my wrist with a freezing hand. "No. I am very well. Are you still reading *Olondrian Lyrics*?"

"Yes. And the *Romance of the Valley*."

She nodded. Her eyes shone with the transparent light of the sky, as if the rain had washed them. "I'm reading, too. I've read your letters. I'm sorry I didn't answer. I've come to you instead. I won't stay long. I'll go back to my real life. You remember I told you I'd built something. . . . This is what I have built. This life."

In the fractured light of the lamp her face looked young, determined, unhappy. There was a recklessness in the way she lifted her chin. "I read. I take notes for my father. I sit in the shrine of the Stone, always reading, watching, gazing into the depths of mystery. The Stone . . . I wish I could show it to you. Perhaps then you would understand. It is black, heavy, miraculous, covered with writing. . . ." She raised her hands, arms wide, delineating a vague shape in the air, then shrugged her shoulders and let them fall.

"I can't describe it. But Jevick—it is a very great thing. Our hope. My father is only the second to attempt to interpret its message. For this reason . . ." She paused and bit her lip, then looked at me and went on quietly: "For this reason it is easy for us to make mistakes. Do you understand? For us, for our cult, it is the beginning. We are still vulnerable—still laughed at, and still hated. . . . We have the support of the king, but of no one close to him. Indeed, his son is one of those who seek most persistently to discredit us. And there is also Avalei's cult. They hate us because we reject what they love: luxury, harlotry, the pursuit of angels."

She smiled at my flushed face. "I know you've met the High Priestess of Avalei. I know everything. We have spies." A tear dropped down her cheek to her lap. "Yes. Spies. We listen at doors, we follow people. My father receives reports every morning at dawn. It's disgusting. . . ."

Reading alarm in my face, she laughed, brushing back tears with the heel of her palm. "Don't worry. You're safe. You believe that, don't you? You know I am your friend."

I looked up into her wistful eyes, her eyes of immense candor. "Yes," I said. "I know it. But I don't know why."

"That's what I've come to tell you," she said. "The reason I am your friend. The reason I won't betray you, even though I know you're running away. The reason for everything." She gazed at me with a frightened smile, and swallowed. "It's strange—now I'm here, I don't know how to begin."

But she did. She did know how to begin. She took a deep breath and looked down at her fingers clenched together on her dark wool dress. Then she raised her head and met my eyes. She leaned toward me like a sister, while the rain closed the Isle behind its resonant palisades.

She told me of the village of Kebreis, the village of Flint, with its roofs of broken slate and latticed windows. A village of cold water and hard rock wedged among the hills of the west, the Fiaduoron, the Dark Mountains. Kebreis: hunched in a fiercely beautiful landscape of clear streams and brilliant skies and the snow-bright pinnacles of the mountains, a landscape whose glitter hurts the eye, whose cold air stings the lungs, its people withdrawn and silent, craving isolation. Many of the men had once worked in the mines. These had tattoos under their eyes where, as they lounged in the café, one might read "Thief" or "Pirate." Among them there was one man who was marked with the blue word "Poacher"—for he had been caught hunting boar in the Kelevain, the Telkan's wood.

He spent six years in the mines, and when his sentence was over he came down from the mountains into the solitude of Kebreis. Like many of the men there he discovered he could live most peacefully in the hills, where his tattoo brought him not calumny but respect. So he settled there and smoked with the others in the little café, drinking sour red wine in the patch of dust under the awning, and he married the schoolteacher's only daughter against her father's will and took her to live in his one-roomed house among the peaks.

The schoolteacher's daughter wore tough cotton clothes like the other women of Kebreis, and in winter a pair of boots trimmed with otter skin. And despite her father's predictions of disaster she never longed for fine linen or servants, never complained when she had to break the ice in the buckets. She kept goats and was sunburned and caught trout and ate potatoes and refused to take even a radish from her father, and the children came one after the other, all of them wild, lanky, singing, adventurous, and strong-hearted like their parents. They were all well-suited to life in Kebreis and free from unhappy dreams. And then there were two girls who died in infancy; and then the last, a boy, whom his mother called Lunre, because he was born in the month of the purest light.

Tialon told me this. She spoke with a trembling eagerness, sometimes pulling at the collar of her dress. She held up her hand when I opened my mouth and went on telling me, hurriedly, as if rushing to catch the story before it escaped. She told me of the thin and lonely boy with the red knees who was plagued by coughs, who cried when he was ill, who lay against the wall under wool blankets with his brothers in the single room divided by a frayed curtain, who suffered in that smoky room and suffered as well outdoors, where he was pelted with snow and unable to run quickly, where his father took him on long walks to improve his constitution and forced him to wade in the furious, icy trout streams. She told me of how he suffered everywhere except in the school where his grandfather, that severe and well-dressed gentleman, who had despaired of all the boy's brothers and sisters, was interested, hardly daring to hope, in this last one, the one with the chronic cough. Lunre. Dressed in the patched clothes of his brothers, and a wool scarf. Lunre who sometimes could not go to school but lay in the corner, pale and languid, watching the frost that formed along the edge of the door when the fire had gone out. It was his grandfather who came to him, leaning on his cane, still muffled in a fur cloak although it was spring, and the streams were rushing bright and cold, and here and there the first of the crocuses peeped through the muddy traces of melting snow. It was his grandfather who came and sat on a stool by the hearth, looking too large and princely for the small room, and offered to pay for the boy to go to school in the capital where the milder climate would give him a chance at survival. Yes, he would go to stay there with a merchant, his grandfather's brother, in the house where his mother had lived for two years long ago, where she had learned to paint and sew but never to speak Olondrian without peppering it with phrases of mountain slang. Lunre's parents agreed, not for the gain, the future prestige, but because Kebreis was killing their last child. And his mother wept over him as though he, the difficult one, the one who was the least like her, was the dearest of them all.

"So Lunre went to Bain," Tialon said. "He was ten years old. Do I need to tell you what happened to him after that? Do I need to tell you of the house of his great-uncle the glass merchant, where they slept outside on the balcony in summer? And his schools—the private boys' school, the University of Bain—do you need to hear of them, of his passion for reading? You have read Firdred of Bain, *On the Nine Textures of Light*, the *Lyrics* of Karanis—and so you know. Is it not enough for you to know that at the age of twenty-one he went to a poorly attended evening lecture and saw my father's elderly predecessor, emaciated and fierce, exhorting young students to join the work of the Stone? And to know, also, that he felt distaste at the sight of that gaunt figure and joined him not because he believed in the dream, but because he could not resist the temptation to go to the Blessed Isle and to walk the halls of the library drenched in myth. . . . It was only later that he became intrigued by the work of the Stone, through the debates held by the scholars who had gathered to serve the old priest. They used to meet in a roof garden full of lavender, at dusk. It was their passion that drew him. And later it was his friendship with my father.

"He was our only friend," she said, touching her hand to her throat. "He was our friend, my father's only friend. Do you understand what that means? He could make my father laugh. He could even make him play the violin. He was the only one who could ever persuade my father to sing—even I couldn't do that, although I loved it. He used to come to our rooms when I was small. He had a special knock, so that we would recognize him and let him in. He would bring a fish or beef heart and cook it over the coals on the balcony. He could make my father eat anything, even drink wine. . . . When he—when Lunre was there my father would sigh and say, 'Why not?'—you see, he would lose his stiffness and become generous. He pretended that it annoyed him, but I could see how happy he was, that it was happiness that made him give in to pleasure. . . . Sometimes when Lunre was there, when I was too little to understand, I would grow so filled with joy I had to scream; I would leap around the house, too drunk with relief to contain myself, and have to be sent to bed early or even punished. You see, our house was so solemn. There was so little room for play. And so during Lunre's visits I would grow wild: I pushed everything too far, I laughed too loudly, I wanted each joke to continue forever. Later I always felt so ashamed. . . ."

She smiled, glancing down at her hands, tracing the lines in her palm, the smudges of old ink. Then she looked up and said: "That friendship was inexplicable. Here was this man, my father—so dour, so shy, so easily insulted—who had recently lost his wife, who had only me. He was in his own type of mourning, which involved a strained sensitivity, an anger which erupted on any pretext, yet somehow he invited this young man to visit him, this student sixteen years younger than himself. How did it happen? I imagine it began in the garden outside the shrine, that high garden with its statues, its narrow parapet, where the followers of the Priest of the Stone used to meet and look down on the battlements of this city in the hour after sunset. . . . The student must have said something, or followed some line of reasoning, which hinted at his solitary nature, his love of classical poetry or his ability to suffer silently, all traits my father admired in him. In him: this youth of twenty-one with the thin veneer of city cultivation over the sadness of Kebreis, with the anxious, slightly affected way of carrying himself which he used to cover his villager's awkwardness. Perhaps that was part of it: they were both awkward, although in Lunre, who was good-natured, this quality was endearing. In my father the awkwardness was cruel. But when they were together it disappeared: they were both completely at ease. . . .

"In those days, Jevick, I truly believe there were more stars in the sky. They used to come out all at once, like a field of snow. And we would sit on the balcony, the three of us, looking at them, and I would listen to my father and Lunre talking. Sometimes they told old stories or Lunre recited part of the *Vanathul,* which he had learned from his father in Kebreis, or my father brought out the *limike* and sang in his clear voice one of the sacred songs, or old lullabies from the country.

Long is the journey homeward,
Weary and worn are we.
Oh, if I fall behind, my love,
Will you look back for me?

That was the saddest song he sang, the one with the simplest words. It was composed long ago on the road called the Trail of Wolves. I remember hearing that song, lying half-asleep on the balcony with my cheek on the tiles in the warmth of the summer night. . . . I could smell so many flowers and also the coals, still red from our supper. We stacked the plates in a corner of the balcony. And later, when I sat there alone, when I was nineteen years old, I could see that there were fewer stars in the sky.

"I have heard that there are people who live happily alone. But I myself have not found it to be possible. I told you that I have built something, and since you came I have realized that what I have built is the shadow of happiness. But true happiness: that is what we had when we were together, my father and Lunre and I, sometimes with my nurse, when I was old enough not to scream with the wild sensation of joy but to sit, ecstatic, to let it wash over me. . . . We cooked, sometimes we went for a drive in one of the palace carriages and picnicked in the woods or walked in the hills, we went to plays organized for the king, and sometimes we wrote plays ourselves and performed them for my nurse on the balcony. By this time Lunre had come to believe in the message of the Stone, and he too had woven and sewn his own robe, although he did not change his name as my father had, which was good, his name suited him: he was with light, and I hope that he has always remained with light. But he had changed in himself. He had developed an intense gaze and the melancholy of hours immured in mystery. Once, from the balcony, I saw him far below in the rain, and I think that he had not realized it was raining."

Tialon paused. She looked wan and remote, as if carved on a fountain. Her eyes were lowered; the lashes cast a shadow. She said: "I used to lie awake at night out of pure happiness, because of an apple, because we had seen butterflies, because he had laughed at my jokes and for a thousand other foolish reasons, while slowly, inexorably, our lives were breaking. They had begun to quarrel, you see—Lunre and my father. They had disagreed on certain interpretations, and my father, who could not bear contradiction even then, had forced Lunre to burn some of his notes. Yes—you do well to look shocked. But worse things happened afterward. One of my father's enemies perished in the Telkan's dungeons—not murdered outright, but imprisoned until his death. And there was—"

She stopped, then went on with an effort, her lips barely moving: "There was a school burned in the Valley."

A breath. Then she went on in the same flat tone: "They were teaching banned books. None of the children could read. Avalei's eunuchs were teaching them by recitation. They were teaching the autobiography of Leiya Tevorova, who claimed to have been haunted by an angel. My father sent them three warnings, and then the Guard, the Telkan's Guard. He told us later that he did not know they were going to burn the school. Lunre called him a liar—my father, a liar. Three children died when the school was burned. Two of them were my age.

"Perhaps it was then that the stars began to disappear from the sky: for I believe whole constellations have been extinguished. They slipped away from us as we were lying awake or sleeping, and they have never come back, not even for a moment. Perhaps they were fading even as I walked back from the library with Lunre, the two of us arm in arm in the dark, in our somber clothes that made us call ourselves 'the two ravens,' laughing in the dim hallways and under the trees. I felt a surge of that wild joy which I had known as a child, and he saw it in me, my excited voice and laughter, and in the turning of one of the halls he suddenly grew still and said to me: 'You should not laugh so; it is too much.' He had never said such a thing to me and I took my arm away from him and we walked in silence back to the Tower of Myrrh. And as we passed through a garden I saw his face in the light of a lamp and it was grim and pained, and unlike the face of my friend.

"The quarrels between my father and Lunre continued and grew worse. My father discovered that Lunre kept secret notes, and as for Lunre, his matchless ability to suffer quietly, which he had developed in the small house in Kebreis, which my father had so admired in him, proved to have its own limits. They shouted at one another, stormed out of the shrine. My father was afraid that Lunre would take his notes to the Telkan, or publish them on the mainland, destroying my father's own work. And Lunre was tormented by his betrayal of his friend, by the burned school, and by the other, unspeakable thing.

"Yes," Tialon whispered, "by the other, unspeakable thing, which I did not discover until he had gone, though I must have sensed its presence without admitting it to myself and without even understanding what it was. I only knew that something, some threat, was hovering over us on that night in the hall when he had told me not to laugh, and again in one of the gardens when I caught my hair in the thorns of the hedge and he, releasing it, stroked my cheek. That was how it appeared: first like that and then on the hill overlooking the sea when we fell silent for no reason, afraid in the light of that threatening sky with the storm coming over the sea; and then at night on the balcony; and then everywhere. Yes, soon this fear, this desolation was everywhere, and I could not look at him without feeling my face grow hot, and he looked at me searchingly and submissively and without hope, and then one day, after eighteen years, he was gone.

"He left my father a letter," Tialon said quietly, "and my father, in his rage, forced me to read it. And so I read how Lunre was going away, was leaving Olondria, but did not know whether he would flee to the north or south of the world. And I also read of his reasons: that he was not worthy to study the words of the gods, as he had betrayed both them and himself. And that, he wrote, he was in the grip of a dishonorable passion. Those were his words: 'a dishonorable passion.'"

The sighing echo of those words hung in the air of the room, the echo not just of what Tialon had said, but of what she had read in the letter on that remote afternoon under the quivering and furious eye of her father. There was a burnt smell from the hills. In the evening she sat on the balcony with her back against the wall, staring into the dark, and when her nurse came out and asked her why she wept she told her that she had only now seen that some of the stars were missing.

"He was twenty years older than I," she said to me in that stone cell in the Gray Houses, seated on the edge of my low bed. "He was—but why am I telling you how he was? You must know." She looked at me, her gaze penetrating, direct.

"Yes," I whispered.

I had thought that she would weep, but she did not. She was like a queen, sitting very straight, her hands quiet in her lap. Only her voice wavered, and a shudder crossed her throat when she said: "Yes. I knew. And how could I not? I did not spend those years, the years of my childhood, listening to him read in the evening light, only to forget the books he loved, the books we loved together. I knew when I saw you with his *Olondrian Lyrics*."

She nodded as if to herself and looked around the room, the rickety shelf with its useless volumes, the bareness and the squalor. The room had grown colder. Her face, turned away from me, was cast in shadow so that I could not see her expression when she said: "And how is he?"

"He is well," I said.

Tialon nodded again. She had the flawless dignity of one sentenced to death. Her story seemed to have drained everything out of her, her terror and wildness and even the resolution that had forced her to tell it. I knew she had told it because she could not give up the chance to say his name, aloud, in the hearing of another, of one who had known him. I sensed this in the way her lips curved to form the word, lingered over it—that it was a forbidden sound in her house. *Lunre*: the call of a water bird, and then the fall of water. A name that means "with light," the last month of the year. She said it now with the sigh of the closing year and then she stood and faced me, her face pale and severe in the cold lamplight.

"I have something for you."

She went to the door and picked up her writing box. She carried it back to the mattress and sat beside me, the box in her lap. Then she sprang the catch and the box yawned open, and she took from it two oily-looking packages tied with string.

"News from the past."

A shrill note in her voice. She set the packages on the sheet. Each was as solid and dense as a cheese. They were bundles of paper covered with a closely written script, discolored with the passage of the years.

"Take them with you," Tialon said. I looked up at her, speechless. Her smile trembled; her eyes were very bright. She clasped her hands in front of her face and looked down, hiding her mouth behind them. "I wrote him over a thousand letters, I think."

"I'll take them."

She swallowed. "Thank you. I'll try to make it easy for you to get out of the Houses."

"And if you want to know more about him," I murmured, "I can tell you—"

She shook her head, closed her writing box, and stood, not looking at me as she whispered: "I have built my life without knowing where he was."

I often think of her like that: with her head half turned away, the curls gleaming at the nape of her thin neck, one hand already reaching down to pick up her umbrella, the other gripping the writing box like an anchor. She seems to hang before me, wavering like the light of a candle, suspended in that breathless, fragile instant. Then the candle is blown out and she is gone, the room is empty, she leaves only a fleeting warmth and a trace of smoke.

After she had gone I remained staring at the door, thinking of the young figure of my master: dark-haired, but with the same steady, piercing, quartz-green eyes, in a black robe that would make his skin seem paler. I thought of him standing among the trees with the rain falling through his cloak in the oblivion of religious contemplation, and cringed with the feeling that I had wronged him by picturing him thus, in his other life which he did not want me to know. But now it was too late: my master, Lunre of Bain, had been irrevocably replaced by Lunre of Kebreis. And the small boy who lay in the corner and watched frost form on the door had replaced all the fantasies of my master's childhood.

There is a courtyard where I imagine my master and Tialon, the tortured man and the adolescent girl: an illusory place with flowers of mother-of-pearl in the swaying almond trees whose leaves are spangled with drops of a recent rain. It is a place of tears. And yet their laughter echoes against the stones, this tall man with the slightly abstracted air, with the solitary smile, in the unseasonable dark wool, and the girl in the short, straight frock of the same material. They are talking under the trees. The girl has hair of dark honey, bound into four fuzzy plaits harassed by the leaves. She is knock-kneed, with the lighted eyes of an evening after a rainstorm and the shapely, fluted ankles of a deer. Again they laugh. Her eyes are quick and lively under thick lashes, and his eyes, answering, wrinkle at the corners. This girl speaks excitedly and precociously about the classics, but she still sleeps in the same room as her old nurse. . . . And he watches her, watches the dazzling light slide on and off of her shoulder, changing as she moves beneath the trees, turning her skin from the color of pale sand to the color of autumn and in the shadows to the color of old silver. Her resplendent skin, which is still the skin of a child. He notices that it is almost the same color as her hair. The difference is infinitesimal: yet in that difference of hue there are desert armies, cities of marble in conflagration. The air is rarefied by the sound of her laugh and the smell of the trees, and then by the sleep and meadows which her arms smell of, as she puts them around his neck and prostrates him with a chaste kiss. A burning memory crackles in his hair. Later, while they are walking, she will wonder why they are suddenly sad, and he will not be able to explain; he will say: "We should not have eaten the mussels. They smell of death. . . ." And they will both want to weep in the dark air.

I see him with the sweat on his brow which has turned the color of tallow and imagine how he will flee to the ends of the earth, putting the fathomless sea between himself and this sweet, incautious girl, interring himself in a country of alien flowers. And never, not even in the delirium of his island fevers, will he allow himself to pronounce the lost child's name. And as for her, she will say his name only in solitude, hugging herself in her small bed, her tears shining in the moonlight.

Tonight the house is quiet. The old nurse sits by the hearth, muttering to herself, half-asleep. The young girl is collecting their soiled plates from the table and carrying them away to the dark kitchen. Suddenly she looks outside. The balcony doors are open, the night soft and humming with the insects of summer. Then there is her startled cry, and the crash of a plate on the floor. She has noticed the disappearance of the stars.

Midnight. The door creaked open and I was instantly awake, fearing as always the witchlight of the ghost. But there was only the dull glow of a lantern, and a hand like an iron scepter prodding me urgently in the neck. "Rise. Rise." It was Auram, High Priest of Avalei, cloaked and hooded. His sleeve was damp and carried an odor of salt. He had already crept down to the shore where a boat rocked on the waves, hushed and lightless, awaiting its cargo: a fugitive saint.

BOOK FOUR

The Breath of Angels

Chapter Thirteen

Into the Valley

The boat slid swiftly through water and night to Ethendria, a city named for the "Lovely Palace" overlooking the sea. We arrived too early to land without drawing undue attention, and dropped anchor within sight of the city's lights to await the dawn. The air was cold, the sea restless; the boat danced at the end of her tether like a foal. I breathed in great gulps of salt and darkness, and remembered buying a ticket to Ethendria long ago, in Bain. The memory lightened my heart: I was moving eastward at last, toward the angel's body. My path was a knot, full of loops and barriers, but freedom lay at the end of it, I was sure. As if to confirm my choice, the angel had withdrawn. She was not far off—I felt her in my heart like a grain of poison—but she had not torn my nights apart since we had spoken in the Girdle of Avalei.

Auram appeared at my shoulder; the spark of my new confidence wavered and grew dim. "*Avneanyi,*" he said.

"I told you not to call me that."

"Why not? It is what you are. But never mind now," he went on smoothly, his voice smiling, his face a hollow in his cloak. The starlight caught his teeth.

"Tell me: are you well?" he asked.

"Yes."

"Excellent, excellent! You have a formidable constitution; or, like me, you are a cricket."

"A cricket, *veimaro*?"

"A midnight creature; the foxes' bard. All night he makes music, but by day he is oh! so tired!"

His hood tilted to one side; he might have been resting his cheek on his hand. I smiled without pleasure, thinking that he was extraordinarily like a cricket: his liveliness and neatness, his black eyes, the extreme fineness of his limbs, even the chirring of his voice.

"As it happens, I prefer the day," I said.

"A pity. But you may change your mind before long—the night belongs to Avalei."

"The night, perhaps. But not me."

"Come, *avneanyi.*" A soft note of warning crept into his voice. "We must be friends if we are to succeed."

He put his hand on my arm, each finger precise and delicate as a physician's lance. His breath smelled faintly of rotting strawberries. "We shall travel light and swiftly. I have but a single trunk, and Miros, my nephew and valet, has been ordered to leave it behind if we are pursued."

I recognized the name of the careless, engaging young man who had first brought me out of the Houses.

"Miros is here?"

"Yes, but it doesn't matter. Listen. We'll avoid inns where we can, at least until the village of Nuillen, at the eastern edge of the Valley, where we shall hold the Market. Is this clear?"

"Yes."

"It may not keep the Telkan's Guard from us. We are a rather conspicuous party—at least, you and I are easily marked. I say this without either humility or conceit, without wishing to flatter or condemn you. We must prepare to face dangers. We must expect to be found."

The boat swayed under me, treacherous.

"What about your lady's friends? What about her power? You said it would be easy."

"And no doubt it will, it will," he soothed me, stroking my arm, the edges of his nails catching in the embroidered jacket he'd given me.

I pulled my arm away. "Speak plainly. Will we be found or not?"

"I cast no bones," he said, laughing. "The Oracle God has no reason to love me. I say that it will be easy, because I believe it. And I say we must expect to be found, because I believe this also."

The sky had grown subtly lighter while we spoke; his hood was black against it. His hands showed white when he moved to fold his arms.

"And what happens if we are found?" I asked sharply.

"For you: the Gray Houses. Indefinitely. For me . . ."

He shrugged, his bright laughter a string of pearls. "I fear no dark place."

Before dawn was full Auram disappeared under the deck, and like day trading places with night, Miros came up yawning and rubbing his eyes. He smiled when he saw me. "Good morning, *avneanyi*," he said, awkward with the word, rubbing his hands on the sides of his plain linen tunic.

"Please call me by name."

"Much better!" he said, visibly relieved. "What was it? Shevas?"

I laughed in spite of myself—*shevas* is Olondrian for "turnip."

"Jevick of Tyom."

"Right! I'll leave your place name alone, if you don't mind—too fine a note for my heavy tongue. But Jevick will do very well."

He pronounced it "Shevick," as my master had—as all Olondrians did, save Tialon, who had a musician's ear. He took my arm and pulled me out of the way of the turning sail, and we leaned on the rails at the edge of the boat together and watched the city take shape. Miros did not resemble his uncle: where the priest was pale and black-haired, Miros had the brown curls and golden skin of the Laths, the people of the Valley. He had only recently joined his uncle's service—to escape some trouble, I understood from his evasions and nervous fumbling with the pearl in his earlobe.

"I don't know a thing about being a valet," he added gloomily. "I only hope we get some hunting in the highlands. If I were home I could hunt in the Kelevain with my other uncles. . . . But it's my own fault. It's always a mistake to leave one's home."

Recalling my own situation, he stammered: "I mean for me, for people like me, uneducated, suited for nothing but idleness. . . ."

I laughed and told him he was right. "I ought to have stayed home myself," I said. At the end of the sentence sorrow clenched my throat.

After a moment I managed: "But you're with your uncle the priest, at any rate. You must admire him."

Miros stared at me, half laughing and half aghast. He glanced about him, then bent to my ear and said in a heightened, roguish whisper like that of a stage villain: "Admire him! I hate him like the cramp."

"Evmeni is Evmeni, Kestenya is Kestenya: but the Valley is Olondria." Thus wrote Firdred of Bain, of the Fayaleith, or "Valley"; and his words seemed to breathe in the air that rushed to meet us at the whitewashed steps of the town. My skin tingled at its touch; my spirits rose. It was too great an effort to be unhappy that transparent morning, thrust from the Gray Houses into Ethendria, a town poised between the Valley and the sea, devoted to the manufacture of sweets, where the very plaster gives off a fragrance of almond paste. Miros dashed off to hire a carriage, leaving me under a tamarind tree with the priest, who sat silent on his traveling trunk with his hood pulled down to his lips; apparently unmoved by the glorious morning, he got into the carriage as soon as Miros returned, and closed the door with a bang.

"Is he all right?" I whispered to Miros.

"What? Him? Perfectly. Look at these beauties!"

Miros was in ecstasies over the elegant, milk-blue horses. He begged me to sit with him on the coachman's box, and I agreed gladly enough. Once he had stowed his uncle's trunk, we climbed onto the box and set off.

A small boy led his goats under chestnut trees by the canal. A merchant, framed by a window, frowned over his newspaper. A girl with a cart of wilted begonias for sale yawned ferociously and scratched herself underneath her slender arm. And then, suddenly, we were among the markets, the overpowering scent of mushrooms and the wild-looking peasants, the *huvyalhi* in robes and crude tin earrings, who rushed at the carriage, shouting and gesticulating, holding up lettuces, sausages, baskets of nettles, and wheels of salty cheese. Miros begged two *droi* from the priest and bought a cone of newspaper filled with tobacco. "Look!" he said, jabbing my ribs with an elbow. And there, gazing at us serenely and with a hint of mockery from among the onions, sat a beautiful peasant girl. . . . In the country both men and women of the *huvyalhi* wear long straight robes, dark or faded to various shades of blue, belted with rope or leather, and the effect of this strangely provocative dress when worn by lovely women has been for centuries the subject of poetry. The soft cotton, when it is old, reveals the outlines of the body. "*Little Leaf-Hands,*" runs an old country song, "*go to draw water again in your old robe, the one your sister wore before you, the one that follows your breasts like rain.*" Miros raised a hand to the girl and she laughed behind her wrist. The carriage jolted forward, pulling through the crowd, the piled radishes, wild irises, hairy goatskins taut with new-pressed wine, and edible fungi like yellow lace. Then we passed the horse graveyard with its blue equine statues and the mausoleum where the dukes' beloved chargers sleep; and then, cresting a little hill, we came upon the bosom of Olondria, undulant and dazed with light.

We were moving away from the sea. On our left hung high limestone cliffs, topped with turf and a few wind-blasted trees; on our right the country spilled like a bolt of silk unrolled in a market, like perfumed oil poured out in a flagrant gesture. The Ethendria Road, wide and well-kept, curved down into the Valley, into the shadow of cliffs and the redolence of wet herbs. The grape harvest was ended, and the country was filled with tumbled vines, rust-colored, mellowed with age, birdsong, and repose. . . . Everything shone in that sumptuous light which is called "the breath of angels": the hills flecked with the gold of the autumn crocus, the windy, bronze-limbed chestnut trees and the *radhui,* the peasant houses, sprawling structures topped with blackened chimneys. The trees and roofs stood out precisely against the purity of the sky whose vibrant blue was a unique gift of the autumn. The dust sparkled over the road, and its odor mixed with the wilder scents of smoke and grasses in the deep places of the fields.

In that lucent countryside, far from any inn, we stopped at a *radhu.* The priest, entombed in the carriage, seemed to feel no need for refreshment, but Miros and I were famished, having sustained ourselves since morning on white pears and figs bought along the road. "We're sure to get something to eat here," Miros said, guiding the horses along the grassy ruts made by a country cart. "Even if it's only *bais* and cabbage. You've never had *bais*? It's what people live on out here: bread made of chestnut flour."

We approached the great, confused shape of the *radhu* among its luxuriant lemon trees, passing a garden of onions and cabbages, a number of broken wheelbarrows, a sullen donkey munching grass in the shade. Excited children tumbled out to greet us. "Watch the horses!" Miros bawled at the little boy and girl and the naked infant dawdling behind them. Their piercing cries accompanied us into a sort of open court, devoid of foliage, sun-baked, thick with dust.

We descended from the coach to the sound of rushing and slamming of doors within the lopsided stone structure facing us. In a moment a boy appeared with a clay pitcher of water, which he poured slowly over our grimy hands. This ceremony took place above the lip of a stone trough near the house, which spirited the water away to the garden. The boy worked with great concentration, breathing hard through his nose. He wore tarnished silver earrings shaped like little cows. Drops from our wet hands sprinkled the earth in that homely little court where blue cloth soaked in a scarred wooden basin, where chickens pecked at the roasted maize forgotten by the children in the shadow of the ivy-covered eaves. The tumbled front of the *radhu* offered a bewildering choice of entrances, arched doorways set at angles to one another: it looked as though a number of architects had disagreed on the plan of the house, each plunging into the work without consulting the others. Indeed, this was not far from the truth, for the *radhu* is a family project, expanding through the generations like a species of fungus. A stocky, bow-legged man appeared at the largest of the doorways and bowed, pressing the back of his right hand to his brow.

"Welcome, welcome!" he said, stepping out and holding his cracked hands over the trough to be washed by the silent boy. "Welcome, *telmaron*! You come from Huluethu, I think? From the young princes? It is an honor. . . ."

"No, from Ethendria," Miros said.

At this the old man's face fell. He wiped his hands on the sides of his robe. "You are not wine merchants?"

"No, by the Rose!" Miros answered, shouting with laughter. "We serve a priest of Avalei. He's resting in the carriage. He'll come out when he's ready. But we, I don't mind telling you, are half starved."

"Ah!" the old man said. His face lit up with a smile again, and he even chuckled as he explained: "I thought you were merchants for a moment—these wine sellers, they squeeze us to death—but Avalei!" He inclined his head and touched his brow. "Greatly is she to be praised. We love her in the Valley, *telmaron*. My own daughter wished to be one of her women, but the temple takes fewer novices these days. . . ." He jerked his head over his shoulder and cleaned his ear with a thick finger. Then he welcomed us under the arch and into a huge old room, clearly the original room of the *radhu*, dominated by a blackened fireplace.

That great, smoke-stained room, its walls unrelieved by decoration, would have been gloomy and oppressive had it not been for a trapdoor in the flat roof, lying open to admit a wide flood of the limpid daylight. Beneath the trapdoor was a generous alcove or sleeping loft; several girls peered down from its edge with bright, laughing faces. The room below was furnished with two iron beds, a few straw chairs, and a wooden cabinet adorned with painted cherries.

The old man's name was Kovyan. He spoke of the grape harvest, spitting into a tin spittoon with such force that the vessel spun in place. A young woman appeared in a dark doorway near the fireplace and called briefly to the girls in the loft. Two of them descended the ladder and skittered away through the doorway, whispering and giving us glances from their immense dark eyes. In a moment they returned with a round mat, laid it on the floor in the middle of the room, and set a stool on top of it. A delicious smell penetrated the air, sweet and hinting at pork fat, and I was embarrassed by the rumbling of my stomach—but Kovyan was overjoyed at this evidence of our hunger and slapped my knee with a gnarled hand as solid as a hammer.

The girls dragged in a wineskin, and Kovyan offered us cups of a powerful, spicy vintage called "The Wine of the White Bees." As we drank, there came a sound of hurried commotion out in the court, and four young men rushed in with an anxious, expectant air. These were Kovyan's sons and the sons of his sister: evidently a child had been dispatched to fetch them from the fields. They had washed hastily in the court, and their beards and long hair dripped with water that ran down to darken the shoulders of their robes. With the knives at their belts and the tin jewelry which reminded me of galley slaves, they presented a rough and even feral appearance; but all of their vigor went into making us welcome. Bows were exchanged and more chairs fetched from the recesses of the *radhu*. The "boys," as Kovyan called them, made themselves comfortable on the squeaking iron beds, drinking straight from the wineskin because there were no more cups. Into this active, convivial atmosphere walked a pair of proud adolescents bearing a colossal bowl on their shoulders.

Miros, enlivened by wine, cheered and tapped his cup with his ring. He winked at me and whispered: "I told you they'd give us something!" The bearers of the bowl, a boy and girl, trembled under its weight as they lowered it to the stool in the middle of the room. Inside it steamed a splendid stew of pork, mulberries, and chestnuts. Eager children materialized from the darkness of the walls. Last of all came

Kovyan's sister, the matriarch of the household: a heavy woman with mocking eyes in a sun-weathered face.

Conversation flared in every corner of the large room, all the men, women, and children talking at once, but only Kovyan made no attempt to lower his excited voice, and so his talk rang out above that of the others. He urged us to visit Huluethu, the country estate to the north of the road, where the "young princes" enjoyed music and hunting. Huluethu was a hunter's palace: venison smoked there every day, and the young men practiced swordplay on the flat roof. "Near the White River," he said, and I asked him if it was the same White River mentioned in the *Romance of the Valley*.

"Is it in the *Romance*?" he asked, wide-eyed, and the family gathered around me as I took out my book and read:

"'*A river is there, which is paved with stars. Its surface is covered with almond blossom; it runs through the fields of my dream like a river of snow. The White River, it is called. It is upon the redness of poppy fields, upon the blueness of fields of lavender. Its water is sweet, and the nymphs who dwell in it are the friends of men. All day they sit on its banks, carding wool. . . .*'" When I looked up, Kovyan tapped his cup in approval. His sister smiled over her coffee, licking her teeth to clean away the grounds.

The light grew etiolated, worn to threads. Kovyan stood and put a match to the little oil lamp on the cabinet. Only when it was dark and stars shone faintly through the skylight did the High Priest of Avalei walk into the room. He strode in without question, without deference, pushing back his hood, his eyes shining, and the *huvyalhi* went to him and kissed his hands, and the life that had begun to enter my veins died out like sap in a fallen tree, and I recalled the presence of death.

The priest sat, refusing wine and stew, taking only a glass of water, a piece of cheese. His terrible, loving gaze beamed about Kovyan's house. "Why not a tale?" he said. "We have a stranger with us, an islander. Let us give him a Valley entertainment."

"Grandmother, Grandmother," the children cried.

Kovyan's sister folded her hands, her eyes amused in the light of the oil lamp. "Very well," she said. "Since our guest admires the *Romance of the Valley*, I will give him a tale from it."

She shifted, her chair creaking. She cleared her throat. A child whimpered somewhere at the back of the room and was hushed back into silence. Then the woman told her tale in a voice both throaty and smooth, like new tussore, while a cat wailed at intervals from behind the wall.

People of the House, People of the House! This tale cannot turn anyone's blood to water.

It is told of Finya the Sorcerer that, sick with illicit love, he journeyed into Evmeni to battle the pirates of the Sea-King; for the people of the archipelago were strong in those days, and proud in their strength, and harassed our people as far as the plains of Madh. So Finya rode to the Salt Coast, where the sea is as white as milk, and the land as poor as ash, and the winds enervate the body. There he destroyed many evil men by the power of sword and magic, and won renown. And this adventure befell him during those days.

It happened that he encamped in an abandoned part of the coast; and with him were Draud, and Rovholon, and Maldar, and Keth of the Spring. When they had passed the night, Finya was the first to see the dawn, and he saw also a white dolphin which had washed up onto the sand. Beautiful was this dolphin as a pearl and well-shaped as a lily, and as it yet lived the youth went down to the shore to rescue it. But as he approached it, the sun, rising over the Duoronwei, struck the dolphin, and it disappeared as if it had been sea foam.

Now Finya was saddened by the fading of such a noble beast, and he hid what he had seen from his companions. Nevertheless, when they wished to press on he expressed the desire to camp in that place a second night: for he said that his wound pained him. At dawn he awoke, and saw the dolphin who seemed at the point of death, and rushed down the stinging sands littered with shells; and a second time the sun rose as he reached the dolphin's side, and the creature, fixing its eye on him, dissolved into the sea.

Then Finya was saddened more than before and would not leave that place, though his companions all were eager to move on. And Draud said, "Surely the wound of the sorcerer is healed; can it be cowardice that holds him back?" Then Rovholon and Maldar and Keth feared that their fellowship would be split, and that Finya would challenge Draud for the insult; but Finya said only: "The payment shall be deferred, Son of the Horse." And they camped a third night in that place, in great unease.

But Finya had resolved not to sleep, and he went down to the empty shore and knelt in the place where he had seen the dolphin. All night he watched, and as the sky grew pale the beast washed up on the shore, and Finya grasped hold of it in mighty joy. Then the dolphin spoke to him, saying: "What have I done to you, Child of Woman, that you repay me with such a grave insult?" And Finya asked: "Pray, where is the insult? I saw your noble beauty and wished to save you from perishing with the light." "Is it no insult then," said the dolphin, "to seize a king's daughter?" "Forgive me," said Finya, "I acted in ignorance." "Nevertheless," said the dolphin, "you shall repay me." "Willingly," said the youth. "Since you have touched," said the dolphin, "do not let go."

Then the dolphin dove into the waves and swam toward the west, and Finya clung to it about the neck. It swam until they reached a beautiful city on a rock, which the sorcerer had never seen nor heard of. Glorious was that city; it covered all of that island of rock, and it was full of good wells, palaces, and gardens, but it was silent: not a soul came out from among its walls, and the chains of the abandoned wells moaned sadly in the wind. "Go up," said the dolphin, "and pass into the central palace. There you shall find a great hall of stone, in the floor of which there is a small hole plugged with a stopper of vine leaves. Pull out this stopper and see what you shall find."

"Willingly," said the youth and clambered from the dolphin's back onto the white steps which led up toward the city. And she stayed in the water, balancing on her tail, and watched him. So many a hero has gone forth into grief.

As he went up the sorcerer marveled greatly at that city, which was vaster and more graceful than any he had seen on his travels. Compared with it the fortress of Beal, which haunted him in his dreams, was as rude as a stable and seemed fit only for dumb beasts to dwell in. Bright were the roofs of the strange city, its pillars wondrous high, its dwellings stately and spacious with goodly foundations and flowered archways; its streets, curved or straight, were well-proportioned, and its silent squares in the shadow of lofty palaces filled him with awe. Very small was the sorcerer in that city immured in oblivion. He climbed the dusty steps of the central palace, the most magnificent of them all, where stone lions gaped at him, but of living things he saw not even a dog. In the center of this palace, as the dolphin had foretold, he found an enormous hall of ancient stone, and the tiny hole stopped with vine leaves. As he was a forthright man, he did not hesitate but bent and pulled out the stopper at once.

The hall shook so that Finya was thrown forward onto his face, and he feared that the palace would topple down upon him. The walls held firm, but more terrible than the earthquake was the voice he heard, the voice of a woman whose resonance turned his bones to water: "Insolent mortal," she said. "Thinkst thou that I do not remember thee? Bitterly wilt thou regret the crime which has stained thy hand this day. This people are set beneath my curse for their pride and the depth of their wizardry, which surpassed that which it is good for mortals to know. Thou hast broken my holy curse; believe that it shall avail thee none. Thus speaks thy destiny from among the stars." "Alas!" cried Finya; for he had offended the goddess Sarma once before and was hated by her. And he heard the ringing of bells.

There were tambourines in the streets of the city, and drums, and joyful flutes; everywhere people were singing, embracing, and dancing with wild gladness. The young sorcerer pushed through the crowds to the very edge of the city in search of the dolphin who had caused him to anger the goddess Sarma. But instead of the dolphin, a beautiful maiden was swimming in the water, clad in white garments which floated about her and mixed with her long black hair. "Help me up!" cried she. And Finya went down the steps and helped her, and she stood on the white steps of her city and wept for very joy. "Thank you, blessed enchanter," said she. And Finya said: "Alas, good lady, why did you cause me to sin against the goddess who already hates me?" And the princess said: "Why, what did she say?" "That you are wicked sorcerers." "Ah, no," said the maiden: "It is she who is wicked; she hates me for my beauty." "That I can well believe," said Finya; for truly the damsel was exceedingly lovely, having bronze skin and black eyes and hair, and a shape to devastate nations. Indeed, he was well-nigh dazzled by her and found her more lovely than any woman he had seen, save only she who haunted his dreams. And the princess laughed and led him into the city filled with rejoicing, where all they passed bowed and did them homage. "Now you shall see," said she, "if ours is truly a wicked city. Stay with me for one year: for I love thee."

So Finya stayed with her in the beautiful city of wells and gardens. And she told him: "This is the city of Nine Wonders. The first wonder is our horses, which are scarlet and shine like roses. The second is our fine white hunting dogs, which can hunt at sea as well as on land. The third is our musicians, who can make men weep until they cast off all their burden of sorrow. The fourth wonder is our light, which is the most delicate in the world. The fifth is our birds, who are wise and speak like men. The sixth is our fruit: the most gratifying to the tongue, and strengthening to the body, of anything one can eat on earth. The seventh is our wine, a delight to the tongue and the heart; and the eighth is the water of our miraculous wells, so pure that it preserves us from old age, sickness and death."

"And what is the ninth wonder?" asked Finya.

"Is nothing to be held sacred?" cried the princess with a laugh; and Finya asked that she forgive his discourtesy. "I have already forgiven thee," she said. Indeed, she had a loveliness that could drive the very gods to envy.

Finya stayed with her for a year and enjoyed every good thing: hunting on land and at sea, and the best of music, wine, and horses. At the end of the year she asked him to stay longer, and he agreed, for he said to himself that there was only despair in his other suit. And he enjoyed the love of the princess, who bore him two fine children, the most passionate hunting of his life, and the wisdom of the birds. All things he enjoyed, save that he did not know the ninth wonder, which he thought must be the most wonderful of them all.

Now Finya still possessed the earring made from a piece of amber which had been given to him in the forest by the witch Brodlian, in which there dwelt his helper and familiar, the *lubnesse,* which was an owl with the sad face of a woman. Once when he was alone in the palace he rubbed at the earring, and the *lubnesse* appeared flapping before him. "O *lubnesse,*" said Finya, "I wish to know the ninth wonder." "Art thou yet unsatisfied?" said she. "Yes," said he: "Without this knowledge I cannot enjoy the other wonders." "Not even thy wife," asked the *lubnesse,* "and thy two children?" "Not even these," said Finya. "Then," said the *lubnesse,* "thou chosest well, when thou didst determine that thou wouldst be a wizard. Hast thou not noticed, then, that for one month out of every year, thy wife doth leave thee, taking the children with her?" "Yes," said Finya: "She goes to the sacred mountain behind the city, for it is her custom to pray at the tomb of her father." "That is as may be," said the *lubnesse.* "When next she goes there, climb the narrow stair to the top of the palace. If her dogs fly at thee, strike at them with a sheaf of wheat, and they will not devour thee. Enter the room at the top of the stair. There will be a fire burning inside, and another thing, and this is the thing that thou must throw onto the fire. Then indeed shalt thou discover the ninth wonder of the city." "May I perish," said Finya, "if I do not so."

Soon enough the time came when the princess wrapped herself in a cloak and said: "I go to pray at the tomb of my father. Let the children come with me, that they may learn our custom." "Very well," said Finya; and they parted. Then Finya went up the narrow stair which led to the top of the palace, a dark and dusty stair which seemed in disuse; great dogs rushed at him, barking and snarling with foam on their jaws, but he struck them with a sheaf of wheat and they lay down and whined. At the top of the stairs he opened a door and entered a small and dirty room where a fire smoked foully in the grate. On the table was something long and black. He picked it up and held it; and it was the long black hair of his beautiful wife.

"Alas," cried Finya, "what is this?" And he threw the hair on the fire. Then a great hush fell on the City of Nine Wonders: the music, the laughter, the footsteps, all ceased, and the only sound to be heard was that of a single voice weeping and lamenting.

Finya rushed down the stairs and out of the palace into the street, and the city was as it had been when he had first seen it: vast, empty, graceful, abandoned even by the mice. And again the chains moaned in the deserted wells. He followed the sound of weeping, and it led him to the sea; and there he saw the beautiful white dolphin, and with her two dolphin pups. And she cried: "Alas, my husband, what hast thou done?" And she wept bitter tears.

Finya, wild with grief, ran down the white steps to the sea. "Who art thou?" he cried. "Who art thou?"

"Alas," said she, "I am the ninth wonder of the City of Nine Wonders."

And she swam with her children out to sea, and was lost.

An owl gave a low, flute-like call from somewhere in the garden. For a moment I thought the High Priest was looking at me, but the light of the oil lamp writhed like a sea worm, casting wayward shadows, and his pensive gaze was impossible to trace. Miros and the others applauded, congratulating Kovyan's sister, exchanging remarks on the poignancy of the tale. Auram leaned and clasped my arm. "From memory!" he hissed in triumph. "All that from memory. She cannot read a word."

I rose, pleading exhaustion, and one of the young men led me into a dark bedchamber. The only light seeped in from the other room. Don't worry, I told myself. Only survive, survive until they bring the body to you and it crumbles on the fire. Flames grew in my mind, great bonfires, suns. The young man slapped the bed, checking it for stability or snakes. He left me, and as I sat down and pulled off my boots I heard the priest's voice clearly from the other room: "Yes, a Night Market."

A Night Market. I lay down and covered myself with the coarse blanket. The others talked late into the night, exchanging laughter. In the morning a watery sun showed me the scrubbed walls of the room patterned with shadows by the ivy over the window. Once again the angel had not come. A painting of the goddess Elueth regarded me from one wall, kneeling, her arms about a white calf. The expression on her dusky face was sad, and underneath her ran the legend: "*For I have loved thee without respite.*"

Chapter Fourteen

The Night Market

The next day we traveled farther into the Valley. And a message ran out from Kovyan's *radhu* in every direction, announcing the Night Market. It would be held outside the village of Nuillen, almost on the eastern edge of the Fayaleith. The news traveled to Terbris, Hanauri, Livallo, Narhavlin, tiny villages in the shadow of towers overgrown with moss. We followed in a carriage, jouncing along the graveled roads. Miros drove, and I sat beside him on the coachman's seat. Sometimes we stopped by the roadside and drank milk from heavy clay bowls, waving our hands to drive away flies in the shade of a chestnut tree, and the young girls who sold milk spoke to us with the glottal accent of the country, clicking their tongues when Miros teased them. They urged us to buy their pots of honey and curd, or strings of dried fish. One of them tried to sell us the skin of an otter. They had lively eyes and raggedly braided hair, always in four plaits, sometimes with tin or glass beads at the tips.

At the crest of a hill, we passed beneath the famous arch of Vanadias, the great architect of the Tombs of Hadfa. The pink stone glowed against the sky, carved with images of the harvest, of dancers, children, and animals entwined with bristling leaves. The intricacy of the carving filled me with awe and a kind of heartache, such as one feels in the presence of mystery. In the center of the arch were the proud words "*This Happy Land*," and beyond it the very shadows seemed impregnated with radiance.

At night those shadows were deep and blue, the *radhui* immense and silent, and the whole world had the quality of an engraving. The carriage trundled past temples and country villas, their white shapes standing out against the darkness, each one spellbound, arrested in torrents of light. A healing light, cool as dew. We passed the famous palace of Feilinhu, standing in nacreous grandeur against the dark lace of its woods: that triumph of Vanadias with its roof of astounding lightness, its molded, tapering pillars of white marble. Miros stopped the horses and swore gently under his breath. The palace, nocturnal, resplendent, stood among palisades of moonlight. Even the crickets were silent. Miros's voice seemed to rend the air as he spoke the immortal first line of Tamundein's poem:

"*Weil, weil tovo manyi falaren, falarenre Feilinhu.*"

Far, far on the hills now are the summers of Feilinhu,
the winds calling, the blue horses,
the balconies of the sky.
Far now are the horses of smoke:
the rain goes chasing them.
Oh my love,
if you would place on one leaf of this book
your kiss.

We watch the lightning over the hills
and imagine it is a city,
and the others dream of its lighted halls
smoking with wild cypress.
Feilinhu, they say,
and they weep.
And I weep with them, love, banquet,
sea of catalpas,
lamp I saw only in a mirror.

The moon is escaping over the land
and only the hills are alight.
There, only there can one be reminded of Feilinhu.
Where we saw the stars broken under the fountain
and saddled the horses of dawn.
And you, empress of sighs:
with your foot on the dark stair.

And she, my empress of sighs. Where was she waiting now with her ravaged hair, her deathless eyes, her perfect desolation? Waiting for me. I knew she was waiting, because she did not come. My nights were silent, but too taut to be called peaceful. Jissavet waited just beyond the dark. The night sky was distended in my dreams, sinking to earth with the weight of destructive glory behind it. In one of those dreams I reached up and touched it gently with a fingertip, and it burst like a yolk, releasing a deluge of light.

People traveled together in little groups along the roadsides, talking and laughing softly, on their way to the Night Market. There was no sign of the Telkan's Guard. I blessed Tialon privately: she must be doing all she could to keep me safe. Fireflies spangled the grass, and a festival air filled the countryside, as if the whole Valley were stirring, coming to life. At the inn in the village of Nuillen, in the old bedrooms divided with screens, the sheets held a coolness as if they had just been brought in from the fields.

We spent two days in Nuillien. During that time the inn filled up until, the landlord told us panting, people were sleeping under the tables. From the window of my room I could see little fires scattered over the square at night, where peasant families slept wrapped in their shawls. On the evening of the Market, music burst out suddenly in the streets, the rattling of drums and the shouting of merry songs, and Auram came into my room bearing a white robe over his arm, his eyes alight. "Come, *avneanyi*," he said. "It's time."

He was splendidly dressed in a surcoat embroidered in gold, its ornamental stiffness softened by the fluid lace at his wrists. Above the glow of the coat, rich bronze in the firelight, the flat white triangle of his face floated, crowned with dead-black hair. He looked at me with delight, as if I were something he had created himself: a beautiful portrait or gem-encrusted ring. His exaltation left no room for the human. I saw in his shining, ecstatic, ruthless eyes that he would not be moved no matter how I suffered.

"Come," he said with a little laugh that drove a chill into my heart. "You must dress." I undressed in silence and put on the robe he had brought for me. The silk whispered over my body, smooth and cold like a river of milk. Afterward he made me sit down and tied my hair back with a silver thread.

The mirror reflected the firelight and my face like a burnt arrow. Under the window a voice sang: "*Gallop, my little black mare.*"

"Have you been studying?" Auram asked.

"Yes."

"Have you committed it to memory?"

"Yes."

My glance strayed to the ragged little book on the table. *The Handbook of Mercies,* by Leiya Tevorova. Auram had brought it to me wrapped in old silks the color of a fallen tooth. "One of the few copies we were able to save," he said, and he pressed it into my hands and urged me to memorize the opening pages. This was the book Leiya had written in Aleilin, in the tower where she was locked away, in the days Auram called the Era of Misfortune. A handbook for the haunted. I turned away from it and met Auram's eyes in the glass.

"Come," he said. "You are ready."

The yard was full of people: word of the *avneanyi* had spread, and now, seeing Auram and me in our vivid costumes, the *huvyalhi* pressed forward. "*Avneanyi,*" someone cried. The landlord struggled through the back door and ordered the stableboys to clear a way to the carriage for us. A careworn man with a sagging paunch and protuberant blue eyes, he looked despairingly at the crowd, which was still pouring in from the street, then flung himself into their midst, moving his thick arms like a bear. "This way, *telmaron,*" he bawled. "Follow me." Auram stepped forward, smiling and nodding, gratified as an actor after a successful play, holding his hands out so that the people could brush his fingertips. No one touched me: it was as if a shell of invisible armor lay between them and the glitter of my robe. "Pray for us," they cried. Above us the sky was dancing with stars. When I reached the carriage my knees gave way and I almost sank to the ground. Someone caught my arm and supported me: Miros. "Hup!" he said, holding open the carriage door. "Here you are. Just put your foot on the step."

I crawled inside.

"*Avneanyi. Avneanyi,*" moaned the crowd.

Auram joined me, Miros closed the door, and the carriage started off. All the way to the common I had the priest's triumphant eyes on me, the cries of the *huvyalhi* ringing in my ears. At the Night Market I stepped down into the grass beside a high tent. Its stretched sides glowed, warmed from within by a lush pink light. All the moths of the

Valley seemed gathered round it, and before it sprawled the booths, flags, and torches of the Night Market.

A great crowd had gathered about a wooden stage in front of the tent, where an old man sat with a *limike* on his knee. One of his shoulders was higher than the other, a crag in the torchlight. He cradled his instrument and woke the strings to life with an ivory plectrum.

"I sing of angels," he called.

Auram held my arm. "Look, *avneanyi*!" he whispered, exultant. "See how they love angels in the Valley."

The crowd pressed close. "Anavyalhi!" someone shouted. "Mirhavli!" cried another; and the word was taken up and passed about the crowd like a skin full of wine.

"Mirhavli! Mirhavli!"

The old man smiled on his stage. His face glittered, and his voice, when he spoke again, was purified, strained through tears. That voice melted into the sound of the strings—for though *limike* means "doves' laughter," the instrument weeps. In these resonant tones the old man told

THE TALE OF THE ANGEL MIRHAVLI

Oh my house, oh men of my house
and ladies of my home,
come hearken to my goodly tale
for it will harm no one.

Oh fair she was, clear-eyed and true,
the maiden Mirhavli.
She was a fisherman's daughter
and she lived beside the sea.

She sat and sang beside the sea
and her voice was soft and low,
so lovely that the fish desired
upon the earth to go.

The fish leapt out upon the sand
and perished one by one
and Mirhavli, she gathered them

and took them into town.

"Now who shall wed our maiden fair,
our lovely Mirhavli?
For she doth make the very fish
to leap out of the sea.

"Is there a man, a marvelous man,
a man of gold and red?
For otherwise I fear our daughter
never will be wed."

He was a man, a marvelous man,
a man of gold and red;
he wore a coat of scarlet
and a gold cap on his head.

He saw the village by the sea
and swiftly came he nigh.
It was a Tolie, and clouds
were smoking in the sky.

Tall as a moonbeam, thin as a spear,
and smelling of the rose!
And as he nears the door, the light
upon his shoulder glows.

"Now see, my child, a bridegroom comes
from a country far away.
And wouldst thou join thy life to his
in the sweet month of Fanlei?"

"Oh, no, Mother, I fear this man,
I fear his bearded smile,
I fear his laughter, and his eyes
the color of cold exile."

"Hush my child, and speak no more.
My word thou must obey.

And thou shalt be married to this man
in the sweet month of Fanlei."

She followed him out of the door,
the maiden Mirhavli.
She saw him stand upon the shore
and call upon the sea.

"Mother," he called, and his voice was wild
and colder than sea-spray,
"Mother, your son is to marry
in the sweet month of Fanlei."

And straight his scarlet coat was split
and his arms spilled out between.
An arm, an arm, another arm:
in all there were thirteen.

"Oh Mother, Mother, bar the door
and hide away the key.
It is a demon and not a man
to whom you have promised me."

They barred the door, they hid the key,
they hung the willow wreath.
He came and stood outside the door
and loudly he began to roar
and gnash his narrow teeth.

"Do what you will, for good or ill,
your child must be my bride,
and I shall come for her upon
the rushing of the tide.

"Do what you will, for good or ill,
ye cannot say me nay,
and Mirhavli shall married be
in the sweet month of Fanlei."

And now the merry month is come,
the apple begins to swell,
and in the air above the field
the lark calls like a bell.

They barred the door, they hid the key,
they hung the willow wreath,
but the sea went dark, and the wind blew wild,
the sky with smoke was all defiled,
and the monster stood beneath.

"Now give to me my promised bride
or I will smite ye sore."
The villagers stood about her house
and kept him from the door.

He rolled his eyes, he gnashed his teeth,
he stretched his arms full wide.
"I shall come again at the good month's end
to claim my promised bride."

And then he struck them all with woe:
a stench rose from the sea,
and the fish no longer left their bed
at the song of Mirhavli.

The earth dried up, the green grew not,
and all were parched with thirst,
and Plague in his white dress stalked the streets
and a gull flew over with swift wing-beats
and cried, "Accursed! Accursed!"

And at last a wave rose from the sea
like the horns of a rearing ram,
and half the village it swept away
like the bursting of a dam.

"Alas, alas," the maiden wept,

"the gods have abandoned me,
for an they had not, our house had gone
to the bottom of the sea."

Now she has braided up her hair
and put on her broidered gown.
"In the morning I go to my betrothed"
she said, and laid her down.

And in the morning she rose up
and went down to the sea.
And she sang a song to comfort her,
the maiden Mirhavli.

And so like starlight was her song,
like a light that cannot wane,
that those who watched her hid their eyes
and their tears fell down like rain.

But the demon rose from the boiling sea
and his arms writhed to and fro.
"Cut out her tongue, for I cannot take her
while she singeth so."

"O demon, I shall not sing again."
But his great arms thrashed the sea,
and the people wept as they cut out the tongue
of lovely Mirhavli.

But as he bore her across the waves
with blood upon her lip,
the prayer that is not formed of words
'gan from her soul to slip.

The prayer most pleasing to the gods
was melted from her soul.
The sky grew bright, the wind blew soft
and the sea began to roll.

The great sea clasped the demon
and the maiden from him tore.
"My promised bride!" the monster cried,
but the good sea bore her on the tide
and carried her to shore.

The monster with his mother fought
in her waves so steep and high,
but at last his strength began to fail
and he foundered with a cry.

The monster with his mother strove
in her waves so high and steep,
but at last he gave a dreadful roar
and vanished in the deep.

The voice of the ancient troubador went on: it told of Mirhavli's wanderings, and of how the Telkan discovered her fainting in the Kelevain; it told of his love for her, the jealousy of his queen and concubines, their false accusations, and how Mirhavli was wrongly condemned to death. It told, too, of the miracle: her voice restored, rising over the sea. It told how the Telkan begged her to return, and how she refused, and was taken up alive by Ithnesse the Goddess of the Sea, to live forever in paradise:

Oh sweet it is to be with thee,
and sweet to be thy love,
and sweet to walk upon the grass
while the dear sun shines above.

Oh sweet it is to tread the grass
while the dear sun shines so bright,
but sweeter still to walk the hills
of the blessed Realm of Light.

As the song ended, a sense of unreality seized me, a curious detachment. It was as if the music had carried the world away. I gazed at the torches that twinkled all the way to the horizon, and found them strange. Then, with a start, I realized that my companions were quarreling.

Perhaps I was slow to notice because they were arguing in a foreign tongue: in Kestenyi, the language of Olondria's easternmost province. I recognized its hissing sound, for my master had taught me the one or two words he knew, and I had heard it among the sailors of the *Ardonyi.* I turned. I could see Miros gesturing, angry in the torch glow. The priest was hidden from me by the wall of the carriage. Suddenly Miros changed languages, saying distinctly in Olondrian: "But how can you refuse? What gives you the right?"

The priest answered sharply in Kestenyi.

"Curse your eyes!" said Miros, hoarse and vehement. "Even my mother wouldn't refuse me this—"

"And that is why you have been separated from her," Auram said flatly. "She means well, but she is weak. Her influence over you has never been of the best. It is common for women to spoil their youngest children."

"Don't talk about her," Miros said. "Only tell me why you refuse. What harm can it do?"

Again the cracked, pitiless voice answered in the eastern tongue. The priest's hand appeared beyond the edge of the carriage, jewel-fingered, trailing lace.

Miros shouted, and I suppose he was told to lower his voice, for he continued in a wild, strained whisper, a passionate outburst of Kestenyi which his uncle punctuated with brief, crackling retorts. Then it seemed as though Miros was pleading. I backed away from him, toward the tent. "Uncle!" he said in Olondrian. "You were young once—you have experienced—"

"You have said enough," said the priest in a cold rage. He whirled around the side of the vehicle, stalked toward me and took my arm.

"Wait!" cried Miros. But the priest dragged me forward toward the door of the tent. When I looked back, Miros was clutching his hair in both hands, his eyes closed. Auram pulled the tent flap aside and we entered the rosy light, and I did not see Miros again until after the fire.

Lamps burned on tables inside the tent. There was grass underfoot, its dry autumnal odor strong in the warmth. There was also, in the center of the space, a high carved chair—brought from a temple, I guessed, or borrowed from some sympathetic landowner of the district. How swiftly they must have ridden to place it here, so that I might sit as I sat now in my white robe, my hands clamped tight on its lacquered arms. Auram was himself again, forgetting his quarrel with Miros. He traced a circle on my brow and whispered joyfully: "It begins."

He went outside. Dear gods, I thought, what am I doing here?

There was a pause in the murmur of the crowd that had gathered before the tent. I only realized how loud that droning had been when it stopped, as one becomes aware, in a summer silence, of the music of cicadas.

Auram's voice rose harsh and pure. "Children of Avalei! Children of the Ripened Grain! Who would hear an *avneanyi* speak?"

"I, *veimaro*!" cried a woman's voice. "I and Tais my daughter."

"Come then," said Auram impressively. "He awaits."

He led them in: a girl, a woman in wooden slippers, a bent old man. "Avalei hears you," he said, and went out.

The woman sank down and advanced on her knees, pulling her daughter behind her with some difficulty, for the girl would not kneel but walked stiffly with a fixed gaze.

"*Avneanyi*," the woman sobbed. She put her hand over her face. It was clear that she had not intended to address me in tears.

I clutched the arms of the chair. After a moment she regained control of herself and looked up, still shaking, drawing her arm across her eyes. "*Avneanyi*," she moaned. "You must help us. It is for the sake of a child. A little child—you know how Avalei loves them."

"Please stand," I said, but she would not. She looked at me wonderingly, as if my slight accent increased her awe. Her daughter, still standing, gazed at the tent wall.

"It's my grandchild," the woman said. "My daughter's son. A little boy—three years old when we lost him a year ago."

"I can't," I said.

She looked at me eagerly, her lips parted.

"I can't promise anything," I amended. "But I will try."

"Thank you, thank you!" she whispered with shining eyes. "Thank you," the old man echoed behind her, seated cross-legged on the grass.

And I looked at one of the little red lamps. I listened to my heart until it grew steady. And I conjured up Leiya Tevorova's words like a smokeless fire.

The Afflicted must sit facing in the direction of the North, which, though it be not the Dwelling-Place of the Angel, is yet the place which draws the Spirit to it with its Vapors, and thus may keep it lingering in its Environs. The Afflicted must then bring to mind a certain Wraith or Image which shall have the form of a Mountain of Nine Gorges. Each of the Gorges shall be deep, ragged, and abysmal, and filled with brilliant and icy Vapors withal. The Afflicted must pursue this Vision until it is well attained, building up the Mountain Stone by Stone. When he has achieved it, he must cause, by an action of Mind, a Tree to grow from each of the Nine Gorges. And the Nine Trees shall have a golden Bark, and various Limbs, of which there shall be Nine Hundred on each Tree: one hundred of Ruby, one hundred of Sapphire, one hundred of Carnelian, one hundred of Emerald, one hundred of Chalcedony; and one hundred also of Amethyst, Topaz, Opal, and Lapis Lazuli; and these shall flash with a most unusual Splendor. When the Afflicted has mastered this—the Gorges, and the Trees, and the Branches which are nine times nine hundred in number—then will he be dazzled most grievously by virtue of the Radiance of that Image, which he will maintain through sore Travail. And when he is able to look upon it without Agony of Spirit, then must he bring into his Vision miraculous Birds, of which there shall be nine hundred on each of the Branches of the Nine Trees; and each Bird shall have nine thousand colored Feathers. On each of the Birds one thousand Feathers shall be jetty black, one thousand white, one thousand blue, one thousand others yellow; and one thousand each of red, green, purple, and bright orange; and one thousand feathers shall be clear as Glass. The Afflicted must perceive these things at once: the Mountain, the Gorges, the Trees with all their Limbs, and the colored Birds. Then shall there come a moment of most dreadful Suffering, which shall be sharp, white, and heated as if in a Forge. And when that Moment has passed, the Afflicted shall no longer see the Mountain, nor any of the things he has lately perceived; but another Vision shall take its place, an unfamiliar Image which shall take a form such as that of a Wood or a Cave. Then shall the Afflicted enter the Cave, or the Wood, or the Strange House, or whatever Image is by him perceived; he shall walk until the Image grows obscured with a gaping Darkness. And in that Darkness he shall meet the Angel.

"Jissavet," I said. "Answer me."

The red lamp burned, and the angel arrived. She stood there in her shift, her shoulders bright as dawn. Her bare feet tore the fabric of the air. Sparks clung to her plaits; her inimical light engulfed the glow of the little red lamp. A veiled light, certainly less than what she was capable of, but still a light intrinsically hostile to life. In the islands we say that death is dark, but I know there is a light beyond that door, intolerable, beyond compare.

"Jevick," she said. Her absorbed, caressing voice. Her expression of longing and the wildness in her beautiful brooding eyes. She raised her hand, and I stiffened and closed my eyes, expecting a blow, but she did not strike. "Jevick," she said again: a glass shard in my brain.

Words came back to me, whispered prayers, ritual incantations: *Preserve us, O gods, from those who speak without voices.* With an effort of will, my eyes tightly closed, my head pressed back against the chair, I forced myself to say: "I have a question."

"I will tell you everything," she said. "I will tell you everything that happened. You will write it for me in the *vallon.*"

I opened my eyes. She hung in the middle air, her hand still raised in an orator's gesture. All about her gleamed a soft albescent fire. She smiled at me, stars falling. "I was waiting for you. I knew you'd call me. You are that rare thing, I said: a wise man from the islands."

I swallowed and stumbled on. "My question. My question is for this woman here, this Olondrian woman. Her grandson is lost. Do you know where he is?"

She stared at me from the circle of her light. She was still so small. Had I stood beside her I could have looked straight down on the top of her head. I sat, frozen, on the Olondrian chair, not daring to move. After a moment I managed to say: "This woman's grandson . . ."

"Grandson," she said. Her glance was like a needle. It was her glance of startling clarity, which I remembered from the *Ardonyi.*

Then her voice clashed against my brain in a shower of brilliant sparks. "What do you want? Are you asking me to find him? You dare to ask me that?"

"Not me. These people. Their priest. He said you could answer—"

"Answer! Do you like to see me? Does it please you?"

She advanced, a golden menace.

"No," I screamed.

"For me it is the same. *The same.* To enter the country again—*that* country—among the living—never! I couldn't bear it!"

She shuddered, throwing off light. I could feel her dread, as strong as my own, the dread of crossing. She clenched her fists. "Write me a *vallon*," she said.

"I can't. Jissavet, these people are trying to help you. They'll find—they'll find your—"

"Write me a *vallon!*"

"Stop!" I screamed, pressing my hands over my eyes. The outlines of my fingers throbbed before me, huge and blurred, the blood in the body like oil in a lamp. Then she was gone.

I came to myself on the ground, in the odor of vomit. "Grandson," I murmured. A face floated over me, tearful, the face of a stranger. An Olondrian peasant woman. My head was pillowed on her knees. "Thank you, my son," she sobbed, her fingers in my hair.

"But I told you nothing."

"We felt her. We saw your torment. *Avneayni* . . ."

I rolled away from her, sat up after a brief struggle, spat in the grass. My chair lay on its side. Two of the little lamps had gone out; another blinked madly on the verge of dissolution. And we—myself, the woman, and the old man she had brought with her—we looked at one another like the survivors of a deluge. The girl still stared at the wall. She stood in that same attitude, as if exiled from life, when out on the starlit commons a storm arose.

At first I thought it merely the noise of the Market. Some new attraction must have arrived, I thought dully: dancers or a wagon full of clowns. Then, as the woman was helping me stand up, a figure burst into the tent, his dark face wild and sweating. "Fly, fly!" he shrieked. "It's the Guard!"

Stains on his robe—earth or blood. "The Guard, I tell you!" he shouted, waving hands like claws as if threatening to tear us apart. A moment his shadow chased itself over the walls, and then he fled. As the tent flap opened and fell, I caught a glimpse of fire.

Then we moved. We ran as one. Not for long—the moment I stepped outside, a rushing figure slammed into me, and I fell. A taste of Olondrian soil in my mouth. When I scrambled to my feet the people who had been with me were gone and the earth was on fire.

Heat blew toward me, crackling, lifting my hair.

The booths were burning. People writhed on the ground, flame-laced, and the dry grass turned to smoke.

Against the firelight, horses. They reared and plunged in the air, screaming with fear and rage. Their riders wore helmets and wielded clubs and did not fall. Their huge silhouettes struck grimly, without hesitation, again and again. Near me a girl rolled senseless, firelit blood in her hair.

Screams wracked the night.

The horseman who had struck the girl turned his beast, whirling his club above his head. "*E drom!*" he shouted. *The Stone*. His stallion's hooves knives in the air, his weapon a blur. I ducked, lifted my robe to the level of my knees, and ran.

We were all running, scattered like mice in flood time. We ran for the fields, the nearby woods, and they chased us, exchanging cries like hunters. The history books would tell of the burning of the Night Market of Nuillen, but they would erase the terror, the stench of blood and soot. And the noise—the noise. Running, I struck my foot on a stone and fell with a splash, up to my chin in an irrigation ditch. The sides were steep enough to provide a chance that a horse would not tread on me if I stayed close. I lay flat in the mud, screams in my ears.

I turned myself sideways, wriggled into the side of the ditch, and plastered my body with mud. A little water flowed past me sluggishly, red with fire. Horses flew over like eagles. My eyelids shuddered, stung by smoke. Toward dawn the fire leapt over me, singeing the field, and was gone.

Chapter Fifteen

This Happy Land

I emerged from the bank, like Leilin the first woman, the Olondrian goddess of clay. The *Book of Mysteries* tells how she rose, "a speaking clod." She awoke in a world new-formed, but the world I entered was old already, incalculably old, smoke-stained, silent. Its hair had gone gray.

Ashes blew on the breeze. In the fog that rolled from the commons, figures moved, bent over like reapers, searching, sobbing names.

I knelt and scooped up a little muddy water from the ditch. My throat was sore, and the water had a charred taste. Then I stood and set out over the field, barefoot, my slippers lost in my flight. I was going back to the commons.

The great tent where the angel had spoken was gone. Its poles still smoldered on the ground.

I walked among the survivors, crying a name, like them. *Miros.* My throat shut up, my voice a whisper. Every effort to shout, every breath, striped my lungs and throat with pain.

I thought I would never find him. I thought he was dead. I could not see the shape of the carriage anywhere. In the center of the commons, where the Night Market had been most crowded, the burned bodies were unrecognizable.

Somewhere near the center I sat down. A booth had collapsed nearby, festooned with long streamers of blackened lace. Coins lay in the ashes on the ground, dark triangles secretive as letters. Beads had fallen from a wrist.

I put my head down on my knees and wept. I wept for those who had died in the fire, who had come to buy and sell, to make merry, to speak with an *avneanyi.* I wept for those whose loved ones were lost on the other side of the trembling door, who would not come again from the land of the dead. I wept for myself. I wept because I was haunted, hounded into the Valley—the cause, against my will, of a great sorrow.

When I looked up I saw a rough youth with a dirty rag tied about his head, and in his pale profile I recognized my friend.

I stood up. "Miros," I shouted. My voice a creak.

He did not know me at first. His gaze slipped over me, anxious and hurried, searching among the ruins. Then I took a step forward and his eyes returned to my face and he ran toward me and caught me in a fierce embrace.

"Jevick!" he croaked.

"Miros!"

"I thought you were dead—"

"Your uncle—"

"Alive, in the carriage, hard by the wood. Come." He seized my arm and began to run. I was slower than he, gasping, my lungs tight. He glanced at me. "Sorry," he panted. "You've got to run. The Guard will be back before long."

"Back," I wheezed.

"They'll have to get rid of the bodies," he said shortly. "Clean the commons."

We ran, the silence broken only by our breath. The carriage stood at the edge of the forest, spared like the trees by the slant of the wind. Its sides were sooty, and there was only one horse.

"Where are we going to go?" I whispered.

Miros looked up from checking the harness. "East. My uncle's servants are coming downriver with—what you wanted. We'll cross on the ferry and meet them in Klah-ne-Wiy."

"Thank you," I said.

He nodded, looking bleakly across the burnt commons. "Let's go."

I opened the door of the carriage to receive another shock. There on the seat lay a bald old man, unconscious, wrapped in a blanket. "Miros!" I said, and he answered from the coachman's perch: "Get in, there isn't time." And I obeyed him, and pulled the door shut with a shaking hand. I sat on the seat across from the old man and looked at him. His face was a mass of stains, as if he had been pilloried in some brutal ritual. I recognized in that withered face, that flat head and pointed chin, the ravaged features of Auram, High Priest of Avalei.

The hair. The hair was a wig. I pressed back against the seat, my heart thudding. The eyebrows were painted on, the eyes enhanced with black paint and belladonna, the wrinkles disguised with unguents, embalmed in powder. The whole man was a creation, re-created every day. The lips, of course, had always been too red. The hands must be treated too: I shuddered at the thought of their touch, their white, elastic fingers. And everything clarified as if a veil had been ripped asunder: the priest's hooded cloak, his unusual, querulous voice. I realized that I had never seen his face in daylight till now. And the thought, coming suddenly, made my hair stand up. I felt my skin shrink, prickling all along my arms as if I had seen Dit-Peta, the island demon "Old Man of Youth."

He did not wake. As we drew away from the fire, into clearer air, the sun shone through the window onto his creased expanse of forehead. For the first time his face had definition. It was human now: touching and impressive as a skull.

He did not wake for five days. Miros cradled the ancient head in his lap and forced a trickle of water between the dry lips. We bought cured meat at a peasant house and built a fire in a meadow and Miros boiled the meat in a metal bowl to make soup. His eyes bright in the firelight, his face drawn. "I told him to die," he said. "The night of the Market. We had a quarrel. . . . I told him I wished he was dead."

"It's not your fault," I said.

"It's not yours either," he countered, watching me sternly through the flames. "I know what you're thinking."

I looked away, at the priest. "He's so old."

Miros laughed then, tears in his eyes. "How old did you think he was?"

"Forty . . . Perhaps forty-five. . . ."

"Forty!" he shouted, falling on his side. "Tell him when he wakes up. . . ." Then he sat up and stifled his laughter, saying hastily: "No—never mention it."

"His energy," I said, dazed. "He walks so quickly, stands so upright—"

"That's *bolma*. You don't know it? The Sea-Kings used to take it, down in Evmeni. It's incredibly expensive. The old man lives on it. Sometimes he chews *milim*, too, because the *bolma* makes him crazy."

"Is it because he's a priest?" I asked.

"Ha!" grunted Miros. "It's because he's an idiotic old camel."

He cooled the soup and fed it to the priest, the liquid trickling down the old man's chin, into the ridges of his neck.

We traveled slowly to spare the horse. The country grew rough and empty. Miros made use of cart tracks, avoiding the King's Road. We drank at a stream and washed there. I found my satchel in the carriage, with all my books and clothes, and Tialon's letters. The priest's big traveling trunk was there too, and Miros's few belongings, consisting largely of tobacco and bottles of *teiva*. I remembered Auram's words: "We must expect to be found." He had lived as he spoke. He had come to the Night Market fearlessly and prepared for flight.

We walked downhill to a stream to gather water. Miros carried the bowl we used for cooking, and I had an empty jar. The jar had once held a preparation belonging to the priest, and when we drank from it the water stung like perfume. Still we filled it everywhere we could. That day the light was tender, and flocks of miniature butterflies hovered in the grass like mist. Suddenly Miros stumbled and sank on one knee. "Oh gods," he said. Sobbing, undone. Water sloshing over his boots.

That day I took his arm and helped him up, I made him drink, I pulled him out of frenzy. And in the night he did the same for me, for the ghost appeared in the carriage where we slept curled up against the chill and I filled the air with wild smoke-roughened cries. She was close, so close. All the fulgent stars were drawn about her like a mantle, and her face shone clenched and angry, a knot of flame. "Write me a *vallon!*" she said. And a landscape burned across my vision, the coast as flat as the sea: her memory, not mine.

"Write me a *vallon!*"

When she let me go I was outside, on the ground. A dark meadow about me and all the stars in place. Miros held my shoulders to stop my thrashing. "I'm all right," I gasped, and he released me and sat panting, a clump of shadow.

"What," he said. "What."

"The angel," I said. I was glad I could not see his face.

"Dear gods."

He was silent for a time, arms about his knees. I sat up, breathing slowly, waiting for the shaking to pass. A wind slipped gently past us, a murmur in the weeds.

Then Miros asked in a low, troubled voice: "Is it always like this?"

"Always. Yes."

And I thought to myself: *It will be like this from now on.* I had refused the angel; she knew that I would not do as she asked; she would hound me across Olondria like the trace of an evil deed. "I am sorry," Miros said, and I scarcely heard him. His words meant less to me than his hand, pulling me up and guiding me to the carriage, and his efforts to make the next day ordinary: his jokes about water, his tug at the reins, his cracked lips whistling a broken tune.

On the fifth day we stopped at a huge old *radhu*. The falling dusk had a tincture of violets. I made out a sprawling building in the gloom: broad sections had crumbled away from it, leaving raw holes, and scattered stones lay about the yard along with pieces of rotten beams. The place had an air of decay, yet goats went springing away through the rubble and a girl came out with a yellowed basin of water to wash our hands. She had black eyes, a restless manner and a firm, obstinate jaw. When we had washed she tossed the water into the weeds.

Miros lifted his uncle from the carriage, and without comment, without a single word, the girl led us into the house. There we found a dark, smoky room with a carpet on the floor. Miros laid the unconscious priest down near its edge.

"What's the matter with him?" asked the girl.

"He's had a fall," Miros said curtly. A moment later he paused and met her eyes. "The truth is, we've come from the Night Market outside Nuillen."

Her eyes widened, but she said only: "You are most welcome, *telmaron*."

Slowly, furtively, the *huvyalhi* came out of the darkness, wearing the faded blue robes of their class. There was a bent, defeated-looking woman, a tall girl with a vacant smile, and an aged man who mumbled incessantly. Last of all came a small girl, perhaps nine or ten years old, whose face had been horribly disfigured by smallpox. There were no men but the demented grandfather, and no infants. The bent woman and the tall girl stared at us with their mouths open.

The black-eyed girl with the firm jaw, who clearly ran the household, brought us wooden bowls of stew and rough tin spoons. She looked no older than sixteen, and her hair hung in four plaits, but she had the capable hands and decided tread of a matron. She arranged the two older women—her mother and sister, I supposed—on a mat and gave them a bowl and spoon to share. Both of them wore white scarves bound tightly around their heads, a mark of widowhood.

The little girl came around with cups of water. She was a lively, graceful creature, with snapping black eyes in her melted face. Miros could hardly look at her, and his hand shook as he spooned stew into his mouth. He asked in a subdued voice about the mumbling old man.

"My mother's father," the matronly girl explained. "He has rheumatism and cramp, and is almost blind with cataracts. But in his day, he was a bull! He plowed the fields by hand and built this room when he was already old. He attacked the *dadeshi* with his big knife—men on horseback, imagine! He used to keep their dried-up ears in a box. . . ."

"Until Kiami ate them," the small girl added wickedly, her lovely eyes flashing at her sister.

The older girl showed her sixteen years in a burst of wild laughter, putting one hand quickly over her mouth.

"Who's Kiami?" Miros asked.

"One of the cats," said the younger girl. "Oh! Grandfather was angry! He pulled our hair. . . ."

The child, utterly unconcerned with her sad and monstrous appearance, regaled us with stories of this most incorrigible of animals. She sat with her legs crossed, her back straight and her arms relaxed, sometimes raising a tiny finger for emphasis. Her speech was rapid, her eyes shone with mischief and intelligence; she was all brightness, merriment, and vivacity. Her sister's black eyes softened as she looked at the slender child with the wonderful strength of character and the rough, reptilian features. The little girl so enjoyed the attention and her own inventiveness that she ended the story prostrated with giggles. Even Miros smiled, and some of the old animation came back to his face as he put down his bowl and said: "A demon, your Kiami!"

When the child went out for more water, her older sister leaned forward and said in a tense whisper: "You've really come from the Night Market?"

"Yes," said Miros.

"The one where so many were killed?"

"Yes."

"Yes," the girl said bitterly. "That is Olondria these days."

All at once her mother broke in softly: "We have no men anymore. Ours is a house without windows. He is the last."

She was pointing her soiled spoon at the grandfather. Her intent gaze, and the strange way she had blurted out the words, cast a pall over the room.

"Yes, Mama," her daughter answered soothingly. "They know." She turned to us. "An accident," she explained. "A part of the house fell on my brothers and killed them, both of them. And my father died before them, of an ague."

"*Bamai,*" Miros whispered—*Bamanan ai,* "May it go out," the old Olondrian charm against misfortune.

"Oh, it's already gone out." The girl smiled, rising to collect the dishes. "Evil's gone through this house. We're safe now. Nothing else can happen to us."

Afterward she led me to a dank, smoke-blackened room. "Thank you," I said. The girl turned, careless, bearing away her little lamp. Through an aperture high in the wall the stars showed white. There was a battered screen, a straw pallet on the floor, a cracked washbowl. Such poverty, such unrelenting hardship. I touched the screen, which perhaps contained, as many old Valley furnishings did, scenes from the *Romance.* The forest of Beal, its trees a network of spikes. Or the tale of a saint, Breim the Enchanter or poor Leiya Tevorova, haunted by an angel.

I closed my eyes and touched my brow to the screen. Fire behind my eyelids. Suddenly a storm of trembling swept over me. My mind was still numb, detached, but my body could not bear what had happened. I sank down and curled up on the moldy pallet.

There I thought of the *huvyalhi* of the Market, and of our hosts in this desolate place. I thought of the woman who had wept over me in the tent. I wanted to do something for them, for these abandoned girls, to give them a word or a sign, to carry something other than horror. But I possessed nothing else. And when the angel appeared, shrugging her way through the elements, born in a shower of sparks, I thought that perhaps this horror itself could become something else, could be used, as Auram had said. That I could be haunted to some purpose.

Her light was dim; she looked like a living girl but for her slight radiance, a crimson aura coloring the air. Beneath the jagged hole in the wall she clasped her hands and gazed at me with a seeking look, an expression of abject longing. There was a stealthy force behind that gaze, a ruthless intelligence that sent terror to the marrow of my bones. A will that would not flag though eternity passed; a strength that would not tire. Yet her eyes were like those of a lover or a child.

She loosened her fingers. "Write," she whispered. A faint smile on her lips. She mimed the clapping of hands with another child, singing an island song.

> *My father is a palm*
> *and my mother is a jacaranda tree.*
> *I go sailing from Ilavet to Prav*
> *in my boat, in my little skin boat.*

I knew the song. The familiar tongue. It occurred to me that only with her could I hear my own language spoken in this country of books and angels. She laughed when she came to the second verse: "*a bowl of green mango soup.*" And I remembered trying to make Jom sing, in the courtyard under the orange trees.

"Jissavet. Stop."

She paused, her mouth open. A frown: cities on fire.

"Jissavet. I need your help. For these people. I'm in a house in the Valley."

The air bent, warped about her.

"Stop. Listen. Such cruel things have happened to them. If you could tell them something. Something to give them hope."

She looked at me with inconsolable eyes. "I can't. I told you. There's a void between—it's horrible. And they are not people like me."

"They are."

She shook her head. "No. You are people like me. You are my people." And again her voice, light and eerie, rose in song. This time she sang of the valleys and plains of Tinimavet, the estuaries where the great rivers rolled in mud to the sea. She sang of the fishermen whose bodies grew accustomed to the air, who could not, like other men, be driven mad by the constant wind. And she sang the long story of Itiknapet the Voyager, who first led the people to the islands.

And when they came upon the risen lands
they found them beautiful,
newly sprung from the sea
with rivers of oil.

She sang of those lands. The Risen Lands, fragrant with calamus. *Kideti-palet*: the Islands of the People.

"*And this shall be the place where the people live,*" the angel sang. "*This shall be the home of the human beings.*"

I remembered it, I felt it—home, with all its distant sweetness—I remembered it through the high voice of the dead girl. One memory in particular came back to me when she sang: that early memory of how I had tried to teach a song to my brother. "My father is a palm," I said. "Repeat!" He said: "My father." "Is a palm," I insisted. But he would not answer. He gazed into the trees, rubbing the edge of his sandal in the chalky groove between the flagstones. As always when he was pressed, he seemed to recede behind a protective wall of incomprehension and maddening nonchalance.

I saw him clearly. How old was he? Six, perhaps seven years old. He was already unable to learn, but my father had not yet noticed. He wore a short blue vest with fiery red-orange embroidery, just like mine. His trouser leg was torn. If I asked him how he had torn it he would not know, or he would not tell me, though the edges of the tear were stained with blood. He would not even complain he was hurt, though he must have cut his knee, somewhere, in a place that would never be named.

"My father is a palm," I said. "Repeat!"

I had seen other children play the game. I had learned it from them, copied the intricate clapping—this was what I had brought for my brother. When I shouted at him a wariness went flitting across his gaze like the wing of a bird.

"You say it," I snarled through clenched teeth, glaring, trying to frighten him—to break through his simplicity and reach him.

He looked away, his eyes uncertain. Did he know what was coming?

My two fists rammed straight into his chest, and he sprawled on his back, howling.

And now, years later, in a strange land, to the sound of an angel's singing, I relived that moment of despair, that attempt to bridge the divide, that terrible reaching, desperate and cruel, when love swerved into violence, when I would have torn the skin from his face to discover what lay beneath.

"Jevick," the angel whispered.

Her eyes met mine, black, secretive, moonless. Her luminous gaze. "Why don't you answer me? Why don't you write?"

Grief and rage, a gathering ocean.

"I can't," I said. "I can't."

"Listen to me!" she screamed.

And the waves fell in a rush.

The silence struck me like a blow. I sat up, sweating and panting, and looked into the lighted face of a demon.

It hovered above me, a deformed face with elements of the human and of the iguana. Its fleshless lips were parted, showing tiny teeth. I shrank toward the wall, cold with terror, and babbled a snatch of Kideti prayer: "From what is unseen . . . from what is afoot before dawn . . ."

"You had a bad dream," the demon said in the language of the north. Its voice was husky and childish, with a slight lisp.

"God of my father," I whispered, trembling. I wiped my face on the sheet. The shapes in the room began to resolve themselves: I recognized the window and marked the position of the screen, and knew that the figure before me was no monster, but the scarred child. She was dressed in a tattered blue shift, made no doubt from a worn-out robe, and her soft hair, unplaited, stood up around her head. She was holding a saucer of oil in which a twist of cotton was burning with a light that fluttered like a dying insect.

"You shouted," she said.

"No doubt I did," I muttered.

"What did you dream about?"

"An angel," I said. I looked up into her face, trying to focus on her beautiful eyes with their vibrancy, their sweet directness. She looked back at me curiously.

"If you have a bad dream, you should never stay in bed. You should get up. Look." She set the saucer of oil on the floor, took my wrist, and pulled until I got up from the pallet. Then she stretched her arms above her head. "You do this. Yes. Now you turn around." Slowly we rotated, our hands in the air, our shadows huge on the walls, while the child recited solemnly:

I greet thee, I greet thee:
Send me a little white rose,
And I will give thee a deer's heart.

"There," she said, letting her arms fall. She smiled at me, brightness brimming in her eyes. "You ought to say it around a garlic plant, but we're not allowed out at night. The others are on the roof. Do you want to go up?"

I nodded and put on my shirt, and the child picked up her meager light and glided soundlessly into the hall. The rooms were black and vacant; we surprised rats in the corners. The air was chill, with the odor of moldy straw. I saw that a *radhu*—often so bright, so cheerfully domestic—could also be a place of stark desolation. The bare feet of the child were silent on the cold stone floors, and the light she held up trembled under the arches.

At last we came to a narrow stairway where the air was fresh and the stars looked down through a triangular hole in the roof. The stairs were so steep that the girl crawled up and I followed the soles of her feet, already hearing soft voices outside. We emerged onto the roof, into the immeasurable night. The sky was littered with sharp, crystal stars. A sliver of moon diffused its powdery light onto the ruined house and the consummate stillness of the surrounding fields.

"Jevick!" Miros cried in a voice so heavily laden with feeling that I knew he was drunk even before I saw him. "Thank Avalei you've come. This is terrible. It's been terrible."

I moved toward him. Vines rustled about my ankles.

"Amaiv!" said a sharp voice. "What are you doing with that light? Put it out, and don't spill the oil."

The little girl blew out the light obediently. "He had a bad dream, *yamas*."

"A bad dream." Miros sighed. "Even sleep is dangerous. . . ."

They sat against the low wall along the edge of the roof, where the vines made a thick curtain over the stone. Miros was holding a bottle and looking down, his face in shadow; the girl with the obstinate chin rested her head on his shoulder. A little apart from them sat the tall girl in the scarf, her legs splayed out and her toes pointing inward. I supposed she was half-witted. I stumbled over an empty bottle as I approached them and then sat down among the vines.

"Careful," Miros said. "If you fall off the roof, *vai*, I'll have killed an *avneanyi* on top of everything."

The girl leaning against him began to giggle and could not stop. Miros held the bottle unsteadily toward me. "There, my friend," he said. "Drink. I've given it all to Laris. We are drinking through her hospitality now."

I drank some of the cleansing *teiva* and handed back the bottle. The scarred girl, like a deft little animal, curled up her legs beside me.

"You should be in bed," the girl with Miros reprimanded her, suddenly recovering from her giggles.

"I can't sleep," the child protested, wheedling.

"You'll sleep soon enough, and then who's going to carry you downstairs?"

"I'll sleep on the roof," said the child decidedly.

"You can't sleep on the roof." The sister had lowered her head like an angry cow. It was this, along with the dogged way she spoke, and her slurred consonants, which showed me that she was very drunk as well.

Miros had one arm around her. He caressed the top of her head, and she nestled back into his shoulder with a sigh. He raised his head and looked at me, and the moonlight showed his features blurred with drink. "This is Laris," he said brokenly. "This is Laris, a true daughter of the Valley. I've already given her two bottles of *teiva*. It was all I had. I'm going to give her everything I own. It will never be enough. Never enough for the Night Market."

"Everything?" said Laris slyly, tugging the neck of his tunic.

"Ah gods," Miros groaned. "You see how it's been, my friend. Drink again. Don't take such little sips; it won't do anything. Let no one reject her hospitality."

"That's right." Laris smirked.

I drank, more to dispel my own embarrassment than from a real desire for *teiva*. The drink made the stars look brighter, cut out of the sky with a tailor's scissors. Dogs bayed away in the long fields.

"Laris, Laris," Miros said sadly. "You don't know who I am." He rested his head on the wall, his features smooth in the delicate light. "Nobody knows who I am," he murmured. "Except perhaps my uncle. Not even Jevick knows, and he is my best friend east of Sinidre."

"I know who you are," said Laris.

"No." Miros shook his head wearily, rolling it back and forth on the wall. "No one knows. Not one of you. Jevick." I felt him looking at me, though his eyes were lost in shadow. It was his cheek that shone, his brow. "You think I'm a gentleman, Jevick," he said hoarsely. "But you are wrong. I have no honor. I forget everything, everyone. I will even forget the Night Market one day. I will forget it long enough to laugh again. It makes me hate myself. . . . I tried to go into the army once. To be sent to the Lelevai. Everyone said I wouldn't go through with the training. And they were right. I drank too much—you know, when you're wearing a sword, they give you credit everywhere—and the way I gambled! Well, I had to give back the sword. For a year I thought I would die of shame. I had proved them right, my brothers, my uncles, everyone. . . . But then—" He shrugged. "I didn't have the courage to kill myself, either. It seemed so much more sensible to go hunting. . . ."

He laughed, but even the moonlight showed the stiffness around his mouth. "The truth is, I have only been good for two things in my life: and those are hunting and *londo*. Even in love I have been a failure. Even in serving a goddess. And that is why, my Laris, I sleep alone."

He kissed the top of her head. "No, no," the girl said dully, clawing vaguely at the neck of his tunic. "I know who you are. You are the man foretold to me in the *taubel*, the man with the long shadow."

"No," said Miros. "I am no one." He leaned forward and pressed the *teiva* bottle into my hand. Then, with some difficulty, he pulled himself away from Laris. He disengaged his arm from around her shoulders with infinite tenderness as she grabbed at his tunic with her blunt little hands.

"It's a mistake," she said, drunk and sorrowful, when at last he had made her hands return to her lap. "You should have loved me, *lammaro.* In this house we have no shame. All of us lost our shame when we lost our brothers."

"Look." She pointed to her sister, the tall girl in the scarf, who sat mesmerized, opening and closing her hands in the dust of moonlight. "She wears a *brodrik,* but she's not a widow. She's not even married." The girl's voice sank to a whisper: "She had a baby, though. We buried it. . . . I know she's prettier than me, but still, my time is coming. Mun Vothis read it for me in the *taubel.* A man with a long shadow, she said. He's supposed to come on a Tolie. But today isn't Tolie, is it?" She looked around at us, her face brightening.

"It's Valie." Miros's voice was muffled, his face in his hands.

"Ah! That's good. Look, Amaiv is sleeping. . . ." We all looked down at the child, who was curled up in a ball at my side.

"She would have been the most beautiful," said Laris.

The next day when we were ready to leave, as I was climbing into my seat, the girl called Laris came rushing out to me. She had not combed her hair, and her scraggly plaits jangled about her face with its broad outlines, its firm, determined jaw. She caught my arm in the shade of a spindly acacia tree by the barren court. "Are you really an *avneanyi?*" she asked breathlessly. And without waiting for an answer she pressed my palm against her stomach, closing her eyes, in a long, sensual movement. She smelled strongly of *teiva* and old sweat, and I recoiled. Laris released me, giving her wild laugh. "Thank you, *avneanyi,*" she said, the shadows of the acacia branches jagged across her smile. "When the time comes, it will quicken me."

Chapter Sixteen

The Courage of Hivnawir

Loneliness was descending on us: we were reaching the end of the country.

It was not, of course, the end of the known world: that place, marked on maps by the dire word *Ludyanith,* "without water," lay on the other side of the desert, beyond the mountains of Duoronwei. Yet the starkness of the hills of the Tavroun, rising about us, dazzled me after the delicacy and warmth of the Valley. For the first time, the road appeared ill-kept. *Go on if you like,* its pitted stones seemed to say. *It is no longer our affair.*

One afternoon we left our horse and carriage at the stable in a wayside inn and walked down to the river to board the ferry. Stones rolled beneath our feet and clay-dust rose on the wind, a single-minded and nameless wind, colder than anything I had known before I entered that wilderness. The priest was now able to walk, but he would not speak or remove his cloak, and clung to Miros's arm with his frail hand as we slipped down to the water's edge. The ferry was manned by slaves. A young girl on the boat, a bride, wept as we pulled away from the shore, trying to hide her face in her dark mantle.

Across that river, the great Ilbalin, I was to meet the angel's body. The river, bordering the highlands like the beads on a woman's skirt, was as sacred to me as it was to the ancient Olondrians and the Tavrouni mountain people, who called it the river of Daimo the God. That water, shining with subdued lights under the gray sky, would carry me to Jissavet and freedom. It stank of fish and rottenness, like the sea. On the deck an Evmeni in a black turban sold images of the gods carved from boars' teeth.

On the other side stood the village of Klah-ne-Wiy. Mud walls, windy alleys, carts and donkeys, cider in the single unhappy café. The walls and floor were black with smoke, and dried venison was sold on strings, and the villagers did not know how to play *londo.* Miros brought out his own ivory pieces and tried to teach them, but they looked at him with suspicion and sucked their pipes. Later he burned his hand trying to turn the spit on the wayward fire and one of them treated him with the juice of an aloe.

Auram crept into one of the narrow bedrooms, beckoning for Miros to follow with his trunk. Then Miros came out again, leaving his uncle alone. I did not see Auram again until the *kebma* hour, when he swept into the common room, his wig purplish in the light of the coal-oil lamps. He wore a dark red costume with a spiked collar and gold-lined cape, and smiled at me coldly with artificial teeth. His eyes blazed. He was splendid, beautifully made like an image of worship. One could believe that he would never die.

After we had eaten, Miros went to sit by the fire. Auram rubbed his waxen, shapely hands so that his rings clicked softly. "You have begun," he said to me. "Have you not?"

"Begun what?" I said, although I knew.

"You have begun to speak to her. I see it in your face."

"I do not know what you see," I said, looking back at him boldly, knowing how my face had changed, become sterner, less readable. But the priest smiled as if he saw only what he had most hoped for, though the light in his eyes, I saw with a start, was made of tears.

"Ah! *Avneanyi,* it is a privilege to watch you—you have discovered, I think, the courage of Hivnawir. You do not know the story?" He laughed, shaking his head so that the black horsehair of his wig rustled. As he spoke he chased the shadows with his hands, his narrow wrists turning in the thick lace at his cuffs. "Hivnawir," he breathed, his eyes sparkling, "is a legendary character, one of our greatest lovers. His story comes from the great era of Bain, when the clans of the Ideiri slew one another in the streets. . . . The time when the Quarter of Sighs was built with its sturdy barred windows, when it was known as the Quarter of the Princes. Bain was a city of vicious noblemen and hired assassins, yes, in the very age of its highest artistic achievements! You must imagine, *avenanyi* . . . carriages studded with iron spikes, and women who never emerged from their stone palaces. . . . Darvan the Old, who was struck through the eye with an arrow in his conservatory, and Bei the Innocent, who had his ears filled with hot lead! Hivnawir was born in that quarter and little is known of him but that, and the tale of his passion from the beautiful Taur, who was forbidden to him not only because she was promised to another but because she was the daughter of his uncle. Our painters adore this story: they have represented Hivnawir as a beautiful, fiery youth with broad shoulders, often on horseback; somehow he has become associated with oleanders and goes wreathed in white and scarlet flowers through centuries of fine art. As for myself, I have always wondered if he were not wan and petulant, a mediocre young man who simply stumbled into a legend! Perhaps he had a drooping lip or wheezed when he ran too fast. But never mind! The goddess forbid we should dabble in sacrilege! We know no more of the beauty of Taur than we do of the splendor of Hivnawir—her portrait was never painted, despite the fashion of the times. Her tyrannical father, Rothda the Truculent, locked her up in a series of stone chambers, like a poor fly in an amber pendant. It is said that she was too beautiful to be looked upon by men: there is the tale of a Nissian slave who cut his throat for love of her. No man was allowed close to her, not even her own relations: Rothda himself did not visit the little girl for years on end! It was the scandal of the city, as you can imagine; they said it was barbarous, and several young men were killed or maimed in their efforts to rescue the damsel. Soon after she was promised in marriage to one of her father's creditors, her cousin Hivnawir became inflamed by the thought of her.

"It is said that he was passing down a hall in his uncle's palace when he heard a girl's voice, sweet and sad, singing an old ballad. He was alone, and he searched the corridors for the source of the music and, unable to find it, finally called out. As soon as he spoke, the music ceased. Then he thought of his cousin Taur; he was certain that he had happened upon the regions of her prison. Knowing this, he could think of nothing else and returned there every day, carrying a taper and pounding vainly on the walls. The more he searched, the less he found, the more he craved a meeting. After all, he reasoned, she is my cousin; there can be no impropriety in my meeting her just once, simply to congratulate her on her engagement! But his determination was more than that which a kind relation would feel. He was stirred by the rumors of her perilous beauty. And Taur, in her carpeted prison, heard the faint cries of the unknown man and drew her shawl about her, trembling.

"At last his persistence began to drive her mad; she was cold around the heart, afraid to play her lyre or even to speak. And her curiosity, too, began to grow like a dark flower, so that her breath was nearly cut off by its thorns. Her women saw how she languished, losing her aspect of a bride, which they had tended so carefully by feeding her on almond paste. 'O *teldamas*,' they cried, 'what can satisfy your heart?' And she answered weakly: 'Bring me the name of the man in the corridor.'

"So it began. Once she knew his name, she became captivated by the thought of her cousin, as he was by the thought of her. The poet says that she ignited her heart by touching it to his; and after that there was no peace for either of them. Taur began to harass her women, demanding that they arrange a meeting, which they refused with exclamations of terror. She became moody and would not eat, but played her lyre and sang, so that the shouts of her distant lover grew in their inarticulate frenzy. 'Bright were her tears, falling like almond blossom'—that is Lian. Who knows where she discovered such bitter strength? Where did this secluded girl develop the strength to threaten to kill herself—to attempt to dash her brains on the wall? One supposes that she inherited the truculence of her father, along with his cunning of a *teiva* merchant . . . for just as he had satisfied a prince to whom he had lost everything at cards by promising him this pure and unseen girl as a bride, so Taur entangled her women in a net of lies and threats so that they lived in dread of the tales she might tell her father. They wept: she was a cruel girl; how could she threaten to say that they were thieves, so that their eyes would be put out with a hot iron? How could she force them to risk their lives, how could she endanger her cousin whom she loved—that unfortunate youth in the corridor? But she would not be dissuaded, and at last they reached a compromise: they would allow her to meet with the young man on the condition that they did not see one another: the women themselves would hold a silk scarf between them, so that the youth would not be deranged by the sight of her."

Auram paused. Outside the sleet was whispering in the stunted trees by the road; a donkey cart went by, creaking. The priest looked dreamily at the lamp, his painted eyes glowing deeply, slowly filling up with the tale's enchantment. "One wonders," he said softly, "how it was. One can imagine her: what it would mean, the voice in a distant passageway. She had books, after all. So no doubt her cousin became the symbol of what she lacked: the sky, the trees, the world. But he . . ." The priest gave me a brilliant, significant glance. "What of Hivnawir? He had everything. Everything: riches, women, horses, taverns, the stars! That is why I said 'the courage of Hivnawir.' It is the courage to choose not what will make us happy, but what is precious.

"Well, the cousins met. They knelt on either side of the silken scarf, neither one touching it. They spoke for hours. For days they met like that, weeks, months, speaking and whispering, singing and reciting poetry. A strange idyll, among the servant women tortured by dread, the lover risking with every meeting a sword in his reckless neck! In the stone room with its harsh outlines disguised by hanging tapestries, in the perfumed air of the artful ventilation . . . The love of voices, naturally, produces the love of lips. Imagine them pressing their ardent mouths to the silk. The poet tells us that Hivnawir outlined her shape with his hands and saw her 'like a wraith of fog in a glass.'"

The priest sat silent now, tracing a scar in the dark old table, his face still haunted by a fluttering smile. He sat that way until the sleet stopped and the night crier passed outside, wailing "*Syen s'mar,*" which is in Kestenyi: "The streets are closed."

At last I asked: "And what happened to them?"

"Oh!" The priest looked startled and then waved his hand, conjuring vague shadows. "A series of troubles—a muddled escape, an attempt on the life of the girl's intended—at last, a sword in the back for the tragic youth. And Taur burned herself in her apartments, having chosen to meet her love and to wound her father by destroying her wondrous beauty. The barb went deep, deep! For Rothda hanged himself in the arbor where, in other times, he had played *omi* with the princes of that cruel city. A famous tale! It has been used as a warning against incest and as a fanciful border for summer tablecloths. But think, *avneanyi*—" He touched my wrist; his teeth glinted. "*They never saw one another face to face.*"

Village of Klah-ne-Wiy, I remember you. I remember the shabby streets and the cold, the Tavrouni women in striped wool blankets, the one who stood by her cart selling white-hot *odash* and picking her ear with a thorn, the one who laughed in the market, her dark blue gums. I remember her, the flyaway hair and strange flat coppery face and the way she tried to sell us a string of yellow beads, a love charm. She pointed the way to the sheep market, and Miros and I bought sheepskin coats and caps and leather sleeping-sacks to survive the cold of the inn.

Cripples begged for alms outside the market. A great bull was being slaughtered there, and expectant women stood around it with pails. One of them clutched Miros's arm and quoted toothlessly: "The desert is the enemy of mankind, and the *feredhai* are the friends of the desert." Geometric patterns in rough ochre framed the doorways, turning violet in the pageantry of dusk. By the temple smoked the lanky black-haired men called the *bildiri,* those whose blood mingled the strains of the Valley and the plateau.

Only once we saw the true *feredhai,* and they were unmistakable. They came through the center of Klah-ne-Wiy in a whirl of noise and dust. There were perhaps seven of them and each man rode a separate skittering mount, and yet they moved together like an indivisible animal. They drove the dogs and children into the alleys, and women snatched their braziers out of the way, and someone shouted as baskets overturned, and yet the riders did not seem to notice but passed with their heads held high, men and ponies lean and wiry and breathing white steam in the cold. The men were young, mere boys, and their long hair was ragged and caked with dust. Their arms were bare, their chests criss-crossed with scabbards and amulets. They passed down the road and left us spitting to clear the dust from our teeth and disappeared in the twilight coloring the hills.

Then the gloomy inn, the barefoot old man shuffling out of the rooms at the back carrying the honey beer called *stedleihe,* and the way that Miros made us pause before we drank, our eyes closed, Kestenyi fashion, "allowing the dragon to pass." And the way we banged on the table until the old man brought the lentils, and later heard a moaning from the kitchen and learned that there was a shaggy cow tied up among the sacks of beans and jars of oil, with garlics around her neck to ward off disease. And the old man seemed so frightened of us and waved his hands explaining that he kept her inside to prevent the *beshaidi* from stealing her. And later we saw him taking snuff at a table with some Tavrounis; he was missing all the teeth on one side of his mouth.

Darkness, smoky air, the dirty lamps on the rickety tables and outside a mournful wail and a rhythmic clapping, and we all went to the door and watched the bride as she was carried through the streets in a procession of brilliant torches. The wind whipped the flames; the sparks flew. The bride was sitting on a chair borne on the shoulders of her kinsmen. I supposed she was the unhappy girl who had traveled with us on the ferry, though her face was hidden beneath an embroidered veil.

But I waited for another, as impatient as any bridegroom. And at last she came. We had then spent six days in Klah-ne-Wiy. She came, not carried by eunuchs and decked with the lilies sacred to Avalei but packed in a leather satchel on a stout Tavrouni's back. They slunk to the door, two of them, looking exactly like all the others except perhaps more ragged, more exhausted, their boots in stinking tatters. They had walked a long way, through the lower hills of Nain, where it was already winter and freezing mud soaked halfway up their calves. And now they were here, at home, in Klah-ne-Wiy. They sat down at a table, and the one with the satchel laid it on the floor beside his feet. Auram put his hand on my arm and nodded, his eyes drowned in sadness. I swallowed. "It's not her."

"Oh yes! Oh yes!" whispered the priest.

My insides twisted.

"Here," said Miros, alarmed, his hand on my back. "Have some *stedleihe*. Or perhaps something stronger. You! *Odashi kav'kesh!*"

"No," I said with an effort. "No." The satchel was small, too small for a human being, unless—and my stomach heaved—unless she was only bones.

"It's not her," I repeated. And then, impelled by some mysterious force: "Jissavet."

"What?" said Miros.

"Quiet!" hissed Auram. "He's calling her!"

"Jissavet. It's not you," I said. The priest whipped his head about, his eyes drawing in light, hoping to glimpse a shadow from the beyond.

"It's not you."

"There," said the priest, alarmed in his turn, "not so loud, we mustn't appear to notice them."

He bent close to me, smelling of powder and cloves, his fingers fastened on my sleeve. "When they go," he whispered. "When they go to bed, in the back. Their room's in the northwest corner. I know it. I'll get the package for you. And perhaps . . ." His tongue, hungry and uncertain, darted across his lip. "Perhaps—now that you have grown stronger—perhaps you'll address her again. Once—or twice. A few words, a few questions. It would mean a great deal to us. . . ."

I laughed. Pure laughter, for the first time since the Feast of Birds. "Oh, *veimaro*," I chuckled, seizing his face, wrinkling it in my hands. I brought it close to my own, so close that his great eyes lost their focus and went dim. "Not for an instant," I told him through my teeth. "Not once."

I released him abruptly; he fell back against his chair. The *odash* arrived, a heady liquor made from barley and served with melted butter. I gulped the foul brew down, fascinated by the battered satchel visible in the light from the dying fire. It lay there, stirring sometimes when one of the messengers touched it with his boot. Her body, rescued from the Olondrian worms.

"Jissavet," I murmured.

And then the door, always bolted, shivered under a volley of blows, and a voice cried, "Open in the name of the king!"

We stared at one another and Auram took my arm, not in panic but with deliberate softness, almost with tenderness. His voice, too, was soft, yet it penetrated beneath the pounding and the shouts at the door, boring straight into my heart. "The road behind the market," he said, "will lead you to the pass. When you have crossed the hills you will see a small river, the Yeidas. Follow that river and it will take you to Sarenha-Haladli, one of the prince's old estates. Stay there. Our people will come for you."

"What are you saying?" I murmured in a daze. The door swelled inward.

The High Priest laughed, shrugged, and brushed the side of his vast brocaded cape. "A marvelous journey. Marvelous and terrible. And perhaps we will go on together. But it is possible that this is, as it were, the last act."

He nodded to the landlord. "Open the door."

The old man lifted the bolt and sprang back as four Valley soldiers rushed into the room. Shadows leapt on the walls. All my thought was for the body, the weather-stained leather satchel that held the key to my future. I ducked beneath the table and scrambled toward it over the earthen floor, but it was gone, swept up on the back of one of the Tavrounis. "Sit down, sit down," the soldiers shouted. But my companions faced them squarely, Auram with his thin hand raised.

"Stand back in the name of Avalei," he commanded. There was a pause, a slight uncertainty on the part of those fresh-faced, well-fed Valley soldiers. Still on my knees, I grasped the Tavrouni's belt. "That's mine!" I hissed. "It's mine! You brought it for me! Give it to me, quickly!"

One of the soldiers looked at me, frowning; Auram stamped his foot to draw his attention. "What do you mean by harassing a High Priest and his men? What has the king to do with me? I am Avalei's mouthpiece. I am prosperity. And, if the hour requires it, I am evil itself."

Even in my dread I admired the old man. Straight as a young willow-tree he stood, his head thrown back, his nostrils curling with disdain. One arm was drawn across his chest, upholding the carmine brilliance of his cape. The hand behind his back, I noticed, clutched a knife.

The soldiers glanced at one another. "We mean no dishonor to Avalei or your person, *veimaro*," one of them grumbled, scratching his neck. "But we have come for a man, a foreigner." He scanned the group and pointed to me with his sword. "That one. The islander. We've come for him."

"That man is my guest," Auram said icily. "An insult to him is an insult to me and through me to the Ripener of the Grain."

"Our orders are from the Telkan," said another soldier, not the one who had spoke first, his dark face swollen with impatience.

Auram smiled. "Our speech begins to form a circle, gentlemen." His finger twirled in the air, its shadow revolving on the ceiling. "Round and round. Round and round. You invoke the king, and I invoke the goddess. Which do you think will prove the stronger?"

"Priests have committed treason before," shouted the dark-faced youth. And it was then that one of his fellows gave a start and dropped his sword. The weapon landed with a thud, and as if a spring had been released a whirr split the air and Auram's knife lodged in the dark soldier's eye.

"Run, Jevick," Miros shouted. "It's over now."

He raised a chair in the manner of one accustomed to tavern brawls. One of the soldiers struck it with his sword, and the light wood cracked and splintered. Miros ducked, fine chaff in his hair.

I sprang to my feet and seized the satchel on the Tavrouni's back. "Give it to me!" He stood his ground, splay-footed, stinking of curdled milk, and we hovered, locked together, for a long moment before I realized he was helping me, attempting to lift the strap over his head. I released him and he whipped off the strap, dropped the satchel, and drew his dagger. His companion sat on the floor, holding his stomach. One of the soldiers had fallen, his head on the hearthstone; in a moment the room filled with the sickening odor of burnt hair.

"Miros," Auram cried. He shouted a few words in rapid Kestenyi and Miros sprang to my side, using the remains of his chair as a shield. "Hurry!" he panted. "Go through the back, there's a door. I'll go with you, I know the house. Ah."

I reached for the satchel, then turned to him as he groaned.

He sank to the floor. A shadow loomed over us, a healthy and carefree shadow with crimson braid adorning its uniform. It advanced to strike, to kill. I dove for its legs and it toppled over me, its sword all slick with Miros's blood slapping on the floor.

The soldier kicked, getting his feet under him. I rolled. A Tavrouni was there, his gray teeth bared, a knife gleaming between them. He sprang on the soldier like a panther. And I—I ought to have taken the angel's body, risked everything for it, my life and the lives of others. But suddenly I could not. I thought: *Too many have died for this.* I thought: *Not what will make us happy, but what is precious.* And I did not lift a dead body from that chaos. Instead I reached for Miros. I seized him with both hands. I took my friend.

I clutched him under the armpits and dragged him into the dark kitchen where a scullery boy with a withered arm lay whimpering in the hay. The large, mild eyes of the cow observed me through the gloom, reflecting the beams of a coachlamp standing outside in the courtyard. The soldiers' coach, no doubt. Miros was breathing fast, too fast. "Miros," I said.

"Yes," he gasped.

"I'm taking you outside. Somewhere safe." I kicked the door open and dragged him into the alley. His bootheels skidded across the hard earth, leaping whenever they struck an uneven patch in the ground. He groaned with every jolt. In the dark I could not see where his wound was, how bad it was, but I saw he clutched his side, and his hands were black in the moonlight. He threw his head back, teeth clenched.

"Miros. Is it—can I—"

"Nothing," he panted. "Nothing. I've had—worse—on a hunting trip."

His words comforted me, although I knew they must be false. I glanced up: another corner among the mud houses. I rounded it, pulling my friend. A crash sounded somewhere behind us, breaking glass. It must be the window of the soldiers' coach, for the inn had only shutters. Auram, I thought. Or perhaps one of our taciturn allies from the Tavroun. I hauled Miros up to grip him more surely, provoking a cry of pain. Faster. Another corner, more silent houses, sometimes behind the thick shutters a fugitive gleam like a firefly in the dusk. My goal was to put as many of those winding turns as possible between myself and the soldiers of the king. They could not track our movements in the dark, and I hoped the earth was too hard for them to gain much from it even in daylight.

At the next corner I paused, gasping for breath in the stinging cold. Miros lay flat on the ground. His head lolled to one side. His hands on his abdomen were lax. My heart gave a spasm of dread, and I crouched to check his breath and found it was still there. I stood again, gulping the cold. The night was silent, littered with stars. This night, this same night stretched all across Olondria, and across the hills I must somehow pass, the Tavroun, said to be the necklace of a goddess flung down carelessly in flight. Dark jewels in the night, a black ridge against the stars. I knelt beside Miros again. When I moved his hands aside, blood spilled from his wound as if from a cup. I stripped off my jacket and shirt, the cold air shaking me in its jaws, put the jacket back on and tied the shirt clumsily around his waist. I feared these maneuvers would do more harm than good; but at least, I hoped, we would streak less blood through the streets of Klah-ne-Wiy. I tried taking Miros's weight on my shoulder, but he was too tall and heavy for me. I was forced to drag him as I had done before.

A fine, icy rain was falling when we reached the sleeping horse-market. The stalls were all dark, closed under covers of goatskin. The tents of the *feredhai* pitched in the square were mostly dark as well; only one or two glowed subtly through the rain. For an agonized moment

I thought of going to one of those tents for aid; these were desert people, after all, traditional enemies of the Laths, unlikely to have ties with imperial soldiers. But I was afraid. I pulled Miros through the mud of the open square and into the rocks beyond.

Cold, exhausted, I hauled his insensible body up the trail. Thorns and juniper branches snagged our clothes. Once I lost hold of him and he slid down a slope of rattling pebbles, coming to rest against the stone wall of the hill. "Off the road," I muttered. "Off the road. We have to get off the road." This thought, its promise of rest, gave me the strength to go on with my task. I slid down to him and gripped his arms once more. "Not yet, Miros. Not yet." Shivering and straining, I pulled him up the hill.

No fire. No fuel. No tinder. I dragged him into a ditch by the trail and lay down beside him. The rain had stopped, and the stars wore a veil of freezing mist. My breath curled in the darkness, white as foam. Beyond it starlight glazed the bare folds of the mountains. The Chain of the Moon.

I climbed the pass. This I have done, if I have done nothing else. I climbed the pass with Miros dragging on my arms. In his pocket I found a little penknife, and I used it to cut a strip from my sheepskin jacket which I looped under his arms and around my aching wrists. I pulled. I pulled under porcelain skies in the shadow of the pine gullies, through a landscape dark, dazzling, and inflexible, the stern cliffs topped by the pink glow of the peaks where scattered geese went flying, filling the air with dim nostalgic cries. It was uncompromising country, home of the short and rugged Tavrouni people, who call themselves *E-gla-gla-mi* and worship a pregnant goddess. Too desperate now to fear anything but death for Miros and myself I knocked at the slabs of bark that served as doors to their crooked huts. There were no villages now in the hills—all had been destroyed by either the Laths of the Valley or the warring nomads of the plateau. The huts I found belonged to taciturn shepherds who raised their goats on the meager vegetation of the cliffs. They showed no surprise when they saw me, and I recalled that bandits were said to haunt these hills and thought that these shepherds must be accustomed to such visitors—wild and wounded men who devoured their *odash* and curds without speaking and robbed them brusquely of food, water, and dried skins. From one I took a tinderbox, from another a length of Evmeni cotton. They sat by their smoking juniper fires, nursing their short clay pipes. One, a fierce graybeard with a broken nose, cleaned Miros's wound with *odash* and stitched it with gut while the patient screamed as if visited by angels.

At last, after days of exposure and hardship, we were rewarded: a door of wonders opened in the landscape. At the crest of a rocky hill, suddenly, a new world lay before us, a blaze of gold, a bleak, profound desolation: Kestenya the savage and solitary, stretched out at the foot of the mountains, the great plateau that led to the birthplace of dragons. A few isolated lines marked it: a roughness hinting at hills, a dry riverbed like the shadow of a wrist. It was the home of the bull, of the stalwart, bristle-maned desert pony. Wolves prowled at its edges through the winters. It was "a shape to make men weep," wrote Firdred of Bain when he first saw it: "exactly the shape of a desecrated sea."

I stood looking down at it, forgetting the wind. Miros, pale as wheat, rolled onto his side and stared over the edge with me. "It is a mystery," writes Firdred, "how man ever had the temerity to enter a place so forbidding and forlorn."

The sight of the desert from the pass had all the mesmeric power of a clear and moonless night resplendent with stars. It provoked the same greed of the eyes, the feeling that never, no matter how long one looked, would the image remain undamaged in the memory. It was too vast, mystic, impenetrable. And yet, as one Telkan wrote, it was nothing: "May Sarma forgive me," wrote Nuilas the Sage, "for I have caused the blood of our sons to be shed for this utterly hostile wilderness, this annihilating void of the east." Perhaps this was why I felt, dazzled, that I could never contain that sweeping vision—because it was nothing, pure nothingness: an almost featureless wasteland, golden, streaked with incarnadine, as Firdred wrote, "the color of a fingernail." To the north the chain of hills stretched on and I saw the city of Ur-Amakir in the distance, poised dramatically on a precipice over the sands, and as I stood gazing at its high stern walls the wind began to shriek and a diamond burned my face. It was the snow.

Book Five

A Garden of Spears

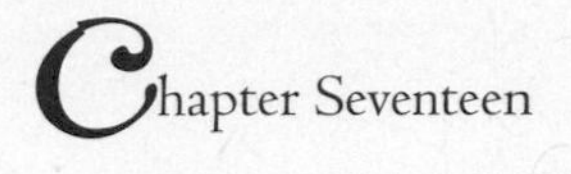

Chapter Seventeen

The House of the Horse, My Palace

The house stood on the eastern side of the Yeidas. It was the last estate, shipwrecked between the farms and the eternity of the desert. It stood in the sparse embrace of its orchard of plum and almond trees and turned its shuttered eyes on the contours of the plateau. There was the library, there the terrace with its stone balustrades, there the balconies caged in iron flowers. I remember even the creak of the gate and the shadow of my hand as I reached for it, in the argentine light of the snow.

We descended and crossed the stone bridge over the Yeidas. Miros clung to my neck, stumbling, too self-aware to let me carry him anymore. We did not speak. We moved on doggedly through a plain of lifeless scrub where emaciated cattle raised their heads to watch us pass. In the distance stood three fortresses, goats searching for grass along their crumbling ramparts. Farther still, the black pyramids of the *feredha* tents. A red cloth flashed among them and disappeared. We reached the wrought-iron gate in the granite wall that surrounded the prince's lands.

The gate leaned, rusting on its hinges, crooked as a leering mouth. We staggered up the path through the desolate orchards. The wind had fallen; Miros's breath was loud in the still air. It seemed to take a long time to reach the house. When at last we did we saw the domes of the roof spattered with crow dung and the shutters with their chips of timeworn paint, the stone walls streaked and moldering at the corners, and the terrace stretching away in the shadow of the naked rose trees. We stood and looked at the house. The sky had darkened above the foothills, and the walls faced us in the gray and grainy light. The silence had a depth, like the stillness after a bell has been struck and the echoes have died away, and one waits for what has been summoned.

The door was unlocked. It gave with a sigh. A breath of musty air, cold as a draft from a hollow hill, caressed my face. "Wait here," I said, lowering Miros to the stones of the porch. He curled up on his side at once and closed his eyes.

I pushed the door wide. "Hello," I called.

The echo mystified me until I stepped inside, into the vast domed hall of Sarenha-Haladli, a name which in the Kestenyi tongue means "The House of the Horse, My Palace," where once the prince had come for the hunting season. A floor of colored stone spread out before me, dimmed by a layer of dust and mirrored above by the painted glass of the dome. Seven arches of red and green porphyry led out of the hall, each enclosing an impenetrable darkness. The palace, as I was to learn, was circular, like a rose, for the rose is an auspicious sign in the highlands. On that first day its lightless corridors, all subtly curved, tormented me with the sinister mockery of a labyrinth.

"Hello. Hello," I shouted, running blindly through the halls. I shouted with weakness, with fever, I think—certainly not with hope. The poignant desuetude of those rooms where the tapestries crumbled at my touch was evidence that no servant lived in the house. No servant, no caretaker, no guide, and only an hour before dark. My thoughts narrowed sharply and my movements clarified, losing their desperate quality. I noted the venerable furniture stamped with imperial pomegranates: firewood. The grand floor lamps in the sitting room contained traces of precious oil. At last, with a cry of joy, I discovered a subterranean scullery housing a porcelain stove festooned with shriveled garlic, where my scrabbling fingers unearthed an old tinderbox, several candles nibbled by rats, a tin of flour, and a handful of blighted potatoes.

I lit a taper and hurried upstairs. The light did little to help me find my way: rather it dazzled me, bobbing along the corridor. Its wasp-gold spark flared over sections of grimy paper emblazoned with heliotropes, the lace of a petrified fern, the shoulder of a carved chair. "Miros," I shouted, my voice absorbed by the dark. I hurried past arched entryways where anxious statues peered out with white eyes, emerging at last into the central hall where the moonlight, flung through the doorway, set illusory crystals in the checkered floor. My bootheels skidded over the cold mosaic. "Miros." He lay where I had left him, almost in the doorway, sleeping on his side. His cheek had a grayish tinge in the candelight, like stagnant water. I pulled him out of the wind and closed the door.

The rooms were cold, mournful, decayed, full of darkness and stale odors, the beds enclosed in cupboards in the fashion of the kings. I shoved Miros into one of these beds and covered him with everything warm I could find: sheepskins, rotting tapestries, carpets heavy with dust. I made no fires; even the taper I held made me uneasy. I pictured its light seeping out across the leaning roof of the terrace. Would it find its way through the brown arabesques of the rose trees to some wilderness where a herdsman would catch it on the end of his knife?

"Water," Miros moaned in his sleep.

I gave him the last of the clear, cold stuff we had gathered at the Yeidas in a Tavrouni waterskin. He coughed, rolled over and slept. I touched his forehead: it was hot and dry. No one had looked at his wound in seven days. As we struggled over the pass I had argued to myself that there was no time to examine it; now I knew I was afraid. Tomorrow, I thought. I slipped into the next chamber and the great box bed, where I tossed on a creaking mattress stuffed with horsehair.

No sleep. No peace. I rose and, wrapped in a carpet for warmth, wrenched open the shutters weighted with cumbersome brass bolts. The moon, unveiled like a mystic revelation above the hills, exuded a silent radiance that made me blink. Olondria was gone; it was a desert night that faced me, still and proud. I was in the empire's most reluctant province, where Limros of Deinivel had remarked: "In this country of perverse inclinations there is no dog who is not a nobleman and no water that is not frozen." But Auram will come, I thought. He will come, or he will send someone with the body. If he has been slain or captured it will not remain a secret. The High Priestess will learn of it, or the prince, and they know where to find us, and they will send a rescue party over the hills.

But Auram did not come. No one came.

I do not know how long we waited in that house adrift on the edge of the boundless plain. I know that the angel came to me most nights, crying "Write" like the clanging of swords, and that I gritted my teeth in that punishment of light. My weakness was a mercy: I fainted soon. I know that I woke, sometimes in my bed, sometimes on the floor, thinking only of survival. I know that I made a number of crude messes of the foodstuffs I had found in the scullery, thinning them with water to make them last. I drew the water from a well in the garden, the frozen chain searing my hands. The pail was cracked, but I found a sound one in the scullery. It knocked against the side of the well with a fat and cheerful sound as, wasted by hunger and fear, I struggled to draw it up. A breath of wind went whispering among the trees, and they quivered, their shadows glancing over the layer of new snow on the ground. The tiny sound, the movement, emphasized the isolation of that place, so iridescent and remote. I grasped the pail at last and rested it on the lip of the well, holding my aching side, waiting for my breath. When I raised my head the trees all looked like shadows and their thorns like mist, and the sun spangled everything with leaves of ice.

I hauled the pail inside the house. Water splashed on the tiles of the main hall as I staggered through, creating bright spots on the floor, revealing the flowers of topaz under the dust, the stars of broken glass, the encrustations of jasper and chalcedony. I made my way into the nearest room with a fireplace, the formal sitting room, a chilly wasteland where peeling damask dangled from the walls, where hectic blossoms seethed in the obscurity of the carpets, and the glass in the windows shivered in the wind. The room had the desolate air of a place avoided by the living, the scene of an accident or an ancient crime, but it had become my haunt because it was close to the main door and contained a wealth of brittle furniture for my fires. Heraldic greyhounds paced through the stones of the fireplace; they seemed to snarl at me as I seized an elegant Valley chair and beat it against the floor, cracking its legs, separating them from the cushions of dark pink velvet, wreaking havoc on the embossed ptarmigans. Sweating with exertion I sat on an ancient *bredis* which had escaped my wrath because its sagging leather was difficult to burn. When I held the tinderbox to the broken chair, the stuffing went up the chimney with a blue flame and a *whoosh* like a cry of alarm.

I warmed my hands at the yellow blaze. There was no food in the house. The *bredis,* I thought reluctantly: I could boil the leather. The thought made my tortured guts writhe in my ribs. And Miros could not survive on boiled leather. He needed meat, milk, healing herbs—perhaps more. The hum of the walls in the force of the wind whose authority flattened the thorn trees kept me aware of the chilling distances outside, the endlessness of the great plateau, its vast impenitent savagery, its dreadful monotony under the wintry sky. For the first time I thought: if Auram never comes. If no one comes. I sprang up to chase the thought away and filled a blackened pot with well-water. I hung it over the fire and pulled at the damask on the walls, which came away in my hands like sheets of the finest cobweb. *If no one comes.* But he would come. I waited until the water boiled, soaked the damask in it, and hung it on the dead lamps to dry. The long strips fluttered in the warmth from the fire. When the water was cool I took the pail and the damask and carried them upstairs.

"Miros."

Each time I entered the room in dread, expecting to find a corpse—but for today at least he was still alive. The door of his box bed stood open, and he turned his head toward me and smiled, and at the sight of that smile relief died in my breast. It was not Miros's smile. It was infinitely more gentle, more withdrawn. "Good news," I said with false cheerfulness. "No stew today." My experimental dishes, which neither of us could swallow without gagging, had been a source of grim amusement during all our time in the house. But now he did not laugh, only smiled more tenderly than before, a smile as delicate and lifeless as the snow.

"I'm going to change your bandages," I said in a trembling voice. "You'll have to sit up for me. I'm sorry."

"That's all right," he said.

It tore my heart to force him to change position, to pull him out of the bed, to tug the bandages where they were stuck to his body. He was as skeletal as the denuded trees in the garden. His wound, sewn up with gut, was a sullen purple, the only color on him. I poured water over it and wrapped it in lengths of tattered damask. Then I put his filthy shirt on again, and his highlander's sheepskin jacket. I pushed him back into bed, cursing myself because I was too weak to set him down gently, and covered him up as best I could.

He was still awake. Usually he lost consciousness during my coarse attempts at nursing. His eyes were large and dark, clearer than the sky.

"Jevick," he said. "I think I'm going to die here."

"Nonsense," I said with all the heartiness I could muster. "You'll be in Sinidre next hunting season."

He sighed. "I'll never hunt again."

"Of course you will."

"No."

He looked at me proudly, and with that new distance and coldness in his face. And everything poured out of him. He spoke of his debts and his failures, and of the woman: Baroness Ailin of Ur-Melinei.

"I am a *balarin,*" he told me bitterly.

A *balarin*: a "sweet, free one": the young lover of a wealthy married woman. In Sinidre he had twice fought with those who had dared to call him this name; he had blinded a man in one eye; he was fined and narrowly escaped prison. But now he admitted that it was the truth. And he was in love with her. He had realized it fully on this journey: if he could not write to her, at least know that she would remember him, he was mad; the simplest actions became unbearable.

"That's why I fought with my uncle at the Night Market," he said, shifting restlessly on the pillow while I knelt beside his bed. "There were letter carriers there. I wanted to send a letter west, and he wouldn't let me. He has no pity; I don't think there's a nerve in his body."

The recollection seemed to stir his blood: a touch of color came into his face. His fingers gripped the blankets with a rush of strength. And as if, having broken his reserve, he was freed from all constraint, he spoke to me of the lady of Ur-Melinei.

His position was hideous, shameful. It was the scandal of his family and the mortification of everyone who knew him. He had met her on a hunting party in the Kelevain; her husband's property bordered on that forest. He had never seen her before. She disliked city society; her own people came from the western fringe of Olondria. She arranged an exclusive society in the country house: there were actors and musicians, hunting, dancing, and masquerades. She rode beautifully. It was whispered that she had Nissian blood. She was very fair, and black-haired like a barbarian. She was ten years older than he, she had three children who were away at school, and her husband was a diplomat of the Order of the Lamp.

It began as a mild flirtation. He was invited to Brovinhu, the baroness's villa, and took part in her amateur theatricals. She cast him opposite herself in such tragedies as *Fedmalie* and *The Necklace,* and swooned in his arms before an intimate audience. "Alas," she said, "thou lookest red, as if thou hast run a great distance." And he answered: "Aye: a gulf separates this hour from the rest of my life." Her husband sat in the front row, clapped his great, hard hands together, smoked cigars, and discussed the Balinfeil with distinguished visitors. Miros had planned to stay for a week; he stayed for the whole season, for the hunting, log fires, and dances on the terrace. And when the baron removed to Belenduri for the winter, Miros, with a few other friends, remained at Brovinhu.

They were lovers. She was the most captivating woman he had known: she eclipsed all the others, the friendly harlots, the high-strung daughters of noblemen. She was strange, sad, willful, seductive, brilliantly educated, an avowed recluse who surrounded herself with friends on her wild property. She refused to allow the grounds at Brovinhu to be cultivated; she loved the desolation of the woods. She would walk in the overgrown orchards with her two long, dove-colored hounds and hunt for coneys and pheasant in the tangled scrub of the fields. A thousand rumors encircled her: that she had been exiled from society for crushing the fan of the Duchess of Sinidre; that she feared to revive a forgotten scandal, a dead love affair, in the city; and the old story of her savage ancestry. Miros adored her too much even to ask her about these whispers, and at Brovinhu, surrounded by her friends, all excellent marksmen, all people who loved air, activity, and the wild woods, he saw the drabness of city society. Who could prefer the stuffy rooms with braziers under the tables, the compulsory visits to elderly noblewomen, to the great, dark hall at Brovinhu where one sprawled in front of the wood fire on thick carpets while the rain beat against the shutters? Who could prefer any place in the world to Ailin's room with the high bed and the lurid Nissian hangings studded with fragments of mirror? In the mornings she would be sitting, smoking at her dressing table. She always rose before he did. Perhaps she never slept.

He spent the most glorious winter of his life, forgetting everything. And then, in the spring, she asked him to go back. "But it's almost summer," he said. He thought he would stay for another season. She refused: her husband was coming back, and her children, for the school holidays. He returned to Sinidre in despair and embarked on the year of torture which succeeded that brief, that paradisiacal winter: a year of secret letters, gifts, jealousy, midnight rides, meetings in parks, in village inns, in temple gardens. He often rode all the way from Sinidre to Ur-Melinei, sleeping in the long grass beside the road, only to be met in the village by her taciturn maid with the lame hip, with a note: "Impossible. Go back at once." He was certain, by turns, that she loved him, despised him, longed for him, tired of him. He suspected her of taking another lover. He haunted the woods around Brovinhu and was almost shot by the gamekeeper, the arrow lodging in the top of his boot. When she refused to have him back for the winter, he knew she was deceiving him; but she wept and said that she was afraid of her husband: afraid for Miros's sake. While he wished for nothing better than the chance to kill her husband honorably, in an open duel.

"You would kill him," she said angrily. "You, an unaccomplished boy, would kill a lord of the Order of the Lamp?"

Miros departed in rage. And then, breaking every rule she had set herself, she came, disguised, to see him in Sinidre.

They had two days. They lived secretly by the docks, in the Kalak quarter, among vendors of raw fish and green tea laden with salt, in the shabby wood houses with nets hung up in the doorways, the shrieking of hungry gulls, the sound of Kalak being spoken everywhere. At the end she looked at him, deadly pale, and said: "Very well. Kill him." It was all that he had asked for. He was ready to kill, or to die. But other forces opposed him: when he appeared at home he was summoned immediately to a *radmakanid*—a family council.

By this time the scandal had reached dangerous proportions. Anonymous letters had been received by his father and his uncles; even his great-uncle the Priest of Avalei had received one on the Isle, and had arrived in Sinidre in a fierce temper. Everyone Miros loved and respected most was there in the spacious sitting room with the polished wood floor, the tall harp in the corner, the room adjoining his mother's latticed garden. They had drawn the curtains and lit only one of the lamps, for the priest liked his surroundings dim. Miros's mother was there, twisting her overskirt in her fine hands, and her brothers, his four successful, strong-willed uncles; her sister, his aunt, who, he thought, looked at him with some sympathy; and his father, and Miros's three brothers and one elder sister. In accordance with Olondrian tradition, it was his maternal uncles and not his father who headed the *radmakanid*, for Miros belonged to their House and would inherit through his mother's family. Chief among them, the eldest and most powerful, was the High Priest. Miros sat quietly before them, his face lashed by their accusations as if by blows, and watched his brothers irritably examining their boots. He was given a choice: enter his great-uncle's service, or join the army. He chose the army, even though soldiers were barred from fighting duels. "I want to be sent far away," he sobbed, later, to his mother. "To go to the Lelevai, to the Brogyar country. . . ." First, however, he had to complete the training in Sinidre, and he could not stop himself from writing to the baroness. He received a brief, constrained note in which she forbade him to write to her or come to Ur-Melinei, which showed him that she had been threatened. He was certain that his family had warned her, coerced her. He wrote again; her next note swore that it was her own will. And now he entered a terrible time of drinking, brawls, and gambling which resulted in his rejection from the army.

After this there was a year of almost suicidal despair. He drank in his bedroom, spent whole days asleep. And finally the woods called to him, and his horses, and his old friends, other young men, lighthearted, simple, and frivolous. He hunted in the Kelevain, riding closer and closer to Brovinhu. He dreamt he would meet her in the forest. His behavior was marked; the *radmakanid* met for a second time, and he was commanded to join his uncle on the Isle.

Somehow she heard of it. She wrote him a single letter, not long, but it was in her own voice, and he carried it with him still. She said she was glad he was going away; she missed him; there was no hunting at Brovinhu. She had been ill and was convalescent. The letter tore him from end to end with passion, elation, and grief; in this state he went out to drink the bars of Sinidre. There he blinded a man who mocked him, calling him a *balarin*. Only his uncle's influence saved him from prison.

"You can't imagine," he went on in a hoarse voice, "what she is like. The fact that she has been ill . . . She is not like me. My brothers laugh, they say she is too sophisticated for me, that I can't possibly keep pace with such a woman. Perhaps they are right. But I believe that she did—that she does love me. Perhaps it was for my sake that she fell ill! As I said, she is nothing like me, her emotions are finer, more turbulent, she doesn't forget anything, she could never forget her sorrow. . . . But I—I am of coarser stuff. I have told you of my unhappiness, but I have left out all my nights at the *londo* tables, the way I could vow to kill myself in the morning and be singing *vanadiel* and laughing in a tavern by dusk. I am fickle . . . my emotions have, I think, no real depth. . . . But hers! She is worth a hundred, a thousand of me. Strangely, this is the one point on which all of us—my brothers, my uncles, myself—on which all of us are agreed."

His hand relaxed on the blanket. A faint smile touched his lips. The light was fading, the sun sinking into the desert. We sat for a time in silence, and then he sang, very softly, a few lines of a comic song I had heard in Bain:

The balarin, the balarin,
What has he done with his boots?
Oh, they're under my lady's bed,
What shall we do?

I had heard the song pouring out of a café, rowdily sung to bawdy laughter and the clashing of cutlery. But Miros sang it lightly, tenderly, in a pensive, faltering voice that broke away at last and was lost in the night.

When it was over, he looked at me. "I'll never hunt again. Even if I live. I'll fight for Avalei as I have never fought before. People say the prince is conspiring against his father the Telkan. Some even say he's preparing an army in secret."

I hushed him, touching his brow, but he pushed my hand away.

"I hope it's true. I hope I live. I'll join him. I will have vengeance for the Night Market.

"If I can't see Ailin again, I'll be as I should have been when she was mine. Someone who doesn't forget. Who keeps faith."

His sentences dissolved, and soon he was raving. I tried to cool his face with pieces of wet damask: the rotting stuff dropped in his hair. I caught his flailing arms, held him, begged him to be still. At last he stopped fighting and lay with his eyes wide open, moonlight in his tears. I sat with him until he was safely asleep, and then I closed the heavy door of his box bed against the cold. I went to the next room, the one where I slept, a place of despair like all the others, stale as a charnel house.

"Jissavet," I said.

"Jissavet."

She bloomed in the dark chamber, illuminating the walls. But she could not see them. It was clear to me now that she could see nothing but me. A crushing and changeless fidelity, like a perfect love affair or the dark, single-minded devotion of a saint.

"Jissavet," I whispered.

She stretched out her hands. She was going to speak, to return to the tales of her past, those disembodied memories. But this time I could not listen. There was no time. "Stop," I said. "Jissavet. Listen to me. I need your help. I must have food and medicine."

"Listen to *you!* I do not listen to you."

Her face affronted, steel in a thunderstorm. Olondrian poets speak of the deadly potency of a woman's frown, but I know what a frown can do, the lowering of a delicate eyebrow, the twist of a lip.

"Don't do this to me," I screamed. "I'm dying."

The light dimmed about me, a shuttered lamp. On my hands and knees I retched, bringing up water and a little bile on the carpet.

"Dying!" she said.

"Yes," I coughed. "I'm dying. We're dying. We're starving. My friend is ill. I need medicine and food."

"I won't go back, I told you!"

"Don't!" I groveled on the floor, a skewered songbird. "Don't, Jissavet . . . You'll kill me, and no one will write your *vallon. . . .*"

Again the light dimmed. I had no strength to rise and lay where I had fallen, rolling onto my back to look at her.

She hovered above me, the red ropes of her hair almost touching my face. I thought I caught their scent: mildew and decay.

"You'll write it?" she demanded, her face ablaze. "If I help you—you and your friend—you'll write my *vallon*?"

"Yes," I said.

That was our bargain: a life for a life. A bargain in which we both suffered: she in the crossing over into my world, I in the crossing to hers. That night she led me through the frozen orchard and told me to dig up the fruits of the hairy vine the Kestenyi call *yom afer*, the "hand of the desert." The snow numbed my fingers; the hard earth broke my nails. I clawed at the ground by starlight like a grave-robber or seeker of buried treasure. The spiny harvest stung my hands, but I soaked the roots in water that night and boiled them at dawn, and they were as soft and nourishing as cream.

She looked at Miros, too: she stepped through the curtain between the worlds and gazed at him. And she guided me out into the foothills of the Tavroun. There, in a cave dug into the hillside and hidden with dried vines, lived a Tavrouni crone with a tin ring in her lip. We shared no common language; I described my friend's trouble with gestures. She gave me a bundle of fragrant twigs and a poultice of twisted grass. I had no way to pay her and mimed my poverty in distress, but she waved me away with the single Olondrian word: "*Avneanyi*."

And then, when I had treated Miros and he was asleep, I went upstairs to the library of Sarenha-Haladli. Squeezed in like an afterthought by the dilapidated observatory, the library had felt-covered walls and a balcony closed in latticework like a cage. The prince had built a Kestenyi collection here, only diversified by some Bainish novels and the works of Karanis of Loi, the books leaning on the shelves like broken teeth. I set my candle down on the writing desk and searched it thoroughly, scrabbling in the drawers. The thought that my light might be seen no longer frightened me: the night was so empty, so vast, reaching all the way to the mountains. I discovered a few pens, brittle as old men's bones, a half-full bottle of ink. I chose *Lantern Tales* from the shelf, for its wide margins.

I sat at the desk in my jacket, dipped the pen in the ink, and steeled myself against the coming light. "I'm ready," I said.

Yes, I called her. I asked her to come. Come, angel, I said. I called her Visible, the Ninth Wonder, Empress of Sighs. Come, I said, and I will show you magic from the north, your own words conjured into a *vallon*. A book, angel, a garden of spears. I will hold the pen for you, and I will weave a net to catch your voice. I will do what no one has done, I will write in Kideti, a language like you and me, a ghost hesitating between worlds. Between the rainstorms, angel, and the white light of the north. Between the river dolphins and the wolves. Between the far south, the land of elephants and amber, and this: the land of cypresses and snow.

So come. Sing to me of Kiem, speak to me of rivers. Pour your memories into my pen. Tell me your *anadnedet*, your life, your death story, as if you were still dying and not dead. Let me do for you what we do for those who are favored by the gods, and die slowly in the islands: let me sit beside your pallet in the firelight, and listen to the tale you long to tell. The story of a life which is revealed, after many years, to have been all along the story of a death. How one lives and goes on living, how one comes to die, under the eye of the vulture, Nedet, the goddess of ashes.

THE ANADNEDET
(I)

The angel said:

I already know about writing. We made maps: maps of the sea, of the waters between Tinimavet, Sedso, and Jiev. And maps of the rivers, the great ones, Dyet and Katapnay and Tadbati-Nut, the ones that made our country of mud on their way to the girdling sea. We made the maps on skins. First we would draw the lines with ashes and water, and later we traced them with a piece of hot iron. For many seasons our house was full of those maps, hanging on the walls, curled at the edges, dark-faced in the rushlight.

If you want to hear my *anadnedet* then you must begin with a map, and it must be a map of the land of Kiem. Of Kiem, the Black Land, wet and shining, the Jawbone of a Cow. I will draw a map for you like this:

There are three rivers, swollen and fed by a hundred tributaries, brown, enormous, pouring their weight to the sea. At the edge of the sea are the shimmering deltas, the dank-smelling lagoons, a landscape flat and liquid and loved by birds. To the north there are deep forests where the rivers rush in silence. To the west the coastline rises in blue hills, where there are terraced gardens and cool air, and a great temple looking down on the villages scattered in the mud.

That is one map. Here is another:

Houses standing up on stilts, skin boats tied to their poles, lying in the mud. The world is wet. There are little waterways, tracks between this house and that, and always the green light reflected up toward the sky. There is the forest, full of the *jodyamu* who will suck your blood unless you travel with chicken bones wrapped in banana leaves, that's what they like, you must lay your offering down on the roots of a tree as soon as you hear them ringing their little bells in the dark. The forest, full of danger, the witches riding on their hyenas, and the souls of the dead disguised as immense fruit bats, and the blood-stained palisades of the clearing where they do the killing when there are wars, earthquakes, epidemics, storms at sea. The forest, close and solemn. And then the rivers, brown and glinting under the trees, where pregnant women go to pray, throwing their beads to Jabjabnot the hippopotamus god, with his bloated stomach and ponderous female breasts. Leave the river, paddle your boat, the great mud flats are shining and they are hunting eels, and the sky is stained with flamingoes. There you can see the old woman filling her pot at the sacred river Dyet, the pot that will strike you blind if you look into it.

That's where we lived, in Kiem. We were *hotun,* the poor, without status. The others called us "people without *jut.*" That is what they called us when I was small, before I began to fall ill: later they called us other names, worse names. No matter what they said to us, my mother smiled at them. Her smile was uncertain, the smile of an idiot. She smiled, twisted her hands in her skirt, looked anxious, began to cry. And then she smiled again. It went on for years.

But he, my father: he was not one of us. My father had *jut,* and his *jut* was some of the strongest in southern Tinimavet. He was a nobleman, the son of a chief, a doctor of birds who had studied with two *tchanavi* in the hills. He could read water. He could read faces, too, and trees, thunder, owl cries, dead crickets. His hair had been silver as long as I could remember. What else can I say about him? I loved him and I still love him and I am like him, always like him, never like my mother.

When I was very small he was not with us. He was with the *tchanavi.* My mother used to talk to me about him. Wait until your father comes, she would say when the others teased me. Then you're going to have *jut,* the best *jut* in the world. Who is my father? I would ask. And she: The king of the rivers. A man from the moon, a prince, a fallen star. And so I was not surprised when he put his head in at the door and I saw his silver hair and beard, like starlight or rain.

There she is, he said.—That was me he was talking about, as he smiled in the rushlight. He had been waiting to see me. He came forward into the room and I said, Look out for the grandmother, and he looked surprised and then laughed: What a quick-eyed girl!

You see, my mother's mother was still alive then, wrapped up in a skin so that she wouldn't scratch herself with her dirty nails. She was wizened, as small as a child, dried up as you would think no living creature could be, utterly shrunken and silent. You could imagine picking her up and shaking her like a gourd, the dusty organs rattling about inside her. I used to pick her up myself and row her about in my boat: me, a child of six. She was that tiny. My father stepped over her and sat with us. Eat something, eat, my mother was saying. There was *datchi* in coconut milk, rice, buffalo curd, a pot of my mother's millet beer. The whole house smelled of happiness and food.

In a moment, my father said. I saw him open his pack and take something out, something reddish like clay in the light. He touched it lovingly with his slender hands, so that I knew: it was *jut*. He placed it gently against the wall.

I go rowing my grandmother. Her little face looks at the sky. We avoid the great canal that leads to the sea. I paddle about in the rushes, beside the green expanse of the rice, in the sunlight and the heat, the paths of dragonflies. The water is murky and brown; my grandmother's face grows dark in the sun, even more wrinkled, but she doesn't mind, nothing disturbs her. I sing to her:

My father is a palm,
and my mother is a jacaranda tree.
I go sailing from Ilavet to Prav
in my boat, in my little skin boat.

Kiem is known for its magic. Even you, the godless of Tyom, call on us to cure your diseases and banish your ghosts. We have powerful surgeons, doctors of leopards and doctors of crocodiles, and doctors of birds like my father, the "men of mist." You can see them going from house to house when people are sick, stately, solemn, sitting upright in their boats, monkey skins dangling, carrying little bags sewn from the skins of frogs, their assistants wailing and ringing copper bells. They can bless musical instruments, take away warts, call down the moon. They battle the witches who ride in the forests at night. If your soul is lost, they can go to the shining land by closing their eyes and search for you, clothed in the gray plumage of herons.

At night they pass in a clamor of bells. We crouch in the doorway and watch them. Their boats ride low in the water, ringed by torchlight. Everywhere there are rustling sounds as people creep to their doors, lifting the curtains, peering down at the glow on the water. The boat stops, is moored to a post, a rope ladder descends, and they climb up into a house. It's not our house. Now there are sighs everywhere, pitying murmurs, secret triumph. In Kiem you are always glad of another's misfortune.

Yes, they are all like that—except my mother. She never understands; she is too stupid to learn how to behave. Her pity is real. Oh! how terrible! she says, wringing her hands, sometimes crying over the sadness of others. She cries over people we don't even know, and worse, over people we do, that ugly Dab-Nin with her slit eyes and curling lip, who spits in the water whenever we pass and allows her son to tip my boat, watching him and laughing, not saying anything. Dab-Nin fell ill when I was thirteen, before I was ill myself. She coughed and lay on the floor with a swollen hip. And everyone sighed and was glad about it, everyone hated Dab-Nin, I'm sure it was a witch who caused her disease. And my mother wept. Oh, the poor woman. Imagine such idiocy. She would be glad if you were sick, I told her. My mother's eyes widened, filling again with wretched tears. Her tears were her wealth, the one thing she had in abundance.

My father did not weep. He was always calm in the face of sorrow, dignified. He knew what it was to be sad. I think he was sadder than my mother, despite all of her misfortunes, because he understood more. He lacked the protection of ignorance. He could not weep at the death of a terrible woman like Dab-Nin, but somehow he was even sadder because of it, because everyone was in mourning for a creature they had all hated, because the world was foul and riddled with lies. He took me in his boat. We went down the stream from Tadbati-Nut, toward the great canal, away from the funeral, the vultures wheeling, the stench of the fire, the smoke creeping into the forest, the clanging of bells and the wailing of many voices. We went out to the sea. My father rowed to where the air was clean and we couldn't hear the funeral anymore. The water was blue and the sun so hot that we opened our straw umbrellas and sat under them, drifting, happy on the great swells. We played *vyet* for a long time, and I managed to beat him once. Then we unwrapped our lunches and ate and drank. We didn't go back until the sun was sinking and there were fires in the village, and Dab-Nin was reduced to ashes.

I know that people noticed it, our avoidance of the funeral, and that it gave them more to say against us. We were suspected of sorcery, of putting *jut* on people. And maybe they were right, at least about me. My father was too good to harm anyone and my mother was too stupid, but I—I was neither a saint nor a fool. I have thought about it often, wondered about it—am I a witch? Testing the thought of it in excitement and terror. In Kiem they often discovered witches who had not known their own natures, who had evil in them which acted without their knowledge, ordinary people, farmers, fishermen, grandmothers, even children, who went to be purged in the forest, screaming with fear. The doctors killed them in the clearing, killed the evil in them, destroyed their *jut*. When they came back they were simple and mild. They walked hesitantly and could not remember things and lived in smiling timidity until they were lost or eaten by crocodiles.

I thought about it then, for the first time: Was I a sorceress? Could I have been the one who killed Dab-Nin? Certainly I was glad she was dead, spitefully glad, exultant: it made me feel strong and happy with light and water. I was happy to be on the sea with my father for a whole day, while that horrible woman sizzled in her own fat. And later I was terrified that the doctors would find me out and take me into the forest to strip me of my power. But later still I thought: I'm not a witch, I can't be one. Or at least I am not strong enough to do much harm. You see, had I been a witch, so many would have died in Kiem, the smoke from the funerals would have extinguished the sun.

While we were out on the water my father told me about death. I still remember his voice, his gentle gaze, the way his hair and face were patterned with light piercing through his umbrella, the way he leaned back in the boat and told this story:

The first man, who was called Tche, was the idea of the rain.

And the first woman, who was called Kyomi, was the idea of the elephant. This creator was not just an elephant, he was the inventor of the elephant, which he made as a shape to contain himself. He was his own inventor.

And the rain made the man Tche. She took her little bone-handled knife and cut his figure out of a piece of deer hide. Then she sewed it all over with pieces of coral and amber and ivory, and when she had finished, there was the most beautiful boy in the world. There has never been a boy as beautiful as the first one, though we like to say "as beautiful as Tche." No one has since made anything so beautiful out of a deer hide. And the rain put Death into his third vertebra.

And the elephant made Kyomi. He made her with his tusk, for he never uses any other weapon. He cut her figure out of a banana leaf and sewed it all over with jade and shells, and one raven's feather for hair. When he had finished, there was the most beautiful girl in the world, and no other girl has possessed even the tenth part of her beauty. And the elephant gave her a wonderful gift: he blew salt into her eyes, so that she had the sight of the gods, by which the world may be truly seen.

All of this happened far away in the Lower Part of the earth, when it was still green land, before the fire.

And Tche and Kyomi were each alone in different parts of the forest, filled with wonder and joy and fear at everything they saw.

Now the elephant and the rain were very jealous of their creations, and their greatest worry was that these two would meet somewhere in the forest. So they held a meeting among the clouds on the top of a high mountain, and the elephant said: I do not want my Kyomi to see your Tche. For she has the sight of the gods, to which his beauty stings like a thunderclap, and if she sees him, she will surely forsake me. And the rain answered: Do not be afraid. For I have put Death itself into the third vertebra of this handsome boy. And I will tell him of it, and of its terrible potency, so that if she touches him, he will flee as if she has tried to kill him. And the elephant said: It is good. And also the girl must know that one cannot love a mortal and yet possess the sight of the gods.

Then the rain went down to the forest and found the boy sitting under a tree, where he was taking shelter, because it was raining. And she said to him: Listen, my son, what I tell you is most important. In your third vertebra you carry Death, which is waiting to catch you. You must take care that nothing touches that third vertebra of yours, especially not a woman's hand, for it would be fatal to you!

What is a woman? asked the boy.

And the rain said: It is a creature like you, only ugly and clumsy and filled with dreadful cunning.

And the boy said: Oh! That is a terrible creature you have described! If I see one, I will run away.

And he went on with his new life, playing in the forest and in the rivers, and making boats and spears and beautiful arrows, and hunting even the flowers because he did not know any better, and sleeping on his stomach so as not to disturb Death.

And the elephant looked for Kyomi and found her down by the edge of the sea, gathering seaweed which she would cook for supper. And he said to her: Greetings, my daughter. What do you think of this sea?

And Kyomi answered with shining eyes: It is beautiful, like a long fire.

Then the elephant said: Ah! That is because you know only the gods. But if you loved a mortal man, how different it would be! Then this same sea, which is to you and me like a fire, or a great mat woven not of reeds, but of lightning, would appear to you gray and flat and even more lifeless than the mud.

How terrible! cried Kyomi. But what is a man?

That is a creature like you, the elephant said, only very ugly, with a great devouring mouth and ferocious nature.

And Kyomi said: Oh! What a terrible creature! Thank you for warning me. If I see one I will run away.

And Kyomi went on walking in the tall forests and down by the sea, gathering seaweed and drinking the dew from the flowers, happier than anyone who has ever lived after her, because she saw the world with the vision of the gods. And one afternoon she saw the boy Tche, and Tche saw her also, and they were far from the elephant and the rain. And Kyomi thought: This cannot be the man of which the elephant spoke, for he is beautiful like one of the gods. And as for Tche, he also thought, The rain did not mean this creature when she spoke of the woman who will cause me to die. And they smiled at one another and Kyomi gave the boy some seaweed and he gave her a hare which he had killed in the forest. No one knows how they came together, it might have been Ot the Deceiver who made it happen, the god in the shape of a chameleon. But they were happy, and they embraced as men and women do, hidden deep in the forest of the lost country.

And Kyomi was looking up at the sky, and suddenly it grew dark, and the trees were all blown out like a series of torches: for she had lost the sight of the gods as the elephant had foretold, and neither she nor her children would have it again. She knew it. She thought: This is the man. And weeping she drew him close, and the palm of her hand brushed over his third vertebra. And Tche cried out and thought to himself in despair: This is the woman.

Then Death leaped out and went clattering over the world.

(2)

The house my father was born in is visible from many places, but especially, on a clear day, from the sea. Lingering in your boat, at the edge of the desolate lagoon, you look up toward the lofty hills of the west. Gardens have been cut into the hillside like steps, fresh and beautiful, gardens of maize and tomatoes, guava orchards, dark green thickets of spinach and cassava, flowering patches of beans, everything tantalizing and blue in the distance. The road is a river of whiteness with small figures staggering along it, men with baskets of charcoal, donkeys with carts, and once a day the old woman coming to fill her pot in the Dyet, ringing her bell to frighten people away. The place she takes the water is there, the temple of Jabjabnot, built above a spring, straddling the cataract. It rises in plumes of mist, etched in the hill, inaccessible. It has many windows through which no one looks out.

Look up farther, along the road. There the houses begin, with their tiled roofs and pillars of carved calamander. Look at that one, the most serene, the one of the greatest elegance: that is the house in which my father was born. In the day its slatted blinds are raised to welcome the wind from the sea; the whole house is open, cool, tranquil, delicious. At night they lower the blinds, and lanterns hang from the corners of the roof, glass lamps brilliant with captive fireflies.

And here is the woman for whose sake he left that house: clumsy and startled as she paddles her boat, running aground on the mud, sometimes preferring to walk, even up to her ankles in the wet earth, because she is awkward with boats, she can't learn to control them. And not only boats. She can't play *vyet,* it's impossible to teach her. She laughs, she waves her hands: I'm confused again! She doesn't mind if you play, she will sit and watch you move the pieces without even the sense to feel envious or ashamed. She knows how to cook a few things, she cooks the same things over and over. Rice and peanuts, *datchi* in coconut milk. She talks about cooking, about a snake she saw, a baby crocodile, or nothing, she just sits there smiling wistfully.

Oh, I know she was beautiful. More than beautiful, famous, even though she was a *hotun* girl, without *jut.* There were still songs about her when I was young; there was a man who used to sing them when he rowed past our house at night. *Child of the sky, beautiful night-hair, supple as a fish. Girl made of honey, disappearing in sunlight.* Those were the songs they sang for my mother, full of her eyes like stars and her hair like a net to catch hearts when she walked with it loose on the wind. The only one who still sang them was that man, who was also *hotun,* a man older than my father with pensive eyes. I didn't like him. But he was only one of my mother's suitors—people said there had once been twenty of them. Oh, I believed it. Why should they lie? People in Kiem never lied for flattery's sake. So I believed she had been a great beauty, even though to me she was this square-hipped, graceless creature with the scar on her forehead where she had once been struck with an oar in an accident. Yes, to me she was this scar, these tearful, frightened eyes, this odor of millet beginning to ferment, this hand with the fingers missing where they had been caught in a leopard trap when she was a child, this inconceivable bad luck. To me she was this terrible luck, this litany of misfortunes. And so, although I believed the tales of her beauty, I did not see how beauty alone could have drawn my father to her, to her poverty, foolishness, and constant affliction.

Once I asked him. More than once. Why did you marry Tati? And he laughed: I've told that story so many times. Or else he said: That's not a proper question for a little girl. But I would insist, and he would always give in.

Out in the waters of the lagoon he said: She was rowing her boat, and I was rowing mine in the other direction. We scraped together—our oars clacking—she nearly swiped my head with hers, frantic to get away, stuck in the canal! Well, she was so serious, and the situation so comical, that I laughed. I didn't know anything about her. I didn't know how poor she was, but I liked the way she laughed when I started laughing. She was so candid, so easy to please. . . .

And in the forest, when we had paused to rest after gathering mushrooms, sitting in the cool shade, he smiled and said: Well, she had lived a different life. I liked to hear about that. I liked her voice, her quiet manner of speaking. I liked the way she cared for her mother. I thought I would like to live with them. Can't you understand that, little frog? No? They had a happy house, peaceful, it seemed to me. . . . There is peace in your mother, like light in a lamp.

And in the doorway at dusk, when we sat with our legs hanging over the side, watching the flickering lights from the other houses, he said: You know it was not always pleasant, living up on the hill. I know it is hard to believe. But we had sorrow. Sorrow is everywhere, of course, but on the hill we had a type which I did not want. I prefer the sorrow here.

Then you married Tati for sorrow? I asked, incredulous.

His face was still, like a tree in the shadows. I don't know, he said.

If my father married for sorrow, then he married the right woman. Sorrow followed my mother like a lover. Her father died in his boat of a fever, his body absorbed into the river to find its way to the sea alone, to rot, to be devoured by the squids. Her brother died of a snake bite, blackening, his leg growing swollen and so pestilential in odor that he could not be kept in the house. He slept in a boat until he died, singing the songs of death and trying over and over to pluck the moon from the sky. And her sister. Her sister was last seen walking at the base of the hills. One of her sandals came to shore two days later. Her basket was found, too, her lunch still wrapped in banana leaves, but no one knew whether she had fallen or jumped.

One could reason about it. There was plenty of sorrow in Kiem, particularly among us, the *hotun,* the low. There was not a family who had not suffered some disaster, an accident with sharks, an attack from the pirates who lived in the caves. A fall, an encounter with crocodiles, a wound that refused to heal. Rape, madness, river blindness, *kyitna.* One could say that my mother was not unusual among these people, all of whom were lacerated with misfortunes.

When I was small I had everything. Mud, guavas, the smell of the sea. We stayed in our boats all day then, lacking nothing. At the fringe of the forest we gathered oranges and sometimes *tyepo* which we would break against a stone, seeking its cream with the tint of young leaves. We made spears and hunted eels and fish in the estuaries; we swam and wrestled, discovered shells and corals, rowed our way to the forest again, made swings out of the vines, shouted, wept, forgot everything, and laughed, and laughed. We, the *hotun* children. We had all been born in the Black Land, but the stigma of having no *jut* set us apart. The old ones who sat drinking sugarcane wine along the canal spat into the water as we passed, an accursed flotilla.

We were Tchod, Miniki, Jissavet, Ainut, Nadni, Pyev. And others: Kedi who died of the fever, Jot who died of the catarrh. These disappeared and we went on playing, not even mentioning them, feeling them only in the cold air that pressed on our backs in the forest. We made slings to kill the little birds with the colorful plumage. If we caught fish, we roasted them on green sticks. Night fell rapidly in Kiem when the sun dropped behind the hills, and the shadows rushed over the land and reached out for us.

I remember all of them. Ainut was the one I loved, because of her soft hair and sober eyes. She used to swim with me near the house. My father called us "the two frogs." He would lower baskets of rice to us on ropes. We loved that, reaching up unsteadily from our boats, pretending that the rivers were in flood, my father shouting to us that we must be careful, pointing to the imaginary crocodiles that made us scream. Sometimes we went far away together, on expeditions to the beaches, where we made houses of palm fronds. Ainut was with me when I saw the indigo sellers from Sedso, the sailors from Prav, and the *kyitna* men of the caves.

When I am very sick, when it's hard to breathe, my father sits beside me. He stays for as long as I want him, all day, all night. He sings to me, he tells me stories, he traces each one of my fingers over and over. The thumb, the pointing finger, the long one. He tells me everything he can think of, helps me sit up and lie down, invents a hundred games to deaden the pain. He lets me lie with my face toward the doorway so that I can look out and we can count the birds that go past and make up their stories. I see his face in the subtle, indoor light, a light that is delicate even in the heat of the day, moth-colored, protected. I see that he is suffering, there are lines going deeper beside his mouth, he's aging, I can't bear it, and I weep. Crying makes it worse. He can't endure what's happening to me. For his sake I stop crying, pretend it's nothing. I smile at him and reach up to wipe the tears which have trickled into his sparse beard. I dry his face with my hair, and we laugh.

The smallest things are enough to give us hope on such long days. We discover whole worlds in the tint of the sky through the doorway. My father plays his flute; the sound is sweeter than the ripple of rain, and sometimes the rain accompanies him and shelters us under its curtain.

In the background, boiling water, carrying dishes, my mother. She walks softly so as not to disturb us. And sweeter than even the voice of the flute is the dream I have: that we live on the hill, pampered and rich, and she is only a servant.

Tell me about the hill, I demand.

He can't refuse me anything. He sighs, plucks mournfully at the threads of his beard. Our doorway faces northwest, you can see a part of the hill from here, but not the temple and not the house with the glass firefly lanterns. I want to hear about that house, to continue the dream I'm having, the dream that smells of jasmine and makes me weep. He doesn't want to talk about it. I force him, and I don't care. Already I believe I deserve more from life.

He says: Imagine a large room. Much bigger than our house, five or six times bigger, with a smooth tile floor. The floor is polished twice a day, they even rub wax into it, and they rub wax into all the slats in the wooden blinds. This room is empty except for the family *janut* set against one wall. Yes, mine was there, on the far left. My father's *jut* was decorated with hanging gold leaves, my mother's with little bars made out of silver. . . . Yes, now you're getting big eyes, just like a real little frog. But what was there for us to do in that room? All alone on the hill, with nothing to look at but the sea, nothing to do but bicker, wait, and die of boredom?

Nothing he says can dismantle my dream. I sift his words in my head, choosing only those which support my fantasy, ignoring all his complaints about the boredom, his father's tyranny, his mother's shallowness and endless deception. I hardly notice the things he tells me with the most urgency, his brothers' fights, the way the servants were beaten, the coldness of all the conversations meant to be subtly wounding, the ruses, lying smiles, and silken cruelty. No. I take the things I want and gather them to myself. The ladies in their gold and orange robes. Their poise as they sit on the shining floor, their skin made supple with coconut oil and wreathed in the aroma of cinnamon. Each of them has a darkened lower lip, tattooed in the manner of the Kiemish noblewomen. They are graceful, unhurried, gorgeous. The wind from the sea comes in and lifts a few strands of their plaited hair; it fills the sleeves of their robes, they are like great butterflies. . . . I dream of them, of their beautiful plates and cups, their delicate food, the oysters and the ginger and cashew nuts, their trips to visit one another, riding in their carts festooned with marigolds, under straw umbrellas. I dream of their lanterns and even the sound of the blinds being lowered at night. The blinds can be adjusted to let in the moonlight. Now moonlight streaks the floor where a lady sits, her oiled hair shining, burning incense to drive away melancholy.

Sometimes Kiem seemed as if it was always the same, unendurable. I don't know if Tyom seemed that way too. The rain, or no rain, or mist, the rice and millet, the buffaloes up to their knees in water, the same river light, overcast, monotonous. Sometimes it seemed like a country where nothing happened, enough to make you drown yourself. I can't stand it, I said to Ainut. And we would go searching for adventures, breathless in the heat, fighting to throw off the shroud of the long rains.

We went rowing our boats. The air was still, without wind enough to stir the reeds. We paddled slowly toward the west, for the world lay west of Kiem, and south: to the east there was nothing but ocean, inhabited by sharks, gods, and the ghosts of the drowned. We paddled beneath the beautiful blue-green hills which rose above us piled on one another like massive cloud formations, both airy and monumental, their cliffs jutting over the sea and hiding the house with the glass lanterns from our view. Below the cliffs there was a stretch of beach, sometimes littered with makeshift huts where sailors and fishermen had camped, or Tchinit the sailors' wife, who slept in a different place every night so that the people of Kiem would not find her and burn her to death. We never saw the sailors' wife, but once we thought we found her camp: there was a broken comb with a few long hairs. We burned these on the beach in great excitement, uttering all the most dreadful incantations we could recall or invent. Tchinit's house was one of those, perhaps, which leaned and collapsed under the rain. And there was the house of Ipa the smith, which always seemed on the verge of disintegration but never fell, where the lonely cripple made bangles of copper wire. We rowed on. We were seeking the farthest, the most deserted beaches. Here we had once found Sedsi indigo sellers, who had given us each a square of cotton dyed the color of a bruise, and from whom we had fled, giggling, when they asked us to lie on their mats. Above these beaches there were caves in the hills, where the pirates lived. We were forbidden to go as far as this shore. There were terrible stories of the pirates, who had mouths in the palms of their hands and tails like monkeys, and lived solely on human flesh.

We rowed on. I'm tired, Ainut said. I was tired, too, but I had been waiting for her to say it first. All right, let's go ashore, I said. We floundered into the warm sea and dragged our rowboats up onto the sand.

The beach was silent. We gathered fronds and wove them into a roof: our boats, tilted on their sides, made the walls of the house.

One side was open, facing the sea. We slept and then rose, groggy with heat, and woke ourselves fully with a long swim. How sweet it was to be free, alone, with no one to call us *hotun* people, no one to spit in the water when we passed, nothing to remind us of our poverty, of the shame of being the children of those who were no better than animals. We grew wilder, bolder, we swam farther, tempting the sharks. Then we raced back to the shore and dashed onto the sand. We danced and sang, we made elaborate headdresses from palm fronds, we practiced fluttering our lashes at vaguely imagined boys. . . . I don't know how I was, but Ainut was different on the beach, with a sudden spirit of mischief and delight—she capered and said silly things that made her shriek with laughter at herself, almost horrified at her own boldness. We made dances, new ones, performing the steps exactly in unison, singing, wearing only our knotted skirts. Then we were suddenly hungry with the hunger that comes from swimming and we put on our short vests and went looking for food.

There was always food on the beach. There were coconuts and sleepy lizards, obese snails dreaming in the tide pools, and higher up there were wild bananas and *datchi,* although we feared the pirates in those regions, and the pariah dogs. But on this day, the day I remember, we were too giddy with happiness to think of those things, and we went up near the caves, chattering and laughing in the long grass, gathering green bananas which we would roast and season with saltwater. Ainut's plaits were wet, and a track of salt lay on her cheek. She was baring her teeth and rolling her eyes, imitating someone. And then I saw the man and my laughter died as if forced out of me by a blow. It was all I could do to draw a breath.

He was standing near the wall of the cliff, knee-deep in the grass. He stood with his hands at his sides and looked at us. Above him there was a gaping cave mouth and a slope of rubble leading down to where he was, the man from the cave. He was dressed in rags and his hair stood up, red in color, red, horrible, stark and flagrant as if it were dipped in blood, and his eyes, worse, remembering it, his eyes seemed without any color at all, silver perhaps or the color of guava peel. Against these colors his skin looked very black. He was a painted man. Ainut followed the movement of my eyes. She stopped laughing and then I moved, my hand shot up and grasped her arm, hard, digging the nails into her flesh.

It was her weakness that made me strong. At first, when I saw the *kyitna* man, my instinct had been to fall, to stop breathing, to die—and perhaps, had I been alone, I would have collapsed from pure terror and they would have carried me off into their cave. But Ainut saved me, she saved us both. We looked at the man and saw a movement higher up, a shadow inside the cave, and the shadow moved into the light, its scarlet hair and beard hanging down in the dust, and Ainut screamed and screamed and went on screaming. Then the first man, the one close to us, lifted his hands and waved them as if to beckon to us, and stepped forward into the grass, and my strength came up and I yanked on Ainut's arm and started running, dragging her, shouting at her to run, to stop screaming and run. We stumbled down the beach. The man was coming after us. Everything came back to me then, everything. My mother's warnings, anxious, irritating, don't go far, Jissavet, do you promise, don't go around to the shore by the caves. I prayed to my father's *jut*. If I get away I'll listen to her, I'll love her better, I'll never disobey her again. Miraculously, we reached the boats. I turned and set Ainut upright and slapped her in the face as hard as I could. Get in your boat, I said. I'm leaving you. Do you hear? I'm leaving you behind.—Sobs, screams, and the bright blue sea. We thrashed into the water, climbed in the boats, hauled on the oars and pulled away, slowly, from that accursed shore.

Even when we were far out on the water, we could still see the man. He stood in the surf, tiny, waving his arms. We could still see the stain of his hair, and we spat in the ocean to clear our hearts of the sight, the impurity. The abomination.

(3)

When I was old enough I asked: Where did *jut* come from?

We were sitting on our pallets in the evening, the light flickering and showing our skin-maps hanging all over the walls, and my father leaned forward, his eyes dark pools, and said:

In the oldest days *jut* lived in the sea. All the separate *janut* and the whole *jut*, it was all there, and all one. The people faced the sea when they prayed, and they knew that something powerful lived in it, and they never teased it or insulted it. Then one day a little girl came, a girl about your size, and she said, I'm going to go and talk to *jut*. And the people said, It is not for human beings to talk to *jut*, and she said,

Very well, but she knew her heart all the same. And when night came she slipped out of the house and went and stood on the cliff, and she shouted down at the sea, *Jut! Jut!*—She stood there stubbornly and called to the sea as loudly as she could, *Jut!* Answer me, *Jut!*

And *Jut* answered.

I'm that girl, I think. I am like the girl who called *jut.* Always outside, always different from people. It's not only that I'm different, it's that I don't want to be different and yet I am proud, almost proud of the difference itself. I won't try to change. When Ainut grows up she will marry a Kiemish laborer, a poor man, but one with *jut.* I'll lie with my face to the doorway, watching the wedding procession go by, already very ill, too ill to get up. At that time, the time of the wedding, I haven't spoken to Ainut for two years, but still the procession goes by our house, that's the way she is, she would think of me even after everything has died between us, she knows I'll be watching her. And I am. She stands in the prow of the boat, with a necklace of marigolds, beautiful. Around her are shouts, confusion, the clashing of spears. She doesn't turn toward me. She glides by with an averted face, remote. And then I lose sight of her in the crowd.

It comes on suddenly, the first times. I'm under the house, untying my boat. Suddenly I can't see anything. Or what I can see is not what's there, I see something like a swarm of flies, white and black, filling up my vision. At the same time, my head grows heavy. I lean forward, grasp the pole. Far away, through the flies, I see my hands. Just as suddenly it clears and I see my mother watching me, holding her basket. Jissi, are you all right?

It's nothing, I say.

Then one day Ainut said: Your hair's red.

What?

Look, right there, she said. She had turned away from the tree. She had put down her basket and was looking at me strangely as I stood holding the pole in the bright sunlight.

Look. She raised her hand, pointed. She didn't touch my hair.

Maybe it's papaya, I laughed, breathless. Maybe I broke one with the pole and it splashed on me.—I raised my hand and felt my hair where she pointed. It wasn't sticky.

I don't think it's papaya, she said. She was always like that, thoughtful, plodding, unromantic, without invention. She looked at me with her sober eyes.

Did we break one? I asked, looking over the ground, still touching my hair gingerly.

I tried to look at my plait.

It's too high, she said. I don't think you can see it.

Then why did you tell me to look?—The rage was already coming over me, the desolation, the covetousness, for life, any kind of life. I touched my hair. It was as if I already knew what would happen, that we would be separated, she and I, that she would go into life, marry, have children and grow old, and I would spend a few seasons stretched in the doorway. My breath caught unnaturally, as if I were getting ready to cry.

Maybe you should go home, Ainut said.

Maybe you should mind your own business, I answered, suddenly furious. You're so stupid. The basket's full of ants.

I did go home, though. I went quickly, expertly through the marshes. I had always had a good hand for boats. My mother was under the house, weaving a cover for the big basket, but my father wasn't there, his boat was gone. I pulled my boat up the slope, my hands shaking, my face hot. I was only fifteen, but still, I knew. My mind raced over my illnesses, my fevers, the times I would vomit and feel faint, and then quickly feel better again. Tati, is my hair red? I thought to myself. But I couldn't say it. I stood there beside my boat, catching my breath. I couldn't say it. My mother smiled; she didn't stop weaving her basket. I couldn't shatter her with another misfortune.

Good morning, good morning, she goes along, greeting everybody, incapable of leaving people alone, nodding to them, good morning, and they turn their backs or laugh at her, insulting, or they spit into the water. Some of them, if they are in a group, pretend to respond to her. Good morning, Hianot, Dab-Nin shouts. Her voice rings across the water, hard and flat, she's standing in the reeds with other women, leering at us. The other women giggle. One of them raises a hand in protest, not sure she wants to participate in this, but hesitant because it's so amusing, that stupid *hotun* woman panting after them like a dog. The blessing of *jut!* Dab-Nin shouts. The women burst out laughing, it's too much. And to you, my mother says. Dab-Nin goes on grinning at us, my mother goes on greeting everyone, and islands of spittle float on the water.

The pestle is thudding beneath the house: it's my mother, pounding grain. The house is full of the brown, overheated shadows of midday, and I lie in the corner under the place where the thatch is decaying, so that a pattern of tiny lights falls on my face. At first, each time the pestle strikes, I feel that it's crushing my skull. But then my mother begins to murmur, singing. She sings only to herself so that her voice has all of its confidence and free expression of sadness, its dark color.

Little one, tender one.
The one I perceived from a distance.
Yes, the one with the quick, tart smile
and the hair pinned with white flutes.
You, fishing and bringing up baskets
of jade and glass fish.
You, scattering ribbons of light
when your laugh unrolls in the fields.
Why do you lead that nightingale
on a thread of your long hair?
Why do they say you love no one?
Why are your dawns so sad?
Is it your death which frightens you,
when it shifts underneath your heart?
Tender one, sweet little one,
orange tree, fire, and ashes.

Not until later did anyone mention the word: Olondria. But even then, in the early months of my illness, they must have considered it, they must have whispered of it in the darkness, agonized over the terrible expense. I had heard of Olondria, a land detached, fantastic, on the other side of the massive northern sea, a land of cold, of *vallon*, where the people were tall and colorless and spoke a language invented by the ghosts. To me it was absurdly distant, so inaccessible that it left me indifferent, unlike the bazaars of Akaneck. When my mother told me that I was to journey there, I laughed. She lowered her eyes, trembling. Don't, she said.

I won't cut my hair, ever. My mother notices it at last—I've been in the house for two days, afraid to go out. The redness spreads from the roots of my hair, as if a blood-touched egg has been cracked on the crown of my head: slowly, obscenely, like that. I say I'm not feeling well, I'm tired of boating, I give any excuse. I sit looking through our water maps, morose. Then my mother notices. She lights a candle in daylight despite the bad luck and holds it over my head, trembling.

Words pass between us. She's quivering, reduced to grief. She presses one hand to her heart, the other gripping the rush candle. No, no, no, she says. I look at her, I'm hard-eyed, arrogant. Why not? I say, scoffing at her. I cross my arms to hide the fact that I am shaking too, I look at her with my head up, tense, defiant. She puts her fist in her mouth, bites it. Tears roll down her cheeks. I tell her: Crying won't help anything.

But what a relief it would be to weep, throw myself into her arms, drench the front of her dress in tears, sobbing in horror, despair—to have her rock me to and fro, crooning, to let myself be broken in front of her, gathered by her, resorbed.

I do not know why such surrender seemed to me worse than death.

So, my mother trembles, staggers, weeps. She puts down the candle, she opens the pot in which we keep the tools, she brings out the old razor wrapped in cotton. She thinks we need to cut my hair, now, perhaps it will grow back normally. I refuse. She stands, aghast. The razor in her hand is like the enemy of my fate: my hair, the confirmation of destiny.

When my father comes home that night there is nothing to eat but cold *datchi*. My mother sits, weeping, in the corner. And I lie on my back, staring up at the slope of the thatched roof, stern, dry-eyed, with my hair in two plaits. My hair, the punishment of the gods. The pelt of the orangutan. Our house has already become the scene of a shipwreck. Fear crosses my father's face, smoothed away at once, he puts his knapsack down and lowers the door curtain.

My mother's sobs grow louder when she hears him come in. He kneels beside her, whispers, strokes her hair. He probably thinks I've insulted her. The thought makes me want to laugh. But I don't laugh, because I don't want to cry.

She tells him, she says, *kyitna*. She weeps in damp heaves. The light moves over the thatch, drawing nearer. His knees crack as he lowers himself to the floor, the light above my hair. Hello, little frog. His voice is unsteady.

Hello Tchimu.—I don't meet his eye, I look straight upward. He brushes his hand lightly over my hair. Then he stands again, his knees crack, and the light moves away. I love him, he is so calm, unflinching, controlled.

He bends down and talks to my mother in a quiet voice. Her sobs increase. He takes a leaf from the pile beside the water pots. He wraps some *datchi* in it and puts the package into his knapsack, and then he lets down the ladder and climbs out to free his boat.

He is out all night. He gathers seven frogs. He kills a leopard. He rows to the west and awakens Ipa the smith. My father pumps the skin bellows, sweating on the night beach, the flames flaring up, the smith hammering. Then my father leaves; he goes to the forest. He seizes crickets in the clearing. He opens his own veins. He bleeds. In the darkness, the rusty, clotted palisades of the dying place. An owl cries: he ignores the terrible omen.

In the morning our house is ringed with charms of dreadful potency. Copper bells tinkle in the breeze. There is a smell of urine and charred bone, and there is blood on all of the wooden stilts which support our house. My mother is cooking porridge over a brazier, inside the room. My father, very pale, sits by the wall. There is a poultice on his arm, and when I open my eyes he smiles, proud, vehement: We are not leaving this house.

I dreamed many times of the man we had seen on the beach, near the pirate caves, the man with the dark face, fox-colored hair, bleached eyes. I don't know how many times I dreamed of him; it seemed like hundreds, and each dream released the same, specific terror. Ainut was always with me, always heavy, always needing to be dragged. It was essential that I protect her. She was myself, the world, she was as heavy as all of the children of the village, she had too many legs and arms. And the man, coming after us. His feet bending down the grass, the precise nature of his breath and shadow. The sea, far away, a strip of blue at the edge of a dazzling beach. The distance was too great. We would never make it.

Now I don't know what he wanted. I think of him with pity. The way he waved his arms, as if pleading with us. And sometimes I think he wasn't pleading at all, that we misunderstood: that he was attempting to warn us, even to save us.

So, my father closed us in. We had that: his supreme courage. Nothing like it had ever been seen in Kiem. This deranged doctor of birds, this lunatic with the *jut* of chiefs, living blatantly in the village with his *kyitna* daughter. Living in front of everyone, with the charms drying all over the house so that no one dared approach, not even with fire, sitting under his house and weaving a mat, in plain view, with the absurd nonchalance of the demented. Wait for a few days, he told my mother, then you can go out again. At first only he appeared, tempting attack. And we looked through the spaces in the thatch and saw the house surrounded, ugly faces, rusty hoes and spears.

Look, I whispered to my mother. There's Ajo Ud. And there's old Nedovi with a torch.—We had sweat on our palms, we couldn't eat, could hardly stand, yet I felt closer to her than I had done in years. I even let her squeeze my arm, happy to make her happy with this graciousness, knowing she didn't expect it. Look, it's Ajo Kyet, she whispered, horrified, moving aside so that I could peer through her place in the thatch.

It was Ajo Kyet. He was the village doctor of leopards. He stood in the boat, his arms crossed on his chest. He did not look the way he did when he sat under his big house near the canal, with a white cloth around his waist—no, he was resplendent with new butter on his hair, and the tails of six blue monkeys hung from his cloak, and his leather belt was trimmed with several bags made of leopard skin, and clouds of incense rose from his long boat. His face was streaked with red. He looked splendid, imposing, and sorrowful. His voice boomed from his broad chest as I watched. Jedin of Kiem! he bellowed, raising his hand. You have brought abomination on us, the curse of *jut* be upon you.

My father's voice startled us, right beneath our feet. Good morning, Kyet! he shouted. The blessing of *jut*!

There was a murmur from the crowd. Ajo Kyet looked sadder than ever. Oh, Jedin, he cried in thrilling tones. Gone are the days when you might call me Kyet. You have put yourself outside, and you know it as well as I do, in your heart. Your *jut* knows. Take your curse and go, Jedin of Kiem.

My daughter is innocent, shouted my father.

There were louder murmurs. Cursed by the tongue! someone cried. Everywhere people were spitting into the water. Some of them picked up clods of mud and touched them to their lips. Only Ajo Kyet was unmoved, pensive. Rarely have I seen anyone look so sad. He went on looking sad and glittering and handsome as he spoke, telling my father in his sonorous voice that it was the gods who assigned curses, just as only the gods could bless. He told my father that there would come a time when his *jut* would fail, and the charms on the house would be as a handful of ash, and the people would know it and they would come with fire and with weapons and obliterate the last trace of our home. He said that my father ought to have known, that he ought to have slipped away with us in the night instead of perpetrating this outrage, spending his own blood to make a sign to all the village that there was *kyitna* here, filth protected with magic. Moral filth, he called it. He was eloquent, noble, stately. We are innocent, my father shouted.

Ajo Kyet shook his head. Innocence cannot survive, he said, in the body of corruption.

(4)

A thousand times I promised myself to be different, patient, kind. I would go out alone, rowing my boat, after she had driven me to rage with her simplicity, after I had mocked her, sneered, or shouted. I would go out alone with only a clay beaker of water. The sea calmed me, the sky the color of mud. I would mutter to myself, arguing, defending her, rowing over that heavy, livid sea. She was guileless, she was good. She had done nothing wrong. Only expressed her pity for Ud's first wife, or interrupted when I was learning a *tchavi's* song from my father, asking how it could rain when there were oranges.

If there was so much fruit, she said, the rains would be over already.—She was under the house, building her cook fire. I was sitting beside my father in one of the grass-bottomed chairs. Of course the rains would be over, I snapped. That's what he's trying to say.

Well, she said doubtfully. But he says it rained for hours.

I know. He means—he's showing the search for the *tchavi.* The way—I paused, helpless. It was no use talking to her.

Perhaps the fruit came early that year, she said.

And the way she said it—as if she were comforting me for the song's mistake, while she squatted, fanning the fire with a reed fan, and my father sat, gentle, not saying anything, only waiting for her to be finished, not even trying to correct her—the way she was so satisfied with nothing, wanted no knowledge at all, only to sow, to dig, to have clean water, content to remain a fool forever—I can't stand it, I shouted, and I untied my boat and dragged it down to the water.

Jissi, my father said. He was disappointed in me. He often said: Your mother is one of the humble. The humble are innocent; they do not need humiliation.

I rowed out to sea. I didn't look back at them.

But now I will never row out to sea again, not alone. And I'll never walk in the fields of millet either, hearing the wind expressing its longing amid the tall grain. And I'll never build fires there to eat stolen fish. No, it's over, from now on there won't be any escape from her, her sighs, the way she squats heavily on her hams, the sloshing, sloshing sound at night as she rinses out her dress, and her odor, that smell of ancient things, of the dark. I can hear her turning over at night, sometimes snoring. She's always tired, she sleeps in an instant, abruptly as a child. The sound of her sleep, her breathing, it's oppressive. The house is so small, there's no air, and I cry because I'm trapped there with her. I cry because I want my boat, I want to be out in the sunlight, I want to look at the sea again, at the mountains, it's terrible when I can hear people talking across the water and I'm alone, never free of them and yet always alone. Yesterday, it's always yesterday that a group of people came, people my age, and stood on the opposite bank and taunted me. Among them were Tchod and Miniki. Throw out your mother's rags, they sang, don't you know that eating them gives you *kyitna?*

In the farthest reaches of the night, Hed-hadet, the rain.

It was the beginning of the world. Hed-hadet began to swell. Bigger, bigger, as big as the mountain of Twenty Thousand Flowers, as big as the moon. No, bigger than that, as big as the ocean, bigger still, as big as the deepest night sky during the dry season. Then she burst, and the world was born in a giant shower of rain, with a great explosion of light and laughter and tears.

The sun and the moon were born then, and the pomegranate tree, and the oil-producing palm tree and the dove. The heron was born, or the thing that made the heron, and the evening star, and the bell and the drum and the thing that made the cricket. Hed-hadet gave birth to the inventor of the elephant and the inventor of the hippopotamus, and the razor and the hoe, and the *datchi* and the millet stalk, and the things which were to create the frog and the donkey.

Then there was a great silence. The rain stopped falling: she climbed back into the regions of the night.

All over the world, the things were looking at one another.

From the distance, chasing its dogs, came the wind.

When we met the sailors from Prav, we were climbing the rocks looking for snails. We had abandoned our boats on the beach below, and they, with their boats, were on the other side of the rocks, smoking dark cigars and making fish soup. We smelled the smoke and crept forward, lying flat on the rocks. We could look down on their heads, sleek hair, bright scarves. They all wore strips of cloth around their brows, tied on their hair behind: to collect the sweat, they explained to us later. I darted my eyes toward Ainut. No, she mouthed, shaking her head, beginning to snake backward stealthily. The sun was bright, the scent of cigar smoke acrid, overpowering. Good afternoon! I shouted down to them.

We were surprised at how fast they were on their feet, their knives unsheathed. I clung to the rocks, giddy with terror and joy. When they saw us the tension eased slowly out of their bodies and they laughed, gesturing at one another, talking in their own language. What are you doing up there? one of them called to us. Come down and eat.—Their Kideti had a smoothness, a watery quality, as if their tongues were gentler and more supple than ours. It was an accent fluid, caressing, unforgettable.

Let's not go, Ainut whispered.

I was climbing down the rocks. You'd better be alone! shouted one of the sailors, knife held up in warning. I saw that it was a woman. She wore the same blue tunic and trousers as the two men.

We're alone, I said. We're just two girls. Come on, I added to Ainut, who was climbing slowly because she was trembling. One of the men took my arm and helped me jump down onto the sand, cool in the shadows. In the background the light leapt on the sea.

God of my father, the sailor said, humorously. You're *chakhet*. Do you know what *chakhet* is?

No. What is it?

Chakhet . . . He waved a hand in the air as if seeking to pluck out the word. The other two were putting away their knives.

Chakhet is brave, the woman sailor said.

No, clever, said the other man.

No, no, said the one who had helped me down. He reached up a hand and helped Ainut to jump down next to me, biting his lip, his eyes narrowed in search of the word. No, *chakhet* . . . When you do something that doesn't need to be done. When you climb a tree because it's tall. When you swim where there are crocodiles, or answer a chief carelessly, just to prove that you can do it—that's *chakhet*.

When you startle people for no reason, said the woman, picking up her cigar and blowing on it to clean off the sand. And make their cigars go out and their dinner burn. . . .

Don't listen to her, said the sailor who had helped us down. She was born like that.

We sat with them in the shadow of the rocks, around their fire. The odors of woodsmoke and smoke from the cigars. And from the clay pot on the fire, too, the smell of fish, peppers, and ginger cooking together, pungent, delicious. My mouth watered; it was rare to be offered such rich food. The sailors had brought the ginger and peppers with them. The one who had called me *chakhet* sat next to me and showed me his tin of spices, pulling it from inside his tunic. He never traveled without it. At sea, he explained, one should always put fire on the tongue, it didn't cause thirst, that was only a rumor. The spices kept one happy, alive, they relieved the monotony. We all travel with spices on Prav, he said. While he talked, the other man, who was older, with a carved, wood-tough face, stirred the soup with a narrow twig, and the woman smoked and looked at us sardonically and smiled. She had a round face, and her breasts bulged under her tunic. The sailor with the spices asked us questions, our names, what we did in our village. I answered, and he tried to make Ainut talk. Once you begin it's easy, he told her encouragingly, and the others laughed, and Ainut looked blank and stolid and tightened her lips. But after a time she relaxed, it was impossible to remain frightened among these sailors who were so free from care, so unruffled, with their easy laughter and indolence as they paused for a time in Kiem on their way to Dinivolim, Jennet, and Ilavet. On their way to somewhere. They told us of the black hills of Jennet, the flowers of the interior whose juice was prized by kings, and the bazaars of Akaneck where slabs of elephant meat were sold and there were golden combs, clocks, and caged dragonflies. And where is your ship? I asked. And they told us that it was up the coast in the natural harbor of Pian, among the hills, and could not believe that we had never been to Pian, never heard of it, it was so close to us, and they looked at us with pity. Poor little millet-grinders, the woman said. She watched us from the distance of her years, travel, toughness, and knowledge, with a gaze that was ironic and sage, sad and amused all at once, with her hair disarrayed by the thousand winds of the sea.

The soup was ready. They put the pot on the sand, and the older sailor unwrapped a packet of banana leaves in which there was thin maize bread. We took the bread in pieces in our fingers and dipped it into the soup. Fire on the tongue. On the sea, light flashed like a warning.

We were wonderful children, strange, vivacious, we amused them. They could not know the source of our dazzling energy, that we were intoxicated with secrets, shame, and buried unhappiness, the unspoken knowledge that we were *hotun* people. The attention, the approval of our elders made us delirious: we sang, we were bright-eyed, witty, impulsive, daring, we gave them everything, showed them our own beach dances, giggled and even spoke impertinently because we knew it would please them. Especially me. It was so easy to be with the sailors from Prav. I felt that I could discern every one of their wishes, and when they laughed and glanced at one another I saw that I had been right, and the thought, the power, filled me with exultation. Ainut followed me; the food and acceptance made her glow. Never could they have encountered such magical children. And wrapped in our brilliant vitality, charging it with a heady essence, was our cry: Don't go, don't leave us, take us with you.

Take us with you. Take us to see the bazaars of Akaneck. Take us to Prav, to the city of Vad-Von-Poi. Take us to live in that city of towers, pulley, wells, and fountains, to be sailors, to wear trousers and blue tunics. Take us to where the women have windblown hair and tapering eyes and smoke cigars, to where they grow hibiscus flowers, the flowers that make the wine you carry in an ancient glass bottle, tied at your waist, underneath your clothes.

They drank. They sang. We tasted the wine in fearful, hesitant sips. The talkative sailor told us not to be shy. The embers of the fire grew redder as the air turned blue, still, silent, leaning toward a motionless dusk. At last they stood, kicked sand over the embers, said they were going back to Pian. I wanted to plead with them, to cry. . . . And the woman shouldered her knapsack with the clay pot bulging in it, and she looked at us sadly and told us what she knew about men and seasons.

Then they were turning toward the sea, toward the red of the sunset, and Ainut, afraid to be out after dark, was clambering up the rocks. The sailor with the spices turned toward me and caught my arm, smiling in the twilight air that was filling with shadows.

The lonely beach. The others turned away. The dark rocks. Salt, the smoke of cigars, ginger, sweat. He leaned down and kissed me with a kiss that arrested time, and then he smiled again.

Good-bye, *chakhet,* he said.

I don't remember his face. It's the only one I don't have anymore, the only face that was lost to me in an instant. The rest, I remember them, Dab-Nin, Ajo Kyet, Ainut and the other children, the *kyitna* man of the caves. I remember them all, I sort through them as if they were shells or beads, lying in the heat in the open doorway, or later, lying inside against the wall, under the worn thatch with its faint and mournful odor of rotting grain. I dwell on them, brood over the details, the hard-faced sailor with his arrogant nose jutting toward his lips, the long eyes of the woman and her polished cheeks and the way her mouth lifted in a smirk, and her sad look. But him, no, I can't remember him, he obliterated his face, the touch of his lips and tongue usurped the place of all other memories. There remains only a trace of smoke, the awareness of blue shadows, a sense of alarm, and the sound of the waves on the shore.

After the crowds cleared away, after the boat of Ajo Kyet went slowly, mournfully, trailing its clouds of incense, and a space was opened around our house, tingling, unapproachable: then, for an afternoon, we were filled with happiness. Perhaps it was not happiness, but for us the emotion of those hours was indistinguishable from true joy. My father climbed up into the house, his eyes wild and his face darkened with triumph, making his hair seem brighter, fiery. We laughed, embraced, the three of us. They had not chased us away. They had not succeeded in ruining us. And I was not feeling very sick, I sat up and ate the meal my mother prepared on the brazier, spinach and fried bananas. We all ate quickly, hungrily, keeping the door flap raised so that the daylight could illuminate the room, and we could see the boats going by, far off on the shining water, the life of the village going on despite everything. My father was full of schemes. First, he said, we'll treat you with *hawet*-blossom, and then with pumpkin flowers when they're in season. Rice-wine too, every day. And meat, if I can shoot something in the forest, or buy from Pato—to thicken your blood. Then we should go out to sea whenever we can, where the air is pure, and you should bathe.—He nodded, chewing; he was glowing with satisfaction.

And all those charms, my mother said. Will they be good forever?

I'll get more, my father said, scoffing from his confidence. I'll replace them. Eat, he said to me, eat all you can.—Then suddenly he was shaking with helpless laughter. That fat sow, he choked. His face when I gave him the blessing of *jut*.

Silence: a subtle darkening in the room.

And Ainut: I never spoke to her again. The last words I said to her: You're so stupid. The basket's full of ants. Perhaps last words are always like that, vapid, inadequate. The last words I said in life were: Hold the light.

What would I have said to her, had I been given the chance? Perhaps I would have told her of her grace, her wonderful steadiness, her beauty unpolluted by vanity, her expression, slightly solemn, yet seeking laughter. But no, I was only fifteen, fresh from adventures in my boat. Perhaps I would have said simply: Remember. Ainut, remember the time we saw the sailors, the indigo sellers, remember when we found the spoor of the leopard. . . .

I would have only those memories. But she would have many others. Now, working in her rice paddy in Kiem, she has her choice of memories, she can remember her wedding night, the birth of her son, the expansion of her small farm. She can remember the first time the man she was to marry smiled at her. Why would she waste her thoughts on me, waste her time in going over a few disjointed memories of a girl she used to play with, who died of *kyitna*?

And yet, I believe that Ainut thinks of me from time to time, perhaps when it rains, or at night when she is afraid. I don't think she flatters me in her thoughts. She must remember the way I bullied her, my restlessness, my impatience. She must remember how I could never admit to any weakness, my imperious manner of a daughter of chiefs, and the way that, if she questioned me or offered a contradiction, I would punish her for days with a cold silence. Finally she would have to coax me back, sometimes with presents, *tyepo,* bananas. I don't think she's forgotten that. And I don't think she's forgotten the three years I lay in the doorway, visible in the light of the setting sun.

(5)

I always thought we would go to the hill. First I thought we would walk there, climbing the ridges, sleeping outside on the way. Then I thought we would go by mule, and later still I thought they would carry me there, Tipyav and my father, in the hammock. No matter how we went, I used to dwell on our adventures. The starlit nights, the camping fires, the dew. And then the first sight of the house, always lit by the glory of the sun, its winged roof sparkling in the pristine air.

One day, after everyone's stopped speaking to us, he appears. He is already old. He taps at the pole of our house. We can't believe it, we look at one another. A dog, my father says, and we go on eating, or they go on, and I watch them. Then the tapping again, discreet but insistent. It's someone, my mother says. Her eyes are full of fear. My father swears. He swears more often now, now that he has had to give up his withdrawn existence and become heroic. I'm trying to draw the curtain aside. My father comes over and yanks it up. Outside, a dark blue evening, blue river light. And standing in the evening, this old man, tall and lean with a tuft of whiskers, chewing his lip, looking up at us.

No, my father says. What are you doing here?

The old man shifts his feet. It's been raining; he's in the mud. He chews his lip. I see that his vest and trousers, though clean, are ragged, and that he's carrying a pair of clean sandals. He looks unhappy and burdened with the hopelessness of Kiem, perhaps senile, at any rate very old. Two stout sacks are lying on a reed mat at his feet. Stealthy faces peer from the neighboring houses.

Holding his sandals, looking up at the sky, the old man speaks. He says that he has come down to find the Ekawi. He says that he has no message, that he has come of his own will. He says that carefully: Of my own will. He says that he's always wanted to come, but he has found it impossible until now, and that he has lived with the shame for years, and that he has no desire but to live and keep on serving his master if his master will forgive him for the betrayal. He speaks in an unbroken stream; he's clearly practiced the words. All the time he keeps looking up at the sky, holding his sandals against his heart. When he's finished, my father swears again, looking down on him from the doorway.

I don't keep servants, my father says. He's furious, trembling with rage. The old man looks at the dark blue sky and blinks. I'm finished with all that, my father says. The word *ekawi* has been banished from my life. I don't want to hear it.

My mother comes to the door. Let him come in for water, she murmurs. My father flings the ladder down, wordless. The old man clambers up, carrying one heavy bag at a time. My mother tries to take one of them and staggers.

He is Tipyav. He will stay with us and help my mother and sleep in a hammock underneath the house. He will never leave us. I don't know how he developed such loyalty, perhaps only in response to desperation. He will be our friend, our doddering uncle, our confidant, the means by which we get news from the village, our messenger, our forager, a back for me to ride on, a backbone for us all, long-suffering, patient. And he will be my mother's servant. That much is decided, that first night. Then you take him, my father shouts. Take him, if you want him. But I will be no one's *ekawi*.

And he swings down the rope ladder into the dark.

He took his boat out that night, and so he wasn't there when we opened the heavy sacks. The old man opened the first one for us, his big, black-nailed hands fumbling with the strings in the rushlight, the contents of the sack shifting and clinking. The mouth of the sack opened all at once, we saw his hand jerk to stop something from falling, but he was too late, it clanked on the floor. We watched it roll, mesmerized. My mother gave a cry. It was a cup, somber and weighty, made of gold.

Let me hold it, I cried. Give it to me.—She was so slow, she picked it up and stared at it with her mouth open. I couldn't bear the sight of that lovely thing in her squat, misshapen hand. I smacked my palm on the floor. Give it to me!

Humbly, she put it into my hands. Oh, it was beautiful, burnished, heavy. I pressed it to my cheek: it was cold, like water. My breath made cloudy patterns over its etched design of triangles and stars, and I wiped it carefully on my shirt. My mother had brought out the razor and was cutting the strings of the other sack, and always, I've always found that moment so strange, for despite our different spirits we were both blinking unusually fast, both of us struggling with our tears of joy. Why, of course you can ask me why, you've never seen our tiny house with the mud walls and thatched roof, the poor skin maps, the water pots repaired with gum, the narrow pallets and murky light, and you've never seen that light when it falls on gold. It wasn't only the golden cups and bowls, the amber necklaces, the beads of jade and coral, the ivory flutes. It was the way the room was changed by the luster of those objects, and the light became like the glow of a thousand fireflies. . . . Suddenly this room, our room, so stifling, so eternally sad, became like a place where things were always happening, a place of enchantments, reversals, lovers' quarrels, impromptu poetry, where the air had the soulful, exciting odor of incense. Oh, look, oh, look, we whispered, laughing and crying. And Tipyav wore such a mournful and awkward smile, as he told us in his shy and halting way of my father's sister, his younger sister who was called Jetnapet. Jetnapet, a beautiful name, it makes you think of the first rains, the smell after all the dust has been washed away. I'd never heard of her. I held her jade bracelet and kissed it, saying, Jetnapet, oh Jetnapet, my aunt! I loved her, I knew all about her, her beauty, her slender wrists like mine, which were so unlike the thick wrists of my mother. I knew how sad she was when she thought of my father, for what she had sent him was as valuable as an entire inheritance.

It's mine, it's my inheritance, I whispered. Then: Give me that, I told my mother sharply, snapping my fingers. I held out my hand, my arm deliciously heavy with rich jewelry, for the bowl she had held up admiringly to the light. What's that? What are you wearing?

She looked startled, confused, ashamed, her hand wandering to the amber at her throat.

Take it off, Tati. . . . Gods, on *you* . . .

We had not heard my father come in: he looked at me aghast, as if I had struck him.

How it was on the hill.

The beautiful lacquered tableware, the jade cups, the decorum, the immobility. My father tells me more about it now that I'm very weak, now that I'm dying, although we don't call it that. During our last months in the village the stories well out of him along with his tears, he unburdens himself to me. He doesn't play the flute anymore, he drinks millet beer, he smells of beer as he unplaits and combs my hair.

It was agony, he tells me thickly, his voice growing older, taking on the uneven texture of the rushlight. My mother, I've never told you about her. God of my father, Jissi, a woman to make you kill yourself, or her, or both. All right, I've told you some. I know I've told you how she never shouted or showed anger, only simpered and smiled. She had been well brought up, what they used to call "hill quality," a child-bride from the mountains up the coast. But listen, how can I tell you. She had a series of servants, always young girls, terrified as rabbits. As soon as one got used to her, showed signs of resignation, my mother would replace her with another. She needed them to be frightened, you see, needed that entertainment in her life of seclusion, someone to terrify. She needed the sound of weeping in the house, from behind the screen where the maid slept. . . . It soothed her, helped her to sleep herself. . . . They were always inseparable, my mother and her trembling maid. Other women, our clanswomen, would visit. My mother had a note at which she pitched her voice to speak to the maid—chilling, penetrating, and yet so soft. . . . The girls lived in terror, it was unspeakable. One of them ran away. The laborers tracked her. Yes, they would have killed her. But she escaped, she must have gone aboard a Pravish ship. I hope she settled somewhere, I hope she found love.

Love, Jissavet. In our house it did not exist. It was the same with everyone on the hill. Love, for our people, was synonymous with dishonor. It was something to be avoided, hidden, crushed. . . . They spoke of it in hushed tones, telling about my cousin who loved a man forbidden to her and drowned herself, or disapproving of a father who doted on his young son, saying the child would be spoiled, would become a weakling. Then I don't want to be strong, I told my mother before I left. That was her complaint, that I was weak. I don't want your kind of strength, I said. Do you know what she said to me? I wish I'd aborted you with *tama*-root.

He strokes my hair softly, my disease, my sun-red hair. It's better here, he whispers, despite everything. I know he means, Despite the fact that you are dying young. On my cheek, a tear. It is not my own.

But she loves you, I said. Your sister.

I think it was true, despite what he said, his hatred of her gifts, his conviction that she was trying to poison his home. She was young when he ran away, a girl of sixteen. He must have been a god to her: this kind, sad-eyed elder brother. She must have wept when she saw that his *jut* had disappeared from the altar, that he was gone. And she had preserved her memory of him for years, hoarded her wedding gold, made cups and bangles disappear, perhaps blamed a maid. Her treasure growing slowly in a cupboard. And then, one day, she thought it was enough, and she found the servant who had most loved him, an old man now, and she said to him: Find my brother. And old Tipyav shouldered the sacks, and she stood at the door in the twilight and watched him, her heart full of pride and love, never knowing how her gift would be received.

Jetnapet, my aunt. I kept hundreds of dreams of her; I thought of her as I lay in the open doorway. I rested my eyes on the cool, marvelous structure of the hill, and I thought: Now, my aunt, you are combing your long hair. You comb it out into sections, each one fixed with a clasp of gold. And now you are trailing your pet dragonfly on a string. Your smooth face, your deep, compassionate eyes. Perhaps you've heard of me, perhaps you even know I'm wearing your bracelet.

My father's mouth cracked. He laughed loudly; the sound frightened me. He drank from his brown gourd of millet beer, and his voice broke when he said: Jissavet, don't do this to me. You have no right.

He closed his eyes: You have no right.

And later, it was during my mother's excitement, her calculations, what we would have to sell to get us to Olondria: my father laughed harshly, sitting propped against the wall with the beer gourd between his knees in the hot night. His laugh woke me. I saw his hair straggling down the sides of his face, his wild eyes, the sweat dripping on his neck. Well, she's proved herself, he said. His voice was far too loud, and my mother looked up guiltily from the corner.

She's won, my father said. My wife is pawing through her ceremonial dishes, my daughter sleeps with a bracelet on her arm. He raised the gourd and drank, his arm swaying so that the whole room seemed occupied by its violent, wandering shadow. His teeth shone wetly when he laughed. Well, Jetnapet! Dream well on your cotton bed, you viper!

Jedin, my mother said.

Oh, the little frog is awake, is she? The little frog . . . He paused and wiped his sweating face on his sleeve. The little one, he muttered.

But we need these things, my mother said. For our journey. She stood holding a decorative ebony box.

Oh, I know it, my father groaned. Open that box, my love, it's full of blood!

But the box was full of coral.

(6)

His hand strokes my brow, trembling over my ruined hair. The odor of millet beer on his breath. Moonlight through the thin gaps in the thatch, and from across the marsh, the sound of drums, a feast. Your mother, he says.

Yes, he told me the truth at last.

Here is another map. It is a map of a face, my father's face. Small bones, a pointed chin, flat cheekbones, just like mine. Two lines between the eyes, just like mine. When he is thinking, he purses his lips in the same way I do. And his frown, like mine, deepens the lines in his brow. A swift smile, a certain noble look, and the intelligence in the eyes, the same, it's mine, it's exactly the same.

Your mother, he said.

Where is she? I asked, suddenly afraid. Where is she? Tchimu? Why isn't she back?

She didn't want you to know, he said, hoarsely, caressingly, his fingers still moving over my hair. There was so little light in the room, only the pricks of moonlight. Outside, the drums, faint voices, the baying of dogs. Go to sleep, Tchimu, I said, speaking with difficulty because of the fear. You're tired.

No, he said. No.

He told me. He insisted on telling me. He said, The truth has its own virtue, which is separate from its content. He said, this is the last story, Jissavet, the last. And it was true. He never told me another story.

There was a girl, he said, a *hotun* girl from a very poor family. Her father died when she was only a child. No, don't ask questions. It is difficult enough. She grew. She was beautiful, like—what. Beautiful like a dream one is unable to remember, with that mystery, that formlessness, that strength . . . and without knowing anything. She never knew anything, in spite of all of life's attempts—well, enough. This girl, Jissavet, when she was close to your age, but a year younger than you are, only sixteen, she went along the pirate coast, looking for snails I think, with her sister. Well, her sister, you know, is dead.

Her sister is dead. But she—she is alive. That is her triumph. And it is a great triumph, Jissi, you know.

He laughed softly, brokenly. Why can't I say it? he muttered. After all this resolution, I still hesitate. . . . You see, it is—what happened, it is the sort of thing the gods should not allow. They should not allow it. But they do. Hianot was captured by the pirates of the coast. She lived with them in the caves for over a year. Sixteen months. Her sister jumped, that is another truth, her sister leaped from the cliffs and was lost. But not she. Do you see the virtue of the truth? You must know what a valiant mother you have. Her courage, her tenacity, are incredible, even more incredible than the beauty of which they still sing in the village. She lived in the caves, injured—they had stunned her with a blow to the head during the capture, the scar is still there. She ran away three times. After each of the first two attempts, they cut off one of the fingers of her right hand. The third time she escaped. She came down from the hill and into the village, like a ghost. She was with child.

He smoothed my hair softly, softly. The odor of millet beer. Tchimu, you're drunk, I tried to say, but I couldn't. A beam of moonlight glowing on the silver of his hair, his face in darkness. Midnight. Anguish. Dogs.

Then you're not my father, I said.

And he: Of course I'm your father.—But I could hear the tremor in his voice. That tremor, I knew it: it was the shudder of fear.

No, I said. You lied to me, you and Tati. You have told me lies.

Yes, he whispered. He sat against the wall, his head hanging. Moonlight dribbled over his slack fingers.

You are not my father at all, I said. And then: The *kyitna*, I have it from him, don't I?

He buried his face in his hands.

When the wound is discovered, the source of the pain, it does not bring pain, because the pain was already there from the first. This is the greatest surprise to me. I cannot believe that I am lying calmly in the darkness while he weeps. I think of the people at the festival, there across the marsh. They're dancing, drinking millet beer from gourds. The old men, already drunk, have been drinking coconut liquor and are staggering to urinate in the weeds. Everywhere there are conversations, shouts. A woman turns. The musicians sweat over their drums and bells. The singer's cries are hoarse; he looks possessed. Beneath a tree two women help another to fix her braids in place. And the young men, the girls dancing in lines, the moonlit laughter and the dogs, the sheen on the water, the fear of snakes, the beer spilled on the ground, the arguments, the secret love among the palms, the hands clapping, the crying child. It's all there, complete, just out of reach. The discovery has hollowed out my spirit and made me light. Now I can hover over the world, now I belong to no one. And all things come to me of their own volition.

My mother, too. She comes back. She has spent the night in the forest, or perhaps in the hammock under the house, a feast for the mosquitoes. I haven't slept. I watch her climb the ladder we left hanging and begin putting charcoal into the brazier.

I'll never talk to her about it. I can't. In that way I am like her, and not like the father who is no longer my father. I don't believe in the virtue of truth. Like my mother, I'm cowardly, I hide, I'm unable to form the words. What would I say? I know that you were raped by a *kyitna* pirate. Why tell her that? She already knows I know. What else would I say, would I ask her about it, the cave, the death of her sister? No, there's nothing in it, no virtue at all. And so those words will never be said, not when my father stops talking and we're alone with only Tipyav to speak to us, not when we make the decision at last and go to the river Katapnay again to board the silent boat with its cargo of oil, not on the journey north, not on the ship or in the wagons carting us ever northward toward those pink-tinged hills, not in the mountains, not in the bleakness of the Young Women's Hall of the sanatorium, not even in terror, in death. Never, never. Up to the end we keep living in the same way. Grain, fire, time to bathe, to sleep. This was how we communicated, though these hollow gestures. Porridge, then *datchi.* And later porridge again.

Somewhere she darts, pauses, runs, trembles, stifles her breath. She climbs down rocks, through sand, through clumps of trees. Through the raw grass that cuts her feet, through the thick bushes, thorns, under branches, fighting her way among the vines. She avoids all paths, the seduction of easy passages. She runs. Sometimes she hides for a time, her heart pounding. Her two hearts. She stumbles, bruises her foot, suffers from hunger, from the heat, from the constant oppression of terror.

I don't know why she goes on. Why not stop, why not lie down and sleep? Even at night she goes on through the forest. Her breath loud, the odor of leaves overpowering in the dark, and the river Dyet so high, too dangerous to cross. She follows the river, picking oranges to suck on the way. She fights against hope, the weakness of that emotion. Then one morning she sees the first fishermen out on the water, and she walks into the village with bleeding feet.

So, you see, I didn't have any *jut,* on either side. That was only a fantasy of my childhood. The lanterns bright with fireflies, the benevolent Jetnapet, the jade cups: I had no connection to any of it. No, it's right, I told him. I believe you. It seems right. — I was satisfied not to belong to the hill. I told him so. I said: I always knew I was not one of you.

Soon after that he lost the desire to speak.

The body of corruption. Is that what I am, Jevick, is that what you think, the body of corruption? No, not you: you spoke to me on the ship, I saw it in you at once, the lack of fear, the absence of superstition. Do you know what it meant, to speak to someone my own age after all those years? For it had been years, over three years. Three years of the mist and heat and fevers and isolation in the body which Ajo Kyet proclaimed filth.

My father said I was innocent. But the gods did not agree. And after all, I was the daughter of a pirate. I was the child of the caves, of brutality, of suffering, humiliation. Cursed by the evil of that dark coast.

Hints, whispers. I remember them, especially now that I know the truth. The cruelty in the eyes, the contempt. You can't know the viciousness of Kiem, no one can know it who hasn't lived there, in that shimmer and draining heat. Sick, unable to move, I remember the women whispering, sliding their eyes toward me and then away, whispering, The mother is so unlucky, yes, that business years ago, and then the aunt, it must be *jut*. The inspired malice of Kiem is such that they would help to hide the truth from me, pretending that I must be protected, in order to increase the pleasure of words whispered just out of hearing: Rape, the pirate coast, her fingers, her child.

Later, in our house, we're so afraid. We make Tipyav come up and sit with us, just sit there against the wall. It's my father, he frightens us, we think that he might die and we don't know how we will bear it if that happens. Already we can't look at one another, my mother and I: we've been like this ever since I learned the truth; if our eyes meet by chance there's a clang, a sound that makes us cringe, the sound of a murder being committed somewhere. My mother finds it hard to catch her breath. We're both afraid to speak. She's clumsier than usual, dropping spoons, catching her feet in my father's blankets, even stumbling over his legs as he lies still, a thin, white-haired old man. Suddenly he's as old as Tipyav, older. His face has no expression. My mother washes him, silently, every night. The sponge, the vacant eyes, it's like a return to the days of the grandmother. She lets down the curtain to strip and wash the lower part of his body.

She does this, but she can't take care of herself. Her hair is filthy and she cries because there are weevils in the flour. I know what it is: it's the man who came as soon as my father stopped talking, the brutal, red-haired man from the pirate coast. I think my mother sees him in the rotting part of the roof, where the rain drips, and in the bananas infested with ants, and in everything that is horrible, perverse, and persecuting her: in the obscene gestures and grimaces of fate. I see him too, everywhere. His face, with its pale reptilian eyes, has conquered my dreams of the hill, of my generous aunt. I think of his shapely wrists, he must be handsome, he smiles at me. Stop it, I scream at my mother. You're driving me mad.

She stops. She puts the beads back into the sack. She's been counting them for hours, it's her only idea these days. We must go to the ghost country, where Jissavet will be cured. I suppose she thinks the gods will lose track of us. Idiot, she's an idiot, and I don't want to leave my father, but I'll go, if only to escape this house, this disintegrating house with its strong odor of sweat, overpowering, and its darkness where we are all losing our minds. I'll go with her, I don't care anymore. Only that day, before dawn, I will hold my father, pressing my cheek to his. And I will be the one to disentangle the strands of my hair from his curled fingers when they lower me to the boat.

The map of Kiem, Jevick: it is drawn in the stars and immortal. It is putrid, already decayed, but it never dies. It is that body of corruption in which, every hour, an innocence meets its fate, a swift and soundless dissolution. I saw the map, I saw how we followed its paths, my mother and I, how we worked together in absolute harmony, how Kiem always needs these two, the one who spoils and the one who submits, how we were made for each other in that eternal design. It came to me, so beautiful it brought the tears to my eyes, with its indisputable, crystalline magnificence. You've ruined my life, I whispered. You've destroyed everything for me. Because of you I never experienced pure happiness. . . .

It was in the Young Women's Hall. She was bending over me, wringing a wet cloth into my hair, dabbing my forehead. Her lips were parted in concentration. I closed my eyes in the odor of her breath, drunk on revulsion and despair. When I opened them I saw the pores in her skin, her huge and luminous eyes, and suddenly, I don't know how it began, I saw the *kyitna* too, how it had followed her all her life, how it had always been the sign of her destroyer. First the man from the caves, and then her child, her own child: we had always been there, as merciless as the gods. At every turn, beating her, mocking her, violating her, overturning her most humble visions, her hopes. I knew my father, I knew the man from the caves, his savage feeling at the sight of her weakness and uncertainty, the same poor flaws which had often driven me to the brink of violence: for Kiem cannot bear the presence of innocence. We hate for anyone to escape the knowledge we possess, the knowledge of the body of corruption. It was her innocence which had deprived me of satisfaction, and my cruelty which had deprived her of all pleasure. The circle was joined, complete. The attendants had already been called, and my mother struggled to hold me down on the bed. I pushed her away, not sure whether I was pushing or clutching at her because her dress, somehow, seemed always caught in my hands. . . . From somewhere far away there came a voice, a demented howling, a most chilling, hollow, almost inhuman sound, like a voice from the other side of death. I am Jissavet of Kiem, it said, over and over. I am from Kiem.

You can sit in the corner. It's all you can do when it starts raining. Sit in the dry corner and watch the water slide on the floor. It finds its way to the doorway at last and joins the rest of the rain, down there, outside. There's thunder, darkness, a cold fog everywhere.

But sometimes—wasn't it true that you would go outside, when the sky had cleared, and run, screaming and jumping to dash the raindrops from the leaves? Wasn't it true that the smell of the mud was buoyant, delightful, excessive—that the yellow light of the flats outshone the sky? And everywhere you could hear your own voice ringing in the cold air, and you would charge through the reeds, which sprang back, scattering moisture. And the sea, still bubbling, angry, glowed with a heavy phosphorescence. You could play with it: its radiance clung to the body.

It's true, I touched that radiance, but then why am I always hungry, why am I always craving more, more light, more life? This life in which I have nothing, only this illness, huge, inscrutable, this illness which has slowly become myself. When I'm alone I think of my kiss, my only kiss, but cautiously; I'm afraid to wear it out with too much remembering, I limit myself, decide that I will think of it only once in a week, in a month. It is my most private memory. When I'm allowed to think of it I close my eyes and concentrate; it's difficult to find that moment again. I start with the sound of the waves, and then I add the pungent smoke of cigars. I lick my wrist to recover the taste of salt. There, it's coming. And there it is. The intoxication of ginger on his lips, the lips of this stranger, this alien. But each time it grows fainter, until the action of memory wears it away, and I trace, in despair, its irredeemable outline.

The ship pulls away from the shore. It is too large to feel the sea. Only at noon do we venture out of our cabin. Then, when the deck is deserted, we lie under an awning, soothed by the humid air. The ocean glitters in every direction.

We burned my grandmother's body on the hillside.

I remember the journey there, all of us in my father's boat, my father rowing smoothly with his long, capable strokes, my mother weeping into a cotton rag. I was feeling important because I had a responsibility: waving a reed fan over the small dry corpse. It was covered with a thin cloth, the weaving loose as if to avoid stifling the old woman in the heat.

Never, perhaps, had Kiem known such a silent funeral. My father had learned the idea among the *tchanavi*. There were no other mourners, no blue chalk, no horns or wailing, and to my chagrin no trays of delicacies. No, only this one lean boat, this man, this woman, this child, walking through the scorched grass, skirting the forest, trudging toward a lonely spot on the hill, bare in the dry season. My mother carried the body in her arms. And my father lit the branch which set the meager shape to crackling on its pyre, while I watched the insects fleeing the conflagration. This is Hanadit of Kiem, he said in a pleasant, even tone. And we release her into the Isle of Abundance.

I think he tried to say something to me: something soothing about death, about the body's return to the wind. But I was bored, hot and hungry, scratching my insect bites, I felt no grief and therefore desired no comfort. The grass of the hill was desiccated and yellow, and swiftly turned black. I began to whine that the smoke had a funny smell. Let's go back, I pleaded, growing petulant when my father shook his head. My mother would not even look at me.

My mother: she was inconsolable, possessed by grief. For this creature, this leather doll with its odor of urine. It was if there had never been a woman on earth so miraculous, so adored, so beloved as Hanadit of Kiem. Tati, Tati, she moaned. For years, as long as I could remember, my grandmother had been incapable of speech, incapable almost of movement, a mere shell, giving nothing to her daughter, placed in a corner like an old gourd. I fell asleep on the grass and then woke wildly, terrified by my strange surroundings, the dark, smoky sky of the hill, and my mother's hideous, jerking screams.

Tati! Tati! she shrieked.

I saw her stumble, burning her hands in the bright embers.

To the end, yes, she was still the same, incompetent, clumsy, bewildered. She babbled and wept in the light of the small oil lamp. I wonder what she saw when she looked at me, if I possessed, for her, the face of the red-haired torturer of the caves. I tried to steady her hand, but my arms wouldn't move. She was tipping the lamp, not paying attention. The tiny flame shrank and crinkled. I heard her calling down the hall in Kideti, a fool to the end, enough to make you weep. Hold the light, I said.

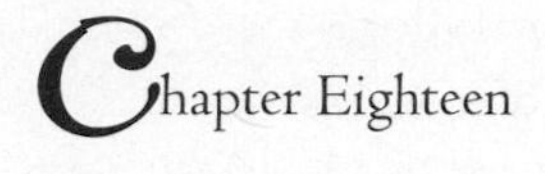

Chapter Eighteen

Spring

I wrote all through the winter. I wrote, paused, went out and walked far over the snowswept plains, a derelict wrapped in a carpet. The crone in the hillside left for her winter quarters in the village, where I could not go for fear of discovery, and I had to search elsewhere for help. The angel flickered above me in the falling snow. She showed me how to hide, when to crawl through the ditches, squirming on my elbows, how to avoid being seen from the grounds of the fortress, where prisoners worked at repairing a crack in the wall, clamped in their wooden shackles. She led me to encampments of *feredhai,* ephemeral villages of women, children, and ancients, the tents pegged fast against the wind. The men and boys were away; they had taken the cattle farther east. When I called out, a woman would raise the tent flap cautiously, shielding her lamp. And they never recoiled from the gaunt foreigner with snow in his long beard but looked at me curiously with their scintillant black eyes, and pulled me inside, exclaiming to one another in birdlike voices, and gave me medicinal herbs and what they could spare of butter and rice. Children watched from raised pallets, muffled in furs, playing with dolls made of tallow. Sometimes my hosts tried to make me stay, pushing me down with hard fingers. "*Kalidoh, kalidoh,*" they repeated. I asked Miros what it meant, and he told me it is the highland word for *avneanyi.*

I smiled. "So they know."

He nodded, head lowered, shoveling rice into his mouth. "Not hard to see," he mumbled.

"No. I suppose not."

He gave a grunt which might have been laughter. His hand on the side of the bowl was so pale it was almost blue, but its grip looked firm and sure. He ate, as he always did that winter, as if someone might take the food away at any moment, as if each meal were a matter of life and death. And of course this was not far from the truth. I had watched him hover for weeks in the indeterminate territory of the angels.

Now he scraped the last grains of rice from the bowl and handed it to me, meeting my eyes. "Thank you."

I nodded. "You look like a true Kestenyi. A bandit."

He grinned, his features almost lost between the hanging locks of his hair and the chaos of his beard. "My uncle won't know me."

The words brought a chill to my heart. I took the bowl and spoon and left him. I know that he had grown used to my strange behavior, my abrupt entrances and disappearances, my shouts in the library upstairs at night, my frequent failure to answer him when he spoke. The angel was closer to me than he: I took her with me everywhere, as the hero of the *Romance* carried a spirit in his earring. I knew her through her close, urgent, volatile, night-breathed voice, the tales she told, her songs with their borders of salt. She whispered to me, she leaned her arms on my shoulders, she pressed her cheek to mine—so that the inconceivable temperature of the eastern winter, the cold I had never felt before, shocking, wondrous, disturbing, seemed to me like the body of the angel. Like her, sometimes, it revitalized my blood on the brisk mornings when the early light was splintered by the icicles; and also, like her, it numbed me when I had sat too long in the dark library, forgetting myself in our otherworldly colloquies.

Now I went up the stairs, to that neglected and shadowy room where the carpet glittered with frost in front of the balcony door. Light came through the doorway, the implacable iron light of the winter plateau, the only light in the room until I called her. I sat in the chair at the desk before my broken pens, the ink-bottle filled with ash and water, the stack of books with her story in the margins. My hand on the stiff leather bindings gray with cold, my shadow faint on the wall. I drew in an icy breath. "Jissavet," I said.

Her voice. Its wistful texture, unrefined silk. "Jevick." Her lights, a series of enigmatic gestures among the bookshelves. And there she was, barefoot in her shift: the black and wary eyes, the childishly parted amber-colored hair.

"You stare like a witch," she accused me with a smile. "If you did that in Kiem, I would spit."

"You wouldn't spit," I said. "You're not superstitious."

"No," she said with a quiet laugh, turning her hair in her fingers. "No, I'm not superstitious. I never was.

"Is that my *vallon*?" she asked then, looking over my shoulder; for she, like me, was now an adept at passing between the worlds.

"Yes," I said, my hand on the books protective, for I could not help but be proud of those lines, wrung as if from my heart. I opened the first one, *Lantern Tales*. "This is Olondrian," I said, pointing to the printed text, "and on the sides—this is Kideti."

"No one can read Kideti," the angel laughed.

"I can," I said. I showed her how I had used Olondrian characters for the sounds the two languages shared. Sometimes I used a letter for a neighboring sound in Kideti: so our *j* sound was the Olondrian *shi*. And sometimes I altered the characters to make new ones: our *tch* sound was also a *shi*, but one that carried a plume-like curve above it.

"Listen," I said. The sun was sinking, flooding the desert with scarlet. It seemed to blaze up unnaturally, casting a threatening glow on the book in my hands. I fumbled with the pages. Suddenly my chest felt tight; distress seized me as I read the opening lines:

> *I already know about writing. We made maps: maps of the sea, of the waters between Tinimavet, Sedso, and Jiev. And maps of the rivers, the great ones, Dyet and Katapnay and Tadbati-Nut, the ones that made our country of mud on their way to the girdling sea. . . .*

"Stop," she whispered at last.

I had not finished the *anadnedet*. My voice faded uncertainly from the air.

"I'm sorry," I said. "I've hurt you." I felt the distress again, more intensely than before. My fingers curled around the page.

"No," she said hoarsely. She was weeping somewhere far away, inconsolable, beyond my reach. The pain it gave me, the sense of helplessness, was so exquisitely sharp I closed my eyes.

"It's a terrible story," she sobbed.

"No," I said. "No. It's a beautiful story. Jissavet? Can you hear me? You've told it beautifully."

"I miss him," she said. "I think he's dead, but I can't find him anywhere."

"You'll find him," I said. "You'll find him, I'll help you to find him. . . ."

Still she wept, devastating me with a flood of grief. So I spoke to her, willing her to be comforted. I snatched my words from anywhere, from the poetry of the desert and the Valley, from the songs of Tinimavet. I imagined I had met her at home in the south. I told her about this meeting, how she rowed her boat on a languid tributary of Tadbati-Nut. I evoked the tepid light, the bristling stillness of the leaves. "And I was riding a white mule," I said, "bringing pepper to sell on the hill. . . ."

And Jissavet, you drove your oar into the shallow stream, arresting the movement of your little boat, and you looked at me with startled eyes, those eyes which have the strange power to penetrate anything: a stone, a heart. I reined the mule in sharply. Can I deny that I was riveted by those eyes, with their low light, their impalpable darkness? By that shoulder, thin and flexible, that flawless skin on which the unctuous light fell, drop by drop, like honey? We were engulfed in the forest, the opaque air was hard to breathe. Your expression altered subtly but unmistakably. You were no longer surprised. You sat up, quickly withdrawing the light of your glance, and faced me instead with a look of offended hauteur. . . . Then I thought, my stare has insulted the daughter of a chief. But what chief's daughter is this who, bold and careless, paddles her boat through the forest alone, regardless of her beauty which must attract the unwanted notice of her inferiors? And I greeted you, emboldened by the fact that you had not rowed away. Then your expression, so mutable, changed again. In it were all the hidden laughter, the irony, and intelligence which, now, you allowed to sparkle for the first time. . . .

Her misery had grown silent. Now she interrupted bitterly: "That's all nonsense. You don't know what you're saying."

But I told her that I knew. "I remember it," I said. "I saw everything that day, aboard the *Ardonyi*."

I told her, too, of the days before the *Ardonyi*, my days in Tyom. In the ossified glitter of the abandoned garden, where the immobility of the trees was as deep and abiding as winter itself, I spoke to her of my parents, my brother, my master. My breath made clouds of fog as if my words had condensed in the air; and when the angel spoke, her breath made light. I told her that I agreed with her father, that sorrow was everywhere, and I described the rain, the frustration, my father's wife. I think she saw Tyom then. She imagined, vaguely, the house of yellow stone on its hill overlooking the deep green of the fields. She imagined my father observing his quiet farm, monumental on the terraced hillside under his reed umbrella. "He must have looked like Jabjabnot," she said. My laughter rang in the frozen air, making the blue trees tremble. "He was," I said. "He was, he was like a god. We lived in terror of him. He was disappointed in us to the day he died."

She did not speak. I saw that I was alone. "Show yourself," I whispered.

There she was, seated on the rim of the fountain, coming into being like the letters drawn in a magical northern ink which is revealed only when held close to a flame. She rested her hands on the edge of the fountain's bowl; her feet dangled.

"Not like that," I said. "In something else. In—a coat. You couldn't sit outside like that, half naked."

She raised her eyes and looked at me gravely.

"I know," I said with a harsh laugh. "You don't feel the cold. You couldn't do this small thing just to please me? You couldn't—just to make it seem—"

She let me talk until, hearing the foolishness of my words, I fell silent.

"Then I'm all alone," I said at last.

She smiled, wise and sad. "Tell me more about your *tchavi*—Lunre?"

"Good pronunciation for an islander," I muttered. "My mother always insisted on calling him 'Lunle.' . . ."

"And was he really from Bain, from that terrible city?"

"That wonderful city," I said. I tilted my head back, looking up through the trees. I glanced at her, her incandescent darkness against the marble.

"I'll tell you his love story," I said.

I told her the story of Tialon and Lunre, and she wept. I told her everything, all of my secret things. I felt myself disintegrating, fading, turning to smoke, becoming pure thought, pure energy, like her. I wanted this dissolution, sought it eagerly. It was never enough. Never, although we clung together like two orphans in a forest. "Now you're not afraid of me anymore," she whispered, shivering. "No," I said, closing my eyes as I reached for her, touching marble.

I could not touch her. And yet she seemed so close, the glow of her skin against my hand, her voice in my ear a private music. I read her *anadnedet* again and again. I wanted to write there too, to inscribe myself among the Olondrian and Kideti words on the page. My own wild poetry scattered there like grain. I thought of her playing with her friends, and I could see her so clearly: satin-eyed, dictatorial. And it seemed to me that she had been made to answer a desire which I had carried all of my life, without knowing it.

Dark nights of Kestenya. Lamplit hours in the library. And that voice, laughing, restless, proud and forlorn. The voice that inhabited the wind and rang in the sun on the trees of ice and occupied the empty space in my heart. I had not known of this empty space, but now I recognized it, and it bled; and I was wretched, distracted, and happy. I ran in the snow, shouted, and broke the icicles on the gate in the wall, stabbing her nebulous image with those bright knives.

And in the box bed I wept. "Stop," she said. "Stop, Jevick, it's over, it's finished."

"It's too late," I choked. "I'll never know you."

"You know me now."

"But I can't do anything. I can't do anything for you. If I'd known I might have done something—found you—"

"Hush," she said. "Sit up, now. Light the candle." She asked me to throw shadows on the wall while she guessed their shapes. This was the way to play *tchoi,* the shadow game of Tinimaveti nights. But as for my angel, my love—she cast no shadow.

Miros was coming back to life. He walked around the garden, first leaning on a stick, then upright, by himself. His face was still gaunt and fierce with beard, but his eyes had regained their brightness and his body the strength to haul water and split wood. To restore his muscles, he had begun practicing *kankelde,* the soldier's art, on a horizontal branch of a plum tree in the garden. He startled me when I came upon him swinging upside down, his face wine-dark, in the figure called Garda's Pendulum.

In the evenings we ate whatever scraps we had in the ravaged sitting room. Firelight flashed on the tangle of his hair. He said: "You saved my life this winter." He said: "I don't know how you did it. It's a miracle."

I smiled and said softly: "You really don't know?"

He gave me a guilty glance. "Well. Yes, I know. But I'm not—I'm not like my uncle."

He tugged at his earring and went on slowly: "Knowing there's an angel in the place doesn't make me want to ask it questions. It doesn't seem right."

I cleaned the last streaks of *yom afer* from my bowl and sucked my fingers. "You sound like an islander."

He shrugged and smiled through his beard. "Perhaps. I don't know."

When the meal was over we stood and he clapped my shoulder, and for a moment, grateful, I leaned into his rough, human embrace.

And then I went upstairs, and read to the angel.

I opened *Lantern Tales* again, old highland stories retold by Ethen of Ur-Fanlei. This time I read not the angel's tale but the story printed there. Its ornate diction recalled an earlier time, before the war in the east. Ethen at the window of her room above the river where she spent several years as the guest of the Duchess of Tevlas, the tall floor lamps on the balcony after dark, burnt *nath* to keep away the mosquitoes, Ethen barefoot, massaging her perennially swollen ankles. *This tale was told to me by Karth, a gaunt manservant with a lazy eye, who claims to have seen the White Crow himself on more than one occasion.* I read aloud, haltingly, translating as I went. Each time I glanced up the angel was looking at me, resting her cheek in her hand.

I read. I read her *My Chain of Nights* by the famous Damios Beshaid, Elathuid's *Journey to the Duoronwei,* Fanlero's *Song of the Dragon.* Limros's *Social Organization of the Kestenyi Nomads,* which calls the east "this vast theater of miserable existences." She listened, a moth at a window. I read *On the Plant Life of the Desert,* by the great botanist of Eiloki, who succumbed to thirst in the sands, with its spidery watercolors of desert flowers such as *tras,* "whose yellow spines are lined with dark hairs like eyelashes." Sometimes she stopped me with questions. I created new words in Kideti: the Olondrian water clock was "that which follows the sun even after sunset." Some books she attended to more closely than others. She grew so still she almost faded away while I read Kahalla the Fearless:

> *What do they say of the desert? What they say of it is not true. What do they say of the dunes, the salt flats, the cities of broken gravel, and the fields of quartz and chalcedony thrown down by the majestic volcanoes of Iva? Nothing. They say nothing. They speak shrilly of the* feredhai, *and they smile and add more pounded cloves to their tea. They are unacquainted with heat and cold, they are utter strangers to death, they speak like people who have never even seen horses. . . .*

I looked up. She was still there, her light pale as a fallen leaf. "I'll have to stop," I chattered. "I'm too cold to go on." She nodded, sighing. "It is a great magic, this *vallon.*" My lips cracked when I smiled; the evening light was rarefied with cold. My breath poured out of me as whiteness, traveling on the draft. I felt it go like an ache, a tearing of cloth. I moved to the balcony doors and saw, in the instant before I closed them, the stars of the desert branching like candelabra.

I read to her from Firfeld's *Sojourns,* too: the two of us wandered together among the fragrant trees of the Shelemvain, and encountered on the fringes of the forest Novannis the False Countess, smoking her beaded pipe among the acacias. We dined at the court of Loma, where women wore tall coiffures made of hollyhocks, and sampled, in the dim greenness of the oak forests, the brains of a wild pig fried with chicory in its own skull, a delicacy of the soft-spoken Dimai. We shivered as we read of the nameless desert in the center of the plateau, which the *feredhai* call only *suamid,* "the place," where no water comes from the sky, not even the snow that falls near the mountains, "and one lives under the tyranny of the wells." And we read of our own islands, of Vad-Von-Poi, the "city of water-baskets." Jissavet's fingers flared above the page. Later, when I was almost asleep, she spoke to me suddenly out of the dark.

"I know what the *vallon* is," she said. "It's *jut*."

The gods must have loved her, and they had taken her.

In Pitot they say the elephant god, Old Grandfather, is jealous. He steals children, he steals wives. This much, he says, and no more. He is the Limiter, the controller of human happiness. He must have seen her; they all must have looked at her, even when she was a child, when she paddled her tiny boat made out of skins. They must have seen her bold eyes and her arms, dark, sunlit, polished, reflected in the brown mirrors of the pools. This girl, small and already so headstrong, with hair in those days of an iridescent black. But with the eyes, the mouth, the expression, with the waywardness and audacity which I would come to love when it was too late, when the gods had claimed her for themselves.

Those years, the years she lay in the doorway: every one of them hurts me, and every hour has an individual pain. Lost hours, irretrievable, hours that I would have taken up and treasured and which were scattered abroad in the mud. Hours in which she lay alone and deserted by her friends. But had I been one of her friends, had I eaten those stolen fish in the fields, had I been blessed, like them, with that inconceivable good fortune—nothing could have parted me from her. Not the *kyitna*, not that hair with the color of poisonous berries, which I would weave into ropes to bind me close to her side, not the hatred of all the world, not the danger of sickness, contamination, which I would have welcomed with tears of joy. Yes, I would have clasped that hair, that waist, and inhaled her frightened breath in the hope that the curse would swell to make room for me, that we might be together, safe, removed from everyone else in the honor and preference which death had shown for us. To be, like her, an aristocrat of death, who would bury us under his scarlet blossoms. To suffer, like her, from torrid fevers. To clutch her hand as I struggled for life, to hear her words of comfort gathering the transparent coolness beyond the stars.

For the first time in many months I prayed to the god with the black-and-white tail, incoherent and extravagant prayers. I prayed that once, just once, the laws of time might be suspended and I might find myself, ten years ago, in Kiem. I prayed that she would stay with me forever, that somehow we would enter the magical, intimate purlieus of her book. And I called down terrible punishments on the playmates of her childhood: that they might first love her memory, and then perish. "Let them die," I begged, "but only after they've suffered as I'm suffering." It seemed to me that the whole world must know of her, must recognize that with her death the universe had altered and the fields, the forests, the rivers were full of ashes.

Is *kyitna* the sign of the hatred of the gods? Or of their love?

Fading, exhausted, she lay in the open doorway. The heavy light, falling across her stomach like a wave, seemed too much for her body to support. Fragile, she was fragile and impermanent as salt. Like salt she would dissolve, lose her substance. And like salt she would flavor everything with a taste that was sharp and amniotic, disquieting and unmistakable. The gods saw. They saw what I had seen aboard the *Ardonyi,* this girl with her piquant, pleasing oddity, her lips from which such strange utterances fell, such as when she had said to her mother, "He has the long face of a fish." They saw the dark and vibrant eyes in which all of her life was concentrated; they knew her erratic moods, her mysterious will, her loneliness which she could not explain to anyone, and her violent rage which had given me so much pain. And they knew more. Into her brain they went, and into her heart. They probed those elusive gardens, those nocturnal roads. They knew the black and sinister wells, the mazes, the sudden traps, and the floating, limpid, inaccessible evenings. Had they not simply recognized, in her, one of themselves? One who, through some cosmic accident, had come to reside on the island of Tinimavet, lost like a star which finds itself, all at once, far from the others. And then the cry had gone out from the Isle of Abundance. And they had crouched, anguished, watching this one who had fallen somehow from the skies. And then with slow and careful gestures, so as not to startle her, they had led her back, and she had departed with them.

"When I was alive, even when I was alive," she whispered to me, "I didn't want to live as I do now."

We went out into the orchard, through the rusty gate, the great flat country glittering before us and the wind rising. The wind, the

Kestenyi wind. I called it "four hundred knife-wheeled chariots," but Jissavet called it "the soldiers of King Yat." It drove the thin snow writhing over the cracked earth of the plain and set the prayer bells jingling on the goat-hair tents. "That one." She pointed. "They've just traded for some lentils and only the eldest of the sisters is there, the one with the kindest heart." I called at the tent flap, hoarse in the wind, and a pair of startled eyes peered out from under joined brows like an island hunting bow.

She exclaimed in Kestenyi, a clatter of sounds. I gestured at my loose jacket. "Please," I said in Olondrian. "Please, my lady, I'm hungry."

"*Kalidoh!*" she breathed and pulled me in where a low fire burned in the center of the floor, sending up a sweet, rough scent of dung. "Sit," she said in a mangled Olondrian, forcing me down on a woven stool. Her gestures were quick, her long, large-knuckled hands in perpetual motion. She adjusted her mantle over her shoulder, flicking its beaded hem out of reach of the fire, and squatted to prod at a bubbling pot balanced in the coals. She said something in Kestenyi, her voice raised. I heard the word *kalidoh*.

"There's another," Jissavet said. "Beside you. Her grandmother."

I looked more closely at the pile of skins on the floor. A thin face watched me, clear-eyed, ringed with fine gray hair.

"Good afternoon," I said.

"No," the granddaughter advised me. "No Olondrian."

The grandmother lay still, staring.

"Look at her eyes," Jissavet whispered.

"I know."

"She isn't dying. She only looks like she's dying. She isn't, though. She's going to live for a long time."

The granddaughter served me lentils and dried meat in a leather bowl. I ate half and showed her my empty satchel: "I need some for my friend." She threw her hands up, scolding as I made to put the remains of the food in the satchel, snatched the bag away and filled it with dried lentils.

"No," I said. "Too much."

She waved her hand dismissively, her face turned away. "For the *kalidoh*. For the *kalidoh*. Not too much."

On her bed the grandmother gazed at me with stricken, watchful eyes. A gold earring curled beside her cheek, lavish as spring.

"Sick?" I asked the granddaughter.

She shook her head.

"No, not sick," Jissavet said, almost in a whisper.

"Jissavet."

A warning in the air, an electricity. Grief.

"Jissavet."

She burned beside me, a bright tear in each eye.

I sank to my knees on the floor, her pain going through me like fire in the grass. "Jissavet."

"Tell her he's dead," she choked. "Her boy. He's not coming back."

I looked up, the fires fading. The granddaughter stared, mouth open, the satchel in her hands.

"I'm sorry," I panted. "The boy is not coming back. He's dead."

She dropped the satchel. "Mima," she cried. A string of Kestenyi words, and then a keening. She drew her mantle over her head.

The old woman did not weep, did not cry out. She lay so still she seemed to be calcifying, turning into stone before my eyes. The light of the low fire sprang back from her cheek, which the terrible hardness descending on her body had turned to mother-of-pearl.

"Grandmother."

Frightened, I crept to her and took her skinny hand. Her eyes were knots of amber that did not blink. Then, unthinking, I whispered to her in Kideti. "There, daughter. It's gone out now. Easy and cold, like a little snake."

The angel, outside my vision, grew still. The weeping granddaughter too; though she whimpered, there was no harshness in her cries.

The air of the room seemed lighter. I heard the gentle crackling of the fire, and a wind sent ripples along the wall of the tent. Just as my straining muscles relaxed, the old woman squeezed my fingers in a vicious grip and burst into a passion of weeping. The granddaughter, gulping, took my place at her side and dried the old woman's eyes with her mantle. The two wept quietly for a long time.

At length I rose, trying not to disturb them, and picked up my satchel.

"Wait," the granddaughter cried, beckoning me back.

The old woman fixed her large light eyes on me. She reached down to the earth and dug a series of careful lines with her fingernail. A wolf took shape, coming into being as I watched, alive in snout and limb, the hairs on its belly distinct. She nicked its teeth into place with a few deft twists and lay back, closing her eyes.

The granddaughter motioned at the drawing. "Gift," she said. "For the *kalidoh*."

I gave her a snake she could not understand, and she gave me a wolf I could not take away. It's fair, I thought, shouldering my satchel over the plain. The wind had fallen; the snowy earth was lighter than the sky, holding the murky luminosity of a coin.

"Jissavet," I said, and she was there, her smile a garland. We walked slowly homeward under the darkening sky.

When I swung the gate open, its creaking seemed to echo.

"What's that?" Jissavet said, and I looked up, sensing a change in the air.

"Thunder."

In the desert a rain of five minutes is like a carnival.

The rains fell in short, sharp bursts, and ephemeral meadows sprang up on the plateau; the snow melted, leaving great empty patches of shining earth and tender flowers of concentrated gold that froze and died in the night. The vines of the *yom afer* turned green and sprouted all over with saffron-colored blooms, giving off an insipid scent, and frayed like pumpkin flowers; the eerie plant called *laddisi* burst forth with its flowers like pungent white stars and its green, obscenely swollen sacks of formicative blue milk. The rains washed the marble terrace of Sarenha-Haladli; I skated across it barefoot, laughing after the angel, the rose trees snagging my shirt. Water lay in the bowl of the fountain like a forgotten hand mirror, and all the trees were studded with buds like knobs of brass.

In a month or less it would all be blown away, replaced by scorching sand, the thorn trees withering through the sapless days; but for now it was ours and we reveled in it, elated by the sudden perfumes, the transitory carpet of the meadows. *And the hills of Tavroun, she wears them like a necklace.* "Show yourself," I said, and she turned for me like a lamp in the ringing fields. The wind blew through her, fresh and startling, spiced with the odor of the plateau, an animating fragrance like crushed pepper. And her laugh went dancing in sparks of light when I told her how I loved her and how silken and volatile she was, and haughty like a black flower. Her arms encircled me, full of the essence of spring. She was so alive, so alive I forgot that the name of the life she lived was death.

"You have to go home," she said.

"Not now. Not yet."

"Soon," she whispered. A chilling sound, a brush against my third vertebra.

Rain pattered on the window, touched with light. I could hear Miros downstairs, singing, hacking up furniture for the fire.

"You have to go home," she repeated, "and so do I. When the time comes, you will release me. I've told my *anadnedet*. I'm tired of the ghost-land. Old."

She hovered by the lamp. It was true, she had grown old. A century of living in her eyes.

"Please, Jevick. It is the last thing."

A movement below in the garden. I froze.

"It's here, isn't it," I whispered, staring. "The body."

Her tears like springtime over the great plateau.

I leaned to the window. Auram, High Priest of Avalei, was coming up the path.

Book Six

Southward

Chapter Nineteen

Bonfire

But preserve your mistrust of the page, for a book is a fortress, a place of weeping, the key to a desert, a river that has no bridge, a garden of spears.

Nothing could have prepared me for the silence that was to follow. Had I been told of it, I would not have believed. Such silences, such griefs, no one can predict them, they come like the first red gleams of *kyitna,* unimaginable until they are suddenly there.

The morning was bright and still. A few white clouds hung on the edge of the sky, a frail scaffolding of mist above the hills. Snow lay in the cracked bowls of the fountains, but already the trees cast denser shadows, bristling with tentative leaves. I swept a space in the orchard clear of snow, built up a heap of broken chairs, and placed on them the pink box Auram had brought with him: a wooden confection adorned with carved rosettes in which the bones of my love had been folded and put away like a musical instrument. The sound of something shifting inside the box knocked at my heart; my hands were sweating, and when I had positioned the coffin I wiped them on my coat. The house observed me, silent. Miros and Auram were there, but no one looked out; they had left me to complete this ritual alone.

I am the last thing you will see, I said in my heart. I am the last, I have carried you in my arms, I have brought you home.

"This is Jissavet of Kiem," I said aloud, my voice taut and strange. "And we release her into the Isle of Abundance."

I crouched beside the pyre and touched it with the flame of an oil lamp, now on the left, now on the right, north and south. At first it would not burn. Black feathers of smoke curled around the delicate pink of the box, and I gritted my teeth, impatient now for a conflagration.

An annihilating transcendence like the death that lovers feel. She was waiting for it, glowing with absolute desire, and her desire made a desolation of the garden, turned the sparkling trees to ash, blackened the marble of the fountains. The books that held her *anadnedet* were stacked nearby on the ground. If the book was her *jut,* then let it go with her. Let it burn, as we burned *janut* in the islands. "Burn, burn," I whispered. "Burn, scorch this garden, flicker in tongues. . . ."

The smoke increased in density: it rolled on the wind, stinging my eyes, smelling of dust, dark libraries, burning cloth. Then a low glimmer, faintly orange in the sun. I tossed my little lamp on the pyre, and the oil hissed up in a ribbon of light.

A startling crack as the wood split. The odor of burning varnish, sparks of livid blue and green along the box. The gilded roses blackening. More loud cracks, making me start. The paint destroyed, flaring up, turning to soot. And then the flames, eager, crackling, devouring. Tears poured down my face. The flames were eating their way to the heart of the box. What was left there, Jissavet, my love. Your broken, delicate bones. Fragile fingers, ankles like cowrie shells. And a ball of hair, perhaps that ball of flame which burst up suddenly like a star, with a coarse, tragic, appalling odor. Other odors were there, despoiling the freshness of the day: something like resin, spices, a tainted revolting sweetness. I covered my eyes with my hands and sobbed, sitting on the ground, one hand pressed on that sad collection of volumes spotted with ink like blood. She's going, I thought in panic. And she was. She lifted away from my heart, tearing it as she vaulted into the sky. Her foot snagged in my veins, ripping away, floating free. She was climbing that dark and trembling ladder of smoke. "Jissavet!" I cried. I snatched up the books and held them to my chest, unable to burn them now, gazing up at the sky. There, where the smoke was fading. Where the sky was the purest, most tranquil blue. Where she had gone alone, no *jut* to take her hand. Lighter than snow or ashes. Where she had entered at last the eternal door, leaving me inconsolable in the silence.

The silence. End of all poetry, all romances. Earlier, frightened, you began to have some intimation of it: so many pages had been turned, the book was so heavy in one hand, so light in the other, thinning toward the end. Still, you consoled yourself. You were not quite at the end of the story, at that terrible flyleaf, blank like a shuttered window: there were still a few pages under your thumb, still to be sought and treasured. Oh, was it possible to read more slowly?—No. The end approached, inexorable, at the same measured pace. The last page, the last of the shining words! And there—the end of the book. The hard cover which, when you turn it, gives you only this leather stamped with old roses and shields.

Then the silence comes, like the absence of sound at the end of the world. You look up. It's a room in an old house. Or perhaps it's a seat in a garden, or even a square; perhaps you've been reading outside and you suddenly see the carriages going by. Life comes back, the shadows of leaves. Someone comes to ask what you will have for dinner, or two small boys run past you, wildly shouting; or else it's merely a breeze blowing a curtain, the white unfurling into a room, brushing the papers on a desk. It is the sound of the world. But to you, the reader, it is only a silence, untenanted and desolate. This is the grief that comes when we are abandoned by the angels: silence, in every direction, irrevocable.

Chapter Twenty

The Sound of the World

When the pyre was a tent of smoke, I walked away.

I walked through the prince's gate and far out over the vastness of the plain. There was no angel to keep me from losing my way. But there was a signal behind me, a smudge of darkness rising to the sky. And at dusk, I knew, there would be a glimmer of light. I walked with my hands in my pockets, listening to my footsteps and my breath. This is the sound of the world. When I turned back at last, the prince's house stood outlined against the bounty of the stars.

Candles burned in the dining room. Great swaths had been cleared in the dust that covered the table. When I entered, Auram rose, throwing back his cape. He bowed, then raised his head again, triumphant and austere. A ghostly bandage glimmered on his wrist.

"*Avneayni,*" he said.

Miros, seated beside him, rose.

"Surely I no longer deserve that title," I said.

"You will deserve it always, my friend!" said Auram. "But come, sit. There is wine, and my manservant has prepared a meal."

I glanced at Miros.

"Not me!" he said with a hard smile, raising his hands. "I've changed professions. I'm going into the army."

"The army," I said. For a moment I was lost; then I recalled the words of his delirium, his dream of the secret army of the prince.

"Come," Auram invited me, extending his good hand. And for the first time I noticed the papers on the table. Bainish newspapers. I walked over and touched the cheap stuff darkened with print, and the ink clung to my fingers like moth dust. At first I could not make sense of the letters: they were too bold, too contrastive, too crude after weeks of the gracefully written books in the library. Then they sprang into meaning like a mosaic seen from a distance, and I sat and huddled over them with Miros.

We read of the Night Market. There were reports of the fire, of the Guard's attack on unarmed *huvyalhi,* of the trampled corpses. There was a report of an *avneanyi,* denied in the next issue of the paper, then revived the following week. I read: "The hand of the Priest of the Stone, too long gripping the fair throat of the Valley." I read: "The freedom to worship." I read: "Shame." There were pages of angry letters, so fierce the paper seemed hot to the touch. It was clear that the winds had turned against the Priest of the Stone.

I looked up. Auram sat jewel-like in his impenetrable disguise, glowing from the exotic stimulant of the Sea-Kings. He smiled. "You see, *avneanyi,* you have given the prince and his allies what they most desire."

"What is that?" I asked, suddenly fearful.

"War."

Miros leaned over the papers, absorbed. The fire hissed, sending up sparks.

"War," I said.

"Yes, *avneanyi.* A war for the Goddess Avalei. A war of revenge, for those who perished in the Night Market, for the *feredhai,* for all of Olondria's poor and conquered peoples."

He lifted his head proudly. Now Miros was looking at him too. "The Priest of the Stone has ruled Olondria too long," Auram said. "Our people can no longer bear it. They cannot bear, anymore, to be kept from all unwritten forms of the spirit."

An edge came into his voice. "It will be a great war, *avneanyi.* You ought to stay for it. To see the libraries fall."

My heart shrank. "Must they fall?"

He shrugged, his eyes an impersonal glitter. "What can be saved will be saved. We are not criminals, but the protectors of those without strength."

"Those without strength," I repeated. My blood ran hot; I stood. I could have struck his face there in that funereal dining room. I could have seized the back of his head and brought that beautiful, bloodless mask down again and again on the oaken table. I could have torn down the portraits on the walls, where the prince's accursed ancestors smirked through the dust with overfed red lips. "But you caused this. *You.* You knew the Guard would come to the Night Market. You set a trap with those you claim to serve. And with me."

"I did," he answered calmly.

"Jevick," Miros murmured, rising and touching my arm.

"I did," said Auram, piercing me with his knife-point eyes. "I did. I am not ashamed. You do not know, perhaps, of the schoolchildren of Wein, who were attacked by the Guard nearly fifteen years ago."

"I do know of them," I said, shaking with anger.

He opened and closed his mouth, off balance for a moment. Then he said: "Well. If you know, then you know that those children were never avenged. No one was punished for their deaths. That is the leadership of this butcher, the Priest of the Stone. And I will not have it."

His narrow chest moved under his brocade tunic; his eyes were horribly steady, holding rage as a cup holds poison. "I will not have it. Now all Olondria knows the truth. The Night Market showed them. I bleed for those who fell there, but not more than I bleed for the schoolchildren of Wein. Not more than I bleed for the province where we now sit, occupied and mutilated for a hundred years, not more than I bleed for Avalei's people, the *huvyalhi* of the Valley. And do not forget that I risked my own life to start the war that will save them. And yours," he added before I could remind him. "And yours."

I sat down and put my head in my hands. I heard the shifting of Miros's chair as he sat, the susurration of the newspapers. I raised my head and looked at him. "And you agree with this, Miros."

His face was stubborn, though his voice shook as he said: "I am Avalei's man."

I stood up again. I walked around the table. My body would not be still. Firelight glimmered on the empurpled walls. I spun to face the priest. "But the libraries, Auram—you need them too! Leiya Tevorova's book, *The Handbook of Mercies*—you saved it from the Priest of the Stone! If the libraries burn—"

"Yes," he said. "Much that we love will be lost. But the memories of Avalei's people, as you know, are long. And the choice that faces Olondria now is a simple one: Cold parchment or living flesh? And I have made my choice."

I shook my head. "That is no choice. No choice one should have to make."

"I agree. But it was forced upon us the moment the Telkan sided with the Priest of the Stone. The moment Olondria chose the book over the voice. Now we must balance the scales."

"The price is too high."

He smiled. "Come. Let me tell you a story."

I shook my head again. My lips trembled. "No more of your stories."

His smile grew softer, more encouraging. He patted the chair beside him. "Come, one more. A story about a price. You will not know it, for it is very seldom told. The tale of Naimar, that beautiful youth . . ."

The story bloomed inside him, inhabiting his body, a kind of radiance. I saw that nothing would stop him from telling it. All through my journey his stories had fallen like snow. He was as full of them as a library with unmarked shelves. He was a talking book.

"Naimar was raised in a palace in a wood," he began in his throaty voice, "the only child of his father's only love. His mother had died in birthing him; the palace was dedicated to her, and it was called the Palace of Little Drops. Those drops were the tears she shed on the newborn brow of her only child, when she held him in the instant before her death. The boy was raised among mournful paintings and images of her: the statues in the garden all bore her likeness. Sculptors had fashioned her sitting, weaving, walking, leading her favorite stallion, caressing the hoods of her beloved hawks. The child was strikingly like her, with his wide eyes and parted lips, his black hair and the anemones in his cheeks! And because of this he came to brood over her, and over death—for he was soon the same age as the lady in the garden."

Slowly I walked around the edge of the table, returned to my chair between Auram and Miros. The priest turned to keep his eyes on me as he spoke. "Then the world lost its savor for him," he went on with a sigh, "and he found no delight in it, neither in hunting, wine, music nor concubines. . . . His father despaired of pleasing him, and Naimar wandered in the woods, wild and woolly haired, and of savage aspect. One day he went to bathe in a stream, and as he was bathing there a Lady appeared to him, clad in saffron-colored robes and beautiful as a rose. 'O youth,' said she, 'stand up from the water, that I might see thee plain, for I am already half in love with thee.' 'Nay,' said the boy, 'what wilt thou give me?' 'What is thy desire?' said she. And he said: 'To escape death, to become immortal!'

"Then the Lady smiled and said, 'That is easily granted.' And he stood, and the water fell from him in streams. And the Lady admired him greatly, and a blush spread over her cheek; but Naimar said: 'Now grant that which thou promised.' 'Willingly,' said the Lady. And she plucked a handful of lilies which were growing by the stream, and took the bulbs, and washed them in the water, and she bade the boy to eat them. And taking them in both hands, he did so.

"'Will I become immortal?' he asked. 'Surely thou wilt,' she said. And as she spoke, the boy cried out, and fell; and the Lady, who was Avalei, looked down at the beautiful corpse that lay on the bank and smiled. 'Thou art immortal,' she said."

In the aftermath of this virulent tale I looked at the priest, aghast. And his red lips parted in his most childlike smile. I sat up straighter, pushed my chair back and turned from the priest to Miros as I spoke, so that both of them could see my face.

"I will tell you the truth," I said, "and if you think me a wiser man than you, and you listen to me, so be it, and if you do not, so be it. Your prince will be a tyrant. He will not hesitate to burn libraries or palaces or *radhui*. He will set Olondria aflame."

Auram inclined his head slightly, a gesture of acceptance. "You may be right. But he will save a future, a way of life. For those who cannot read, he will save the world."

I knew it was true. A certain world would be saved, but it would no longer contain the Olondria I knew.

No more battles, I thought, no more arguments. I held out my hand to the priest, and he placed his own inside it, white driftwood barnacled with rings. So frail, so cold, with a bandage on the wrist.

His dark eyes questioned me. "Forgiveness?" he said.

"No," I answered. "Farewell."

A night of desert stars and silence, poignant as a breath. I sat on the bed and watched the open window. No angel tore the air. The sky was motionless, complete above the sleeping mountains, seamless as a glass. I did not close my eyes, because when I did I saw Miros screaming in battle, blood-streaked mares, Olondria on a pyre. I saw war come, and I saw myself far away, in a courtyard of yellow stone, with no one to bring me messages from the dead.

The heavens turned. A dark blue glow came to dwell on the windowsill. Slowly the shapes in the room emerged from the dark as if rising from the sea. There was the mantelpiece, there the door.

There was the wrought-iron table and the stack of books that held the *anadnedet.* And there was my satchel, rescued by the priest, with all my books inside: *Olondrian Lyrics,* the *Romance of the Valley.* The record book where I had scribbled my agony in Bain. And the packets of Tialon's letters, heavy as two stones.

He had brought them for me. When his Tavrouni allies had killed the soldiers in Klah-ne-Wiy, he had had the presence of mind to collect my things, this precious satchel and the angel's body, and he had hired a servant and suffered his broken wrist to be tied in place by a local doctor. A group of soldiers met him when he came out of the little mud clinic. Auram smiled at them, his disdain as gray and icy as the sky. They took him to Ur-Amakir, the nearest city, where he was to be tried for treason and the murder of the soldiers. He would be very glad to oblige, he said. News of the Night Market had reached the city; crowds gathered chanting outside the jail where he was held. Realizing that his oration in court might spark riots, the Duke of Ur-Amakir accepted his claim of innocent self-defense and released him.

And he came to Sarenha-Haladli with the body, as he had promised. He was, after all, a man of honor.

I stood. My bones ached with a sorrow older than myself. I went to the table and put my hand on a book to feel something solid. It was *Lantern Tales,* in which Jissavet's words murmured like doves. I remembered her telling me: *I know what the* vallon *is. It's* jut. Now she had helped start a war in a far country to liberate those who could not read, the *hotun* of Olondria. I wondered, for an unguarded moment, what she would have said. But I knew that this was not her war. Nor was it mine.

I packed the books, put on my boots, and set the strap of the satchel on my shoulder. There was already enough light to see the steps. Downstairs in the dining room, where the shadows of the rose trees streaked the windows, Auram's Evmeni manservant was boiling coffee. Soon Miros came in, supporting the arm of the hooded priest with a new tenderness, a reverence. We sat together in the lightening air. The servant gave me a glass of coffee clouded with white steam. Its flavor was earthy, stinging, coarse: the taste of Tyom.

Difficult, difficult, difficult!
Difficult to carry these blankets

and these curds, threads, skins and splendors
into the Land of Red Sheep.
Maskiha spinning your wool,
spin the sun into blankets for me.
For all night I am lying alone now,
in the shade of invisible spikenards.
I go to where the water is sweet,
and the peaches are of carnelian.
Someone tell me why my road
is eternally strewn with ashes.
And why in the doorways of the sky
there are girls whose palms are rivers of milk,
bursting, flowing, dissolving like snowflakes
over the Land of Red Sheep.

Miros sang as we traveled in the priest's carriage along the cart-tracks, the country altering slowly, kindling with the sparkle of orchards in flower. Soon the track grew wide and level and bordered with fragments of brick, and there were more sheep and fewer cattle in the fields. Far away to the south waved the blue fringes of a forest. Birds filled the air, geese and swans flocking around the reservoirs. Honeysuckle drowned the balustrades of the country houses, and bildiri villages smoked in clouds of alabaster dust.

The sun brought the color back to Miros's face; the meals we ate in the villages filled out his frame. He was almost himself again when we reached the southern Tavroun. As we rolled beneath the ancient aqueduct into the town of Tashuef he was singing a *vanadel* that made the priest's servant snigger. And when we went out that evening to a tavern called the Swan, he appeared altogether restored, tall and fresh. We ate a Valley meal of *kebma,* sour cream, and mountain olives, followed by a dish of apricots and quails. After a bottle of insipid wine we began on the white-hot *teiva* with preserved figs floating thickly in the bottle, and listened to the Evmeni musicians playing their long guitars and violins among the streetlamps and shadows of trees. It was like an evening in the Valley. Only the dryness of the air, the peculiar echoes of the sounds, and the aloof and solemn propriety of the patrons at other tables, made it clear that we were still among the mountains. We removed the tablecloth and marked the little table with chalk, and Miros taught me the elementary rules of *londo* and promptly won six *droi* from the purse the priest had given me and shouted to the waiter: "Another bottle. And bring us some chicken livers."

Turning to me he grinned and said: "I know I owe you my life. But you owe me six *droi*."

"You may have the *droi*," I said, "if you will take care of your life."

His face grew pensive, showing its new hardness under the lamps, a touch of age. "I will care for it, body and spirit," he said.

Afterward we walked through the stiff brick streets of the town, passing doors where the names of the owners hung in brass, singing *vanadiel* to the barking of chained mastiffs and the tolling of a bell in the temple of Iva. We saw no rubbish pits or decaying backstreets. All was trim, definite, contained. The shadows lay very straight and black. We compared the town to the nomad camps where refuse fell haphazardly, submitting to the purification of sand.

Under an old arcade he said: "This is a city of emptiness. Look, there's no one awake in the whole square. No late-night carousers, not even a soldier. Look at the benches, all alone. And that house with all of its shutters bolted. This is a place you could bring a woman to with complete discretion. She'd wear a Kestenyi mantle in the streets. I don't think anyone would question you, or even notice. . . ."

"Would she come here with you?"

"Never," he laughed.

He did not mention her again. And now we stood at the inn where lamplight fell on the whitewashed steps, the sleeping geraniums. He gripped my shoulders and saluted me with kisses on both cheeks, calling me *bremaro beilare*, "my poor friend." I was already forlorn, thinking of traveling without him. A grumbling servant answered our knock at the door. Dawn was breaking as we walked to our rooms, and Miros's outline seemed to waver in the cinder-colored air.

And in the morning I left the town of Tashuef, I left Kestenya. I boarded a riverboat called *She Lies Weeping* and leaned on the railing squinting at the wharf, the merchants and soldiers swearing, the crates of fish being swung overhead on ropes. There was the carriage, Miros seated on the box with the driver, both of them waving. Miros had wrapped his head in a scarf, Kestenyi-fashion. I saw rather than heard his good-byes, his mouth open and shouting. Of the priest I saw only a bony hand at the window.

"Good-bye," I yelled back, knowing they could not hear me. The river swelled beneath the vessel, wide and full, a milky blue beneath the sky. The hills rose smothered in grass and flowering thorn on either side, and over them the peaks of snow hung shining like foam.

We passed the Land of Gum, the Land of Willows, the Land of Mice. Far off in the pallid east glimmered the Sweet and Bitter Lakes. The villages had names like Weam, Lilawu, Elwianab—Evmeni syllables rounded and dropping like honey. South of Wun there were camels imported from the desert of Waob; at Welawion I saw the first elephants. And yet the effect was not one of excitement, but of fatigue, for the land continued gray, mud-hued, and oppressed by a salty wind. Often I saw men asleep in their boats, their lips white with salt. In coastal pastures enervated sheep chewed colorless grasses. In the distant east the fringes of the Dimavain waved like flags of dark blue silk, exuding the same refreshing seduction as the mountains.

Orange trees, date palms, the colocynths Fodra called "the flowers of sleep." At Ur-Brome I boarded a ship for Tinimavet. My satchel, my clinking purse, and my sore heart. It was trying to live again, that heart: it throbbed in me like a scarlet bruise. Ur-Brome reeked of smoke and sewage, in full sun but somehow failing to absorb the light, its flattened squares preserving the dullness of fog. As we pulled away from the shore a feeble clamor went up from the crowd on the quay and a woman beside me wept beneath her parasol.

Inscrutable country of the north—ravishing Olondria! Suddenly, as we pulled away on the sea, she unveiled the beauty of that coast with a limpid gesture of the light which seemed to contain a coy and voluptuous smile. A wash of blue poured over the sea that had been so thick and gray, a blue of dazzling, ineffable tenderness. And the city took on the delicate colors of a bed of roses on the brink of death, those exquisite pinks and whites. The ivory of worn seashells glowed in its walls, and the faded gold of tapestries, and another, elusive color, the gray of chalk—a frail and etiolated color, more precious to me than the rest because it seemed to contain the essential Olondrian sadness. The woman beside me sobbed with renewed despair, throwing back her head, her sunshade drooping, two bright tracks descending from under her lashes. While on the waves the Salt Coast grew still whiter, more fragile, more luminous—and at last it was only a nimbus on the sea.

Chapter Twenty-One

Jissavet's Alphabet

"Ah!" my mother said. "What's this? You're thin. And you have a completely different face."

We sat in the courtyard in the soft air of the evening. The sky was a dark turquoise and the first stars already floated, detached and pale, as if they were not real stars but only reflections. It was the end of a day which I had spent on the back of a gaunt and sullen donkey I had purchased at Dinivolim, coming down through the forests and rubber plantations into the shimmering tea country, and at last to the cliffs of Tyom. My household was not expecting me; Jom saw me first, bellowed, charged, and crushed me to his heart in the front courtyard, and my mother ran out to meet me with a look of fear, her hair disheveled, her hands still gleaming with the grease of the kitchen. A servant was sent to fetch Lunre, who was away; others hurriedly prepared a reception for me, filling the courtyard with flowers. Now we sat there on cane chairs in an atmosphere of relaxed festivity which I recognized as the absence of my father.

"I'll soon get fat again," I said, holding up my empty plate. A servant took it and held the cloth and the bowl for me to wash.

"Fat again!" she said. "You were never fatter than a little mouse. And all of your fat, you carried it on your whiskers. . . ."

"Yes, we must fatten you," said my father's wife, wiping her narrow hands on the servant's cloth, smoothing her long skirt. She sat very straight in the growing darkness, not bending into the shape of the chair. The last rays of the sky shone on her high and polished plaits. Her face was a lean shadow. "How else can we find you a bride?" Her laugh clattered, an old spoon falling on metal. "Not that it stopped your foreign tutor. He's still as thin as a cricket, and we celebrated his wedding during the Sea Days!"

I turned to Lunre, shocked. He wore an abashed, uncomfortable smile, and I imagined that he was grateful for the darkness. "True," he said in a low voice, in Kideti, glancing away at the trees.

I stared at him. "But where is she?"

He rubbed his jaw.

My mother answered gently: "Lunre lives in his own house now, on Painted Mountain."

"You moved away," I said in Olondrian, dismayed. And he answered in the same language, his hands moving in the dark like drifting leaves. "I couldn't stay here forever, with no one to teach. I would have told you later, but . . ." He shrugged, eloquent in silence. The servants brought two braziers from the kitchen, and the reddish light revealed a demure smile on the face of my father's wife.

"Congratulations," I told Lunre in Kideti.

He looked at me, his face serious, filled with gratitude in the dimness. "Thank you," he said. He reached and grasped my hand, then patted my arm as if to feel that I was real, was here beside him. "Jevick," he murmured. His voice hummed out in the twilight, his same voice. I had forgotten how thin it was, ragged in the upper register. Had I described his voice I would not have said that it had that worn quality, as if its fabric was stretched, on the verge of tearing. I would have told of another voice, smoother, nobler, more restful, yet when he spoke it was this voice I recognized: this weather-beaten voice, shredded by winds like the voice of an old sailor, brought him close to me in a dazzling instant. I knew him through his voice, despite his hair, grown longer and bleached salt-white, tied at the nape of his neck in the island fashion, and despite his vest with the Tyomish designs, his drawstring trousers and leather sandals, the costume of a fisherman of the cliffs. His voice was the same, his lanky body, the way he sat with his elbows on his knees, his sad necromancer's eyes. He played with a leaf, burning it on the coals, and the redness lit his fingers until they were incandescent with hidden blood.

We spoke. We spoke of nothing, fish and fruit trees and the gossip of Tyom, an old man's death, a number of betrothals. My father's wife, loyal to her bitterness, made only comments whose innocence concealed their essential cruelty. She was a dagger thinly sheathed, as always, only slightly subdued by the thought that I, the Ekawi, could send her away. And only this gnawing fear, evident in her strained and watchful pose, made her pitiable and therefore bearable. Her laugh rang out unnaturally, so that Jom whimpered with distress and my mother looked at her co-wife with concern. My mother, incapable of malice, even in self-defense, who humbled herself in order to soothe

the first wife: "Look at your son's clothes," she said, teasing, and my father's wife, not unaware of the kindness, sniffed coldly. "Ridiculous attire," she said. "Even his tutor doesn't dress like that." A smirk twisted her iron face in the moonlight.

It was my mother's genius, this passionate sensitivity that made her capable of knowing others better than they knew themselves. When Lunre was ready to go, we walked with him to the arch of the courtyard, a servant following with a Tyomish lamp, a bowl of oil. The light was florid and agitated, a light by which one could never read, its nervous color bouncing in all directions, lighting up my master's smile and then, leaning against the wall, the pole which he took in his hand, grasping it firmly. It was a *bolkyet,* a stick in which a narrow blade was hidden. He twisted the handle, revealing a streak of white. "In case of thieves," he grinned, snapping it closed, and my mother said approvingly: "Yes, Painted Mountain is far." I looked at her and saw, by her earnest eyes in the transient light, by the tender curve at the corner of her mouth, that her thoughts were the same as mine: she knew that Lunre would never have occasion to use the *bolkyet* he leaned upon so proudly. For any islander coming upon my master in the dark, even the most brutal and wayward criminal, would flee from his spectral countenance and supernatural height and from the pallor that indicated a lack of blood. Yet I saw that, since he had moved away, my mother had flattered him for his brusque courage in going armed among the forests, and that Lunre, who would never have admitted to physical vanity, was pleased to be seen as a man to be reckoned with. This glimpse of their new lives, so full of grace and generosity, affected me like the sight of a beautiful painting, like one of those dark and melancholy paintings of Olondria in which only a tiny corner is laden with light. There they stood, surrounded by darkness under a distant moon, lit by the thick and glancing rays from the bowl, the white-haired man with his pale and gentle eyes as changeful as water, and the woman, black-haired, barefoot, lambent with smiles. Then he put his free hand on my shoulder and kissed me on both cheeks, saying in Olondrian: "Welcome, friend of my heart." He squeezed my shoulder and turned, the servant lighting his way out to the gate, his angular shadow sliding over the path.

"He is a good man," my mother said when he had gone. "You should be happy that he has found a wife."

"I am happy," I said.

She linked her arm through mine, turning with me to walk back to the chairs. "My little mouse . . ."

The words affected her suddenly; it was clear she had not expected it. I heard the catch in her voice, and she fell silent. Then she laughed tearfully: "How silly I am! And look, Jom's taken off his vest—it's getting colder, he'll be chilled. . . ."

Jom had indeed removed his vest and stood before the orange trees with his powerful chest and shoulders lit by the moon. My father's wife walked toward me with her brisk, constricted steps and knelt on the flagstones to receive the touch of my hand. I touched her formidable hairstyle, which was barbed like a sea urchin, and she rose, muttered good night, and walked stiffly off to her room. We could hear her scolding one of the servants. Footsteps pattered, a light flashed. Then the house was dark, submerged in silence.

"Jomi," my mother said. "First One, what have you done with your vest? No, leave him," she said to me, touching my arm. "He likes it. And he's only happy because his brother is home. Aren't you, Jomi. Aren't you, my little squirrel . . ."

Her little squirrel, her little mouse. When she spoke to us her voice overflowed with love, a love that was naked, glowing, transparent, the same pure ardor that poured from her eyes when she looked at us, that lit up the curve of her cheek, inexhaustible, never flagging in strength. This love existed only to give itself, an eternal fountain. And now, it seemed to me, that my father was dead, she was free to bestow her love without the fear of being mocked or of exposing us to the danger of his jealousy. Moonlight fell in the courtyard, a white rain, immobile, diaphanous. Jom put his hands into it and rubbed his face. He went through all the motions of washing, scrubbing his hair and the definite, vivid contours of his bricklayer's physique. Soft moans escaped from him, and his laugh which was quiet and strangely flat, devoid of all but the most private emotion. A laugh like the chuckling call of a dove. He was still far from me, so far, whitening in the moonlight like a statue.

The following morning I rode to Painted Mountain.

My mother had described the secluded spot where Lunre had chosen to live. I rode up through the vivid and varied greenness of

Tinimavet, the dark green of the mango trees, the yellow-green of the coffee bushes. The canna lilies, not yet in flower, had leaves of a cool and opaque green; the papayas, throwing their white trunks toward the sky, were crowned with a green that was almost blue. Lunre's house stood alone at the end of a dusty path, its thatched roof sheltered by an enormous flame tree.

I dismounted in silence, my satchel a weight on my shoulder. The house was small, isolated, looking across the valley, surrounded on all sides by trees and dwarfed by the heavy arms of the flame tree kindling its myriad torches in the shadows. It was strange to see my master emerge smiling from the doorway, stooping to pass underneath the hanging thatch. He clasped my hand and greeted me in Olondrian, and the daylight showed how tanned with the sun he was, how white his hair.

"A beautiful morning," he said. "As always, here on the edge of the valley! Often I stand here, just looking out, just looking . . ." And he put his hands on his narrow hips and squinted over the valley where the sunlight poured on the misty green of the farms. "Beautiful!" he repeated. "Sometimes I can see all the way to Snail Mountain. Ah, but come—come in." He motioned me toward the open door, wearing a bashful, unfamiliar smile. I ducked inside and he followed me, pulling shut a door of unfinished bark.

"A shame to cut off the view," he said. "But Niahet says it lets in the flies." The room was dim and cool, with screens of woven reeds on the windows; but even in the poor light I caught the anxious glance he darted at me, his sudden firmness of purpose in saying "Niahet." I did not know what to do with myself and stood holding my satchel in front of me while Lunre urged me repeatedly to sit down and finally seated himself on one of the woven mats on the swept earth floor, hunched and awkward, all gangly arms and legs. It was clear that he was not yet accustomed to sitting on the floor, but he managed to make himself comfortable by leaning against the wall. I sank down on the mat across from him, my back to the door, the satchel beside me. "So, here I am," he said.

He smiled at me, his teeth white in the gloom. Flecks of sunlight clung like gold dust to the screens in the three windows. Aside from the mats there was no furniture in the room but the old sea chest, its blue paint peeling, set against one wall. A few books were stacked on top of it and, I saw with a curious throb of the heart, a simple *jut,* veiled to the waist, its spraddle-legs fashioned of copper. It must belong to the wife. It presided over my master's books in squat, enigmatic silence: one external soul watching the others.

"Welcome," said Lunre, cracking his slim knuckles in the old manner but with an overattentive air, a suppressed agitation, and I knew that he was nervous and sought my approval, that for him this visit of mine was of the most profound importance. The brilliant green of his eyes was flecked with shadows of uncertainty, bits of flotsam dulling the flashing waters. And his gaze was no longer quiet and direct: it moved, glancing here and there, at the bare walls or the attenuate streaks of light.

"Ah, Niahet," he said abruptly. His voice was unusually loud. She came in, pushing the curtain aside with her shoulder, holding a wooden tray. She was not beautiful, nor very young, though she was twenty years younger than he. She knelt before me with practiced grace.

"Hot date juice in the morning," Lunre said, still in that strange loud voice, and switching into his accented Kideti. "I know it's unusual, but I find it so—I like it so much."

I kept my eyes lowered. My face was hot.

"Ah, thank you," he said as the woman turned and knelt before him and he took his cup of date juice from the tray. I sat holding mine: its smell was heavy, dark, nostalgic, it reminded me of childhood fevers and sleep. The woman rose. I realized that I knew her, only by sight, as one knows almost everyone in Tyom: she was the daughter of small farmers, the pudgy one, the quiet one. Her brother worked as steward on a neighboring estate. She did not speak to me, of course, though Lunre gazed at her hopefully, and also, I noticed, with a mild affection. She went out with her back erect, planting her solid, bare feet on the floor, her heels glowing like yellow soapstone.

"A wonderful," Lunre said. His voice was hoarse and would not rise. He cleared his throat. "A wonderful woman," he said.

I sipped the sticky drink. My courage almost failed me; like Lunre, I did not know where to look. Here he was, married to an illiterate islander, having discovered a richness in the soil of Tyom. *Once you have built something—something that takes all your passion and will—it becomes more precious to you than your own happiness.* There was no way to begin, so I began clumsily.

"Thank you for lending me books for the journey," I said. "But you might have suggested Leiya's autobiography."

He raised an eyebrow, maintaining his smile though his gaze was very still. "Ah?"

My laugh clattered. "A joke. Of course you wouldn't have sent it with me. You knew it was banned, like her other books. *The Handbook of Mercies,* for example. I had a chance to read that one, while I was away."

He set his cup down on the tray and sat with his head bowed, frowning at it. When he raised his eyes, the pain in them went straight into my heart.

"I gathered from Sten that something had happened to you," he said quietly. "Something I may not have prepared you for. I am very sorry."

"Don't," I said. "I didn't mean—I didn't want to complain. I just didn't know how to say—I met someone. She gave me something for you." I clawed at the satchel, tore it open, and pulled out the two pink packages tied with string. "She gave me these. She asked me to bring them."

Lunre looked at the packages. He blinked at them. He touched them. For a moment he seemed not to understand their significance. More than this: it appeared that he did not know what the letters were, what writing was, that he had forgotten how to read. Then, without warning, his breath caught and his face went pale to the lips. He grasped at the packages with feeble fingers. And as I stared, my heart pounding, I heard him groan: a low and terrible sound, ghastly and grating, a sound to chill the blood.

He groaned. He clutched his side as if I had stabbed him, crumpling so that his head lay on the mat beside the fatal letters. His cries desecrated the homely innocence of the little house, profaned the green tranquility of the hill. They were ugly, bestial, appalling, their anguish obliterating all kindness, all decency. His hair was against the letters, his hands covering his face. When I crawled to him and took his shoulders, he fought me. "No. You have done enough," he shouted, thrashing in my arms.

"Hush. Hush," I said. I did not release him until his first torment had passed. Then I lowered him gently to the earthen floor. The woman, Niahet, did not emerge; I imagined her pacing her humble kitchen in an agony of fear.

"Hush," I said. He lay on the floor, still shaking, and I placed my hand between his shoulder blades in quiet authority. I willed him to endure the pain with a wisdom born of the desert, of the winter, of the evenings of the dead. Yet tears rolled down my cheeks, and my heart struggled. It seemed to me that I was a servant of death, that desolation followed wherever I passed. I remembered Tialon's brave despair, the bodies burning in the Night Market, Olondria lying under the threat of war. I had drawn that line of destruction across the north, and now I had brought it home with me to Tyom, to Lunre's house. A curse, I thought. A curse. And then I seemed to hear the angel's voice. *Stop, Jevick. It's over now. It's finished.*

"I shall never be able to speak of it," Lunre whispered.

"I know." The glinting screens on the windows wavered; I blinked to clear my vision. "You do not need to speak of it. But you will read the letters."

"I can't. I can't go back."

"I know. But you will read."

Then he sat up slowly like an old man and drew his knees in close. A superstitious terror in his face. He stared at the letters before him on the ground. "I never thought this would happen to me. It's like looking at a noose. . . ."

"No," I said. "A door."

"A door," he repeated. New tears slipped from his lashes and down his cheeks, but I think he did not know that he was weeping. Where was he looking now with his bright eyes, devoid of color in the gloom, shot with a hard, abstract brilliance? Into his old world. Where in the days of triumph and certainty he had walked in a dark robe through the gleaming halls, carrying his writing box, and rain had fallen among the trees of the roof gardens, melting the light of the lamps. There he had walked with an angel at his side. And now he looked at me. "*Tchavi!*" he said. One word, half a whisper and half a cry. It carried wonder and an anguished plea. He took my hand, bent over it, pressed it to his brow. "*Tchavi. Tchavi.*"

I imagine his departure from the palace. He's in a room, one of those small clean rooms of the Tower of Myrrh, a pallet on the floor, a few gnarled, half-melted candles, the open windows showing the sleeping fields. The first birds have begun to sing, and the fields are blue with mist, but he still has a candle lighted, on a chair, and by its light he is carefully turning books over in his hands and then packing them in tall, scuffed leather bags. He has not yet acquired the legendary sea chest he will purchase in Bain, perhaps in the Chandler's Market. The candlelight caresses his silver hair, then sinks and loses its way in the folds of his voluminous dark robe.

It is the same robe that filled with rain under the trees when the priest's daughter watched him from a high window, and now he reaches behind him and clutches its fabric in two handfuls and pulls it smoothly off over his head. It lies on the pallet, crumpled like a skin. It smells of the earth, of the wild roots he used to make its dye, of the winter rain that fell while he wove its cloth, of the wicks of lamps, of the dusty curtains in the shrine of the Stone. He stands naked, his ribs lit by the flicker of candlelight, and looks outside at the fields where the shadows are deepening. Then he bends to untie the knot of the limp cloth traveling bag which has gathered dust in the corner for nine years.

The knot will not untie. He snatches at it with icy fingers. Finally he severs the string with his teeth. It leaves the taste of ash in his mouth, and he reaches into the bag at last and pulls out the clothes, the white shirt, the tapered trousers. He is still thin as he was years ago and the clothes fit him well enough, but he does not fit them: his body is awkward. From the bottom of the cloth bag he removes, and puts on with clumsy movements, the rings and the earrings set with veined blue stones.

By the time he reaches the southern pier the hills will be blazing with light, and his earlobes, unaccustomed to the jewelry, will be sore. But now as he touches the earrings tentatively they do not feel painful, only heavy, with the dull weight of any stone. Soon he will not notice them at all, as when he stands in our courtyard and the sun of the islands fills them with liquid radiance, and the boy who converses with birds reminds him suddenly of their presence by reaching out for them and crying "*Katchimta*": Blue.

And I, too, I changed my clothes. I put away my Bainish suit and slipped into my Kideti trousers and vest. A cloak against the rains, though it was still bright and hot outside when I went to the altar room and reached out for my *jut*. A shiver of dread went through me in the instant before I touched it, and I laughed because I had never cared for my *jut*, that little claw-footed shape with the jade handles. I had never cleaned it, never oiled it, never prayed over it. "Come," I told it, smiling, and hefted it in one hand. It was heavier than I had expected, as if its insides were solid clay. When I turned I saw my mother in the doorway, and she gasped and put her hands over her mouth, her eyes filling.

"Don't go," she cried.

I held the *jut* close to my side, my cloak falling over it. "I'm glad you're here. I was going to look for you before I went. I knew you'd miss my *jut*, if no one else did."

She was not listening, could not hear me. "Don't." She rubbed my shoulder, tears bright on her cheeks.

"I'll come back," I said. "Soon. In a fortnight, perhaps. I'll always go, but I'll always come back."

"I shouldn't have let you go." She gripped my collar, her eyes fierce. "I know something happened to you there. I'm not a fool. When Sten came—he said you were ill. What kind of illness? He wouldn't tell me—he didn't know, he said . . ."

I put my arm around her and kissed her hair.

"And now you're going. With your *jut*. And I should be proud. . . . It's a blessing, a *tchavi* in the family. . . ."

Her tears soaked into my vest. I waited, knowing that at last she would raise her head, push back her hair and try to smile. And when she did I smiled down at her and told her again that I would come back when I could, soon, perhaps before the long rains. And I walked out with my *jut* under my cloak. I crossed the farm, greeting the laborers who waved to me from the fields. This happy land, I thought, this happy land. I passed the row of storage rooms, secluded under calamander trees, their doors chained shut. I went on walking, far from the village, out to the cliffs where I used to go with Lunre, the briny rocks like spines under my sandals. My *jut* fell soundlessly, the sea too far for the splash to reach me. About me mountains hung like palaces of cloud.

Tchavi, they call me now. Not Ekawi, never Ekawi. They follow me through the village when I come down from the mountain. Children, precious as water after my months among the peaks. Breathless women begging me to come into their homes for a meal. *Tchavi, Tchavi.* A ragged procession follows me down the road, and people glance at one another and say: "He is going to his *jut.*" And others say: "He has no *jut.*" But no one knows for certain. I stride toward the yellow house, leaning on my staff. There, for a short time, I will stay. At home. I sit with my family, I walk, I read. I exchange the books I took into the mountains for new ones. I visit Lunre and Niahet his wife. I talk with many people, whole and *hotun.* And I remember Jissavet.

No, she will not come again.

I look for her on the evening paths the color of mist, at the corner of the house where moisture trickles. At this corner, behind the bushes where direct sunlight never falls, this corner of permanent shadows, mildew, decay. I breathe the dense nocturnal odor of jasmine, the smell of the rain-soaked wall. "*Autumn comes with a whisper, smelling of stone. . . .*" But there is no autumn here, and there is no angel, no dark butterfly on the roof, no glancing and inexplicable light.

I walk under the dripping trees. Across the sky the blood of my heart is spread in the shape of her fine, receding footprints. Like doors of fire, opening and closing. While in the courtyards of Tyom the braziers are lit and the old men wheeze with laughter.

I lean on the fences, looking for her. A lamp is lit in a nearby house and a dark shape moves from the grass to the little pathway of broken bricks: a clay jar in her arms, she passes, one leg and then another leg. Her queenly back, the oblique light on her heel. I am ready to cry out; I make a movement and she turns. Her face is surprised in the dusk, no more than eight or nine years old. Of course, I recognize the house, it's Pavit's youngest daughter. I have always known those windows smothered in leaves.

Afternoons of Tyom. Drunk with the heat I stagger up from the hour of rest, my head throbbing, my mouth dry. I stumble into the courtyard, already vaguely looking for her in the water jar, the cup held to my lips, the heavy light on the stones. Flies buzz around me, rumors of her in the shadow of the wall. I narrow my eyes, gazing into the sunlight, and the heat and sweat on my lashes make me believe I see her incipient form, radiating luster among the hibiscus. But she does not come, she never arrives. She is always on the point of being, never crossing over again into life. When the storms roll in from the sea, I sit in the doorway of the hall while the rain unleashes its demons in the darkened courtyard.

And now, how glad I am that I did not burn this stack of books, this poor vestige of her, pathetic as a stray hair! For I am like those lovers who keep obscure and grotesque charms, a maize-cob gnawed by the loved one, a tick scratched from her ankle. Such is the angel's *anadnedet*. I kneel at the table in the schoolroom, reading in the oily gleam of my lamp, for the light that enters from the garden is not enough, only the faded light that penetrates the curtain of rain. In the resonance of the downpour I review her passionate language. "There's thunder, darkness, a cold fog everywhere." The poverty of the words does not deprive them of significance: sometimes I think they are almost, almost enough . . . almost enough to call her up again, real, before me, with her flashing eyes, her sumptuous, unreachable skin. So the lover invents his own religion, praying over his treasure of discarded fingernails. The *anadnedet* has no more power than these—perhaps less. Yet I adore it; to touch its pages gives me joy. There, at the corner, a stain of ink shows where I started when she suddenly spoke to me in the midst of my hurried writing. Wonderful stain, peaked like a star. And all these creased and dirty pages, dry and porous in the light of my lamp. I bend down close: they smell of smoke as they speak to me of a watery temple, maps "curled at the edges," "immense fruit bats." Jissavet does not live within these words, she is not contained by them. What would she say of this rainstorm, had she lived? No, I will never know how she would respond to this crash of thunder, if she would start, laugh, or run outside into the garden. Still, I read. When the rain stops I can hear the sound of the pages turning, a sensuous sound like a woman turning in bed. A whisper beneath the dropping of water from the wet leaves of the garden hedge and the echoing clamor of the disturbed cockatoos.

I am like no other *tchavi* in the history of the islands. When I visit Tyom, children come to me in the old schoolroom. They come with pens of *tediet*-wood, with hibiscus-flower ink in leather bottles, with stiff paper lifted out of a slurry of leaves. These are made by the yellow man who lives on Painted Mountain, a mad old codger who gives them to anyone who asks. Only the children ask. In the schoolroom they show me the words they have written during my absence, whole stories in Kideti, embryonic poems. This alphabet was developed in Olondria, I tell them, but it is our own; it was used to pen the first work of written Kideti literature. *The Anadnedet,* by Jissavet of Kiem. This is why we call it Jissavet's Alphabet. At the end of each lesson I read aloud from this seminal work. And I introduce them to others, books I have translated from Olondrian in the most violent and sacrilegious form of reading. And I tell them: This is a journey to *jepnatow-het,* the land of shadows. Do not mistake it for the country of the real.

Perhaps even the land named in the books is no longer real. Terrible rumors reach us from the north: libraries burning, devotees of the Stone dragged into the street. Perhaps, one day, Tyom will become the last refuge of books. I do not know. I read. I take the children of Tyom hunting with Firdred, spearing boar in snowy Olondrian forests. Together we enter the dark-shuttered castle of Beal. And Fodra takes us to Bain, to the white walls overlooking the sea, the eternal flavor of olives. Then I look up: the light has changed, the children are restless with hunger, we have all lost another afternoon of our lives, gaining nothing but an enigmatic glow: for the cup I lift now is not merely a cup but carries on its glazed surface the shadows of sails. And this lintel, suddenly it's darker, as if magically aged. And the flowers of the courtyard, exhausted with heat, hang on their stalks like handkerchiefs forgotten after a midnight ball, like sashes lost at romantic assignations. In the same way, perhaps, I am still influenced by the angel, subtly, hazily, as the tide responds even in the dark of the moon. Sometimes she comes to me in dreams, and it is as if I have been permitted to enter the huge and vanished doors of childhood.

My lost rose, my distant bell! What was that feeling of happiness, welling up unexpectedly under the sorrow? I was in the schoolroom after a lesson; my mother was there; the room was hot and bright, the walls yellow with light from the open doorway. I stood, shaken with joy, concentrating on the feeling as if analyzing a new and delightful taste. It was the angel: the pure heat, the warbling doves in the sunny garden, my mother's golden face lit by the walls.

"What is it, younger son?" she asked me, laughing.

What is it? Yes, what is it? It is the reason I walk the mountains after dusk, unable to bear even my tattered shelter of dried grass, and watch the fireflies pulsing over the forest. Oh, will she not come? Can they not call her, those roving lamps? No: I am alone in the sultry air, in the faintly violet darkness, in the odor of damp leaves. But I go on waiting for her. I look for her still.

Acknowledgments

This book took two years to write and a decade to revise, and it's impossible to thank all the people who helped me along the way. However, special thanks are due:

To Anna Jean Mayhew, for her helpful comments. To the "Smiling Authors": Kerry Dunn, Sheryl Dunn, Richard C. Hine, Marla Mendenhall, Jarucia Jaycox Nirula, Dwight Okita, Steffan Piper, and Robert L. Taylor, for constructive criticism, advice, and moral support.

To Gavin J. Grant and Kelly Link of Small Beer Press, for making it happen, and for the magic editing touch.

To Kat Köhler, my partner in crime.

To my parents, who passed on their love of words.

And to Keith—first reader, loyal critic, mapmaker, and inspiration—who was there when it all began.

Sofia Samatar is the author of the novels *A Stranger in Olondria* and *The Winged Histories,* the short story collection, *Tender,* and *Monster Portraits,* a collaboration with her brother, the artist Del Samatar. She is the recipient of the William L. Crawford Award, the Astounding Award, the British Fantasy Award, and the World Fantasy Award. She teaches Arabic literature, African literature, and speculative fiction at James Madison University and her website is sofiasamatar.com.

ALSO AVAILABLE FROM SMALL BEER PRESS

These interconnected stories are set in an opulent quasi-historical world of magick and high manners called the Republic of Califa. The Republic is a strangely familiar place—a baroque approximation of Gold Rush era-California with an overlay of Aztec ceremony—yet the characters who populate it are true originals.

"Packed to the gills with clever wordplay, bizarre characters and outlandish events. . . . in or around the Republic of Califa, an alternate, Aztec-influenced version of the Golden State from the 19th century, where magick is part of everyday life." — Michael Berry, *San Francisco Chronicle*

"Like discovering a new language, dark and magical and far more fun than the one you grew up speaking. Califa and her denizens sizzle to life on the page in all of their blood-soaked, candy-colored glory; *Prophecies, Libels and Dreams* is a wonder."— Kelly Braffet, author of *Save Yourself*

paper · $16 · 9781618730893 | ebook available